"I serve Temujin, Genghis Khan,"

the shaman said. "I have sensed the will of the spirits, I know that Temujin is the Son of Heaven and destined to rule over all the world. I cannot stand against the spirits, but it is I who will rule through him, in the end. That is the only revenge I can grant you, sworn brother of Temujin—that you will see the great Khan grow ever more regretful as his conquests increase; that he will be haunted even at the height of his power by the ghosts and spirits of those he betrayed, and that, because of his fear and remorse, he will give me whatever I want and do whatever I wish him to do."

"That will be enough punishment," Jamukha replied, wondering if the shaman could sense his fear of the smothering darkness in which he was embedded. Invisible ropes held him, and he understood that Teb-Tenggeri had bound lum with a powerful spell. To attempt escape would be risky; if he failed, Teb-Tenggeri would bind his soul even more tightly, and see that he never got another chance to fly away from him.

Jamukha had what he had wanted, a chance to keep his promise to haunt Temujin. But already the hatred that had flared up inside him burned less brightly, replaced by a growing fear.

—from "Spirit Brother"
by Pamela Sargent

More Imagination-Expanding Anthologies Brought to You by DAW:

MAGICAL BEGINNINGS *Edited by Steven H. Silver and Martin H. Greenberg.* How and where did such writers as Andre Norton, Peter Beagle, Ursula K. Le Guin, and Mercedes Lackey get their start? Now you can find out by reading the stories that began their careers, some well-known classics, others long unavailable. Each of the sixteen stories included has an introduction by its author which offers insight into the genesis of both the particular tale and the individual writer's career. And all of them serve as fascinating examples of the richness and range that the fantasy genre offers to both writers and readers.

DAW 30TH ANNIVERSARY FANTASY ANTHOLOGY *Edited by Elizabeth R. Wollheim and Sheila E. Gilbert.* In celebration of DAW Books' thirtieth anniversary, here are eighteen original stories by some of the authors who have helped to make DAW the landmark fantasy publishing house it is today. Includes stories by Andre Norton, Melanie Rawn, Tanith Lee, Jennifer Roberson, Mercedes Lackey, Tanya Huff, and many other top authors in the field.

VENGEANCE FANTASTIC *Edited by Denise Little.* From a young woman who would betray her own faith to save her people from marauding Vikings...to a goddess willing to pull down the very heavens to bring justice to a god...to a deal struck between Adam and Eve and Lucifer himself...to a "woman" who must decide how to rework the threads of life...here are spellbinding tales that will strike a chord with every reader. Enjoy seventeen unforgettable tales from some of fantasy's finest, including Mickey Zucker Reichert, Michelle West, Nina Kiriki Hoffman, P. N. Elrod, Jody Lynn Nye, Elizabeth Ann Scarborough, Mel Odom, Kristine Kathryn Rusch, Gary A. Braunbeck, and more.

CONQUEROR FANTASTIC

Edited by
Pamela Sargent

DAW BOOKS, INC.
DONALD A. WOLLHEIM, FOUNDER
375 Hudson Street, New York, NY 10014
ELIZABETH R. WOLLHEIM
SHEILA E. GILBERT
PUBLISHERS

www.dawbooks.com

First Printing, April 2004

1   2   3   4   5   6   7   8   9

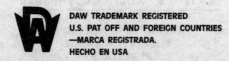

ACKNOWLEDGMENTS

CONTENTS

INTRODUCTION

Pamela Sargent

T he past, even the most recent past, can be an elusive
quarry, difficult to capture. In fact, our own personal bi-
ographies are constantly being rewritten in our memories.
We may subtly reshape past events that we think we remember clearly. An insignificant incident suddenly takes on
greater importance; an occurrence that was once mysterious
or obscure is brought into the light by newly discovered facts
and becomes comprehensible.

All such memories are shaped by our images of ourselves
and what we believe; they hinge on our view of our world
and our own places in it. They can often be lost to us, or
glimpsed only as pieces of what was. As the historian Doris
Kearns Goodwin discovered when writing a memoir of her
childhood as a fan of baseball and the legendary and beloved
Brooklyn Dodgers: ". . . my own memory was not equal to
my expanding ambition. Some of my most vivid private rec-
ollections of people and events seemed ambiguous and frag-
mentary when subjected to the necessities of public narrative.
If I were to be faithful to my tale, it would be necessary to
summon to my own history the tools I had acquired in inves-
tigating the history of others." (*Wait Till Next Year,* Simon &
Schuster, 1997.) Goodwin ended up having to interview her

former neighbors, gathering material from local archives, and reading contemporary newspapers in order to write about her own experiences accurately.

That Goodwin and another bestselling historian, Stephen Ambrose, were accused of plagiarism not long ago, and then confessed to having paraphrased the work of others too closely and of setting down lines verbatim without proper attribution, reveals that even those trained in recapturing the past can run into problems. As journalist David Gates put it in a news story on the subject: "If you're a historian and you didn't actually witness this or that event, you reconstruct and retell it based on your own interviews, somebody else's printed account or both. In other words, you combine quotation with paraphrase, and it's not surprising when the two get mixed up . . ." ("No Ordinary Crime," *Newsweek,* March 18, 2002.)

The historical past, even for the most painstaking historian, is much more elusive than one's own personal past. Those eras for which we have detailed records must to a certain degree be imagined. Extensive records of what people wore and ate, the work they did, the games they played, the dwellings in which they lived, and their known beliefs don't give us a true and fully formed picture of their inner lives. Diaries, journals, and letters may come closest to opening up the minds and feelings of past people to us, but such documents can be as selective and subject to distortion as our own memories. We also lack extensive records for most human history. Our prehistoric past must be pasted together from bones, shards, and pieces of tools; and the ancient past imagined from those monuments that still stand and those documents that have survived.

All of history is a compilation of stories told and retold, reinterpreted, revised, and rewritten as new evidence comes to light. To write fiction about the past requires learning enough about the period one chooses to write about so as not to violate what is known; that much is obvious. But because we in the post-industrial world live in an intellectual climate that is largely rational and that is fed by our scientific and technological developments, we may be tempted to view the past only from that rational perspective. Does the purely realistic piece of historical fiction truly reflect the past? Or does it instead only mirror our image, formed by our own worldview, of what the past might have been like?

Some would contend that historical novelists are essentially writing only about their own times, or that they cannot help writing about their own times as much as about the past. But one way in which the writer might escape that restriction is to take on a mental outlook completely unlike her own, one that treats older beliefs as if they are a kind of reality. Here is where historical fantasy can provide a useful tool in envisioning the past; I would even argue that in many cases the historical fantasist may come closer to capturing the sensibility of the past than the writer who is completely grounded in realism. Can a realistic story do justice to a past in which shamans, witches, gods, spirits, magic, miracles, unseen forces, and hidden conspiracies were almost universally believed in and accepted? The fantasist may be closer to giving us a feeling for past people and the mental universe in which they lived by using the devices of fantasy; and the fact is that much of this magical and conspiratorial thinking still survives and flourishes among people of our own time. It is a rare late twentieth or early twenty-first century person who harbors no superstitions at all.

Fantasy also seems a particularly appropriate way to approach the stories of the conquerors of history whose stories live on in the memories of millions. To imagine oneself as all-powerful, to dream of controlling the lives of many others and of being remembered long after death is certainly a common enough human fantasy and one of the most alluring.

For this anthology, I began by asking writers for stories featuring historical figures such as Alexander the Great, Julius Caesar, Genghis Khan, Napoleon, Hitler, Stalin, or any other conqueror from any culture who happened to interest the writer. I was also looking for historical fantasy rather than alternative history, although the line between the two can often be hard to draw (as it can be with such other related forms of fiction as magical realism, science fiction, and dark fantasy). The conqueror could be the central character of the story, a supporting or minor character in the tale, or even off-stage, as long as the story hinged on his or her presence in some way.

The authors in *Conqueror Fantastic* responded with the following fascinating and inventive tales, in which we catch sight of personages as removed in time and culture as Alexander the Great and the Native American warrior known as King Philip, Genghis Khan and a Japanese empress, Lyndon Johnson and Napoleon, Adolf Hitler and Hernando Cortés, Robert F. Kennedy and Saladin—to name only a few of those who appear in these pages. Every one of the writers in this volume succeeded in the goal that both the historian and the writer of fiction share: to depict some of the facets of our human experience and to make us see ourselves and our past in a new light.

TO THE GODS THEIR DUE

Michelle West

We begin with an atmospheric and moving story nar-
rated by Alexander the Great, a tale that can be
read as both the story of a conqueror and as a
Greek tragedy. Michelle West's novels include
Hunter's Oath, *Hunter's Death*, *The Broken Crown*,
The Uncrowned King, *The Shining Court*, *Sea of Sor-
rows*, and *Sun Sword*, all published by DAW; she
also writes a book review column for *The Magazine
of Fantasy & Science Fiction*. As Michelle Sagara,
she is the author of *Into the Dark Lands*, *Children of
the Blood*, *Lady of Mercy*, and *Chains of Darkness,
Chains of Light*, all published by Del Rey. She has
also written under the name of Michelle Sagara
West, and has published over forty pieces of short fiction. She lives with her family in Toronto, Canada.

T o watch the woman who wears snakes, twined like living jewelry across the slender width of olive arms, is to
watch drama at its finest; women act upon the stage seldom,
and queens both never and always.

She wears paint like a fine mask, but she does not hide her features; she *made* them, and walking through the noisy streets, they command the attention of the crowds that became spectators the moment she set foot upon the palace road. Her hair is dark, and she wears it long, tresses straightened to the small of her back. She wears gold around her throat, and gold upon her brow: the crown. Gold crown.

In her youth, she wore it with pride and with a wild passion; I remember her well. I touched that slender crown; I pulled it from her head, disturbing her hair; I perched it upon my own, and was dismayed when it fell to rest like a necklace and not an insignia of office. She was patient, then.

Now she is hollow. The two, patience and hollowness, seem very alike. But only to me, and only because I see it in the way that she moves.

Understand that I have always loved my mother. I have loved the wild splendor of her voice, the passion of her anger—when it was not directed at me—the sensuous play of her hands across the moving backs of the snakes she so coddled. I have loved her ferocity, her certainty, the beauty of her unfettered pride. Perhaps it is her pride that I best loved, and it pains me to see her don it now, for it is as hollow as she.

Did I love my father?

Not so easy a question to answer. As a child, yes. All children love their fathers. But he was distant: king, the scion of distant gods. She was present. She brought to me the teacher I best loved and the teacher I least liked, bidding them give me what she thought she could not teach me herself: skill at arms and upon a horse, and the ability to endure in the most Spartan of environments.

Ah. There. She has reached the body of the traitor. Pausanias. The man who murdered Philip of Macedon.

Ah, mother. I watch.

Hephaestion comes to me, stands by my side. I feel his palm upon my shoulder, and I lean against that brief warmth for a minute.

"Alexander," he says softly. But his face is turned streetward, and he, too, is caught by the macabre procession. "Alexander, come away."

Mute, I reach up and push off his hand. "You cannot protect me," I tell him. "Not today. Not here."

He says nothing.

"Hephaestion, leave me."

He does not move. But he does not touch me again. If he did, I would turn to him, and I cannot. This is my first sacrifice, and I must bear witness to it. So I have been told, and I believe this much at least. If he touches me again, I will order him to leave, as king and not as lover, and he, Companion and bodyguard, will have no choice but to obey. He does not press me.

But I hear the changes of his breath, the ragged rise and fall of his chest. Arrogant, he is called. Pretentious. Vain. He is all of those things. But he is so much more than that; he is not unlike Olympias herself, my mother.

"Could you do this?" I ask him idly, for she has the whole of my attention.

It must be so hard for her to stand before Pausanias thus, her people—her people again, now that I have gained the throne—gathered at her back in mute witness to her spectacle. Her hands are steady when she raises them to her forehead and steady when she removes the crown from her brow. It catches sunlight, as she no doubt intended, and it shines like the glinting edge of turned blade.

She must be bleeding, my mother; she must be. And she has never been a woman to grieve privately; never been a private person. All of her life has been an open stage, and I have deprived her of that, for she stands there, before the dead, and she pays him honor.

The man who killed her husband.

And such a pathetic death. I witnessed it at a safe distance, for I had been ordered to attend my father at the wedding of my uncle; we two Alexanders were to be his sole honor guard. I accepted this commandment, I played at being the dutiful son; it was the last time that I would be required to do so.

My uncle's shock was real; his cry of shock and dismay twin to my own. Before all of the assembled nobles of this kingdom, and those to the east and the west, Pausanias drew short sword and ended my father's life with a single blow.

He fled. As arranged, he fled. I watched him and waited; the bodyguard would not be far behind.

He was caught, of course; killed almost instantly. That, too, was expected. My hand was not the hand to kill him. I understand necessity and treachery—how could I not? In Mieza, among kin, these things are played out time and again when the throne is the prize. But not even I would reward such loyalty so poorly.

He died quickly.

Then the first act of the spectacle: his body, defiled, was put on display before the palace gate. The wedding was not to take place; the guests, in shock and disarray, retreated. The king was dead, and he had left in his wake four possible heirs: Amyntas, the prince for whom he served as regent—a regency that was never to be ended; Arridheaus, the half-wit son of a low-born courtesan; and his son by Eurydice, his new wife, a Macedonian woman of good breeding, quiet beauty and a family of generals. That son, like Amyntas before him, would never rule—but through him, Attalus, one of my father's Companions, might.

Had he only one heir, he would still be alive.

That he loved Eurydice cannot be in doubt. She was of his people, and she was, as I have noted, an exemplary woman. Had she come to the court as a lesser wife, had she remained a mistress in good standing, things would now be different.

But when she was with child—her first—he repudiated my mother.

Attalus was pleased. And with wine, grew bold. In my father's hall, while I stood in attendance, he said, "Perhaps at last we will have a legitimate heir."

I will kill him for it, but not now.

Now, I watch as my mother kisses the golden crown and places it upon the brow of the man who murdered her husband.

The crowd murmurs, their faces turned toward the palace gates as if they expect the king himself to return from the dead at such an outrageous offering. But the gates are still.

I am still.

She loved my father. That is the truth, all of her angry bitter words notwithstanding. She tolerated Eurydice, as she had tolerated all of my father's mistresses; she treated her kindly. And she was repaid so poorly for that kindness. Ah. She removes her dagger now, and with infinite care, she cuts the bonds that hold the lifeless body to the gates.

She speaks; I cannot hear her, but I know her well: I know what she says.

Hollow words, passionate words, she offers the dead. Blessings and thanks for his avenging of the wrongs done her by her husband.

I mark them. Hephaestion has turned away. He cannot watch. I watch for us both.

"Could you do this?" I ask him again.

He shakes his head. "Your mother is stronger than I," he says, words shaky, knowing her pain. "If your murderer stood at the gates, I could not honor him."

"Not even if I discarded you so callously? Not even if I deprived you of all honor, after your loyalty and your years of service to me?"

"Not even then," he says quietly.

"Why?"

"Because I would always have hope."

"Of what?"

He knows why I ask. But he is silent.

"Hephaestion, answer me."

"That you would return. That you would understand the folly of your choice. That you would remember why you needed me."

"Need you?" I ask, the words light.

He would catch my arms, if he were just a bit bolder; I would then send him away. He is still. "I need to know that I am necessary, Alexander. To you. I think the day I stop being necessary—"

I nod. "You did not understand my father."

"No. But it is not your father who I love."

The body is free of the gates. She struggles with its weight, for Pausanias was not a small man. Even handless, footless, he is not small. The flies about him part, as if they were a living veil. There are no clouds in the sky; azure opens above, like a great eye. She has no way to hide her tears; they glint across her face, they fall across the contours of her aging skin.

She has never looked old to me, until this moment.

"Alexander, she will see us. We must leave."

"No."

"Why?"

I would tell him, but I cannot. Not yet. She is not yet finished.

When I was young, and my father was away with the army, she would speak of him. Her voice, her words, return to me, dimmed by memory. I see him as I saw him then, unstained by time or death: eyeless, where the arrows of an archer almost ended his life, but unbroken and unbowed, his hands twisted in the mane of his finest horse, his sword raised high, his expression one of determination, exultation. War defined him.

It defines us all; there is no other way to win immortality in this most mortal of places. What he began, I mean to continue.

But if war defined him, it did not denude him of charm or mystery; she loved him, bitter weakness that it was, and loves him still: Philip of Macedon. King of all Greece, if the Greeks could but own the truth of the title.

The body is upon the ground. She calls for the palanquin that carried her, and with effort, with strain, the snakes twisting as if they are her only muscles, she lifts the burden she has taken upon herself.

"I was wronged," she says, her voice now the trumpet call, the sound of war. But whether it is a call to advance or retreat, they cannot tell; they step away. The powers of a wronged woman, from Hera to Medea, permeate our myth, define our knowledge of women: she wears this history like a mantle, for the crown is gone, and although she will take the title of Queen again, she will never lift the tiara.

"I call upon you to witness it: I was wronged. The gods have judged; the gods exonerate me." She lights incense in braziers upon the long poles that quarter the palanquin, and sweet smoke rises in wreaths about her face, nestling in her hair, obscuring the stench of decay.

"You will honor this man, and this man's memory, for he was but an instrument of the gods, and what the gods decree, only the gods may decry."

Sheep are brought now, at her command. She takes her dagger again, cutting not rope but sinew, flesh, vessel; blood spills as the bleating of the lamb is silenced by wind and death. She bathes him in this blood, anoints him with this sacrifice. She does not leave the task of separating the gods' portion from ours to another; she performs the whole of the rite.

To the gods she burns skin and bones; to the people who stand closest she offers the meat. She herself tastes it, but it is bitter to her.

Ptolemy comes through the crowds in his armour, his left shoulder shielded, his right exposed. "Alexander, what is this madness?" he says, his anger and confusion distorting his otherwise pleasant features. "Why do you stand thus? Why do you allow it? Do you not know what they will say?"

"They will say nothing."

"They will say nothing *to you*. But across the length and breadth of Macedon—and all of Greece—she will be known as the hand behind the dagger that killed the king."

Ptolemy is not a fool. But he admired both my father and my mother, and his emotion overrides his sense.

She is my first sacrifice. "Yes," I tell him calmly, while Hephaestion struggles and regains his composure. "That is surely what they will say."

"You cannot allow this."

I laugh. It is a bitter laugh, and it is a genuine one. "Who among us—even including my father—could ever command

Olympias? She is of the line of Achilles, and her determination knows no bounds."

"It is not for determination, but for rage, that Achilles was known," Ptolemy says.

There are reasons why I wanted no Companion but Hephaestion this day. "Achilles was known for his greatness. His prowess could not be equaled."

"Achilles may have been known for his heroism, but do not forget," Ptolemy replied, "that this hero chose to shelter among women in an island harem for his safety."

"True enough. But when he at last chose his fate, he did not hide that way again."

He is bewildered by the moment, by the loss, by the magnitude of the task that awaits us. Were he not, he would understand. He makes to leave, and I raise my hand. "Do not disturb her, Ptolemy."

It is the King's voice that I use; the voice of a friend has been buried beneath the cold, and yes, the anger of the moment. He bows at once.

"I have not forgotten what waits us. But I must attend my mother this day. When she is past this frenzy, she will be spent, and then she will listen to reason. But you have served me well, and were the situation not so urgent, I would acknowledge it now, and with great ceremony.

"I cannot spare you. Send for Attalus. If he attempts to resist, have him killed immediately."

He bows again, and when he rises, it is with renewed purpose. We are brothers, my Companions and I, and we are hunters.

She is finished. The body begins to move. It halts once in the streets; her voice rises and the men who carry the palanquin fall at once to the ground at her feet.

They take Pausanias to my father's body, and my mother pauses before it. She sends them away. But she cannot dismiss the witnesses who have trailed after her, ragged or resplendent, although I have no doubt that she would be rid of us in a moment if our presence did not suit her purpose.

She reaches out. She touches the crown upon my father's

still face. Touches his face, his folded hands, the sword by which he made kingdoms, and destroyed them. All are still. But even before death, they were beyond her.

She does not dishonor the body. It would be theater, yes, and it would provide strength to the legend that she builds this day, but she cannot bring herself to that final act.

Instead, she bends over him a moment; her hair falls across her face. What she says, no one hears, and even I cannot pretend to know it; there were things that passed between them that I could guess at, and things that will never make sense. That she loved him, that she could *still* love him, after his treachery, is one.

She burns Pausanias there, covering him carefully with oil before she lights the torch. They will call her murderess. But they will forgive her much, for she is once again Queen of Macedon, and until I take a wife, there will be no other.

Oh my mother. I loved you, and I love you still; had it been your hand raised against me, had it been your voice that had carried command, or your womb my successor, you would not now lie in state, as Philip does. I have known you and your pain for the whole of my life.

And I will carry it with me when I travel east; I will not forget it, I will not be free of it. I know that of all the enemies you have made at court, not a single one has hurt you as much as I have. But he would have taken the throne from me, and it is mine.

Hephaestion's eyes are now dry. "Alexander," he says. "It is over."

"Yes, over." I turn to him wearily. "But there is more to come. My mother will not wish to speak with me."

"Then you—"

"I will return to her chambers, and I will wait there. If she asks it of you, tell her that you do not know my whereabouts."

If he were a fool, I would not love him. He does not say, *does she know?* He does not ask if we have spoken; we have not. She will not ask me, of course, if I had my father assassinated. She will not ask me a question that I will not answer. She is proud, that way.

But he knows that she knows.

Because if she did not know, she would not have come to the body—to either of these bodies—in this fashion; she would have come in rage and fury; she would have defiled the dead, rather than praising him, and she would have held my father's face in her hands and wailed like a lost beast, until at last someone came to take her away.

When I return to the palace, Aristander of Telmessus is waiting. He is not a young man, but neither is he old; his hair is dark and white, and his eyes are blue. He bows, his beard brushing robes, as I enter his presence.

"Yes," I say, before he speaks. "I have done as you commanded."

"I do not seek command, my lord," he replies gravely. "I have never sought it. I see what I see, and I offer what advice comes from that vision; it is for the mighty to determine whether or not the advice is pleasing or sound."

"It is not pleasing," I tell him. "Of all the advice that you have given, there is none yet that has been so unpleasant."

"If I were to speak only pleasantry, Alexander, you would not now have me. You will build your legends, as your mother is building hers, but you will build them from a foundation of strength. I am no keeper of history, no keeper of public record; I am a poor orator, a poor actor, and a feeble historian."

"They say you have cast your spells upon me."

"And they say that your mother is a murderer."

"Enough, Aristander. Why have you come?"

"Only to see what I see," he replied, remote and respectful.

"And is what you see pleasing?"

"What I see is truth." He bowed. "The gods have always demanded their sacrifices. But they do not demand *sheep* or *goat* from a great king. Of what value would these things be to such a man?"

"Little."

He bows again. "I will leave you to your mother. She is coming as we speak, and you had best be away if you would see her at all."

I walk down the long hall, but I stop a moment, then turn to see the faintest of smiles cross his lips. "You will be a great king," he says quietly, but the heights of the hall catch his words, magnifying them. At another time, this would please me.

And perhaps in truth it pleases me now. But victory is distant and loss is near, and as my mother before me, I am fixed by the immediate.

When she comes, the snakes are gone. Her hair is wild; her hands have been at it, and her eyes are streaked black with bitter tears. Her face is lined, her skin sallow. She should have returned in triumph to Mieza, the jewel of Macedon. But although she knows victory, the field is not to her liking.

Her eyes widen when she sees me. I rise at once; I have waited until she has drawn close enough that I might prevent her flight if necessary.

"Alexander."

"Mother." I want to hold out my arms, but she will not come to me. She does not hold out hers; instead she crosses them against her breast and tightens them.

For a moment I understand why cowards lie.

I have always understood why kings do, and I have always understood when a lie is meaningless, when it serves no purpose.

She has always loved my father. Philip. Philip the fire lord. Philip, the Lion of Macedon.

That was the whole of her truth until I was born. Then it was half, half of her truth, for she was no longer simple wife; she was mother as well.

As mother, as keeper of my secrets, as protector of my heritage and the beginning of my life, she has done what she must to save me; to give the throne, to give my tenure, its cleanest start.

She looks at me. As if she does not understand me, or as if

she wishes that she did not. It is . . . painful. I have taken wounds in war, but they were of no consequence. This, this is self-inflicted. Necessary.

For a moment I think she will ask me why. But she does not; she knows why. Instead, she bows her head. "Let me ask of you only one favor," she says.

It is not what I expected. "What favor? What favor would the Queen of Macedon ask of her king?"

"Eurydice," she says.

I could pretend to misunderstand her. I know of her terrible jealousy, her great anger, her insurmountable loss. But I will not do this; I will not lie to her.

"I cannot."

"She is blameless in this. All of the choices made were Philip's or Attalus's. She had no choice."

"No."

"Kill her son, if you must."

"And what then? If I had killed yours, would you forgive? Would you forget?"

"She is not I."

"No. But she is Macedonian, and if she is quiet, she has courage and conviction. The son, I cannot spare. And because I cannot spare him, the mother is too dangerous."

"Alexander—"

Silence.

"You have no wife."

I nod.

"You have no heir. A king needs heirs. Adopt this child; take Eurydice to wife."

"You say that to me?"

She is silent.

"You are queen. There will be no other while I live."

She lifts hands to her face. "Then let me do it."

I shake my head. "You have done enough."

"I will be blamed for their deaths. Let me—"

"No. I forbid it."

"As king or as son?"

"As whatever it takes; you will abide by my decision in this."

She is bitter, bitterly angry. She is white with it. She does what no man alive would dare: she slaps me. The sound rings, resonant, earned, in the empty room. "Get out."

I bow to her. I start to speak, and she stops me with a gesture.

"Do not speak to me of love," she snaps, for she knows me well.

As she is forced to obey, I too am bound. I leave her, wondering if I will ever see her again.

In the months to come, I am busy. The Athenians cause me grief, but they are hampered; they do not understand kings, but I understand them. Aristotle gave me that much. Greece is suspended between the choice of two evils: Sparta and Macedon. Her people have long memory, and Sparta is not likely to gain their support or their sympathies.

I have destroyed Thebes, for its insolence and because of all of the cities, she is most hated. There is threat in the deaths that have come from her city, and the slaves taken there will carry it in tales to their new masters. I need not speak the threat aloud. It has been heard.

But it is not in Greece that I will make my fortunes known; not in Greece that I will earn the only immortality a man earns in these diminished times. No more can Heracles ascend to Olympus; the gods are distant and they speak slowly and seldom.

No, I will go east.

She comes to me when the army is gathered. I had not expected that. It moves me; I cannot speak of it now. I see her, and she is indeed the queen that she was, but she has become like my father: distantly regal.

I would stay, if I could. But my father's ghost is restless, and in the silence the of the army lies his strongest accusation. They were his men. To make them mine, I must take them from this place, the scene of the worst of my crimes.

Did I love him?

I close my eyes.

I dismiss the bodyguard; they hesitate. Only Hephaestion stands by me as she approaches. He does not fear her dagger; he does not fear her poison. She will never threaten me with death.

I dismount; Bucephalus is restless and eager to move, but he will wait.

"I did not think to see you here."

She says, "I did not think to come."

"But you did."

She nods. Her eyes are too round, and too clear, as she gazes at my face; we are of a height. She reaches out and touches my face, her hands caressing the curve of my cheek. There is something familiar about the movement, but it is not until she is done that I realize what it is: she touched my father's body in just such a way.

She does not speak the words. She does not say, *you are both dead to me now.* She is not a merciful woman; she knows that I understand.

Knows that I must have watched her performance.

I catch her hands. "I will write," I tell her, my voice a little too loud.

"I," she says softly, "will write as well."

And she will. She will write of things of little consequence. She will speak of politics, of war, of the state of the nation. She will complain about Antipater, for he is garrulous and not over-fond of her. But she will never offer me what she offered me before the death of Philip.

I will miss it.

I do not think she knows how much. I no longer have a way to tell her.

"Alexander," she says, her eyes hollow. She steps close now, close enough to touch, but she does not sweep me into her arms; she dashes that hope, and adds to the burden I carry.

"Beware the Furies."

*　　*　　*

It is Aristander who tells me where we must travel next, and it surprises me, but it does not displease me. Troy. We must go to Troy.

"Why?"

"Two men of great note died in Troy," he replies.

"You will perform a divination there?"

"I? No, Alexander. You will perform it. But it must be done; I will read what is writ there, and I will tell you what I see."

"Troy is not on our path."

"Troy is the heart of your path," he says quietly. "But if you decide against Troy, I will still travel by your side. The army is waiting, and it is strong enough to gain some portion of the east."

I walk out of the royal tent, and I look out, across the wide plains. The men are not yet in marching order, although they are preparing: the Companion Footsoldiers in armor that is yet new; the Companion Cavalry and their sparse attendants; the shieldbearers, the Companions, the bodyguard. They wait upon my command.

Parmenion, my father's most favored general, stands to one side of the tent. He kneels, although he is almost sixty and well past the suppleness of youth; the gesture is solid, but there is no grace in it.

"We make a pilgrimage," I tell him. "To offer sacrifices at the site of one of our greatest victories. I wish to make an auspicious beginning, for I mean to make the Persians pay for their slights to Greece."

He nods. He is loyal. He is competent. He is the only one of my Companions who sought the conquest of the eastern kingdom as readily as I, and his support was essential to the campaign, for many of our men did not wish to cross the eastern borders to a foreign country.

For that reason, his son Philotas commands the Companion Cavalry, and Parmenion himself is second only to me; the left wing of the army is his personal purview.

Aristander comes out of the tent; Parmenion stiffens. They are not friendly, these two. Few of the soldiers trust Aris-

tander, and Parmenion defines the soldiery. I bid him take his
men and follow where I lead.

He meets my gaze for just as long as his rank—and his importance—allows. Then he nods and leaves to mount his
horse.

"We will not linger," I say quietly. "Speed is of the
essence."

"Yes," Aristander replies, cryptically.

There is so little left of Troy that it is hard to lend credence
to old tales from a distance. But some of its majesty and its
history endures in the ground and the air above the outlines
of its ruined walls, and as we approach, the men murmur.
Some speak; some sing. Words and wind entwine until the
whole of the coast seems to sing the lay of the passage of
years.

I am not immune. I know my history, and my legend; I
know my lineage. I understand well the value of Troy, for it is
at Troy that the greatest of Achilles' battles was fought: with
himself, and with his enemy. Of all of the books I was to study
under the stiff and condescending tutelage of Aristotle, it was
the one upon which we could both agree—and disagree.

My youth, he said, told against me; but my age—and wisdom, should I live to gain it, would reveal all, in the passage
of time. Against such an understanding, I have travelled with
the copy of the *Iliad* that he made with his own hands.

I do not know what Aristander seeks; I do not know what
manner of divination he will perform in this place. Upon the
ships that carried us here, I slew a bull in the name of Posei-
don, and I offered the god thanks for our speedy and safe
passage to these ancient shores. I did not need the advice of a
mystic to perform such action; I am king here, and all of my
brothers are under my care. The gods must be propitiated,
and no hand is higher than mine.

But of the sacrifices to be made at Troy, Aristander says
nothing. There is a temple to Athena which is still famous,
and of course I will stop there, but it is not to Athena that
Aristander looks. What then?

Your life now depends on what you next choose; by that choice, you will be known.

The shore approaches, and I have no answer.

Two deaths. He spoke of two deaths. But there were many, surely.

Hephaestion comes to stand by my side upon the deck. "Well?"

"I do not understand why he speaks of two men."

"It's not the two, it's the choice."

"But who? Ajax?"

He says, quietly, "I have never searched for heroes."

I look at him for a long time. "Patrocles," I say at last.

He smiles. "Patrocles, is it?"

"And Achilles."

"Two deaths?"

"The only two deaths of note: Patrocles, for Achilles. And Achilles."

"For Alexander." He smiles.

"All right. But I will *never* lend you my armor."

He laughs. "And I will never have need of it, if you do not choose to skulk in your tent. There is no Agamemnon here; no King, no lord, but you."

"Do not make light of it, Hephaestion."

"Why?"

"Because the only death I will not bear is yours."

"What greater honor will we have than death? We are warriors, not shepherds. All of our lives will be measured by that fact."

"Then let it be measured when we are both well past the age of Parmenion."

He laughs again. "Parmenion will perish when Macedon does. The shore is at hand. Come, then. Achilles."

"And Patrocles."

It is to the tombs of Achilles and Patrocles that we then go. We strip ourselves of armor, of cloth, of every encumbrance; we run, in strength, to the stone temples that stand in memory of our greatest hero and his companion. Let the gods see us; let the gods judge.

To the shouts and the cries of the army, we make our obeisances, pay our respects, offer our sacrifices, and when we are done, we take up arms and cloth again. But not armor. The armor goes to the temple of Athena, to be dedicated to her, goddess of wise counsel and war, in this ancient place.

I am greeted by villagers; they offer me golden crowns and wreaths, they speak my name with awe and respect. And fear.

But something gives me pause. I pass beneath the shadow of another temple, and there I stop. "Wait, Hephaestion," I tell him quietly. With less ceremony, with more gravity, I approach the tomb of Priam, King of Troy.

There I kneel, as if the shade contains the ghost of that ancient man. I speak quietly. I remember his role, and Achilles, in this place.

No man interrupts me; even Hephaestion is absent, as Patrocles was when these two men met. But when I rise at last, Aristander waits, brazier in hand.

He nods quietly. "You have chosen," he says.

"What do you see here?"

"I see," he says quietly, "that you have not paid honor to Hector."

"Hector was our enemy."

"Indeed. A noble hero, and a man who was bound by duty, by honor, and by love." He bows his head. When he lifts it again, he says, "You will have victory, Alexander. You will have victory beyond the measure of any. Even the accomplishments of Philip will pale beside yours."

I should be pleased.

But there is, about his words, a shadow, some hint of Aristotle, some ghost that I do not understand.

"Tell the men."

Aristander bows, and obeys me. In the distance, I hear jubilation. But it is distant, and I think, for no reason at all, of Olympias, and her endless loss.

*   *   *

If I do not now speak of battle, it is not because there was none. My brothers and I were hunters, warriors, the pride of Macedon. We were invincible. Aristander had never yet been proved wrong, and he spoke that day with an authority that he seldom chose to wield. Therefore I sought to spare little; not my men, not myself.

The Persian army was heavy with servants and camp followers; it moved slowly, when it chose to move at all. It was large and unwieldy and unused to the rigors of the road, and upon this fact, much depended.

Of Granicus, Aristobulus and Callisthenes have written at length. I will not add to their tales, however embellished and prettified they might be; we met Darius, and we triumphed against his greater numbers and his sluggishness.

We met again at Issus, and again, we were to triumph, although in both of these instances, Darius himself was lost to a retreat that we could not hinder.

But at Issus I will make note of the most precious of the Great King's possessions to come into my hands to date.

I speak not of golden baths, nor of gold itself, although in truth we were much in need of the latter. I speak not of plunder, although plunder was to be had, and the army required at least some small reward for their efforts.

I speak instead of Sisygambis, mother to Darius, and Statira, his wife; of her daughters, and of her son, a boy of no more than six.

They were weeping when we came into their camp, and no small wonder; the forces of Darius had been squandered, and he presumed lost.

"Leonnatus, go to the women and see that they are both secured and *unharmed.*"

Leonnatus bowed and left, taking a small detachment of men with which to enforce my command. I was both weary and aware, as I am often weary and aware after battle; I had been injured, but the injury itself was minor, of little note.

I looked to Aristander.

"As you will," he said quietly. "There are no omens to guide you, Alexander. The women belong to Darius; they will make hostages, they will make bargaining tools, or they will be something entirely different. I am not a warrior; it is not the spoils of war I seek, but the story inherent in it." But his eyes were keen and clear, a hawk's eyes.

"I will see them," I told Hephaestion. "Follow."

Hephaestion nodded.

And so it is that we came to this dwelling. What has been said is true: the women weep. I hear their voices clearly, and they are deep and almost ugly with grief and fear. But it is not simple fear that motivates them; the grief itself is genuine.

Leonnatus awaits me; neither he, nor his men, have entered. They know that this was the preserve of Darius, and that I, who would claim his kingdom, now own what waits within.

I hesitate, although that hesitation is not marked; it is measured by silence and stillness, and perhaps by desire. I am not unmoved by what I have seen; there are riches in this encampment that make all of the finery of the country of my birth seem paltry by comparison. To be a king in Macedon seems a shadowy thing, and I have killed for it, and would kill again.

But I do not know what it means to be king in Persia. Not yet.

I pull back the hangings that serve as door, and Hephaestion alone accompanies me as I enter.

The eldest of the women steps forward instantly. Her bearing is perfect; she is both regal and graceful as she bows to the ground and pays obeisance at the feet of the man she presumes to be king.

Hephaestion stares at her bowed head, her supple back, in consternation; his gaze darts toward me and back. It is awkward. How awkward, I do not appreciate until later.

But there are few witnesses, and it is to Hephaestion that she has offered her gesture because Hephaestion, in the eyes of man, is all things I am not: Tall, handsome, graceful, possessed of a certain quality that defies description. What she has seen in him, I see in him, and I do not begrudge her.

But one of her slaves has seen this interplay, this subtle exchange that passes between my Companion and me, and this woman now speaks, halting and uncertain, in a voice so softspoken that I do not understand the words.

She lifts herself, this woman who was once queen, and there is no colour at all in her cheeks, save what has mixed with the residue of tears.

Behind her exquisitely turned back, I see two girls and a woman who is not much older than myself; she is striking, her skin gold, and her hair as dark as night. She holds her daughters by the shoulders, ready to bend them to earth if they do not rush to meet it; ready, perhaps, to pull them from my reach if I am too forward with threat or doom.

But it is the shadows by her feet that are of more interest; a third child, hidden in her skirts.

Young, I think, and most certainly a boy.

Darius's family.

The oldest of the women now meets my gaze, and she falters, losing precious grace and certainty.

"No mistake has been made," I tell her, and I reach out to take her hands; they shake in mine. "For he, too, is Alexander, the closest of my allies, and the only man I have ever trusted completely. In paying him your respects, you honor my choice.

"You are Sisygambis. I am Alexander. Your son is my chosen enemy, but I bear you no malice."

She lowers herself again to the ground, this time in my shadow. "You have been queen, and you are mother to the king; you are worthy of honor, and where I can, I will extend you that honor, and demand no less from any man who owes me allegiance."

She lifts her fair face, and there is colour to it now, although she is turned from the light. She does not have the look of Olympias to her; she misses the harshness and the flame, the force and the fire.

Not for the sake of her life would Olympias choose to honor the man who would be the death of her son. This woman and she are not the same, but I feel a kinship there, perhaps because I am long away from home, and long away from my mother.

I lift her to her feet. She meets my gaze, holding it above the edge of a demi-veil. Measuring my words in the stillness, she is silent.

"What do you intend?" she says at last.

"I intend," I reply, "to be king."

Her eyes close; her hands cease their trembling. When she opens both, she looks at me for a long while, and I see myself as she must: sweaty, blood-stained, dirty and grey.

"We have had word of your conduct in Caria. You placed Ada upon the throne, and she offered you the legitimacy of adoption."

"She chose to honor me, and I chose to accept the honor offered."

"I cannot offer you what she offered."

"No. But your presence here is honor enough."

She says, "He is my son." And gesturing the young queen forward, she adds gravely, "This is my daughter, Statira. She is sister and wife to the Great King; the closest of his kin. The child is her son."

"And Darius's."

"And his, as well."

I smile at the boy. He hesitates, but he is clearly a coddled child; a boy who has never been taken to the edge of harshness. Without me, he might have been king.

I did not suffer Eurydice's child to live, nor Eurydice. But this is different: I have no claim to this throne but the claim of conquest, and therefore no other legitimate heir is a risk to me.

I spare the boy. It is a gift to the Queen Mother, and she understands that it is, indeed, my gift. Her expression, in the lamplight of the coming evening, is soft and steady.

"You are not what I expected," she says at last.

"And what did you expect?"

She hesitates for a moment, and then says quietly, "Philip of Macedon."

"And am I to be found wanting?"

"Had I the choice? Had I the choice, you would be Philip, for he would never have come so far, and fared so well. You come, lion of the west, and you bring the shadow with you."

"She does not trust me," I tell Hephaestion, after I have made the rounds of the tents that house the injured. I have tended my duties here; I have made my sacrifices to the God of Healing and the Lord of Gods.

"Should she?"

"She is no threat to me."

"Is that your way of saying yes?"

I hit his shoulder with half my strength. He laughs, well-pleased.

"You disapprove?"

"No, Alexander, I don't. It has never been your way to measure strength by the weakness of those you subjugate."

"Meaning the women."

He shrugs. "You have a weakness for women."

"Funny. That's not what Olympias said."

"Olympias?"

"She said I had a weakness for you." Before he answers, and he is measuring a reply, I tell him, "I consider it a strength."

"Earn her trust," he says quietly.

"How? I mean to kill and depose her son."

"I know. And she is no fool. She knows it as well."

We spend the evening together, and then, before dawn, I rise.

She is waiting for me. Her daughter, and her grand-children, are nowhere in sight, but they are not of concern. The young seldom are. Some consider them beautiful, but they seem unfinished to me, things with potential but without power.

Sisygambis has power. It rides the crest of her perfectly balanced shoulders, the elegance of her turned wrist, the cool neutrality—especially that—of the gaze she turns up to meet mine. Although I could take that power from her in a moment, power of the type she possesses is not one that can be bestowed; it is for that reason that it fascinates, and always has.

She is seated, and upon such a chair as would be a throne in the lands of my birth. That such a chair could exist so close to a place of war makes me wonder what we will find in his palace, in his many palaces, where craftsmen have laboured long on works that will remain enshrined where they stand.

"What do you desire of me, Alexander?" She uses my name, and not my title. Nor should she; I have taken territory but her son has not yet fallen into my hands. Just a hint of amusement shows in the corner of her eyes, her lips. "I am far too old to be a worthy wife, and if I am not mistaken, it will be some time before you take one."

"Oh?"

She does not elaborate, and I do not press her, thinking of all of the lectures I have heard from my own distant mother.

"I don't know."

"That is not a good answer. For we—my daughters, my granddaughters, and I—have learned that it is only by offering what is wanted that we maintain our grace and our position. Is it not so in your lands?"

I think of my mother. "To some, perhaps."

"Are we to be kept for bargaining?"

"I am sorry, but there will be no bargaining."

She is silent. "Then for status?"

"Certainly for status." I meet her gaze; she does not falter, does not dissemble.

"You cannot rule these lands," she says softly, "and be son of Macedon. If you seek to retain what you gain by conquest, you will have to *be* of Persia."

"And you can teach me that?"

"I . . . do not know. You are not my son. You are not like my son."

I bow my head. "He cannot survive this," I tell her softly.

"I know."

"And can you forgive me his death?"

"I . . . am not certain," she says. This, too, is truth. She is so unlike my mother.

"Will you try?"

"I have little choice in the matter."

"You have all choice in the matter," I reply, desiring no evasiveness. "What I have granted to you, I grant you in fullness; you are not my pawn; you are subject to my laws, but not my will."

"And my daughter?"

"She is your daughter."

"She is not to be married to one of your generals—your satraps?"

"No."

"And her daughters?"

"I will not marry them to consolidate my own position," I tell her quietly. "I will not marry them against the choice of their queen."

"You will have a queen in Persia who is not your wife?"

"You are Queen," I tell her quietly.

"And your own wives?"

I say nothing. She bows her head gracefully. "I have spoken at length with your Aristander."

The room is suddenly cold. "Why?"

"There is a journey that you must make," she says quietly. "What it makes of you will define you."

"And that journey?"

"You must go to the oracle in the desert oasis of Siwah."

"Another oracle."

"An oracle," she replies, "that is revered here. Siwah knows no political connection, and it owes allegiance only to its own truth." She rises, and then pauses, gazing at me again. "You must think me a poor mother," she says at last, "who does not plead for her son, or defy the man who intends to be his death."

"No," I tell her, and it is truth, although Olympias would never tender such an answer and have it contain any truth. "I do not know how to judge you."

"Nor I you. Perhaps it is best to let time and experience

lend us that grace. Go to Siwah, and I will wait upon the answer that you receive there."

She tests me once, but it is a minor test. The tribes who keep the hills in their wandering numbers have extracted, for years, a toll from the Great King in return for unmolested passage through their lands. It is not a toll to my liking, for what a hundred thousand men cannot keep, a handful of bandits will not hold against me.

But they come to the Queen Mother, and they plead their case at her delicate feet, asking for clemency and mercy.

I am not present for that meeting, although I have allowed it. She comes to me.

"I have been asked to intercede on behalf of an old people and an old tradition," she says, with only Hephaestion and Parmenion as witness. She bends knees to the covered ground.

"Will you speak on behalf of bandits?"

"No. Only on behalf of those treaties which have bound my family for generations."

"And what would you have of me?"

"They require no toll of you or your army," she replies.

"Good."

"But they would continue, as they have, their taxing of the merchants and the others who pass through these lands. And they would continue unhunted by your armies."

"And would you have them do so?"

"I have pledged them what support, meagre though it might be, my title has left me."

Clever woman. She raises her face; Parmenion's eyes are as narrow as a blade's edge.

He looks to me; he knows that hunting scattered men through the hilly terrain is the work of months, and that men will be lost who otherwise might serve against the greater threat; he also knows that in allowing this, I cede authority to a captive. He says nothing.

"Tell them," I say, "that by the grace of the Queen Mother, they are to be spared for their insolence, and that while they conform to the treaty they have offered her, they will be allowed to continue as they have been."

She does not look surprised. Nor does she look pleased. She gathers herself, leaving the ground behind only after she has pressed her head to it, acknowledging the greater difference between our ranks.

Hephaestion says, "Was that wise?"

"Who can say?"

"But you don't regret it."

"Not in the slightest."

He laughs. "Be careful, Alexander."

"I am."

I am Alexander. I am Alexander of Macedon. I am hegemon of the Greek League. I am the son of Queen Ada in Caria, her only heir. I am the King of Asia.

But of these things, I have already spoken. It is in Egypt that the world is changed, or that the meaning of Alexander is changed, for it is in Egypt, with its towering monuments a proof against the passage of time, that I am met as son of god, that I am revered as living god.

I had not thought to treat this seriously. Of the golden baths and the yards of silk, the gold and silver, the jewels and treasures that have come into our hands with each loss that Darius has taken, I have seen only the pragmatic: I will keep my army. To my men, I have been generous, but in truth it is an easy generosity: I intend to have more, much more, than the simple wealth of days.

But upon the banks of the Nile, within the streets, and upon the great steps of the palace that is both temple and monument, all things shift uneasily beneath my feet.

Aristander is by my side. He has been silent these many months, speaking not in the riddles of prophecy or vision, but in the wry, sparing comments of an older man. But he, too, feels the shift in the winds, as if they were divine, and he, too, is changed. Or changed again.

The black eyes he turns upon me, crusted by brow that is

black and white, are eyes I have seen before, but I had thought them swallowed in Macedon, consumed at last by Troy.

No. He bows before me, and before the brightly robed, wizened priests who come, in glory and grandeur, to offer me the crown of pharaohs; he abases himself, as one might abase oneself in the presence of high priests and their hidden, insidious lords.

I have been offered the open gates of many cities upon the Royal Road; those that have been closed, I have opened myself, and at cost. But those cities become as ghosts, a dim memory; this one, this great, dry place, with its warm heat and the green of its cultivated banks, becomes all of my reality.

I fear the heat, and the fire; I turn to Hephaestion. His eyes, as Aristander's, are dark. He does not abase himself before me; I have never required that of him. But he is silent; the weight of history has sealed his lips, depriving him of words.

"You are the son of Nectanebo," the priest says. "You are the true son of the last pharoah of Egypt; the last pharoah to bear the blood of Ra in his veins. We welcome you home, Great King; we ask you to intercede with the gods on our behalf, for our voices have been almost stilled in the hands of the lesser men who have claimed rulership of these lands."

There is hope in these people, but more: certainty.

I look to Aristander. He rises slowly. And I hear his words, his dark words, although no one else looks askance.

There is another sacrifice to be made, Alexander. The gods are waiting.

It is therefore to Siwah that I will travel: Siwah, at the behest of Sisygambis; Siwah at the behest of Aristander.

Siwah, on my own behalf, made strange by the heat of the desert and the heat of Egypt, by the glory of my dreams of this Alexandria, which will surely be the greatest of all the cities that bear my name. People make offerings not to gods, but to *me,* and in my name, I accept their honor, and I honor them in my own fashion. I make offerings to Apis, to the gods that have long been shunted one side by Darius, Great King no longer. I offer the priests the power and respect that is their due.

But I do this through a fog, a golden fog; it has settled upon me like a drizzle, a rain, an unknown veil. I cannot lift it, and if I am honest, I do not wish to do so.

Not since Heracles has man ascended, escaping the bonds of his mortality.

But surely, I have done what Heracles has not?

"Not yet," Aristander says softly, as if all thought, even mine, is known to him on this day.

If I am the son of a god, then the only crime for which I might be judged is no longer crime, and the Furies do not wait upon me in their grim judgment.

The women are of little interest to me; I leave them behind. All save Sisygambis, who asks leave to accompany the army upon this quest. I grant it; in the end, there is—as I promised—only one thing that I will not grant her.

Two, for if she begged death of me, my answer would be no. She might seek it by her own hand, but she would not receive it by mine. I have come to value her, and I throw away nothing of value unless there is something to be gained by its loss.

In the desert, the winds come upon us unaware, and we are almost lost to the blinding light of the sun, the suffocating heat of the desert day, the chill of its terrible, barren night. Aristander saves us; Aristander becomes the guide who leads us to the oasis of Siwah.

He walks like a ghost. His feet barely touch the ground; I cannot see them in the whirl of desert robes beneath his sandals. If he casts a shadow, it is also swept aside; were I a man to own fear, I would fear him. But I own none. I have come to the desert shrine in need of answers, and if my life is forfeit in the attempt, so be it. It is not the first time I will place my life in the balance; not the last.

No life is worth living if it must be lived timidly and without passion. Not even a god's life.

*   *   *

"Son of Amon, Great King, Lord of the Two Lands, I greet you."

The man that greets me, surrounded as if in a dance by other men, is not old, is not young; he is caught between these two states, in a perpetual prime that radiates outward from his center. He casts a dwindling shadow down the stairs as I approach, and I am caught in that shadow, revealed by it.

If Aristander's gaze has been the heart of all mystery, there is, in this man's gaze, the promise of answers, of an end to questions.

I do not kneel before him. Not here; not beneath the sun's gaze, not before the gathered assembly of my generals. Nor can I fail to do him honor, for in this place, this distant place, his is the power; I am the supplicant.

As if he can hear me, and perhaps he can, he takes my hands in his, and bows his head. In the heat, in the sun's trickery of light, his skin gleams like metal, like scales. I have touched the serpents in my mother's chambers; they have touched me. I know what they feel like.

"Come," he says. "The journey you must undertake, you must undertake alone. Will you enter into the temple? You must leave behind your arms and your armor."

I unbuckle my sword and lay it across the steps, careful not to place it before his feet. The armor is less of a loss, for although we are no longer besieged by the desert, the heat holds dominion. This, too, I lay across the steps.

Hephaestion comes to stand at my side, and the priest raises his head, his eyes half-lidded, as if against light.

"Alone," he says softly.

"Guard my sword, my shield," I tell Hephaestion. "Let no other touch it until I emerge."

Hephaestion frowns, but he also nods.

I follow the priest into the temple.

Incense is burning. I cannot place the whole of its scent; it is heavy, cloying, something that might better be drunk than inhaled. But beyond this veil of smoke, there is light; the stone of the temple has been cut in several places, and light gapes like bleeding wounds across the flat, stone floor. There are hollows here where feet have passed, a hundred, a hundred thousand, times, over and over in some prescribed dance that will remain forever closed to me. But they mark a path, they mark time. I hesitate as he walks these subtle grooves, and he stops.

"We are not yet finished," he said quietly. "Follow or stand."

I do not follow his path; it has not been my way to follow the well-trod ground before; to seek safety in the comfort of numbers. Even when the army has been at its strongest, I have been at its head, the lion's jaws, and not its wayward tail.

I cross the length of this open hall, and the priest watches where I have chosen to place my feet.

"Very well," he says, when I reach him. "There are many ways to cross a desert, and as long as they lead you to the oasis, no man can offer argument." He does not frown.

"But beyond this point, there is no path to follow, no path to abjure. You have made your way here. You must make your way out." He claps his hands. Thunder answers, and lightning.

He is gone, and when I turn, so, too is the door. One by one, the windows—those slashes in stone, those careful cuts, close; darkness descends in a circle that can be traced by its growing strength.

But I am not afraid of darkness. I am Alexander. I have come for answers.

Will I rule Asia?

Light opens up beneath my feet; stone grates against stone as I listen. I have no weapon, here; no shield; no bodyguard. I am a man of scant stature, but I *am* a man. From out of the shadows comes shade; it drinks in the light until it has assumed a form that I recognize. Blood has dried across robes meant for ceremony and not for war, and his expression is forbidding and remote.

Philip of Macedon.

I stand my ground. I have come for answers. If this is the whole of the answer I am to receive, it is still the truth.

"You murdered me," he says; his voice is a voice that has urged men—the men I now lead—to victory time and again.

"I saved you once," I reply. "Were it not for my intervention, you would have died on that field, and I would have come months earlier into my manhood."

He says nothing.

"Will you set the Furies upon me? Will I be hounded as parricide? I think not. What are the Furies, after all, but a stain upon immortality, a sting in the tail of legend?"

"I have not come to argue with you, Alexander."

"You never argued overmuch. You made your decisions."

"And you have made yours. Will you now forsake the bloodline? Will you now ascend? Will you be the son of Amon in the East?"

"Can you offer me that?"

"I offer nothing but the truth."

"You are not here for vengeance?"

"Of what use is vengeance to the dead?" He laughs. It is not a kind laugh. "Of what use is *anything* to the dead? I have come. If you have the courage to face me, you will have what you desire."

"Your advice? I have had my fill of it, and if that is all that is offered—"

"You will leave? How?"

There is only silence, but I hate to offer him that. "I don't know. But I rarely know until the battle is joined what the course of that battle will be. Plans are like dreams; they vanish when you wake."

He smiles bitterly. "What would you know, Alexander?"

"Am I your son?"

"You are no son of mine."

He has said just those words before. But they carried a different weight, then. They do not fill me with fear; they do not fill me with anger. They do not threaten my future.

"And my father?"

He says, "You are as you have chosen to be: son of Amon,

Pharoah of Egypt, Lord of Two Lands, while you are worshipped as such. Worship will transform you, Alexander. It has already begun. All power that gods know is gained by worship, and those gods that fail to find worship, fail. That is how gods die."

It is not to speak of the death of gods that I have come, but his words strike me; they are cold.

"Will I rule all of Asia?"

"You will rule," he says remotely, "all of the land you have taken, and all of the land that you take. But you have chosen a hero's path. You may not turn from it, now. The time for peace has passed you by."

"What do you mean?"

"You will know. When battle is offered, you will win only if you join it; there is to be no victory afforded you in any other way."

"I will win any battle I join?"

"Yes."

"I will be King of Persia?"

"Yes. Yes, as was prophesied in Gordion, you will be all these things."

I bow. I bow to him, and then I tell him, quietly, "You may go."

It surprises me when he does, although I cannot say why. I feel a loss when the light becomes the simple light of sun, stretched and cut along the smooth floor.

Aristander is waiting for me when I emerge.

"You have made your second sacrifice," he says quietly.

"Have I?"

"Yes."

"What have I given up, seer? My father? I said my farewells to my father before I left Macedon."

"Do you not know?"

"It is not my custom to ask questions for which I already have answers."

"It is," he says wryly. "And men have died when their answers do not match the answers that you have."

He is unchanged. I did not expect that. I do not know why. "I have never played that game with you."

"You did, Great King. The first time we met. You sought to catch me out, to play me for a fool, if fool I was."

"You passed. Prove that you are not a fool now. Answer me."

"Your mortality," he says. "You have sacrificed your mortality."

"I would that all sacrifices could be so pleasant," I tell him, thinking of Olympias.

"Not all sacrifices make their price known immediately," he replies. "Understand what it is that you have offered."

Siwah is silent; night lies upon her palm trees, her native greenery. Beyond the fecund stretch of land, desert waits. And within the encampment, Sisygambis waits as well.

She bows when she greets me, but it is not in gestures of subservience that I am interested; I wait until she rises. From the ground, she meets my gaze; she holds it for a while, and then she lowers the lids of her eyes, dropping her chin.

"Sisygambis."

"Lord."

"What do you see?"

"I see," she says softly, "the death of my son."

"That is all?"

"No." She rises. "I will teach you."

"Teach me?"

"What it means to be the Great King."

Her words do not come to me at once, as if they were a single sentence; they come in broken fragments, until they form a whole. Understanding is seldom this difficult. "You could forgive a man the death of your son?"

"A man? No. But you are no longer that, and against the gods, only fools rail." She rises. "I make no demands of you. But I ask—I ask for—"

I lift a hand. "Your daughter, and all of your kin whose lives you value, I will spare. All save his."

"If you—" She stops herself for just a moment.

"Sisygambis, speak plainly."

"If you come upon my living son, and it is within your power to do so, give me the chance to bid him farewell."

I nod, and she leaves me.

I wonder, then, what cost Aristander spoke of, for it seems to me that I have gained much by shedding the mortality that he feels I have undervalued.

We meet Darius again on the field. He has his cavalry, and they are mounted and armed in a foreign manner; he has his infantry, and although they are poor they stand arrayed in great number. But the pride of his army is to be found in his chariots; in their great, bladed wheels and their fearless horses, their determined charioteers, he has placed his greatest faith.

I am eager to test my own against that faith; for after all, we two kings tested faith again and again when we faced each other across the mass of men bristling with armor and weapons, each having chosen their lives and their deaths.

He has his strength in numbers. I grant him that; I will grant him nothing else.

Parmenion stands to my left; Philotas, his son, to my right. "They have cleared a road for their chariots," Philotas says neutrally.

"They have cleared a road for the Companion footsoldiers," I reply. He nods; the footsoldiers are at their best when upon level ground; it is on hilly terrain, or when the rocks are too broad, that we take our greatest casualties, for it is difficult for them to walk in lockstep, abreast, with their weapons, three yards long, in an even, undinted line.

The Persians travel in a line that is many hundreds deep, and many wide; it is not the formation Parmenion favors, and I understand why; there is no mobility in it, no ability to react.

Sisygambis comes to me. I did not expect to see her, but as Olympias before her, she goes where she feels she must, and I do not deny her the privilege.

"Will you plead for your son now?" Philotas asks. He will pay for that, but later.

She does not answer him. Instead, she says, "We will wait with the royal tent and the baggage; we are no good in war." She hesitates a moment, and then says, "You have honored me, Alexander. I honor you in my fashion. Go with the gods."

I bow. I do not know what it has cost her to say this, but I see it a moment in the stiffness of her bearing. She leaves me in silence.

The armies begin to move.

Many of my own will die here; many of my brothers. They will lift sword and spear in my name; they will hold shield steady, although those shields be riven by arrow and spear; they will stand their ground, keeping to their formation, stepping over the bodies of the fallen to take up the positions that the battle decrees. They will do this independent of me, but for me, and I grieve and exult at their loyalty.

I go to speak with them, and to ride with the cavalry.

"If indeed I am son to the great god Zeus-Amon, he will show us his favor today, for although their numbers are greater by far than our own, they have only a man to lead them—a man who runs, who has always run, from battle."

In Gaugamela, I make the kingdom mine. But I am not willing to rest there; I order the men east. They are weary, but they have triumphed in my cause, and they know me now.

Months have passed. I do not feel them. I have fought; I have taken injuries. But the time itself is inconsequential.

The men, though, are weary. They have had victory, and they have had plunder beyond their greatest dreams, but while my heart turns to the plains of the distant east—the realms that lie beyond the understanding of our greatest historians, our most noteworthy travelers—theirs turn to the land they call home. Macedon.

"Not even your father would have sought so wide or vast

an empire," Hephaestion tells me. His voice is heavy. I look at him.

"My father?" I answer, cool now. "My father has no need of such a paltry kingdom."

He takes a half-step back, and his eyes are wide. But they narrow as I wait. "Alexander, the jungles are wet and hot, and our swords and armor rust almost the moment we have cleaned the cursed water from their surfaces. The fevers here are strange; the rain worse than the whole of Darius's three armies.

"What you have achieved in these lands will never be equaled—but I tell you now that the Macedonians will not continue beyond the border of the Beas." He gestures; the river lies before us, and beyond it, the heart of a new land. I know so little of it, and I would know more.

"Will they disobey me if I order them on?"

He hesitates. "It would break something in them," he says at last, but quietly, "to disobey their king. But you have adopted strange titles, and strange dress, in these lands. You ride upon elephants, where we have the time to march with them; you adorn yourself in the colors of the east."

"They are a gift."

"It doesn't matter."

"Hephaestion?"

"It will break something in them, but they will be broken by their own choice; they will not cross the Beas. If you go, some handful of us will journey with you, but no more, and it is not upon a handful of men that you will build your greater empire."

"And the Iranians?"

"They will follow you. The tempers of this land do not drive them to despair."

I nod.

Aristander, uncharacteristically silent, speaks now. "You cannot turn back without cost," he says softly.

"I cannot go forward without an army."

He says nothing; his silence is loud.

"I will make another; we will return to the Beas. I am

young, and the years will afford me the time to build an army of *men.*"

Hephaestion almost cringes at the way I use the word. He has never questioned me about the Siwah Oracle. He has never denied me the divinity that I chose there. And he has never feared that the taking of these two things has changed me beyond recall. But he has never acknowledged the change, either.

"Aristander, go out. Go to those craven, tired men, and perform a divination in my name. I will join you."

"What question would you have me ask, Great King?"

"Whatever question you deem most suitable."

He bows.

When he leaves, I am free to vent my rage; it is deep and bitter. Sisygambis is not beside me, and there is nothing to hinder the words that I speak only in the privacy of my tent.

"I am guaranteed victory in battle," I tell Hephaestion, "and not in retreat."

"By who?"

"By the gods," I tell him bitterly. "And the gods are unbending."

"They do not care overmuch for the fate of men," he replies.

"And have my men lost all faith in me?"

"They have lost no faith in you. They have lost faith in themselves, in this place. Had they lost faith in you, they would not have come to plead; they would have come bearing arms. They follow their king, Alexander, but they cannot keep up with him. Let them rest a while in your shadow; let them gather strength; those that are weak, send home. But you will break faith with them if you choose the Beas."

"Or they will break faith with me."

He says nothing.

Aristander's offerings provoke a bleak response. I do not ask him what they mean, or what they portend. Instead, I offer his warnings to my men. I tell them that they are the gods' portents, and the gods have told me that if I cross the

Beas, it will go poorly. Where I would not, of course, bow to the demands of men, the auguries of the gods cannot be disdained; I tell them that we will turn back.

It is a way of saving face, and Hephaestion knows it at once. Perhaps the Macedonians know it as well, but if they do, they are wise enough not to accuse me of such subterfuge. Instead, they offer me tears, gratitude; they look to the west as if all of the distance we have traveled together could be crossed by the simple intensity of a glance, and then they retreat to their tents to begin the chore of packing.

The rains are heavy, this day; the air is so humid it seems strange that rain falls at all.

But after my men have gone, I look to Aristander. His gaze is bleak.

"What have you seen?"

"The price you will pay if you do not ford the river," he says quietly.

"How heavily does it weigh against the price I must pay if I do?"

"That is not for me to decide," he replies. But his wariness is answer enough: the cost will be high.

If I could force them on, I would. But the other words of the Siwah Oracle weigh heavily upon me; I need these men, and not simply for the strength of their arms, for those are failing. I need their faith. They believe in me. And no god exists without the raw strength, the visceral strength, of that belief.

"Can I lead them back in safety?"

He says nothing.

And so we come at last to this place. Miles have passed beneath our feet as we walk the ocean's shoreline, sand giving way to rock, and rock to sand, and all giving way to salt.

The fleet has not come. It is the first time that this has happened, and I wonder if the fleet has been destroyed by storms in the open sea, or if Nearchus has proved traitor. He has not come.

The monsoons have come instead, and the ocean harbors

them. But the water falls upon the shoreline, with no life to give it purchase, and I wonder if the jungles have become a less bitter memory for my Macedonian soldiers. The heat here is dry, and the swords do not rust so readily, but green has given way to gray, gold, and blue; we are surrounded on all sides by water we cannot drink and land we can take no sustenance from.

The ships that Nearchus had command of were to carry the food the army requires; we have a dwindling supply that we have carried upon our backs, or the backs of the pack animals that I allow. I have waited here two days, and for each of those days, the food has diminished. We can find water, if we dig for it, or if we search some miles inland, but the water will not sustain us.

"Alexander." Hephaestion bows. He is given leave to come and go at will, and he passes into my presence like shadow.

"Nearchus?"

He shakes his head.

"We cannot wait upon the ships," I say at last.

"Can we go back?"

"We don't have the food." Hephaestion knows this. Knows it, and must hear it again, or he would not ask. "The army has passed over the three hundred miles from Pattala; what we *could* take from the land has been taken. There is no forage, and no further food, to be found there; to lead the army back that way is certain death."

"We cannot go forward."

"We have crossed desert before," I tell him.

"Not this desert. It is said—"

"I know what is said. But if we go inland, we will hit Jhau, and there are provisions there, if scant, that have not yet been plundered."

"The Jhau tract is not known for fertility."

"No. But there is hope that way. And back? None. Tell the men that we must move. We have spent two days here, and we could ill afford those; we will not waste another day's provisions. Gather water."

* * *

They pray for rain.

It is a twist of fortune; the rains that were to defeat the Beas crossing are suddenly a great cause for nostalgia. Skin cracks and weathers beneath the harsh glare of the sun. The tribes of the Jhau will remember our passage through their skeletal lands, for we have taken what we needed: everything. And we have given them only death in return, although the promise of wealth and supplies has left the lips of the generals who were cruel enough to hold out hope.

The dead that we have left behind are not only native; they are ours. The children have difficulty with the pace of the march, as do the pack animals. The women bear it in silence, and I can see, when I turn to look at the vast and straggling army at my back, that many of these women have chosen to bear the burden of their children for as long as their legs will allow it.

It is not long; it is not that long. Two days, at twenty miles a day, and I see fewer and fewer of these. The children weigh less as the days progress, but their mothers shed weight as well, and some of that weight is not their own. We cannot afford to stop; not for rest. We march during the night, and we sleep when the sun is at its peak, but the moon is bright, and the skies cloudless; there is no mercy in darkness.

They look to me.

I feel both their faith and their fear, and both are scalding, burdens almost too heavy to be borne.

On the third night, Aristander comes to my tent. He is gaunt and tired with travel, but his eyes are still the same: they speak of mystery and of vision, and the two are inseparable.

I would shake answers from him, but I must conserve my strength. In truth, I am weary; the wound that I took in Tyre seems reluctant to heal, and it bows me when I can least afford it. I will not take water from the mouths of my men, and drink is in scant supply. In the distance, the shortened screams of pack animals falling are followed by silence; they will be slaughtered, eaten, sacrificed to the soldiery.

I will take none of them.

"Aristander."

"Alexander."

"Why have you come?"

"We are a day's march from the bed of a dry river."

"Dry?"

"It will fill. Even in this vast and barren tract, the rains fall. But they fall in fury, and nothing holds them back. The riverbeds are dangerous."

He waits.

No; the sounds of the falling animals are not the only cries I hear. But they are the only ones I wish to identify in this place. I have led them here. I.

"You cannot save them all," he says softly.

"Can I save any of them?"

"At a price."

"Name it. Name it quickly."

He looks to Hephaestion then.

I will not sacrifice Hephaestion. "Hephaestion, go."

"Go?"

"Stand guard. I will speak with Aristander alone."

"No."

"That is not a request, Hephaestion."

Once before, once, he stood at my side while I bore witness. He hesitates. The only witness to his disobedience is Aristander, but things have changed. It is not with a king's voice that I speak, for I do not think that would move him. It is . . . a god's. *"Hephaestion, leave me."*

He stares at me. His face is still and smooth, although new hollows adorn his cheeks. "Alexander . . ." He leaves us.

I turn to Aristander. I am weary, now.

"You cannot save them all," he continues, his eyes as sharp and clear as the distant stars. "But you can save some third."

"How?"

"You are general here. You are king and god. The gods have drowned whole cities, or buried them beneath the lava's flood. If the supplies are saved, if the army is winnowed, you will feed some thirty thousand. But no more; no more than that." He looks to the walls of the tent, and beyond it. He speaks, to me and not to me. The words drift back as if from a height or a distance.

The river. The rain.

"Choose," he says. "And by your choice be known."

"Is this, then, the sacrifice that is demanded of me?"

He says nothing.

"Why, Aristander?"

"You ask me that?"

"Yes."

"Because you are as a god, and you are the only fate the army knows."

"Leave me."

He does not hesitate; he is not Hephaestion.

But in the wake of his departure, I consider his words with care. I consider dying here. I think of the women, the children, the way the one carries the other until both fall.

In the Makran desert, I make my choice.

The riverbed lies before us, its walls both wide and hard. It is a grave, a grave open to air and the sight of the gods who might watch. I know that they watch with a remote interest; that they watch without mercy. The quality of a god's mercy will never be trusted again.

I know, for I have taken such mercy as is offered, and I have swallowed it whole. I do not know to whom gods pray, but I pray, now, that it will not devour me from within.

Or that it will take me quickly.

I have set the royal tent within the center of the riverbed. I stand within it, and beyond me, circling the tent in the tatters of their own smaller quarters, the women and children bed down for the night. The children are few, and they are weakened now beyond my ability to measure.

The men wander among their wives, but they will not stay long; I have ordered them up, beyond the walls of the small canyon. Those who obey my orders will have no cause to thank me; those who do not will have no avenue of complaint. I am not harsh. I, too, wander among the women.

They have never raised spears, except to clean them; they have never lifted sword; they have not walked into the death offered by the armies of my enemies. But they have offered solace and comfort to the men who have, these shadow wives; they have borne children, and kept pace with the soldiers that they have been chosen by.

I would spare them, if I could.

But it is better this way. To watch them dwindle and die invokes some echo of the helplessness that moves me; it breaks my men in a way that war-wounds, that sieges, that even the great elephants, have not.

So, I choose.

As if it were a battlefield, this vast desert, as if nature itself were a king who I know will not grant me the mercy of burying my dead, I lay out a plan of battle; I choose the flank I might sacrifice in order to attain victory.

I bide here, among the women, while the rains start in the north. My tent, my flag, all of my possessions, are nestled among them, an illusory gesture of safety. Only the supplies have been moved to higher ground, but in times of scarcity this is not unusual; it takes trusted men to guard the supplies that will feed what remains of the army. Those who have eaten too well in the first days of this grim march will soon be without, and if the supplies were not well guarded, they would become too much of a temptation. I have already had seven men put to death over a simple matter of food.

Hephaestion joins me in my tent. Although we have taken little comfort from each other in the past two weeks, old habits assert themselves when we pause to rest; our guard is dropped and we seek those things which we hope will lend us strength.

But not tonight.

Tonight, when he enters the long corridor of the tent, I stop him with a gesture. He pulls up short, too distant to touch, or to be touched.

"Alexander."

"No. I need you with the men."

He is silent. He knows me. He knows me too well.

And yet I see in his face some doubt; what he knows, he no longer trusts. It hurts me, but the hurt is so slight compared to the burden I have chosen to carry that I cannot address it now.

"Later," I tell him. "Later, you will understand everything."

He has always been a more patient man than I.

The rains come.

But they come not as torrent and not as storm; they come not as relief from the endless thirst and heat of the desert, but as proof that the answer to a prayer can be a cruel gesture of divinity. Water, like a moving wall, passes through the river bed. There is some warning, but it is the warning of thunder before the lightning falls. In Macedon, we have no such storms, no such graves, no such stretches of endless heat, endless cold.

Who among us could have predicted the flood that remade the river?

I hear it, for I have been waiting. I leave the tent in which I have sequestered myself; my side aches, troubled now by the ghost of the worst of my wounds. I hear the shouting, diminished as it is by thunder, the voice of water.

I am not afraid of water.

I am not afraid of anything but this: what I have chosen to do, what I have done, what I bear witness to. Do the gods judge their own?

I stand in the lee of the tent, in the heart of the storm and invite the only possible answer to that question. Let the waters come. Let the miracle follow. Else, let me be swept away with these people that I have always kept safe, at the back of the army, behind the lines of battle.

They do not have the time to cry out; they are swept away by the water. The tent is torn from the ground, its moorings struck as if by the fall of rock. I feel the water upon my face, my back, my hands; I feel it upon my legs.

But here, a miracle: I am Alexander, the Great King, son

of Amon, Lord of Two Lands, and the river passes me by. What prayers I have made have been answered.

Grief is our companion as we continue our trek through the desert. My men have learned a bitter lesson with the passage into evening; there is not a riverbed in the whole of Gedrosia that would tempt them to risk a similar loss. They waste water for tears, and their throats are raw with screams, with hoarse shouts; not a few were washed away in a vain attempt to save from the waters what the sun and the desert would have taken anyway.

The responsibility for the loss is not theirs.

They do not descend into savagery; they do not lose honor in deserting the weak and the helpless. I set the march at twenty miles a day. I come from the floods, wet, but whole, and they follow me.

Perhaps this is why I was spared: they follow me. They look to no other for commands. I promise them that I will lead those who can march through the length of the sandy valleys and into Carmania, where supplies await us.

Those who can, march.

But not all of the men who survived are fit to march; they fall by the roadside; they sleep on their feet. Some one or two who have fallen by the wayside in exhaustion might wake themselves in time to join the main body of the army; those who are lost from its tail, are lost. The desert buries our dead. That is the worst of our disgraces: we have not honored our fallen.

Aristander, thinner now, is still alive. He stumbles and rights himself, time and again; the desert does not defeat him. I do not care.

But I look for Hephaestion, among the Companion Calvary, many of whom will go horseless for months. Or forever. He is there, dwindling, but steady. He meets my gaze and looks away; this is to be repeated during the long week that we tread the sands.

We lose our way when the sand, carried by howling wind,

rises. We lose our brothers. But at least they lie buried; their faces are not turned skyward in accusation.

The desert strips away pretensions. It does not differentiate between the young and the old. Each step taken is an act of faith, an act of will. And it is by such faith, and such will, that we find our way through to Carmania.

I wonder what gods feel, if they feel at all.

The desert changed us. The desert changed me. But more than that, worse, the desert changed Hephaestion. And he was the only truth that remains of my early life.

I did not notice it at first. I cannot clearly say why. For a long time after we escaped the Makran, the desert lay in my heart, and in the heart of all that I chose to do. Only in the absolute finery of the Persian court, with its colour, its glitter, its profusion of exotic life, was an oasis to be found. There, and in the cool evenings in the quarters of Sisygambis.

She is not my mother, and I am not her son, but I have lost the one, and she the other. She does not ask me to speak, when I have no words to offer; she does not ask my advice; she does not wait upon my orders. She is not wife, and she is not mistress; she has not ruled me; she has not served me.

But she is quiet this evening, and when I, too, am quiet for long enough she says, simply, "You must make peace with Hephaestion."

"We are not at war."

She bows her head, for it is not her way to argue; not with words. But her silence has textures. "I will not ask you what occurred in the desert."

"Have you asked Hephaestion?"

She doesn't answer.

"Sisygambis?"

"I do not understand the friendship between you," she answers at last. "I have never understood it. At one time, I may have disapproved of it."

"And now?"

She looks up and she smiles; it is lovely, but elegiac. I do not like the look.

It is to Aristander that I go.

He is waiting for me. "Aristander, I would speak with you."

"I know." His eyes are dark, his expression sombre. His hair is whiter, an artifact of the Makran.

"I will not offer you anything else. I *will* not, do you understand?"

He meets my gaze without flinching. "It is not to me that you have made your offerings. It has never been to me."

I am silent.

"Then I will offer nothing else. I will be content."

"Godhood is not so easily withdrawn, Alexander, once it has been granted."

"Gods perish without followers."

"You will never be without followers," he replies. Remote, now. "Already your court is more Persian than not, and the Persians offer you reverence that your own men never will. Mortality will not define you. It will not dog you."

"It is not the fear of mortality that dogs me now. I tell you, I tell the gods themselves if they are listening, that I will not sacrifice Hephaestion to them."

He bows his head.

Hephaestion.

Although he exists in the splendour of the Persian court, although he has adopted the same manner of dress, the same clipped beard, the same gold, he is gaunt, and there is a hollowness to his face that will never leave it.

He is wealthy now; wealth defined not in the meager trappings of the home of our youth, but in the glory of Babylon. But the gold itself does not shine for him; it is cold around his throat, his wrists, in the hollow of his throat.

"Hephaestion." We are alone. It is hard, in the court, to be alone. It was never this hard in Macedon.

He hears me, and drops at once to his knees; he offers me

the kiss of obeisance, the gesture of the lesser to the greater. It does not please me.

"We are alone here," I tell him, shaking my hand free of his grip. "Formalities of the court need not be observed."

He bows his head a moment, and then he rises—but he stands a few inches away from the tips of those fingers.

I am at a loss for words, and words seldom fail me. Even action is remote; I am bound by the distance he places between us.

"Hephaestion."

"Alexander."

His eyes skirt the ground, the lavish carpets, the decorations woven by slaves. In the light, he casts a long shadow.

"You fear me."

He is silent.

"Why? Have I given you cause to doubt me?"

"I do not doubt you," he says, but heavily, as if even these scant words are wearying. "You led us across the desert. You brought us home. You brought us," he continues, looking up, "here. The men that return to Macedon return as rich men; they would not have had a tenth the wealth had you not chosen to travel east. Had your ambitions been the ambitions of a . . . lesser man." He looks at me, then. "I miss Macedon," he says softly. "Do you?" The words are a challenge.

I do not know how to answer that challenge.

"I know what you did," he continues. "I understand the choice you made."

"Then understand—"

"I could not have made the choice you did."

"Hephaestion—"

"But I would have shared the burden of it, had I been given leave."

"I did not want—"

"I know. Alexander, ask me why."

"Why?"

"Why I miss Macedon."

I shake my head, staring at him, seeing the lines that the sun and the wind, the sand and the rains, have worn in his face, in the corners of his lips, his eyes. He is not a young man any more.

"In Macedon, you were Alexander."

"I am Alexander now."

"No. Now you are the son of Amon, you are the Great King. There is nothing of Macedon in you, nothing of home. You sit upon a golden throne; your feet cannot be seen to touch the ground when you summon your full court. You wear—*we* wear—robes that would have been dresses, fodder for the richest of our generals' wives. We wear rings, and necklaces, and bracelets; we adorn ourselves in finery that would once have been used to pay soldiery, feed men." He shakes his head. "I knew what you were. I do not know what you are."

I have not changed. But I cannot say the words. I have never lied to Hephaestion, and I do not know how to begin. Because if I must lie, it is over.

I reach out to touch him; he stands, he bears the weight of my hands. But he does not lift his arms, does not lean into the warmth of my palms; does not offer me any like gesture.

"Achilles was the son of a god," I tell him quietly. "the greatest of our heroes."

"He is less of a hero than Alexander," Hephaestion replies. And then he looks at me, his eyes wide, unfettered by lid. "Achilles needed Patrocles."

"I need Hephaestion."

"No. You think you do. But if you could make such a choice, and bear it, you have no need of me."

"You are my heir."

"You will have children. You are married. Roxanne expects no less."

"I am not concerned with her expectations."

"You are not concerned with *any* other expectations. I have nothing of value to offer you. I cannot speak this foreign tongue, and I cannot sing its songs, tell its tales, unravel its bitter politics. This world is not my world, and the only place I have in it is yours."

"And is that not enough?"

"I am not a *woman,* Alexander. I am not a *wife.* I am—I was—a man. What man could easily bear to become superfluous, to become some court's decoration? I offer you loyalty, but even that—even that is given you by others whom you favor. The eunuch. The queen. The successors. There is not, now, anything that I can give you that you cannot find within yourself."

He turns away.

It seems only yesterday that he stood by my side while I watched my mother in the streets around Mieza. Only yesterday that I sent for him when Eurydice bore her son. The deserts are farther away, and less welcome, than either of the earlier memories.

But I can unearth more: our lessons at the side of Aristotle. Our lessons in the light and the dark of our chambers. Our promises, our vows. Were those artifacts of youth? No. We shared our secrets, our conspiracies, and the burden of my guilt. But gods have no need of guilt. All that they do is beyond judgment.

There is a lesson here, and I have not learned it.

Or I have not wished to learn it.

Two men. Two men.

I have the copy of the *Iliad,* bound by Aristotle, and carried in safety these hundreds of miles. It has been years since I last read it, and I seek solace in the myth that once informed my life.

Two great men died at Troy. Choose.

Achilles. Achilles and Patrocles.

But the pages whisper their denial as they shift beneath my fingers.

Achilles achieved what he desired, given the choice. Hector failed. But it is Hector's name that draws the eye, where once I spurned it. Hector, older, and trapped by the duties and the responsibilities his family laid upon him.

I have long despised failure. I despise it now. But I turn those pages until at last I can read no more, for Patrocles has donned the armor that he was never meant to wear, and Patrocles has left the side of Achilles for the last time.

Hephaestion will not live.

"No," Arisander says.

I did not summon him, but he stands in my presence as if commanded to it.

So I speak, out loud, Aristander my only audience, his eyes as dark as they have ever been.

"Achilles achieved what he set out to achieve."

"Yes. He gained a measure of immortality; his name is remembered, and because it is remembered, he leaves a legacy for those who follow."

"Would you have had me choose Hector?"

"I? No."

"Would you have chosen him?"

He is silent.

"Speak, Aristander."

"Achilles achieved what he desired. But what did he desire? Hector failed. Is it not by failure that you have judged him?"

"Yes."

"Then judge him, Alexander, and let him go. He is not for you. You are far from home, and no ties to family, no duty, no promise to honor those that have come before you now binds you."

"And had I chosen Hector?"

"You would not now have all that you have."

"What do I have, Aristander?" I lift a hand that is heavy with gold, with eastern gems.

"What the gods have," he replies, and I see pity in his face. "Your name will be spoken across tens of thousands of miles, by millions of people. Your legacy will spur men who would not recognize either of your worlds to deeds that might not otherwise have been attempted. You will be admired. Men will strive to live up to what you have built."

"And that is all?"

"That is all."

"And if I now want more?"

He says, gently, "What more could a god want? Love? It is ephemeral. Ephemera. Let it go."

"And you?"

"What of me, my lord?"

"Have you seen what you desired to see? Have you found some truth in the whole of my tale, beginning to end?"

He closes his eyes, denying vision. But he nods. He nods, and then, for the first time, he drops to his knees and bows his head at my feet.

I am Alexander.

I am alone.

Hephaestion did not wait for me; he died while I presided over the ceremonies and the games that have come to signify my prestige in these lands.

The only person who would have understood the loss—or perhaps the only person whose understanding I could have freely accepted—is in Macedon, and closed to me now; the first act of this long war. What I did, I bitterly regret now; for she has lived ten years in the shadow of such a loss, and the loss came to her by my hand. If I knew how, I would ask for her forgiveness. But if I were she, I would not now extend it. I wonder if she is happy.

I know why Achilles chose to accept the offer of something beneath contempt, dying enclosed in the halls of a half-ruined temple. I understand why he surrendered the body of the man who had destroyed Patrocles, giving it over to the keeping of Priam, aged father, and one of the few who remained alive to mourn and grieve.

I give Roxanne the child she desires. I give my men the positions that they covet. I drink what they offer me, eat what they choose to place before me.

I know that I will not survive it.

I will go to the halls that the gods call home.

I will speak to them, and if they listen—ah, if they listen, I will ask them for the waters of the Lethe. I will be cleansed, and I will wake in fields that only the dead know well. I will look for Hephaestion there, for surely he must be there, among the heroes of our youth; there and waiting for me to pick up sword, to shed the burden and the trappings of greatness.

He must understand me, now. He must understand what I failed to understand in the days of a youth that was defined by his presence. He will be happy to see me, for I will come to him as I was, and the body of Persia will not stand between us.

But if the gods do not listen? If the gods do not grant my request? Where will I wander then, and for how long? What must I see, what must I preside over, what pleas will reach me in the long, cold halls of the peaked mountains until at last I am forgotten and I am free?

INTENSIFIED TRANSMOGRIFICATION

Barry N. Malzberg and Bill Pronzini

Here, in their first sf/fantasy collaborative effort in over twenty years, two writers offer an imaginative glimpse into the mind of a President Lyndon B. Johnson obsessed with both the Vietnam War and that mid-twentieth century conqueror, Mao Zedong. Individually, Barry N. Malzberg and Bill Pronzini are masterful and prolific writers; together, they have collaborated on thirty-five short stories and the novels *Night Screams*, *Prose Bowl*, *The Running of Beasts*, and *Acts of Mercy*. A collection of their collaborative crime stories, *Problems Solved*, was recently published by Crippen & Landru. Among Pronzini's solo achievements are over fifty novels, four nonfiction books, and numerous articles; his honors include three Shamus Awards, a Lifetime Achievement Award from the Private Eye Writers of America, and six nominations for the Mystery Writers of America's Edgar Award. His most recent

books include the novels *A Wasteland of Strangers*,
Bleeders (in his "Nameless Detective" series), and
Nothing but the Night.

Malzberg, a respected figure who has influenced a
number of science fiction writers, was the first recipi-
ent of the John W. Campbell Award for best novel of
the year in 1972 for *Beyond Apollo*, and also won a
Locus Award for a collection of essays, *Engines of the
Night*. His many notable novels include *Herovit's
World*, *Guernica Night*, *Conversations*, *Galaxies*,
and *The Remaking of Sigmund Freud*.

L et me remind you of the way it was before he tried to
seize absolute power, declare a state of national emergency, enact martial law, create nuclear holocaust. Feverish
times, those, and heady stuff for the aides-de-camp of whom
I was the closest. But that was a little way down the line; we
were still living in "normal" times then. Or so I tried to tell
myself.

Lyndon and I would have our early morning conferences. I
would creep in to find him in a bathrobe, the war reports
spread over the bed, glasses high on his head, open bottle of
bourbon on the sideboard. Here, he would say, more often
than not. Join me. Have a short one.

Impossible to tell if he had stopped late or was starting
early. Or had never stopped at all, that often being Lyndon's
way in those times. No, I would say, I don't think I should do
that.

It's the Lincoln Bedroom, Lyndon said. This is about as
private as it gets. You don't think old Abe would mind, do
you? If it hadn't been for booze he never would have got past
Gettysburg. What's wrong with you? Have one, it will
change your perspective.

I don't want to change my perspective, was what I wanted
to respond. If I fall into thinking like you, Mr. President, we
are all surely doomed. It is only I who is keeping you from
conflagration.

But I didn't say that. I was not interested in heavy response in those days. Call it prudence or cowardice, I did know it would only lead to forms of confrontation I could not bear.

China, Lucky Lyndon said. China's the key to all of this. What we should do is send our bombers over the borders and nuke them. Defoliate the bastards. Force ten million Red Chinese on bicycles to change their goddamned routes to Ching Chow.

Dangerous stuff, I said. I had to say something to this; I couldn't just keep still when he was talking like this. They'll have to respond, they'll come off the mainland and attack the West. They might even come here and attack us.

It was good advice, prudent or cowardly. I was Lyndon's closest advisor then. Such being an inaccurate description, since Mr. President took no advice from anyone; but he said nearly every day that he liked having me around, I reminded him of human weakness and stupidity, qualities he needed to keep in mind at all times if he was truly going to be a good president.

That's true, he said. You might get a strike back, but wouldn't that make Thieu happy anyway? Lyndon laughed, sighed, drank. Got to make him happy; he's our boss man.

I said nothing. Often it was better just to let him vent this way. Most of the things he threatened never got done and the ranting helped divert dangerous energy. That was the theory, anyway.

Well, he said, what do you think of that?

Making Thieu happy? I don't think anything of that at all.

In fact, Lyndon said, I'd rather take care of New York. That's a faster way through. But I'm a reasonable man. I don't think we could cover the public relations damage. Hah-hah. That's a joke, son. And seriously, the fallout would come pretty near Washington. We'd be coughing up shit between the acts.

Here, he said, after I had looked back at him for a while, saying nothing. Take these goddamned papers and get out. What fun are you, anyway? Don't you have anything to say

for yourself? You're just another of the goddamned ap-
peasers.

Verbatim transcription, more or less: that was Lucky
Lyndon in 1968, right after the Tet offensive. That was how
he had been talking for some time, ever since he had been
compelled to declare martial law just to get the streets
cleared, to protect the lives of the citizenry. It wasn't his
idea to do that, it was the peace demonstrators. He remained what he always had been, he was fond of saying—
the man you could trust, your president, our president,
proclaimer of the Great Society.

But the nukes, the damned nukes.

He kept threatening to use them but he never did. The bicycling Chinese, ten million of them, remained safe. That
made him, in his eyes, a temperate, a kindly man; he had
stayed his hand, stayed the power. But had the Chinese
shown gratititude for this? No, they had foxed him again,
they had come all the way into the north and were running
the magic show there, sending the Viet Cong on a spirit run
south to the damned places. If he was going to nuke them at
all, he should have done it then, as soon as they took over the
campaign of the north. But even then he had been temperate,
had let the demonstrators cow him.

Martial law is a fact, though, whether you use nukes over-
seas or not. Even if you don't use them on your own population. That is a tough fact: weapons win, power wins. My job
was to compile the dossier, to list all of the facts that made
martial law necessary. It wouldn't have happened if Lyndon
hadn't been forced to it; I was responsible for gathering all of
the reasons behind the forcing, you see.

So: remember Atlantic City? Fannie Lou Hamer got television time and media attention for her black alternate Missis-
sippi delegation even though she had no legal position. That
was Lyndon's doing; he protected her. Remember Eugene
McCarthy? It was between him and Humphrey for the vice
presidential nomination, Lyndon's choice: watch him scram-
ble! He wanted it as badly as Humphrey did, he had his private conference with Lyndon and I listened to him beg for it,

politely. No one should ever try to claim it was otherwise. The only reason he let himself put up for the opposition is that Lyndon had disappointed him.

Don't forget Atlantic City then. Don't forget the Gulf of Tonkin, either, the vote that came out of the Senate 97-2 authorizing Lyndon to take all the action necessary. Remember the speech in July of '65 when he announced the call-up? No one wants to send the flower of American youth to die in a foreign land, he said. Of course no one did; why did he even have to say this? But he said it very clearly, so that there would be no more mistakes.

I remember all of these things vividly. That was my job, remembrance. Combing the dossier, compiling the evidence. From my memory to the Halls of Truth. If I were not there to have compiled it, who would? Of course it cannot be said that any of this did me particular good. Who cared about any of this, even the martial law and the suspension of the Constitution? The origins are shrouded in mystery, as they say. The same as Lucky Lyndon: nobody would care about him, either, when he was out of office.

That was what I told myself, anyway, in the days before I began to realize just how bad the situation was—the situation with Lyndon, I mean, the depth and potential consequences of his disintegration.

Only those close to him saw it clearly. Lady Bird, a handful of his advisors, and me mostly clearly of all because I was the closest. He was drinking more and more heavily, demanding that I drink with him, just the two of us locked together alone in the Lincoln Bedroom. He wouldn't take no for an answer, he screamed obscenities at me when I tried to argue, so what choice did I have? None, no choice at all. He was Mr. President, how could I refuse to drink with the leader of the free world, the proclaimer of the Great Society?

His breakdown escalated rapidly, more rapidly than I could have imagined. It was not just with me that he broke into sudden violent, unprovoked, often senseless rants; he did it during meetings with his advisors, with the Joint Chiefs, with poor Lady Bird who was so confused and frightened that she retreated into herself, refused to have anything to do with anyone, perhaps convinced herself that everything was perfectly normal with Lyndon despite the irrationality of his diatribes. He cancelled a Cabinet meeting and a national press conference without explanation or apology, and no one but me knew it was because he was too drunk to appear. I was the only one who knew the truth. I was the only one aside from a few Secret Service agents who knew when he took to roaming the halls at night, muttering and grumbling and hurling invective at nonexistent dissenters.

Worst of all was his obsession with the Red Chinese.

He claimed that they were secretly planning to launch a nuclear attack against the United States. There was no intelligence to support this, but be believed it anyway. They're going to nuke us, he kept saying, stumbling around Lincoln's bedroom, waving his glass, the ice cubes tinkling like wind chimes. Don't you see it? Don't you understand? It's as clear as branch water. They're planning to nuke us, and there's only one answer for that. Nuke the bastards first, defoliate the whole goddamned country.

Holocaust, I said, conflagration. I was trying to be reasonable, to maintain my composure, but how could I help but be affected by all the liquor he insisted I consume? It's unthinkable, Mr. President.

The alternative is unthinkable, he said, and belched. Have another drink, he said.

Please, Mr. President . . .

Call me Lyndon, he said. He winked at me, poured another shot of bourbon into my glass. Let's not stand on ceremony here. We've never stood on ceremony before, have we?

We can't unleash nuclear weapons without provocation, I said. We can't become the aggressors. It's madness.

Are you saying I'm mad?

No, no . . .

Admit it, that's what you think. You think Lucky Lyndon's gone around the bend. He squinted at me over the rim of his glass. Well, you're wrong! he screamed. And all at once he was in the throes of another of his ravings, his face shiny red with drink and passion, his eyes luminous with dementia. I've never been more sane. I see the truth, even if Connally and the rest don't, I know what has to be done and I have the power to do it. I am the power, I'm the President of the fucking United States of America, leader of the free world, don't tell me I'm crazy!

I'm not, I said, I am only trying to keep you from making a terrible mistake—

Mistake! Did I make a mistake declaring martial law, throwing all the goddamn protestors in jail? Did I make a mistake in the Gulf of Tonkin? It's time for action, I tell you, real action—time to stop shilly-shallying and start puckering the hog's ass. It's time for the nukes.

Please, Lyndon, I said, please just stop and think what it would mean. Holocaust, chaos, anarchy—

Bullshit. Don't tell me what it would mean, don't tell me I can't do what I know is right. I'm going to tell McNamara to tell the Joint Chiefs to get the bombers ready. Or maybe I won't, he said slyly. Maybe I'll just push the button myself, boom, no more Red Chinese bicycling to Ching Chow, no more Yellow Peril threat. I can do anything I believe is necessary. I'm the President, and a goddamned Texan to boot. If I want to push the button, then I'm going to push it. Who's going to stop me?

Call it cowardice, but I did not argue with him any more. It was useless, he was beyond reason. Mad. Of course he was mad. Pressure, liquor, ego, power. Weaker men had gone mad with far less provocation.

I had no doubt that he would carry out his threat. He was the President of the United States, he could take any action no matter how insane and despite all the fail-safe measures. Suspend elections, declare a national state of emergency, send nuclear warheads screaming into the heart of China and slaughter millions upon millions of innocent people. Destroy what it had taken mankind thousands of years to build, possibly even blow up the entire planet.

He had to be stopped, before it was too late. I knew that, and as much as it pained me, as much as it made me weep in-

side, I knew that there *was* one person who could stop him—
I knew it beyond it any doubt when I found the gun.

It was in a drawer in the closet of his private bedroom.
This was the evening of the Big Rant, the self-granted man-
date to nuke the Red Chinese, not long after he passed out on
the bed. I went rummaging in the closet—a whim, the guidance of a divine hand, the reason is unimportant—I went
rummaging and I found the gun. He must have brought it
with him to the White House from Texas, he was always
fond of such things, guns and dogs and outdoor barbecues
and the rest of it. It was a big gun, a Texas-size gun, a Frontier Colt with a long barrel and an ivory handle. And all the
chambers, like all the waiting bombers, were loaded and
ready to fire.

I stood holding the gun in my hand, at once repelled and
fascinated by it, and I knew what I must do. It was monstrous, it was unthinkable, poor Lady Bird, poor daughters,
but there was no other choice, it was for the good of all
mankind.

Not assassination—euthanasia. Mercy for him, mercy for
us.

Tears coursed down my cheeks. Lucky Lyndon? No, Unlucky Lyndon. A man who knew that he had been cheated—
cheated by Harvard, by McNamara's band, by the Kennedys
great and small, by the press, by the Lowensteins and Mark
Lanes, finally by the Vietnamese. Thieu's gang weren't
worth a damn, didn't want to fight, didn't want anything to
do with the war, ran for cover. That was the Army of the Republic of South Vietnam, the Arvins, jokes really, press-
ganged peasants there to provide a cover for Ky's graft: the
whole thing was a racket. But once you got trapped by a
racket, there was no way out, you became a racketeer yourself or they swallowed you.

That had been his thinking. I knew how Unlucky Lyndon
thought. None better than me, none more trusted and quali-
fied. The last one left. Chuck Robb, the son-in-law home-
land-detailed, couldn't even protect his own daughter's
husband. Connally, George Reedy? They saw him that last

night in June, Connally still reminding him of the attack every time he looked at the Governor (and knowing that the demonstrators wanted to do to him what they had done to Kennedy in Dallas); Connally saying, Give it up, Lyndon, get out. We're all going to get eaten on this, I can't go out in front of the press any more and defend this. Get out now while there's still time. And Reedy, the son of a bitch, nodding and nodding. He had to listen to this crap right there in the Oval Office before he threw them out.

I could see it happening then, the disintegration. I could see it when he wouldn't tell anyone what he was going to do, not even McNamara or Rusk, not even Sam Rayburn, just began to draw the orders. I could see it when I came into the Oval Office late and found him there taking notes and babbling about martial law and cancelation of elections. Cancelation of elections! This was after RFK had jumped in and when all the polls showed McCarthy winning in Wisconsin; you might be able to cancel elections as a winner but not as a loser. They'd never have let him do it. The country would have been on fire.

I'm on fire, he said to me that night. The Lowensteins are on fire. The Chinese are on fire, too. They'll come in and destroy us. Remember Tet? They took the Embassy, they had our flag down.

I remember, I said. That was when they were telling you the war was won.

It was won, he said. Tet was bad public relations. We drove them out, we had the Embassy back in a day.

That was then and this is now, I said. It's too late. Too damned late for the lies, for overt action. It's over. Whether you win or lose, there's no longer a battle when a win looks like a loss.

Bullshit, he said. I'll lock you up, too, he said. You traitorous son of a bitch, I'll put you in a reservation with the Lowensteins. With Abie Rubin and the Reverend. I don't have to take this shit from you, of all people.

Oh, I knew it back then. I knew the truth about him. I knew how mad he was and how mad he would become. I knew what I was going to have to do before it was too late. I just wouldn't let myself admit it until the situation became as intolerable as it is now.

You understand, don't you? I think you understand. I had to protect the country. I did it for the country, I did it for the free world, I did it for all of mankind.

I lifted the gun, the Texas-size Frontier Colt. It wasn't easy, my hand was shaking, I didn't know even up to the instant I pulled the trigger if I could do it. But I did. I did what I had to do.

In those last few seconds he opened his eyes and looked at me. With great and terrible sadness he said, You were the last person I could trust.

Well, I said, you were wrong. And I placed gun to temple and blew out his my our brains.

THE LION HUNT

Janeen Webb

Before the rise of Alexander the Great, his father
Philip of Macedon dreamed of unity among the
Greeks and of conquests in Persia. In this story,
based on actual events, we see how fragile this
king's hopes were and how easily events might have
gone another way. Janeen Webb is one of those un-
usual people who can both teach literature and write it.
She holds a Ph.D. in literature from the University of
Newcastle and is Reader in Literature at Australian
Catholic University in Melbourne; her criticism has appeared in *Omni, Foundation, The New York Review of
Science Fiction, Science-Fiction Studies, The Age*, and in
several standard reference works. She has also won the
Aurealis and Ditmar Awards for her short fiction and a
World Fantasy Award for the ground-breaking anthol-
ogy *Dreaming Down-Under*, which she edited with Jack
Dann. She is now writing *The Sinbad Chronicles*, a se-
ries of novels for young readers; the first volume, *Sailing
to Atlantis*, came out from HarperCollins in 2001, and

the second, *The Silken Road to Samarkand*, was published in 2003.

T he wedding feast at the palace of Aegae was in full swing. King Philip looked out over his crowded hall, surveying the lavish banquet with pleasure. He could afford to be generous: this marriage of his daughter Cleopatra with the prince of Epirus was politically advantageous by anyone's reckoning. Not that he had given the happy couple any choice in the matter: matrimonial alliances were, as he had firmly told his weeping daughter, a matter of policy, not inclination. The nuptials were proceeding as planned.

Philip appeared relaxed, sitting easily in his high-backed chair of honor, its sides elaborately carved with his emblematic lions, its seat draped with cloth of gold. Beside him was his son, Alexander, a tall and muscular young man who carried himself with the lithe grace of an athlete and the absolute assurance of one who believed in his own divinity. The two looked unmistakably alike in their ceremonial finery: the same curling hair, the same straight noses and sensual mouths, the same intense dark eyes (though Philip wore a patch to cover the empty socket of the one he had lost at Methone). Father and son were laughing together, but even at their most convivial they dominated the high-roofed feasting hall, both exuding the comfortable power of men used to iron-fisted control.

Philip's guests reclined on couches beside low tables laden with delicacies. The elaborate appetizers had been cleared away, and now there were golden platters laden with roasted meats, both flesh and fowl; and there were trays heaped high with fresh-baked breads. Soft-footed serving maids moved among the diners, pouring water from golden pitchers into silver basins so that guests might rinse their hands, replenishing dishes and bringing ever more varieties of exquisite food. Others offered glistening fruit piled onto serving dishes and delicious pastries dripping with sweet honey on silver plates. Young men with sieves and cups filled mixing bowls to the

brim with the finest Thessalian wines, and constantly refilled
the golden goblets of the revelers. The aromas of spiced
foods mingled with the perfumes of the company, filling the
banqueting hall with a rich miasma of warm scents, the smell
of indulgence.

And when, at last, it seemed the guests could eat no more,
Philip called for music. The chief bard of the court took up
his lyre, and the mood of the feast turned toward song and
dancing. More pledges and toasts were drunk to the future of
the noble couple, and the royal revelers grew increasingly
raucous. It would be a long night.

The courtier Pausanias slipped unobtrusively from the
room to an elegant antechamber. Away from the hubbub, he
leaned against a marble pillar, savoring its smooth coolness
after the stuffy heat and stifling scents of the feasting hall.

"Just look at him!" he said, gesturing in the direction of
the king. "The man's a heavy drinker, even by army stan-
dards. He'll be in his cups tonight, and who knows what secrets he might betray to that sharp-eared young bridegroom
he's so proud of snaring."

"Easy, friend," said Hermias, stepping from the shadows
and holding up his plump hand in greeting. "He's much more
likely to bed that serving girl he's been fondling all evening.
One of the privileges of rank," he added wryly. "The king is
a physical man."

"Maybe," said Pausanias. "But I like it not."

Hermias considered the fastidious little courtier for a moment. He shrugged his shoulders. "There are some pretty
youths here tonight, if that's your fancy," he said slyly.

Pausanias let the issue drop. "Not tonight. I have business." From the folds of his tunic he withdrew a small leather
bag, a bag heavy with silver tetradrachmas. He tossed the
pouch to Hermias, who caught it deftly.

"Polybus sends you greetings," said Pausanias.

Hermias tucked the bag out of sight. "The coins are
good?"

"From Philip's own mines at Mount Pangaeus." Pausanias
chuckled. "I tested them myself."

"Thank you, friend."

"Don't thank me yet," replied the courtier. "Polybus also reminds you that the matter we spoke of is now close at hand. Are you still with me?"

Hermias paled. "Are you set upon this course then?"

"I am. After the wedding, there is to be a royal hunt. The opportunity will serve."

"I never thought it would come to this." Hermias massaged his temples with anxious fingers, thinking hard. "A little information, here and there," he said. "That's all you asked for. A little palace intrigue. It seemed of no real consequence."

"You were willing enough," said Pausanias.

Hermias fidgeted with his tunic, smoothing the folds over his portly bulk. "Philip has always had his enemies," he said. "Everyone gossips. What harm in making a little profit from it?"

"What harm indeed," replied Pausanias dryly. "You've grown soft and fat enough serving two masters."

"Look," said Hermias, his voice edged with panic, "Philip's a man of sensual appetites, it's true: but they don't interfere with his rule. He's a magnificent leader."

"Yes, yes," said Pausanias, "nobody doubts his abilities. But his time has come. He's just announced a war against Persia, and he'll drag all Greece along with him. The confederacy has agreed to it, of course." He was beginning to pace now, moving softly in the shadowed room. "It's simple enough, my friend," he said at last. "Everyone knows that this anti-Persian crusade is Philip's way of enforcing Macedonian domination. If he controls this war effort, he controls all Greece. Polybus wants that stopped, and soon."

"But," countered Hermias, "Philip's an extraordinary general. His army would do anything for him. And he's in good shape. He'll probably pull it off."

"That, my friend," said Pausanias, his tone heavy with exasperation, "is the point. A victory for Philip would only consolidate Macedonian power. Athens and Corinth and Megara are already nervous, and the Phocians still hate him for the way he treated them after the Battle of the Crocus Field."

"Then why not kill Parmenio?" said Hermias. "He's the key to all Philip's military strategies. And he's here for the wedding feast. I saw him."

"Because Philip would just get another strategist," said Pausanias. He shook his head as if to clear away his frustration. "Don't you see?"

"No," said Hermias, nervously twisting his carnelian signet ring as he spoke. "I don't. What's so bad for us about another foreign conquest? It keeps the kings and generals a long way from home, and the rest of us can get on with our lives without interference. And we've done well enough from Philip's victories, you and I. Aegae prospers, and his people with it."

"Think," said Pausanias. "What happens if Philip doesn't win this time? What if his grandiose scheme fails, and the rest of us pay the price? Persia will take its revenge. Do you want to see Greece overrun with Persian troops? Your precious Aegae in flames?"

Hermias was silent.

Pausanias pressed his advantage. "Then spare me the hypocrisy for once, Hermias. Win or lose, one way or the other, Philip's war on Persia is a political disaster for the Greek confederacy." He paused, calculating, then went on: "And it's not as if he's an innocent in matters of intrigue. Those mines of his have financed more than one assassination in the name of diplomacy. He knows how the game is played—just look at the wedding guests in there." Pausanias jerked his thumb in the direction of the feast. "Those nobles from Epirus wouldn't dare say a word against any of it. Philip's totally and completely unscrupulous when it comes to bribery and corruption. They've all been well paid." He paused for breath. "What I'm saying, friend, is that this whole empire runs on plots and conspiracies. Philip expects it."

"And Alexander?"

"Will inherit. But he is young yet. He is strong-minded like his father, and the army will follow him, but the mourning period will give the other states some respite. Alexander will have to re-organize, and he will need to win popular consent if he is to rule. That all takes time, and time is what we need."

"I still don't like it."

"I don't see that you have a choice. You're implicated, my friend. You're bought and paid for." Pausanias casually drew a long knife, testing it against his forefinger. "You know we can't risk a security breach." His voice was low now, menacing.

Hermias sighed ruefully. "Put it away, *friend*," he said. "We both know you won't kill me here."

Pausanias nodded, letting the tension ease. "And your hand in Polybus' purse ensures your silence," he said. "You cannot betray me without implicating yourself, and Philip's justice will be swift and merciless if he scents treachery. Either way, you will die. I ask you again, Hermias: are you with me?"

Hermias sat down heavily on the nearest couch. His shoulders sagged, and he cradled his head in his hands for a few moments. When he looked up once more, his face was bleak.

"Tell me what you need," he said.

The morning of the hunt dawned fine and clear. All the palace servants had been up before sunrise, baking and packing and preparing delicacies for the hunting party. During the heat of the afternoon the king and his guests would rest in tented pavilions, and in the cool of the evening they would dine under the stars. Several heavily loaded wagons had departed yesterday, so that all might be ready for the royal party. The grooms had also been busy: the pride of Philip's stables, the glossy high-necked horses that were easily the best in all Greece had been brushed and combed and readied for the day's work. They were led clattering into the forecourt, an extravagant gesture of generosity to those guests privileged to ride them.

Philip—dressed for the hunt in leather leggings and battle-skirt and his favorite iron corselet studded with golden lions, his sword buckled at his side—was up long before his guests, striding about the palace forecourt, giving instructions. His son joined him, arm in arm with his new brother-in-law, who seemed more than a little uneasy.

"I've never hunted a lion before," the prince of Epirus was saying.

"A noble adversary, to be sure, but no different from other beasts in the end," Alexander replied. "And this particular beast has taken one or two calves from my father's farms. It has learned to stalk its prey too close to our people. So the king wants to kill it before it ranges nearer to his horses—there are many foals this season, grazing in the high pastures." He sighed. "I sometimes think he loves those horses better than anything else in this world, including his wives."

The prince managed a smile. "I'm still nervous," he said.

"You'll be fine. Just ride with the pack, and pull back if it gets too dangerous. No one expects heroics. The more experienced hunters will corner the lion, but the kill belongs to my father today. It's the custom." Alexander grinned broadly. "Relax. Here come our guests."

The hunting procession was quickly assembled. As soon as the riders were mounted and had taken up their weapons, the party set off for the mountains. Philip rode at the head of the column, followed by his noble guests and surrounded by elite guards from the hetaerae cavalry with their distinctive long lances. General Parmenio, the strategist, was with them today: he nodded cheerfully to Alexander as he swung into his place in the line. The servants followed behind in their carts: they would travel directly to join their fellows in setting up the day camp, while the hunters ranged freely over the hills in pursuit of their quarry.

The early morning summer breeze was cool, bringing scents of wild thyme and honey as the procession followed the winding road that led to the hills above Aegae. The steep road climbed steadily, and the sun had risen high in the sky so that men and horses were all sweating freely by the time Philip halted, reigning in his mount in a space where the pass widened out onto a grassy plateau. The king sat motionless in his saddle, shading his eyes to look back over the rich patchwork of green pastures and the shimmering silver-greys of olive groves. Below him, the shining thread of a little stream cascaded over mossy rocks, on its way to join up with the wide river that snaked through the valley. He leaned forward to pat the graceful neck of his favorite horse. All peaceful, all calm.

The stillness was broken by a single shout: "Lion!"

The cry went up from Philip's left, where a line of trackers emerged into the sunlight from the shadow of the beech trees on the high ground. And the hunters were off, their tiredness forgotten, urging their horses up the rocky slope. They raced along the ridge, a curving line of superb horsemen, with Philip and Alexander riding hard on the wing with the best and boldest of the guards. Philip shouted with joy as they crested the hill and saw the quarry plunge headlong down the slope on the other side, making for the safety of a rocky outcrop that ended abruptly in a waterfall. It was a descent that would make the bravest hesitate—a sharp, uneven incline overgrown with saplings and scrubby bushes, the slope pockmarked with animal burrows that spelled death for any unlucky horse. Many of the nobles, the bridegroom among them, hung back. But the king did not pause—he sounded his horn, and the leading hunters wheeled, giving chase under the trees. The undergrowth was thick, the ground sharper than it looked with treacherous shards and stones. The smell of leaf-mold was strong in their nostrils as they raced, ducking under overhanging branches, skittering on loosened ground. The mountain gorge echoed to the thunder of hoofbeats and the din of hunting horns, and the riders' whoops of fierce joy echoed and re-echoed from the valley walls.

The hunt ran hard, and now it was Alexander in the lead, sending the stones flying as his horse cleared a fallen tree. Down and down he went, Parmenio close on his heels, and Philip rode with them, plying the whip. The horses were flecked with foam now, panting with effort. But the riders never hesitated: they ran their mounts until, in a narrow cleft where the roar of the waterfall mingled with the roaring of the lion, the quarry was brought to bay, trapped by Alexander and Parmenio against water and rock.

The lion had turned, crouched ready to spring, its back protected by an overhanging rock, and a dark cave behind. It could only be reached by way of a narrow path between the rocks and the river. Alexander shouted to Parmenio above the clashing of weapons and the yells of the hunters following in the rear. He motioned to the general to take the inner edge. He himself edged his mount beside the rushing waterfall. The sharp stink of the lion's lair made the horse skittish, shifting its feet and sending loose pebbles cascading down the rocks. Alexander steadied his mount. Parmenio was already in position.

Wordlessly, on either side of the trapped lion, the two men lowered their lances, thrusting at the beast, forcing it forward. The animal was a huge male, powerfully muscled. It swiped at its tormentors with long curved claws that could rip a man apart. It was winded, but its snarls of defiance made it clear that it meant to fight.

Philip rode his mount straight towards the waiting beast, cheered by the shouts of his men, now arriving in the rear.

"Phil-ip, Phil-ip," they chanted. "A kill, a kill."

The king reached the clearing and leapt from his horse, throwing off his riding cloak and brandishing his bright blade. The golden lion studs on his corselet flashed in the brilliant sunlight as Philip, the lion king of Macedon, strode forward to meet the tawny king of beasts in deadly combat.

The great lion was instantly aware of Philip: it roared a challenge, revealing sharp yellow teeth. Then it gathered its strength and sprang straight at the king. But Philip was ready for it, shouting his own battle cry. In the shock of their meeting he stuck his point straight into the beast's neck, driving the blade up to the hilt, so that the lion's heart was split in two. The beast died snarling and thrashing, and Philip was bloodied to the shoulder. He leaned against the rock for a moment, gagging on the vile, hot smell of the dying lion. Alexander and Parmenio flanked him, still wary of the great beast.

Philip straightened, and turned, triumphant, to the cheers of his followers. The blaring of hunting horns and the shouting and hallooing of men celebrating the kill made a deafening din in his ears. He did not notice the sudden clatter of hooves on the slope above him. He was holding both arms aloft, accepting the homage of his men, when a mounted guard came charging down the mountainside, his long lance spearing straight at the king where he stood, vulnerable, astride the lion.

"No!" Alexander acted instinctively, leaping from his horse and knocking his father aside. Philip rolled free, and came up quickly, sword at the ready. Alexander staggered, but stood firm, the lance quivering where it stuck in the exposed flesh of his upper arm. A dozen swords flashed, and the assassin toppled from his horse to lie dead at the king's feet.

"Fools," said Philip. "I needed him alive. I need to know who paid him."

"You'll know soon enough, my lord," Parmenio remarked dryly. "Such things are never secret for long." He poked with his foot at the dead man. "This piece of filth is wearing a guard's uniform. You can leave me to interrogate my men," he said. "There will be no further incidents today, I guarantee it." He turned then to Alexander, his face full of concern. "You need a surgeon," he said bluntly.

"It's nothing," said Alexander. "A flesh wound. My man will see to it when we reach the pavilion."

"Even so," said Philip, "you must let us take care of it for now."

Alexander nodded, gritting his teeth against the pain as Philip himself withdrew the bloody lance-head and bound his son's wound with a strip of linen.

"This may be bad," Philip said quietly. "The tip is discoloured."

"And we have a long climb back to the day camp," said Parmenio.

"I'll be all right," said Alexander. "It will take more than a lance wound to kill the likes of me." He grinned confidently. "Don't worry. I can ride."

"You'll have to," his father replied.

*   *   *

There was none of the joy of the chase as the hunters picked their careful way back up the treacherous slope. Parmenio had detailed two of his men to fashion a rough sled from branches so that the slain lion could be dragged back to camp, but the king had lost interest in his trophy. He was concentrating on his son, riding slowly beside him, watching with grave concern as Alexander began to sweat and shake. By the time the party reached the top of the ridge once more, Alexander was clinging to his horse's mane, scarcely able to stay upright.

"Shock," said Parmenio.

"I hope so," Philip replied grimly. "I hope so."

The field surgeon had been summoned, and he met the hunting party on the plateau. He had brought a wagon that would carry the wounded man to the king's pavilion.

"Gently," he said, as Philip helped his son down from his horse. Alexander pitched forward, and Parmenio had to lift him bodily onto the straw-filled wagon where he lay still, exhausted. "He'll need rest," the surgeon went on briskly. "I've brought wine to cleanse the wound, and blankets to keep him warm while his body recovers from the shock. Though I must admit I'm surprised a flesh wound has taken him like this—he's a strong young man."

"It's more than shock," said Philip, his voice pitched low. "It's poison. I'm sure of it." He held out the lance-tip, wrapped carefully in linen torn from his undershirt. The surgeon reached for it, barehanded.

"Don't touch the point," said Philip quickly.

The surgeon faltered, then took the weapon gingerly, turning it this way and that, sighting along the edge.

"I did not wipe it," Philip said. "Do you recognise that coating on the blade? Can you tell me what it is?"

The field surgeon paled. "No, my lord," he stammered. "I can see that the edge is chipped, so it may have scraped on bone. But there is a lot of dried blood on the weapon, and I am no apothecary to tell one tincture from another." He gathered his thoughts, and added: "I do have herbs I can infuse to try to draw out poison when we reach the camp, if that is what you wish. And I can bleed the wound."

"Do it," said Philip. "And keep the business to yourself. There may be more than one traitor in this camp. I'll hold you responsible if any more harm comes to my heir. Do you understand?"

"Yes, my lord," said the surgeon, swallowing hard. "I'll do my best."

"You'll do better than that," the king said darkly. "My son must live." He turned away abruptly, striding across to where Parmenio stood, deep in conversation with his most trusted guards.

"I've already arranged an escort," the strategist said as the king approached. "No one will get near Alexander."

"Thank you, old friend," the king replied. "Will you walk with me a moment?"

"Of course."

The two moved out of earshot of the anxious guards. "My men know nothing," Parmenio said. "The assassin was a last minute replacement, when the youngest of the regular troupe was too ill to ride this morning. They say the boy was fevered and vomiting—and that they thought nothing more than that he had drunk too much wine last night. But now . . ."

"Now they are solving the riddle," said Philip.

"Now they are ashamed not to have prevented it," Parmenio finished quietly. "But with all the unfamiliar faces at the palace for the wedding, they did not think to question too closely."

"Peace, Parmenio," Philip said wearily. "I'm not blaming your men. There'll be no scapegoating or punishment in their ranks."

Parmenio breathed a sigh of relief. "A wise decision, my lord. If there's to be fighting, we'll need their goodwill."

"I know," Philip replied. "But I doubt there's an army at our gates. This smells more of petty intrigue—one of Polybus' plots, I'll wager." His voice hardened. "We'll find the men he has suborned, of course, and they will die." He stopped for a moment, tense with anger. "But Parmenio," he went on, "if he has murdered my son, I swear by Heracles my ancestor that I will raze Polybus' miserable city to the ground. And he will live to watch it burn, before I personally send his paltry soul to Hades."

"Then let us hope it will not come to that," said Parmenio. "We are already at war with Persia." He touched Philip's arm. "Come, my lord, we will watch Alexander's progress together. He's a strong man, and we must hope that it will be enough."

It was a difficult ride. Wary guards surrounded both their king and the trundling wagon where Alexander groaned in pain at every misstep that jolted him. The sun was sinking in the west by the time they had made their slow journey to the high plain where Philip's household servants had pitched the king's pavilions. Alexander was rambling incoherently, his body wracked with spasms as he struggled against the poison in his veins. He was carried gently to a couch in his father's tent, where the surgeon set to work, trembling under the king's unnerving scrutiny.

Outside, the mood of the guests was somber. When evening came, servants washed and poured and served up laden platters for the hunters, but there was no feasting in the firelight. People talked in low whispers, eating and drinking but little. It was as if the world was holding its breath, fearful of what was to come.

Philip sat by his son's bedside, willing him to live, watching him fighting for his life. But as the night wore on, the spasms became more violent and Alexander's heart weakened. The surgeon could do nothing. Just before dawn Alexander was wracked by a last seizure, too great for even the strongest mortal heart. And the heir to the lion throne of Macedon lay dead.

The morning star shone pale in a lightening sky and the cool mountain air carried echoes of early birdsong as Philip, hard-faced, strode from the tent and ordered an immediate return to his palace. The hunting column became a slow funereal procession, with the wedding guests holding their mounts to a measured walk behind the wagon with its burden of sorrow, and the guards keeping careful watch over all. Philip rode, as was customary, at the head. He would not let them see him grieve, not his new son-in-law and these courtiers he had bought for so much silver. He would deal with his pain and loss in his own time. Would deal with that, and with his son's murderer. Vengeance, that was Philip's motto. And Philip was a patient man. He could wait.

The people of Aegae were outraged at the loss of Alexander, at the loss of so much promise, so much talent, so much spirit. They wanted blood. As Parmenio had predicted, public indignation quickly overrode paid loyalties, and the conspirators were not difficult to discover. Hermias did not resist when the guards came for him. It was whispered in palace corridors that the fat little court official seemed relieved to have been found out. He wept copious tears, and readily gave up Pausanias as the instigator of the conspiracy. And now he sat quietly in his prison cell, waiting for the day of his execution, knowing that his family would not come, that there would be no hemlock to ease his traitor's death.

The more wily Pausanias had fled from the palace on the day of the assassination. But he had not fled far enough. He too was soon exposed and dragged, bloodied but still alive, into the presence of the king. Only the intervention of Parmenio's guards had saved the man who had hired Alexander's killer from the rough justice of a jeering crowd, but it had been a violent passage, and his right arm now hung limp and useless at his side from his obviously dislocated shoulder.

Parmenio gestured to one of his men. "Fix that," he said.

The guard took hold of Pausanias' shoulder, rotated the arm, and pulled.

Pausanias fainted.

Another guard emptied a pitcher of water over him. Pausanias regained spluttering consciousness just as the king spoke to his general:

"Why?" Philip asked.

"Not for mercy," Parmenio replied. "The shoulder's a

common enough injury among lance bearers. It's best to set it quickly." He looked with undisguised contempt at Pausanias, sprawled wet and bleeding on the palace floor. "We went to a lot of trouble to get that piece of filth here alive," he said, "and I assumed you'd want him coherent enough to answer a few questions. He'll stay conscious now."

"I see. Get him up, then," said Philip.

Two guards hauled Pausanias to his feet, and stood impassively, supporting him.

Philip bent forward intently. "Why?" he asked simply. "Why try to kill me?"

"For the good of Greece," Pausanias grated.

A guard struck him heavily across the mouth. Pausanias wiped away the trickle of blood with his left hand.

"Hold," said the king. "We are civilized men here, not torturers. He will tell us. He wants to tell us. He wants to justify himself. All traitors do."

Pausanias spat.

The guards looked straight ahead, impassive, unmoving.

"We know it was Polybus who paid you," said Parmenio in a matter-of-fact tone. "We have arrested the courier. He has told us a great deal. He will die with you, of course."

Pausanias sagged, but straightened his body with visible effort. "Then you don't need to ask me," he said.

"Oh but we do," said Philip coldly. "We want to hear everything you have to tell us. And you will tell us."

The questioning went on late into the night, and Pausanias, wracked by pain and venomous with anger and liberated to speak his mind by the certain knowledge of his own imminent death, told them a great deal. Told them more than he knew. By the end of that night, Philip was sure. Parmenio the strategist was already laying plans against Polybus. There would be war in Greece.

But first there would be a royal funeral. Alexander's bones would lie in his father's tomb, so many years in the making against inevitable death. Against, as it turned out, the wrong

death. King Philip would have to build anew—if they gave
him time.

The funeral procession would begin just before sunset, but
Philip had come early from the palace, to make a last inspec-
tion. He rode slowly, flanked by Parmenio's anxious guards.
The road to the tombs was full of busy people, but the throng
parted easily before the king's men. All along the roadside
were the usual signs of a festival in the making: traders setting up their booths to sell amulets and charms and souvenir
coins hurriedly cast with a rough likeness of Alexander; food
vendors already turning spitted animals, starting the slow
cooking process that would feed the crowds; families staking
out likely picnic spots; beggars arriving. There were rich
pickings at royal funerals.

"He shouldn't do this," one guard muttered to his partner.
"It isn't in the plan. He has enemies everywhere."

His friend shrugged. "He's the king. He knows he is
watched. What difference does it make to us?"

"The difference," hissed the first, "is that we could find
ourselves fighting off assassins in the middle of all this lot."
He gestured vaguely at the milling crowd.

"Not even the Athenians would try it on the day of the funeral," his friend replied. "Besides, everyone thinks the king
is up at the palace, preparing to lead the procession. No one
will pay us any special attention—there are royal guards riding everywhere today. Relax."

They rode on in silence.

When they reached the gates, Philip halted. He turned to
the leader of his guard. "Have the courtyard cleared," he
said. "I want everyone out—priests, carpenters, stonemasons,
everyone."

"Sir."

The soldiers were efficient. Within minutes artisans were
scurrying from their last-minute work, leaving the dusty
space deserted.

"Now leave me," he said.

"But sir," the captain of the guard began, stammering.
"Our orders are . . ."

"I give the orders here," said Philip. "And I want a moment alone with my son. Have your men watch the entrance. Nobody enters. Is that clear?"

"Sir."

Philip dismounted, and handed the reins to the captain. "A little space of time, that's all," he said quietly. "Then you may escort me back to the palace. Understood?"

The man nodded.

Philip entered and paced about the enclosure, noting the details, checking that his orders had been obeyed. The pyre had been built high, overlaid with sweet-smelling boughs and piled about with small offerings. The larger ones would come later, with the pomp and ceremony of the procession. Inside the palatial tomb, beyond its forecourts and antechambers, Alexander lay in the main room, ready for his last parade. The gleaming mosaics on the chamber walls were lit by bracketed lamps which would burn untended for the correct ceremonial period. Philip noted with satisfaction that the depiction of the fateful lion hunt had been completed—though some of the shining tesserae still looked wet in their settings. The mounted figures of Alexander and Parmenio would now grace this tomb for all time, lances poised forever above the snarling lion.

In the center of the chamber was the funeral couch, a thing of exquisite beauty, cunningly carved and decorated with beaten gold leaf and beautiful ivory miniatures of men and beasts and mythical creatures. The king smiled sadly to see a little herm from the gymnasium amongst the side-carvings, reminding him of happier times when he had brought Aristotle to Pella to educate the boy. It all seemed so long ago now, and such waste of spirit. What were all his plans to conquer Persia, to build an empire, without his son to inherit it, to carry it forward into history? Philip sighed and looked up, inspecting the accoutrements. The bed's canopy was wreathed in cloth of gold. All was as it should be—all that the trappings of wealth and power could make it.

Finally, Philip approached his son. Alexander lay in state, a crown of gold oak leaves on his brow, his body dressed in

the gold-studded corselet and battle skirts of a royal warrior
beneath the drape of the purple cloak so stunningly embroidered in thread of gold. His had not been an easeful death.
He would burn as a soldier. Young, well muscled, dead before his time, Alexander looked every inch a king, lying there
in all his majesty.

There were tears in Philip's one good eye. He reached out
to touch his son, briefly, brushing his hand across the waxen
cheek. "It should have been me," he said softly. "This death
was planned for me. And you will be avenged, I swear it."
His voice cracked. "Your assassins burn before you this day,"
he went on, "to make their miserable sniveling excuses to
their gods. But they are only messengers. I will find their
masters, and they will pay for this deed in blood and death.
Polybus will pay with all that he holds dear. This I promise
you." He bowed his head, and sighed deeply. "Go well, my
son. Your ancestor Heracles awaits. All is prepared for you."

He stepped back then, and walked away, straight-backed
and purposeful, to where his captain stood waiting.

"I'm ready," he said simply.

"Sir."

Philip remounted, and rode back to the palace in brooding
silence, unmoved by the noise and bustle of the crowds that
parted before him.

At sunset, robed and magnificent in the trappings of his
state, King Philip of Macedon rode out once more, this time
at the head of the funeral procession. A huge crowd had gathered along the route, watching in respectful silence as their
king came forth to preside over the pyre of his heir. Behind
him, on the best of Philip's horses, rode Parmenio and the
palace guards, pacing slowly—and alert, always, for any sign
of disturbance. Next came black-clad women mourners, tear-
ing their hair and strewing ashes; and then there were all the
nobles of Philip's court and ambassadors from neighboring
kingdoms, richly dressed and riding in horse-drawn car-
riages, and bearing costly gifts for the pyre. But by far the
most magnificent spectacle of all was the funeral cart that
bore Alexander himself. Drawn slowly by a team of strong

warriors, their muscles bunching with effort as they pulled, the richly decorated cart carried the prince of Macedon on his carven funeral bed with its trappings of gold and purple. Beside and behind him were more ranks of marching warriors, their tall lances bearing purple flags in honor of their prince.

The long procession of mourners moved with its own slow, inexorable rhythm. The outer areas of the funeral arena were already packed with jostling crowds of people anxious to witness the ritual, and attendants scurried to and fro, ordering the final arrangement of offerings. There was an expectant hush as Philip, still flanked by his guards, dismounted and climbed the stairs to his place of honor in the center of the tiered royal stand that had been built beside the pyre. At his nod, the business of unloading the horse-drawn offerings began, and the nobles processed to their places. Finally, Alexander's cart arrived: it was drawn slowly, and with infinite care, up the ramp to its place at the very top of the pyre. The warriors withdrew. And all was ready.

Philip raised his arm in salute. His voice rang out, clear and powerful, as he spoke a eulogy for Alexander, spoke of how the world was forever diminished by this great loss. Finally, he spoke the formal words of parting, and the priests began their rituals. As the sun dipped below the horizon, the moment came: the ceremonial torch was touched to the base of the pyre, and greedy red flames crackled from it. The air was suddenly full of the smell of burning, of oil and wood and flesh.

And Philip watched, standing tall, stiff-necked, untouchable in his grief. He watched the long succession of precious offerings as they burned, and watched unmoved as the corpse of the assassin and the other still-living conspirators, staked at the four corners of the pyre, were taken ignominiously by the flames. He had had their tongues cut out, lest they defile his son's ceremony with their death cries. The fire burned greedily until, almost at the last, he witnessed, dry-eyed despite the stinging smoke, the burning of four magnificent horses in the conflagration—a last gift to his favorite son, his heir. The pyre roared and gouts of red flame leapt skywards as Alexander himself was finally consumed in all his gold and finery.

And it was over. The king turned away then, leaving the priests and the attendants to their work, to the sifting of the cooling ashes and the separation of bones and the final sealing of the tomb.

Philip would not look back. Behind him lay the smoking ruins of the future. And Alexander dead.

OBSERVABLE THINGS

Paul Di Filippo

Paul Di Filippo pays tribute to fantasist Robert E. Howard (with a brief nod in the direction of H.P. Lovecraft), several early American historical figures, and his own hometown of Providence, Rhode Island, in this inventive fantasy tale. His thorough and detailed knowledge of fantastic fiction is regularly on display in his columns for *Asimov's Science Fiction*, *The Magazine of Fantasy & Science Fiction*, and a variety of other print and online publications. His short fiction, praised by, among many others, Harlan Ellison, William Gibson, and Bruce Sterling, has appeared in several collections, including *Ribofunk, Lost Pages*, and *Strange Trades*, which was a *Washington Post* Notable Book for 2001. His other books include *The Steampunk Trilogy, Ciphers, Fractal Paisleys, Joe's Liver*, and, most recently, *A Mouthful of Tongues* (Cosmos Books) and *Little Doors* (Four Walls Eight Windows). He shares his Providence home with his companion of nearly thirty years, Deborah Newton.

Now that I have at long last, thro' simple Rolling Away of the weary Years, attained my threescore and a lustrum and acquired the status of Elderly Relick, honor'd and revered (yea, even feared), but likewise equally unlisten'd to, by Younger Generations busy with the affairs of a new Century, I am naturally disposed to cast my Eye backwards o'er the course of my life, questioning whether Events which once loom'd large as Mount Ararat in my Mental Apprehension did indeed hold all the Significance with which I once imbued 'em, and whether certain treasured Beliefs of mine, Polestars by which I erstwhile directed my Conduct and Career, were as trustworthy as I deemed, or whether these glittering Arrays of interlocking Axioms and Suppositions were not in fact Edifices built upon the Shifting Sands of Happenstance, Misunderstanding, and Deceit.

Chief among these Eidolons, perchance falsely dominant, I number my quondam Faith in the Existence and Prevalence of Witchcraft. Doubts as to the Mundane Workings of the Prince of Darkness thro' his mortal Slaves first began to trouble me shortly after the Trials at Salem, wherein I play'd no small Part. Convinced then that "an Army of Devils is broke in upon the place which is our very center," I staunchly maintained that Spectral Powers rampaged at will up and down our Earthly Stage, and that every Prayerful Man had a Duty to crusade against 'em.

Presently, however, in my Dotage (and I suspect in my weary Bones that I will not live much longer, certainly not managing to equal the vast Pile of Years once surmounted by my father, whose Christian Name "Increase" betokened his very longevity), I begin to doubt myself whether or not the Celestial Forces commonly make such Extraordinary use of Mortals as Actors in their Unknowable Dramas, imbuing 'em with Supernatural Powers for Good or Evil. I myself have, I now honestly aver, never in my Maturity witnessed any Occult Manifestations among the Pitiful Wretches accused in Salem or elsewhere and which would qualify without reservation as Extramundane. Certainly I would have no hesitation at this late date in abandoning all Credence in the Supernatural, were it not for one certain Man and the Events he brought in his train.

That Man was named Solomon Kane, and I met him when I was but thirteen years old, and all of Christian New England seemed doomed to Merciless Extinction at the hands of the Salvages and their Dreaded Conqueror, King Philip.

'Tis said, Reader, that the Spaniard De Leon quested after the Fountain of Youth in the Bermoothes and elsewhere, yet had he but considered the Power of Man's Memory to restore his Vanished Infancy as if not a Day had passed since he wore Bunting and Lisped his Cradle Songs, then would the Balked Romish Explorer have realized that said Prize dwelt nor further off than beneath our Pates. Thus when I in my Expiring Years cast my own Sensibilities backward down Time's Stream, I am instantly restored to the inquisitive and fleet-witted yet shallow-experienced and Headstrong Young Lad who once believed that he could understand any Observable Thing, and who found the World a Condign Marvel for his Seething Brain.

The Clime during that August of the Year of Our Lord 1676 had been a most unnatural one for the Colonies, Steamy, Enervating and Mephitic, as befitted the horrid Travails we Poor Souls in the English Israel had been undergoing for the past several Years. Betimes it seemed that we upright New World Denizens were suffering the fate detailed in Deuteronomy: "wasted with Hunger, devoured with Burning Heat, the Teeth of Beasts against them." For two years now we had been battling for our Very Lives against the False Indians who had once befriended us, and with whom we had lived in tolerable Amity for some Decades. The Causes of their Bellicosity were numerous and hard to parse. An Enduring Catalogue of Innumerable Grievances had existed prior to actual Combat on both sides of the Affair, and the subsequent War had occasioned a Host of others. Slaughters and Outrages had been frequent during the course of the Struggle, and Blood both Pagan and Christian had flowed like Wine among the Nazarites.

At this Juncture, however, after much Tromping up and down the Countryside by Armed Militias, after many Grievous Setbacks and Retreats, Burnings of Homes and Stockados, Slaughter of Livestock, Despoiling of Grain and Fruit, Captivity of Innocent Maidens and Babes, the Tide seemed to have turned against the Tawny Tygers and in favor of the White Man. The Perfidious Canonchet, one of the Salvages' chief Sagamores, had been recently captured and executed, his Dying breath an Unrepentant Curse upon his Betters. Weetamoo, the Squaw Sachem, pursued across the Taunton River just days ago in her Canoo, had Drowned and Perished Utterly, her Head Alone paraded on a Pole thro' the Lanes of Taunton to Exultant Cheers. The Various Tribes Allied against us, the Bulk of the Nipmucs, the Narragansetts, the Wampanoags, and many lesser Clans, facing not only we English Lions but also our allies, the Mohegans and Mohawks, had been driven either Westward or Northward or into Guarded Encampments.

Yet one Redoubtable Foe remained uncaptured, and he the most Fearsome, Clever and Undauntable Specter of all. King Philip, Warrior Son of Massassoit, Sachem of the Wampanoags, known before his English Christening as Metacomet. He it was who had Brew'd all the Storm amongst his Kith and Kin, he it was who had Wrought such clever Strategems agains us, oft o'erwhelming our Superior Forces by Guile and Cunning. Now, 'tis true, Philip seemed helpless, a Portrait of the Chastized as we read of in Amos: "he who is stout of heart among the Mighty shall flee away naked in that day."

Yet just so long as Philip lived, so long would our Future Safety be uncertain. Prospects that the Renegade could Regroup his forces and return Some Faroff Day to Harangue and Belabor us again were all too Large, especially if he turned for help to our Rivals, the French and Dutch. (And may I interpolate here, Reader, Merest Mention of the well-known Irruption Twelve Years Later of just such Salvage Deviltry around Saco, Pemmaquid, Casco and Elsewhere as proof of the Undying Enmity of these Redskins, as chronicled in my own humble tome, *Deccenium Luctuosm*?)

Moreover, there weighed in the Balance evidence of King

Philip's Supernatural Allegiances. Many and many a time had reports come of Uncanny Forces at work on the side of the Salvages. Ill-faced Omens had oft abounded before Various Indian Attacks, viz., Uncouth Storms, the clouding of the Moon and the Sun, St. Elmo's Fire, the Appearance of Unnatural Beasts and the Disappearance of Common Game Animals. Such Tokens of the Dark Allies invoked by the Indians unnerved us, rightly so, and made Philip's Death all the more Imperative.

It was in this Spirit, and with this Aim, that a group of Statesmen, Militiamen and Common Citizenry stood eagerly upon Hammett's Wharf that August Day in Newport, chief Establishment of the Plantations of Rhode Island, awaiting our Savior from across the Sea.

Standing atop a Tarry Piling and thus elevated above the Mass, with the Undimmed Eyes of Youth I was the first to spot the Ship we all anticipated, and gave a loud "Hulloo!"

"Here she comes! The Black Gull approaches!"

A general Stir went up among the Crowd congregated under the Unnaturally Blazing Sun. Even my own Father, ever a Figure of Stern Sobriety, evidenced a more agitated Mien neath his formal Wig, betokening a Ferment of Hope and Trepidation, than I had ever before seen him exhibit. He turned to Major Pynchon and said, "Let us pray that Kane has seen fit to answer our pleas. If this ship indeed bears that most fierce and noble of Puritans, we are saved, forsooth."

I clambered down from my Bitumenous Perch, as the Stout Full-rigged Vessel drew e'en closer, and from the expectantly gathered Souls there began to arise a general unseemly Hubbub. Major Sanford and Captain Goulding, Major Gookin and Captain Church, took it upon themselves to quiet the Ladies and Husbandmen and their Babes, lest Solomon Kane receive a Wrongful Impression of our Character, deeming us less Stoic than the situation demanded.

Before much longer, Hawsers flew thro' the Air from the creeping Ship and the Black Gull was Warped into place alongside Hammett's Wharf. Navvies heaved a Gangplank

up and over to bridge the Gap twixt Ship and Shore, and a
Collective Suspension of Breath preceded the actual appearance of Solomon Kane.

When the Man Himself materialized like one of the Four
Spirits of heaven mentioned in Zechariah, that Suspension
turned to a Gasp.

Used as we all were to the Sober, Respectful, Crowfeather
Garb of our Preachers and Leaders, we still received a Shock
upon first sighting Solomon Kane. For he was Attired in a
Manner that had not been General for at least an Hundred
Years. His Unadorned, Closefitting Garments harked back to
the days of Good Queen Bess. From Slouch Hat to Unsea-
sonable Mantle to Worn Boots, he presented a Stygian Form.
Exceedingly tall, with long arms and broad shoulders, Kane
exhibited features both Saturnine and Powerfully Focus'd. A
kind of Dark Pallor lent him a Ghostly Visage, counter-
pointed but not relieved by the Thick Hedgerow of his
Brows.

And his Accouterments! Warlike and Vengeful in the extreme, raising in my Brain thoughts of the passage in Psalms:
"two-edged swords in their hands, to wreak vengeance on the
nations and chastizement on the peoples . . ." A Wicked Un-
scabbard'd Rapier depended from his wide leather belt, into
which were thrust Twin Pistols. But the most Curious object
carried by the Adventurer was a kind of short lance or Stave
of Ebony Wood, its Pommel carved into the shape of a Cat's
Head, its sharp tip stain'd with some Ocherous Substance.

At my elbow a Rude Fellow unknown to me whispered to
his Companion, "'Tis said Kane was peer to Raleigh and
Drake in their prime, during the century long gone."

"Aye. I have it on best authority that his Afric exploits
earned him undying youth from Pagan sorcerors."

"If so, that fabled benison sits heavily on his shoulders."

I felt a righteous indignation in my Youthful Soul against
the words of these Hayseed Poltroons. To my eyes, Solomon
Kane was Justice Incarnate, the most Proper and Vengeful
Christian my Gaze had yet to encounter. Moreover, he radi-

ated an Aura of Romance, like a figure out of Spenser or Malory, a Dark Knight on a Perpetual Quest.

With Unreasoning Certitude, I knew then that I would follow this man wherever he led, and do whatever he bade, if he would but Consent for me to be his Page.

Kane broke the Awe-ful Silence occasion'd by his entrance with a curt speech: "I have arrived as agent of thy solace, Brethren." Then he set foot on the Gangplank and began his descent.

Our Leaders were already moving solemnly toward the base of the Plank to usher Kane ashore, and the Visitor had nearly reached their warm Solicitude when the unexpected happened.

From the wat'ry gap twixt Wharf and Ship, a long scaled green Arm shot upward, and clamped its Mossy, Long-nailed fingers around the ankle of Kane's right Boot!

Before anyone else could summon up the Wits to react, Kane had whipped forth one of his Antique Pistols, and instantly primed and fired it straight into the Form of his Attacker!

The Unearthly Hand convulsed and withdrew, releasing Kane. Women screamed, and Men hastened to peer over the edge of the Wharf to descry the Nature of the Assailant. By virtue of my small size, I managed to push to the Vanguard.

The Humanoid Creature had been mortally wounded, staining the Harbor's Waters with its dark blood. Its Mortal Frenzy made Full Apprehension of its Lineaments impossible amidst the Froth, yet I thought to Glimpse a Barbed Tail and Webbed Hands. Upon its Expiration, the Chthonic Creature floated for a Short Moment, revealing its Naked, Reptilian Backside, before sinking like a Stone.

Kane had calmly replaced his matchlock. No expression of either Dismay or Triumph clouded his stony features.

Kane uttered his assessment of the Attack with plainspoken Certitude. "A child of Dagon. Your suspicions of Indian complicity with ancient demiurges were not misplaced, my friends. Let us adjourn to some quarters affording more safety than the open air, and we can begin to plot our campaign against these abominations."

Major Pynchon was the first to regain his Composure. "By all means, Master Kane. We have adopted the house of one of our most esteemed husbandmen, Benedict Arnold, nigh to Spring Street, as our headquarters. Refreshment awaits us there."

En masse then, I staying close to my Father's side, so as not to be summarily dismissed from the Council of Grey-beards, we set out up the Low Slope toward Spring Street, leaving at our back the waters of Newport Harbor, once so innocent and accomodating, yet now revealed to be the Lair of the Unspeakable.

All cram'd into the Narrow Quarters of the Keeping Room in Benedict Arnold's stout gambrel'd House hard by the Old Stone Mill (which some averred had been builded by Norse-men before e'er White Men arrived on these shores), we Set-tlers held Solomon Kane at our Worshipful Center as if he were the precious Beating Heart of our Body Politic. After his Masterful Display at the Wharf, he had commanded all our Respect. I was reminded of the passage in Luke, where the Christ is led into the council of priests and scribes and asked to furnish proof of his identity. Our Lord replied engi-matically then: "If I tell you, you will not believe; and if I ask you, you will not answer." Yet still He carried the Day amongst the Disbelievers, and just so did Kane, despite his Stern Silence, evoke our Affections and Belief. And even the most Curious Statements he was later to make could not shake our Reliance on him.

Arnold's demure wife and dainty daughters served a mod-est Collation of Small Beer and Pasties, which were but spar-ingly consumed. Truth to tell, no man among us was particularly an-hungered, as the enervating Heat of this most ungodly August robbed one of all Appetite, and the Close-ness of the Room only accentuated the oppressiveness. I my-self was able to down only three or four of the handy Meat Pies, whereas under other circumstances my Youthful Stom-ach—a Demanding Master whose Mature Edicts would lead to a later Corpulence of Frame—would have not been sated without Twice that Number.

Drinking only from a Tumbler of Well Water, his Stomach apparently set Sharp only for Fighting, Kane surveyed us silently, as if we were but Tools arrayed for his Handiwork, and he deeming how best to employ us.

The first order of Business was to make Suitable Introductions of all the Figures of Some Account in the Affairs of the Colonies to our Honored Visitor. We had here assembled men from Plymouth, Connecticut, Massachusetts and Rhode Island and the Providence Plantations, each of the Polities that had suffered from the Depradations of the Salvages. Major Pynchon took this Affair into Hand, and Singularly Conducted each Colonist to shake the hand of the Brooding Puritan. Soon 'twas my Father's turn, and I trailed expectantly in his Wake.

"Mr. Kane, this stalwart man of the cloth is the Reverend Increase Mather, Pastor of Boston's North Church and President of Harvard College."

Father shook Kane's hand, and I awaited Acknowledgment of my Presence in turn. When such Token was not shortly forthcoming, I thrust forward and offered my own Hand, speaking boldly to the Corvine Adventurer from abroad.

"Cotton Mather, Sir, and most delighted to meet you."

To my surprize, Father discharged no Public Rebuke upon me, but smiled at my Presumption.

"You will forgive my son, I hope, Mr. Kane, for he is something of a prodigy. Already enrolled in the College at his tender age, he exhibits more wit than many an elder I could name."

Kane fixed upon me then a Stare of such Directness and Probing Intensity that I felt like moist, defenseless soil beneath the Farmer's Plough. I fancied he was reading a direct Impression off my very Soul, estimating the Cut of my Inner Qualities and Weighing 'em in some Obscure Balance.

Evidently I passed Muster, for Kane gripped my outthrust Hand with fervor and replied, "The blood of righteousness flows strongly in this one. Let him be a part of our councils."

Elated at this warm reception, half-dazed by Kane's Glory, I somehow retreated to the Periphery of the Crowd, where I watched and listened attentively to the following Discourse.

It fell to my Sire to give a Concise Summary of the Atrocities conducted by the Salvages, clothing the Stage of the Debate as it were with the Gory Curtains that would frame our Final Campaign. He spoke as Fervently as if he stood behind his wonted Pulpit, blasting Sinners.

"Many an innocent soul has lost his very scalp to these barbarians after being cruelly struck down from behind. Defenseless babes have had their brains dashed out upon tree trunks. Women have been trammelled and dragged at several removes across the harsh countryside as mere chattel of their redskinned captors. Why, recounting the tragedy at Nine Men's Misery alone would keep us here all day! And occasionally the cruel ingenuity of the tawny tygers has surpassed all boundaries of the imagination. There was one harmless fellow named Wright, whose strange conceit was that so long as he held his Bible, no harm would befall him. A praiseworthy belief, yet one that should have been supplemented by more practical measures. For when his salvage assailants understood the tenor of his defense, they but laughed coarsely, then slit open poor Wright from waistcoat to windpipe and inserted the Holy Book into his very guts."

The whole Room was Aghast at the repetition of this ofttold Tale, and one of Arnold's daughters swooned, dropping a Pewter Pitcher upon the stone floor with a loud Crash. But Kane evinced no comparable Reaction, instead admonishing us in a matter-of-fact yet grim Manner.

"Citizens, you may spare me your accounts of the simple grotesqueries that limited mortals may inflict on one another. I have stood beneath the Moon of Skulls and climbed the black stairs of an eldritch ziggurat to a sacrificial altar where an unnatural beast slavered over a naked princess. I have trod the streets of a city of vampires, the lone living man. I have wrestled with a murderous ghost who inhabited an English moor and was wont to rend his victims to small shreds. I have lived for months among a race of winged demons, fanged like wolves, who yet came to call me brother. Man is ever the sport and sustenance of titanic beings of night and horror. These primitive assaults by your rude tormentors are as piss in a tempest, compared to other bloody insults the cosmos holds in store for us. No, what matters most is not the atrocities performed upon you, but your manner of reply."

The Host of Militiamen and Counselors was taken aback by Kane's Implicit Diminishment of all the Wrongs they had so long Clasp'd close to their Breasts, and were silent a while. Then Major Gookin spoke.

"Why, we have but answered 'em in kind. Upon capturing the lowest Indian soldier, we have performed upon 'em apposite punishments, such as the breaking of their fingers and other bones, and the pressing of their chests with heavy weights. Ofttimes we employ our allies the Mohegan as our sanctioned executioners, for they know precisely what excruciations will justifiably extract the most pain from their stoic renegade compatriots. When possible, such as during our magnificent success last year in the Great Narragansett Swamp, when we attacked the winter encampment of the salvages, we have slaughtered their women and children and destroyed all their stores, the selfsame indignities they have inflicted on us. And of course, we regain some small measure of our lost economy by selling some captives as slaves in the Indies."

Kane smashed his pewter Tankard down hard upon the Board, causing all of us to jump as if Pitchforked. His face expressed naught but Disgust.

"This is not how you conduct a war, my brethren, but rather how infants wage a childish game of tit-for-tat. No wonder this petty conflict has persisted for so many years. Simple footsoldiers have no say in the duration or direction or intensity of the campaign. Abusing them earns you only the increased enmity of their race. But if ye make the leaders your target, you cut the problem off at the head. Champion against champion, that is how such a matter must be resolved, and how I myself intend to settle it."

Major Sanford took Offense at this Upbraiding. "Think you us utter nincompoops? We have chased Philip and his fellow sachems up and down the countryside, and we slew each pint-pot Caesar as directly as we could. Now only Philip is left, and our best intelligence has him hiding within a few leagues of our very seat here. But he is proving impossible to corner, thanks to his extraordinary assist from powers beyond our ken. That is why we have enlisted your aid, relying on your vaunted experience with matters arcane."

The Starkfaced Puritan accepted this Counterblow with a surprising Temperance, cogitating upon Sanford's words for a full minute before finally saying, "Still and all, I maintain that 'tis your own unwise conduct that had prolonged this altercation."

Now stepped forward a man from the Ranks who had till this moment held Silence. People parted for him, opening a Path to Kane. Some gave way out of Deference, others out of Disdain, as if reluctant to let this man's touch Ataint 'em.

When the man had approached close to Kane, he extended his hand and offered his name.

"Roger Williams, Sir, and glad I am to hear you second the very sentiments I have been long pouring into the deaf ears of my peers. Their stubborn brutality has watered the thirsty root of this needless conflict with copious blood. And now my beloved Providence, that lively experiment at the head of the Salt River, is all burnt, save for three dwellings, because of the arrogant insensitivity of my comrades. I had parole from Philip himself for the safety of my settlement, but such treaties were expunged by a surfeit of betrayal, pain and unnecessary cruelty."

Kane studied Williams for a moment before clasping his hand. "You are the fabled heretic, Sir, cast out of the Massachusetts colony for your deviant preaching."

Williams faltered not, neither in Glance nor Grip. "Indeed, such an ignorant label has been applied to me, among others even less charitable. But what I preach is merely a brotherhood and equality of all the races, a sensible chariness to-

ward all earthly authority, and a reliance on our inner voices
in matters of conscience and action."

Releasing Williams's hand, Kane uttered a Judgment that
ill consorted with the Prejudices of fully half the Audience.
"Your ways are not mine, Sir, but I fully respect them. You
are an authentic gentleman and visionary. I will not seek to
enlist your help in this crusade, but I ask that you do nothing
to hinder us from accomplishing the destruction of your erstwhile salvage netop."

With his use of this Aboriginal Word meaning friend,
Kane gave some hint of the Depth of his Intimacy with New
World Matters.

Williams sighed in a Dis-spirited Fashion. "I acknowledge
your tact and good will, Sir, and altho' I could have wished
you might be dissuaded from your bloody pursuit, yet will I
give my bond not to stand in your way."

"In return," Kane replied, "you have my vow that when I
am in striking distance of Philip, I will endeavor to withhold
a mortal blow. Let us snaffle him and bring him to justice in
a civilized manner, proving that our virtue is the greater.
There will be no torture enacted upon Philip's person, so
long as I can help it."

"My thanks, Mr. Kane. This is the most I could expect."

Williams departed the Arnold Lodgings then, and Kane
made a request we found most curious.

"Is there one among you who has stood in Philip's actual
presence? If there be more than one, let me speak to the one
who has done so most recently."

A buzzing Consultation ensued, and finally a Verdict was
reached. Major Pynchon said, "Sir, there is a goodwife now
resident in this town named Mary Rowlandson. In February
of last year she was taken captive by the Indians in a raid
upon her garrison, and at one point was interviewed by Metacomet himself, all before attaining her present liberty. Shall
we fetch her?"

"By all means."

A Messenger was Dispatched, and men took the occasion
to venture outside, to stretch their Legs or enjoy a Bowl of

Pipeweed, altho' little enough Relief from the Actual Heat was to be had, with the fully leafed Trees unstirring in the heavy stagnant Atmosphere. I myself remained inside, casting sly but constant Glances upon the Object of my Worship. Kane bided the interval like a patient predator, a Wolf or Catamount with an Eternal Perspective upon Events, or even like God Himself, Who, as we read in the Second Letter of Peter, regards a day as a thousand years and a thousand years as but a day.

Finally Kane chose to register my Ardent Eyebeams and motioned me to his Side. Tremulously I approached. Once within his Orbit, I made so bold as to ask a Boon, most especially now, whilst my Father was Absent. "Mr. Kane, I want to come with you when you strike out after the heathen prince."

Kane's Smile resembled a Hawk's Beakish Grin. "The little scholar desires to experience the warrior's lot? Not so wise a wish, young Cotton. Should your face be flecked but once with your foe's blood, you may well find yourself casting aside your primers in favor of the gun and the sword. And that is not a fate I would wish on anyone." Kane's eyes clouded over momentarily, as if he were watching a Parade of Phantasms from a Softer, more Luxurious Period in his own Career. "Had I heeded my own earliest inclinations, I might have become a simple schoolmaster, and never known the pains and tragedies I have endured. A wife, a fixed abode, children of my loins—all foreclosed to me now. But forsooth, absent also would have been the harsh glories of righteous conquest and retribution against sinners. And I surely would not be here speaking with you now, but long ago moldered to dust in my humble grave."

At this Juncture Kane negligently fondled the Cat-headed Stave at his waist, and my Eyes widened as I bethought to detect a Faint Glow emanating from the Fetiche.

There came a stir at the Door of the Room, and Kane summarily ended my short Interview. "I will not trammel thy spirit, Cotton. Every man must learn for himself which path he will tread. Let us see what eventuates. Stay alert, and take whate'er chance Dame Fortune presents."

Flanked by the returning Crowd, Mary Rowlandson entered the room. A short, pretty, chaste Woman of no great years, who yet evinced upon her Lineaments the Marks of her Travails as captive of the Indians, she came timorously into the presence of our Guest.

"Mary Rowlandson," said Kane decorously, "you received an audience from the Wampanoag sachem Metacomet during your captivity?"

"Yes, Sir, that I did. At first I was greatly afear'd of him, for he presented a fiercesome sight. He stood outside his rude wigwom, exceedingly tall, with mighty thews. He was girded with wampom, the Indian currency, and his stern face was bedizened with garish dawbs of paint. But once he began to speak, in a calm and respectful manner, I someways lost my fright. He inquired as to my treatment, and I made complaint about the poor food afforded us, recounting how we slaves subsisted most days on naught but ground-nuts and hirtle-berries. Hearing this, Philip issued orders that we be given meat, bear or venison. Likewise, he ordered replacements for our tattered stokins and shoos. When my audience was concluded, I retired with a fonder impression of him than I had expected to retain."

Kane seemed to come to some sudden decision. "Mary, you and I must now adjourn to a private chamber, where I intend to make use of your prior proximity to our enemy. For I have a method of ascertaining his current whereabouts thro' the spiritual bond established twixt you and the salvage. Mr. Arnold, where may we obtain the requisite privacy?"

Benedict Arnold hastened to say, "Pray employ the bed-chamber my daughters use."

Kane stood, and escorted Mary Rowlandson to the designated Chamber.

Immediately I made for the Outer Door, but reckoned not with my Father's intervention.

"Cotton! Whither are you bound?"

"Ah, Sir, I—to the privy! 'Tis urgent!"

"Very well then. But stray not!"

Clutching my Privates as if to contain the Impulse to Micturate, I hastened outside.

Reader, I will confess to being no Plaster Saint in my Youth. As the Case was with Holy Augustine, the Tugs and Lures of the Flesh exerted their Devilish Sway over the immature Lad I once was. I oft-times sweated blood over my Sins of impurity, in the Wake of their Fulfillment, but could not find it in myself to firmly Excommunicate the Urges, so that I would, after some Days' piety, fall once again into the Slough of Onan. But at the Moment when I dash'd forth from the Arnold Household, I had cause to bless the Muddier Wellsprings of my Constitution, for it was these selfsame Peccant Ways which now afforded me a chance to spy upon Kane at his Conjurings.

I had removed from Boston to Newport many a Time before this day, accompanying Father on business matters concerning his Investments in the Carib Trade, viz., Molasses, Rum, and Slaves. And we were often hosted by Benedict Arnold, one of Father's partners. In my aimless lonely Rambles about the Yard whilst boring Mercantile Affairs were conducted, I had discovered a small Chink or Slit in the outer wall of the House, a Gap which fortuitously gave upon the bedroom of the Arnold girls. Shielded by a dense stand of Pipeplants, whose lilac blooms would oft perfume my Vernal Peeping, this Spyhole had granted me many a Sweet Moment of Carnal Delight, as I witnessed the girls Making Water in their Chamberpots, or adjusting their Petty Coates and Stays.

Now I planted myself firmly before this Coign of vantage and was rewarded with the following Spectacle.

Mary Rowlandson sat on a sturdy straight-backed Chair, whilst Kane stood behind her. Their Speech, if any, I could not discern. But what Unfolded next made mere Words exiguous.

Kane laid his Left Hand upon Mary's collarbone, his Fingertips trailing tantalizing close to the Slope of her Bosom. I experienced a momentary Twinge of Suspicion. Was our

Unassailable Puritan going to give way to his own Base
Lusts and Molest his Subject? How could I follow him with
Honor then? But no, Kane's Right Hand rose into view,
clutching his Feline-Top't stave. That Instrument began to
emit a Verdigrised Phosphoresence, a Lambent Glow that
cloaked the actors in a veritable Corpselight. Kane uttered
Something then, forcefully invoking Assistance or com-
manding Materialization.

Slowly, slowly, a third figure began to Cohere out of Thin
Air. Surrounded by an Identifiable Landscape of Marshy As-
pect, the Wraith gradually assumed its Wonted Lineaments,
and I suddenly knew I was looking at none other than King
Philip Himself.

Reader, you may rest assured that I felt at that Pivotal Moment like King David viewing Bathsheba nude at her Ablu-
tions, all a-tingle with Mindless Exaltation. But as the
Horrible Figure of Metacomet acquired more and more So-
lidity, my feelings transform'd to those which Actaeon must
have felt, stumbling upon Artemis at her Sylvan Bath: a
sense of Trespassing on the Cosmically Shrouded.

And when the Moment arrived that King Philip's puzzled,
roving Eyes seemed to fasten on my Spyhole and engage my
own Orbs in Spiteful Recognition, I nearly Fainted from fear.

Kane, howsomever, was nowise Discommoded by the
Ghost. The Puritan's next actions were easy to interpret: he
adjured the Ghost to speak. But this Astral Semblance of
Metacomet, I soon saw, was no Obedient Smoak, but rather a
Spectre of some Volition and Malignance. Philip's only response to Kane's Adjuration was to Glower most Fearsomely
and fasten his hands around Kane's throat!

Then ensued a brief but violent Tumult, as the two War-
riors Contested against each other. Freed of Kane's steadying
grip, a Drain'd Mary Rowlandson fell insensible to the
Floorboards. My Heart was in my Gullet as Metacomet bent
my Hero backwards, as if to crack his very Spine. But then
Kane swung his Pagan Stave against the Skull of the Salvage
King, and the Unnatural Apparition exploded in a Blaze of
Light.

After spending just a moment longer at the Chink, to As-certain that Kane yet Breathed and was making a Full Recov-ery, I hastily returned to the Gathering inside, making a Shew of buttoning my Trews.

Evidently, sounds of Kane's Struggle had penetrated to the Assembly, for much Consternation was a-brew. Majors Pyn-chon and Gookin stood poised to burst in upon Kane. But just then the bedroom door opened, and a weary Kane emerged, half-supporting his stun'd Female Accomplice.

Kane held up one hand in a Gesture of Reassurance. "All is well. I contended with the spirit of our enemy, and altho' he escaped me, I won the knowledge of his location, leaving him all unwitting of the theft, and, consequently, complacent of his own security. Philip is ensconced in the miry depths of a certain swamp at the foot of Mount Hope. We will set out under cover of darkness to bring the rogue down. But till then, let us all rest and prepare. I myself am sore fatigued."

Master Arnold conducted Kane to his own Bed. A General Exultancy reigned, albeit tinged with Sobriety at the Assault yet to come, as men slap'd each other upon their Backs and assured one another that at long last the Days of Terror were at an end.

Never prior to this Fateful Night had I ever considered myself to be one of the Sinners assailed by Paul in his Sec-ond Letter to the Romans. A Preacher's son, ever alert to maintaining Public Probity and a Cleanly Conscience, I had so long trodden the Path of Righteousness that by now such behavior was Second Nature to me, even as my Rectitude earned me Cuffings and Taunts from my Rowdy Errant Peers. Yet assuredly my actions of but a scant hour pass't had caused me to Plummet into the ranks of those Sinners casti-gated by the Apostle, for Paul numbers among such Fiends as murderers, gossips, slanderers and inventors of evil, those who are "disobedient to their parents."

And so I had been.

But now, as I rode Unseeing thro' the Stifling August Night, bundled beneath the very Cloak of my Hero as the

Mighty Steed loaned to Kane carried us north to Tripp's
Ferry, in Pursuit of the Greatest Villain and Conqueror these
Arcadian Shores of the English Zion had yet known, I could
not by any Dint of Conscience Regret my sins. For had I
obeyed my Father's commands to remain behind in Newport, I would have missed all that Violent Glory that was to
come, and thereafter Reviled my Overpunctiliousness for all
Eternity.

At least such were my sanguine Feelings as I clutched the
taut-muscled midriff of Solomon Kane whilst we gallop'd to
our Destiny. Hang the Consequences till the Morrow!
Tonight I was my own Man!

Kane had not Stirred from his Needful Sleep until well
past eleven of the clock that eve, and the assembled Soldiers,
Farmers and Tradesmen had grown restless as Hens before a
Storm, despite busying themselves with the preparations of
their Weaponry and the Stoking of their Guts. But when the
Grim Cavalier finally emerged with his Surly Magnificence
Restored, and commanded, "Let us be off!", all Impatience
and Incertitude vanish't, and a Lusty Huzzah spontaneously
shook the very Rafters of the Arnold homestead.

As the men marshalled outside in the starlit Yard amidst
the snorting Horses, Father approached me.

"Cotton, I have arranged for Faith and Charity to attend
thee while we elders finish this dangerous and sordid matter.
You need not go to bed at all on such a momentous night, for
I know your curiosity as to our success would certainly keep
you awake. But I do trust that you will make the most of
your time with the Arnold girls, perhaps by regaling 'em
with some of your lessons in natural history. Share with 'em
the exciting news of the fossil record of God's abortive creations, those uncouth beasts which Noah spurned, and which
perished afterwards in the Flood."

At any other time the Enticing Prospect of being alone
with the Arnold Daughters would have commanded my
whole attention. But tonight I was not to be Fobbed off so
easily. Yet I made no Objection to my Father, but merely

nodded mutely. Insofar as I kept Silent, so I chopped my logic, I could not be afterwards deemed a Liar.

As soon as Father exited, I made my same Privy-Desirous Excuse to the Arnolds, and was outside amidst the restlessly tromping Troop.

Spotting Kane, I acted unhesitantly. Racing to the side of his Horse, I thrust up my hand.

"Take me with you!" I whispered in a husky fashion.

Wordlessly Kane complied, hauling me off the ground with One-Handed ease. As I swung up into the saddle, he adjusted his long Mantle to Enshroud me, and the Deed was Done, with no one the Wiser.

Beneath my Woolly Concealment, bereft of any Actual Sense of the passing Terrain, I mentally rehearsed our Progress northward thro' Middle Town and Port's Mouth, along the sizable island whereof Newport occupied the Southern Portion. Our Terminus would be Tripp's Ferry, the Connexion to Mount Hope and Bristol on the Mainland. How I would avoid Father there, I could not say, and simply Entrusted my Survival as a member of the War Party to Luck and to Kane's Patronage.

After nearly an hour's hard Riding, we made the Slip wherefrom the Ferry wontedly departed. A messenger had been dispatched while Kane yet slumbered, and the Ferrymen awaited us, eager to do their part to end the Depradations of the Wampanoags and their kindred. The flickering light of Cressets and Torches filtered thro' the Weave of Kane's cloak, and I anticipated being Caught out upon perhaps some necessary Dismounting. But Kane simply trotted us onboard the rocking Ferry, taking up a Station at the Prow, and after another ten or so Horsemen followed, we poled off, leaving the rest of our party ashore until the craft returned.

I could hear the Oarlocks Engaged as we reached deeper Waters, and the Chaunts of the Laboring Scullers as they drew us across the half-mile of salty channel. The devilish August heat had hardly Abated with the fall of night, and the Closeness of my Little Tent made my eyes droop. But what

Chanced next pulled me out of my drowse as surely as a Fisherman yanks a Cod from its Wat'ry Parlor.

"Mr. Kane," Major Pynchon said in a trembling voice, "what make you of those fast-moving clouds?"

When we had left Newport the begemmed nocturnal Skies had been clear as Ice. But obviously not so now.

"I like them not, Major. They recall to me the boiling stormheads which I saw accrue when an Ethiop sorceror of my acquaintance named N'Longa sought to dishearten his foes by magical means. Plainly these stormheads too are of supernatural origin."

A voice I did not recognize said, "I was with Captains Henchman and Prentice as we marched from Boston to Dedham last year to succor the garrison there, and we were overtaken by an eclipse of the moon. We all saw then strange portents on the moon's darkened face. A bloody scalp, an Indian bow. If the Tawnies can brand their evil upon Luna's very brow, what chance have we against 'em?"

"Nerve yourself to greater confidence, soldier!" Kane demanded. "Have ye forgotten you ride with God on your side?"

Some Instinct caused me to slip out of the Saddle then, to free Kane for easier Maneuvering. And 'twas well I did. For, as the Clouds clustering overhead began to Rumble and Spit, discharging crackling Lightnings as well, we were attacked!

"Watch yourselves!" yelled Kane, before Anyone else had taken Cognizance of the Assault upon us.

An enormous dripping Tendril as of some Unknown Leviathan of the Deeps, sucker'd over and round as a Hogshead Barrell, Hoary with Barnicles and Seawrack, burst from the water, arc'd thro' the air, and slapped down athwart the Deck, narrowly missing men and horses, who had scuttled away from its descent, thanks to Kane's warning. Horses scream'd, men curst, and a volley of Shots crack'd the night. But mere Musketballs seemed to have no effect upon the Creature, and the Awe-some Limb rose skyward again for another Plunge.

Kane was unhorsed now, and standing full beneath the

shadow of the Kraken's Appendage. He flourished aloft his Cat-headed Stave, which Instrument commenced to Fulgurate in the manner I had earlier witnessed.

"Back to Hell with ye, demon! Back to the infernal depths!"

Pride in Kane's Staunch Demeanor and Apprehension that he would not Prevail against this Monster warred in my Juvenile Breast. Then all was decided, as a Lance of Cold Flame jabbed outward from Stave to Tendril. A smell as of one of our traditional Clam Bakes multiplied an hundredfold filled the air, the Monst'rous Limb flailed about in obvious Pain before sliding away beneath the Turbid Waters, and silence descended upon the scene. At the same time the Unnatural Clouds began to Dissipate, and the Stars once more Smiled down on us.

Recovering with Admirable Alacrity, Major Pynchon soon had the Rowers back at work and order restored. In some further minutes the mainland beckoned us from no large distance. I came up to Kane, and was instantly heartened by his Praise.

"You did well to give me my liberty at the crucial moment, lad, and you did not quail before the hideous unknown. I do not believe anyone will raise any objections to your continued presence tonight."

"Thank you, Sir. I was inspired by your own noble bearing."

Kane returned me no Smile, but simply said, "If I exhibit no fear, young Cotton, it is only because all such emotions have been burnt from me by unfathomable hardships and privations. Anyone witnessing the horrors I have seen—assuming those hypothetical witnesses survived—would exhibit the same stoicism. I have no choice any longer in what I do, and this paucity of options represents a missing civilized luxury the lack of which I sometimes sorely regret. But such is my lot, and I am mainly content."

Leaving me to ponder this Chill Assessment of his Own Damaged Soul, Kane moved off to help with the docking. Soon we were on dry land.

Two Worthy and Vigorous men now separated themselves from the Mass of welcomers, introducing themselves as Captain Church of Plymouth and Captain Williams of Scituate. They delivered an Account of their forces, which included a

Contingent of Praying Indians. These Friendly Salvages stood in a Cabal a ways off from us White Men, and I instantly mistrusted their Obsequious yet oddly Threatening Mien. In their adopted Civilized Garb, the Uppish barbarians seemed both Traitors to their own Race and Unreliant Allies, neither Fish nor Fowle, a Pack of Trained Apes or Dancing Bears.

"Mr. Kane," said Williams. "Thanks to your veritable intelligence, we have been able to encircle the bog and insure that Philip and any of his remaining myrmidons remain cloistered within. We await your subsequent direction."

Kane uttered then the chilling Words we had all been anticipating, but which nonetheless still Pricked our Courage. "There is naught for it but to enter the horse-repelling swamp afoot, in pairs. The separation of our forces will allow us to beat every bush most thoroughly. But the treacherous conditions underfoot, which the Indians know intimately, will confound and undo many of the teams. We can only pray that whoever of us meets Metacomet will be up to subduing him. Let us but agree to raise a commotion upon sighting our prize, and I will immediately hasten to aid whichever brave Ajax first grapples with the villain."

"Shall we wait until daybreak?" asked Captain Church.

"By no means. As soon as the rest of our party is ferried o'er, we strike."

Father arrived with the third Boatload of men, and I shall not recount the Bitter Upbraidings I thereupon received. I made humble yet cogent Response, employing all the finer Logic with which my mentors at Harvard had imbued me, citing the duty of every citizen, however Juvenile, to protect our Commonwealth. When mere Females could exhibit such Courage as to ward off their Vile Attackers with a scuttle of live Coals, could a strapping Youth such as myself do any less? Suffice it to say that not only did my words soothe and convince, but Kane's account of my Behavior under the Kraken's Buffets earned me Grudging Praise (once Father's Apoplexy abated), and also at last the Miraculous Privilege of Penetrating the Very Marsh itself, and in no other role than that of Patroclus to Kane's Achilles, to continue Kane's Grecian Simile.

In the end, Father seemed actually Prideful of my new Station in the Scheme of Things. He laid a hand on Kane's shoulder, signalling his assent to my new status, and bade the Puritan earnestly to keep me safe by his Side, asserting that no other Warrior could offer his Cherished Son more Protection than Kane. Kane returned a simple, "That I will endeavor to do," and then we moved out.

The hour was now nearly Three in the Morning, and already hints of Aurora's debut were discernible. We welcomed even this negligible Lessening of darkness as an Aid to our Progress.

I carried no Weapon, but my Utility amidst the Thickets soon became apparent. Being Lighter and some'at more Nimble than my Protector, I served as Scout, probing ahead with a long stout Stick and testing the Hummocks and Tussocks that would serve us as Stepping Stones into the Depths of the Bog. This Service freed Kane to concentrate his Hunter's Senses on both repelling any Attack and Ferreting out any Hidden Salvages.

Not wishing to advertize our Presence too far in advance, we carried no Light, nor did any of the other Teams. Moving thro' the Sepulchral Gloom and Heat, with its Squelching Muck, Slithering Serpents, Apparitional Trees, and Hordes of Disturbed Insects, some of which made known their Appetite for Human Flesh, I felt like Dante Essaying some Lesser Circle of Hell, with Kane my Militant Virgil.

Now passed an Indeterminate Period of Time, an interval wherein my Sensible Universe narrowed to my own harsh Slogging, labored Breathing and tensioned Nerves. However, I drew Courage and Stamina from Kane's unfaltering Harrowing of our Swampy Environs. Rapier in one hand and Pistol in t'other, he stalked behind me like some Avenging Angel out of Judges or Zechariah, and I felt utterly safe within his Sphere of Protection.

Every now and then a distant Shot would resound, and I would pray that one less Salvage befouled the Earth, and also that our own men Fared Unharmed. But as time passed and no Hulloo summoned us to confront the Chief Object of our

Search, I began to despair that our Fiendish Quarry would escape us once again.

In our unyielding Progress, Kane and I reached finally a largish expanse of solid ground, a little Islet sequester'd in the heart of the Swamp. Its O'ergrown Marge concealed its Interior from our eyes, and we penetrated cautiously.

But all our Deft Secrecy availed naught, for King Philip awaited us in full Cognizance of our advance, standing with Solemn Gravity upon a patch of clear Ground.

A grey Dawn now nearly nigh allowed me a good picture of the Formidable Warrior. Tall as Kane, the fearsome Metacomet wore his pursuit-tatter'd buckskins and robe as if they were Ermine or Sable. His painted face, all majestic angles, seemed hewn from our own New England granite or a block of lignum vitae. Strands of Wampom bedizened his brawny chest, across which he confidently cradled his Musket, Indian-fashion. A Rude Tom-a-Hawk, its Shaft carven with Pagan Glyphs, Feathers depending from its Butt, hung from his waist.

Ignoring me utterly, Philip spoke first, his Manly voice resonant with Suppressed Rage, Black Despair and a most curious Forlorn Indifference to his own Fate. Of Fear I heard no syllable, but yet much of Intelligence and Refinement. Let me confess now that, by the end of his Speech, I had gained new Respect for our Opponent.

"What cheer, fellow Mage. After our spirit battle, we come face to face at last. Your reputation for independence and courage has reached me across the wide waters, yet I find you now entered into the service of these small men, who are all too timid and inept to confront me themselves. I see a proud lion yoked to a plough."

Kane responded soberly. "The choice of mission is my own, Metacomet. No man commands me. As ever, I respond to the sheer injustice of the situation."

King Philip spat upon the soggy soil. "Injustice! Where were you then when my people were enslaved and humiliated, when they were arrested and imprisoned under false charges, when my brothers were executed and my sisters mo-

lested, when our lands were stolen from us? Is it only the suf-
ferings of white men that can elicit your outrage?"

Kane seemed Stung by this Jab. "I have fought on behalf
of all races and tribes, Metacomet, the sons of Ham as well
as the sons of Shem. But by the time I learned of this war,
your side was clearly in the wrong, having overstepped all
bounds of civilized combat. Enlisting wicked allies, you
turned your back on all courts and treaties—"

Philip's face contorted with anger. "Instruments of the
conquerors, prejudiced against our kind from the start! And I
piss on your ridiculous rules of war! Only victory matters."

Seemingly reconciled to the Futility of any further Argument, Kane assumed a more Agressive Footing. "Let us have
at it then, King. Each cause will find embodiment in its
champion, and victory will go to him who strikes hardest.
And should it be within my powers to subdue you without
dealing a mortal blow, I am pledged to do so, having given
troth to your netop, Roger Williams."

"You must do what you deem honorable, as shall I. But I
pray you, let us abandon our firearms, and allow our human
muscles to hold sway."

King Philip nobly suited Deeds to Words then, and tossed
aside his musket. Kane followed suit with his brace of Pistols
and also his Rapier. Into his hand came the Cat-Headed
Stave, its weird Radiance now matched by the cousin'd
Glow from the Tom-a-Hawk.

Then Kane and Philip closed upon one another.

I watched Enrapt as the well-matched Fighters circled
each other warily. But I was not prepared for what eventu-
ated when their Weapons clashed.

An enormous Report like a barrage of Thunder issued from
the smash of Fetiche against Hatchet. Jags of harsh Lightning
shot skyward, illuminating the Scene as brightly as Noon. Neither man seemed disconcerted by the titanic Repercussions of
their Contest, but, quite to the contrary, became e'en more fully
Embroil'd in a Fantastic Dance of Death, darting around and
about, each seeking a way thro' t'other's Defenses.

Once more my Heart was Socketed firmly in my Windpipe, as I observed my Worshipful Idol strive so Manfully, amidst the St. Elmo's Coruscations. From the Fringes, I watched this Eldritch Display with mute Fascination, unable to assign Dominance to either Combatant. But this much I knew: the Contest would not long go uninterrupted, for surely every Interested Participant within Leagues must be hastening to this very spot, drawn by the Tumult. If Kane would indeed settle Philip's Hash, it must be soon.

But then came Tragedy! Forced backwards, Kane stumbled upon a Root, and momentarily lost his Vigilance. Into that narrow crack of Inattention, Metacomet plunged! A blow from his Tom-a-Hawk was only partially deflected before coming into Heavy Contact with Kane's Scull!

Now Kane measured his lanky Length upon the clammy Ground, Stunned and Bleeding. A Yawp of Sympathy and Alarm escaped my own Lips. My Beloved Conqueror had been felled, and All was Lost lest I could save him! I estimated how quickly I could reach one of Kane's discarded Pistols, but before I could move, Metacomet bestrode my prostrate Hero like the Colossus of Rhodes and raised his evil Axe.

"I took no such pledge of mercy as thee, Kane. Prepare to meet thy false God."

At that instant a Shot rang out, and King Philip plunged Rearward to the ground.

Into the clearing stepped one of the Praying Indians, named most inaptly, as I later learned, Alderman. He it was whose Cowardly Shot had ignobly finished the Great Sagamore, once the Bane of our Land, piercing the Body of the proud Leader precisely where "Joab thrust his darts into rebellious Absolom."

I rushed to Kane's side, seeking to Succor him. But his Wound was Gouting much blood, and he remained Insensate. There was little enough I could do, save cushion his Head and stroke his Gory Brow.

Within minutes, the Islet was crowded with exultant Soldiers. Somehow, between 'em all, both Kane and the corpse of Philip were Borne out of the Marsh.

*　　*　　*

Patient Reader, there is little enough more to indite in this Account anent the most Stirring Moments of my Young Life, now so far removed from my current Feeble Estate.

The fate of Philip's Mortal Remains is well-known. Beheaded and quartered in the Punishment long reserved for Traitors, he was denied sanctified Burial according to either Christian or Pagan Customs. His mounted Head was on display at Plymouth for twenty-five Years or more, and served as Grim Warning to his Dis-spirited and Dis-sheveled brethren.

This Brutal Decomposition of his Opponent, which Kane's Incapacitation made him unable to prevent, most assuredly occasioned Kane's Deepest Regrets, tho' he spoke not ever of it.

As for Kane himself, he recovered admirably, despite the Severity of his Wound, proving once agan that while one Man may die from cracking his Tooth upon a Plumb-stone, another may survive an Hatchet buried in his Scull. And I shall eschew False Humility enough to reveal that it was I who had the Inspired Notion to place his Stave upon his Bosom during the initial Stuporous stages of his Recovery. Indeed, the Magical Wand seemed to act as a Sovereign Incitement to his Speedy Healing. Before a fortnight had passed, the Old Puritan was ready to return to his Native Shores.

We made our Goodbyes at the same Newport Wharf where I had seen him step ashore, what seemed like a Small Eternity ago, so rich in Incident had the brief days been.

Kane clasped my hand firmly, regarding me from under his crumpled Slouch Hat with an iron Gaze.

"Think you still, young Cotton, to follow in the warrior's footsteps after all the gruesome things you have observed?"

I made ready Reply, having given much Consideration to this question while Kane recuperated. "No, Sir, I do not. I will most likely become a preacher, I think, like unto my father. The Reverend Cotton Mather has a nice sound to't. In that profession, I deem, a man's hands may remain virtuously unbloodied."

Kane neither disputed nor affirmed this Sentiment, but simply Saluted me, and Sailed off.

THE EMPRESS JINGŪ FISHES
(Jingū Tennō, Late-Fourth-century Japan)

Kij Johnson

This elegant story is told in a few carefully chosen brush strokes, becoming a prose poem in which we glimpse the outline of an empress's life. Kij Johnson is the author of the novelette "Fox Magic," which won the Theodore Sturgeon Award for best short story of 1994; her short fiction has appeared in *Analog, Asimov's Science Fiction, The Magazine of Science Fiction, Realms of Fantasy, Amazing Stories,* and other publications. In 2001, she published her first novel, *The Fox Woman* (Tor), a fantasy set in Heian-era Japan, and won the International Association for the Fantastic in the Arts's Crawford Award for best new fantasy work; a companion to that novel, *Fudoki,* was published in 2003. She has held editorial and managerial positions at Tor Books, Dark Horse Comics, Wizards of the Coast, and Microsoft, and has taught writing at Louisiana State University and the University of Kansas. After several years in Seattle, Washington, she and her husband, writer Chris McKitterick, now live in Lawrence, Kansas.

T he empress Jingū fishes. The little mountain stream before
  her is fast but smooth, and clear enough that she can see
an *ayu*-trout near the bottom, though it is nearly hidden by tree-
shadows above and the busy pattern of the river bed below:
gold and russet and gray rocks, waving tangled weeds. The
trout does not see her—or does not care whether she sees it—
only hovers there, as unconcerned and self-absorbed as the
gods.

She is not hungry, for she has just eaten. Beside a small
slender stone as long as her thumb, cooked rice spills from a
tipped cedarwood box, the remains of her meal. She picks up
the stone and tucks it into her sash; she will need it later, and
it will be just the right size and shape. Jingū knows this as
clearly as she knows the death-name of the unborn son in her
belly, or the date of her own death, forty years from now.
Past and future are equally immediate to the gods, and thus
to her, their shaman, to whom and through whom they speak.

Half a year from now, she will be in the kingdom of Silla
on the Korean peninsula, completing a task the gods have set
her. It will be bitterly cold, a pale-skied day with snow in the
air. Though it will be six months before she sees it, she
knows that Silla's capital will be built on the Chinese plan,
its walls twenty feet high and roofed with tile to protect
against flaming arrows, roads from the gates scattering
across a treeless plain—a perfect place for her to draw up her
troops. Though she is pregnant with her son, who will be
due—and overdue—by then, Jingū is on horseback at their
head, dressed in armor, her long hair tied close in a man's
style. Her bow lies across her horse's neck, and she runs a
crow-feathered arrow between her fingers. She longs for the
Sillans to attack, longs for their king to open the gates of the
capital and ride out to meet her. She has wanted this since her
husband Chūai died. The gods demanded he take Silla; when
he refused they killed him. She cannot avenge herself on the
gods, but aches to kill someone, anyone.

That is half a year from now. Now, this instant, she looks
at the trout suspended in water as clear and cold and pitiless
as the future.

*   *   *

Eight years ago. Jingū is to be married. She kneels on a litter hung so heavily with silk and paper and tree branches that she can see nothing; but she sees anyway. This is the emperor's temporary palace; though it is only a month before they move to the next place, the many wood-and-plaster buildings are solidly constructed, with graceful tall roofs. Her husband the emperor will be called Chūai when he is dead, and this is his name to her even now, before she has seen his face—though she must remember to address him as "husband" or "your highness." The future is uncomfortable enough to a woman who is born to it, and she knows already that he will be afraid of the gods that speak through her, that he will ignore them and die.

Her robes are heavy with appliqué and silver. The dangling headdress ornaments tickle her face when she tips back her head. The soles of her shoes are hung with silver charms shaped like fish. Her bracelets of shell are narrow but so deep that they form broad flat disks around her wrists. She cannot walk, cannot pick up anything. Her wedding-dress is nearly as heavy as the armor she will wear eight years from now, after the gods speak and her husband dies.

Her husband has other, older, wives and even two grown sons. This will be a problem when her son is born. For a time, anyway: she sees her stepsons' deaths, unavoidable as soon as they raise arms against the boy. Her son will prevail and become emperor. Many generations from now he will be a god, the god of peace and then the god of war, Hachiman. She smiles and touches her still-virgin belly: it is quite appropriate that his mother will conquer a land across the sea for him.

Five months from now. Jingū crouches alone in a shrine, a building sunk half into the earth, its roof many men's height over her head. The roof's supports make strange angled shadows against the morning light that sifts from the steep triangles of the eave openings. The air is thick with the scents of horses and hot metal, latrines and cooking fish: the

smells of an army. Outside the shrine she hears her warleader
Takeuchi talking with her guard. It is Takeuchi who will stop
the rebellious stepsons for her, but that is years in the future,
and Jingū has a war to fight and a son to bear before then.

She does not pray for her troops' safety in crossing the sea
or a victory in Silla, for she has seen these things already.
No: she is nine months pregnant, and her child frets to be
born. The contractions drive her to her knees, panting. Her
urine runs into the hard-packed earth; snot and saliva and
sweat drip from her face. She prefers not to embarrass herself
in front of her troops. The privacy of the shrine is welcome.

Jingū has been careful to show none of the weakness that
can come of pregnancy, though hers has not been an easy
one. Her chest hurts, and her bowels, pelvis, legs, back—
everything. She finds herself panting at even slight exertion.
Her breasts have begun to weep, and the cotton with which
she binds them chafes. Inside her, Ōjin grows large and
kicks, searching for a comfortable position.

Things have grown a little easier for her since her son
dropped in her belly: it's easier to breathe, easier to move.
The clear fluid seeping from her loins to stain her saddle has
been only a minor inconvenience.

She wears the torso of her armor, though its slim metal
plates are very heavy, and, since she is still in Japan, their
value is only based in her troops' morale. There are ordinarily four panels that would cradle her torso, front, sides and
back; but she has removed a side panel, claiming that her
belly is too great to secure the fourth piece. In truth, she simply chooses to lighten the armor by removing some of it, and
it is easy enough to see that the panel turned away from the
enemy will be useless. The weight: she already carries sorrow heavy as stone bracelets, and her child like iron in her
womb.

When the contraction ends at last, she collapses on her left
side—the unarmored side—tears leaking to the ground. "Not
now," she says aloud, to the gods and her son. "Wait. When
I've returned from Silla: then."

She has brought with her the slender smooth stone she

found beside the trout's stream. She slides it into her vagina, a cold weight that warms eventually. The stone frets; gods are not all great gods, and this stone longs for its icy riverbed, for the company of its fellows. It has no choice but to stay, for she wraps hemp cloth tightly around her loins to hold stone and child in place, and ties a knot.

The stone, the army, the horse before the walls of Silla's capital—they are in the future. In the meantime, Jingū stands on the riverbank and eyes the trout. It remains supremely unconcerned with her shadow over it, her loss and anger, her war and the forty years of her life that stretch beyond, each day without Chūai. The fish does not care. "You bastard," she says aloud, and sets out to catch it, though she is not hungry.

Like every woman, whether peasant or empress, she has a needle, though hers is of silver, a treasure from over the same sea she will soon cross. She draws it from her sash, and bends it easily between her fingers, to a hook shape. It looks fragile, but will be sturdy enough for the trout, which is small.

The gods have taken even luck from Jingū; there is no serendipity to the fact she snagged her robe on a *sakaki* shoot when she walked to the stream's edge. She crouches and rocks back on her heels, and worries at the frayed thread, tugging until it starts to slide past its fellows. Its absence leaves a tiny flaw in the fabric, a puckered line that is more sensed than seen. When she has pulled half a dozen strands of the dark silk, she twists them together, and when this is done, she tugs on the thread, hard as a fish fighting to live. She will not lose this trout because she underestimates the power of denial and despair. It holds. She threads the bent needle and ties a knot.

Problems with the natives. It is a year ago. Jingū and Chūai are well content with one another, though Jingū already mourns him in her heart. The blurring of present and future has consequences both large and small: unexpected minor

advantages have been Jingū's ability to sexually please her
husband from the very beginning, and the passion they share
even after seven years of marriage, fueled on her part by the
knowledge that he will die soon. And not so minor: the two
older wives are nearly forgotten, and it is Jingū who travels
with Chūai now.

Chūai (though she remembers to call him "beloved") has
for several years fought with the Kumaso, ill-mannered and
independent-minded locals from an island of Japan, who refused to pay their taxes. The battles with the Kumaso have
been inconclusive at best—it is never easy to force recalci-
trants to battle on their own terrain—but Chūai remains confident. He has called a council of his generals in Na, a
strange little barbarian town on the island. Jingū walks the
hills outside of Na, weeping, waiting for the dream that she
knows is coming.

Still, when the dream takes her it is like a rape, and she
awakens screaming. Her husband holds her until her muscles
unclench and the tears begin. She speaks then, the gods'
voice scraping from between her clenched teeth. *"Ignore the
Kumaso,"* it says. *"There is a rich land across the water to
the north and west: Silla. Take it."*

Chūai has seen her weakness in the hands of the terrible
gods before this; he knows that they tell the truth through
her. But he is emperor, and understands (better than the gods,
perhaps) the intricate exchanges of power and influence that
are necessary to rule a land. "Why?" he says softly to Jingū.
"It has taken years to bring this together. We can't leave this
campaign to start another somewhere none of us have seen."
The gods do not permit her to say what crowds in her mind:
because they will kill you.

In the morning, Chūai leads Jingū to the tallest hill they
can see from Na, and together they climb it. There are no fish
on the soles of her shoes this time, and it is a simple walk, if
long. The autumn sky is very blue, the oak and maple trees in
their first startling change from green to gold and red. For an
instant she pretends that she and Chūai are not emperor and
consort but ordinary people gathering sticks or hunting, free

to live as they wish, to say without constraint, "Do that," or, "Don't do this." The illusion is gone as quickly as it comes; there is no rest from the gods. They come to the hill's top and look around them: the island they stand on stretches away to the south and west; to the north and east is the main island of the empire. To the north and west, where Silla is supposed to be, is nothing but water and sky and a few fishing boats, small as fallen leaves on a lake. "See?" he says. "There is nothing there, nothing to conquer, nothing to point to and strive for. Whereas here—"his sweeping arm encompasses the hill, little Na at its feet, the island they stand on—"are the Kumaso. Enemies we can see and destroy. Which do you think my commanders will see as the wiser course?"

"The gods—" she whispers past her strangled throat.

Chūai rubs his face with his hand. "The gods are unreasonable, and they are not all allies. Even the gods can be treacherous."

She knows this better than he ever will. The words come out in a rush: "They will kill you if you do not."

He touches the tears growing cold on her cheeks. "You've already seen your life without me, haven't you?" She cannot meet his weary eyes. "Then I am already dead."

Some months later, the gods do kill him, with a Kumaso arrow in the chest, an infected wound, and a quick (if uncomfortable) death. There are times in the last days when he asks about the future, but she has nothing to tell him, for none of it has to do with him, none but the barely-begun son in her belly: Prince Homuda, who will be Ōjin after he has died, and then the god Hachiman.

Knowing her husband will die is not the same as losing him. She is numb as she stumbles through the purification retreat and rituals. Past and future are meaningless to the gods and thus to Jingū. The pain never lessens: each moment of each day contains the first shock and the endless ache of his death. Forty years before she dies.

A fish is not seduced by bait: when it grows hungry, it eats whichever mosquito egg or dragonfly happens to be closest.

If one is fortunate or destined, one's bait looks like the fish's preferred food, and it happens to be closer than any other mosquito egg or dragonfly at that moment.

But it is chance that fish and bait are in the right places at the right time. There may be no fish there, or a different fish, or the wrong bait, or the fish may not be hungry. The woman who hopes to catch a fish knows she offers nothing to the fish that it cannot find for itself—and better, for her bait comes with a hook and a thread, and death.

The spilled rice on the ground is cold. Grains stick to her hand when she picks one up and presses it onto the needle. It looks a bit like the tiny things that live at the water's surface and become mosquitoes.

She stands slowly, and looks down into the stream, down at the shimmering motionless uncaring trout. "You bastard," she says again. "Prove to me that I should go to Silla."

Jingū knows what the gods want. They toss their demands at her, knowing she will meet them: a dozen shrines to this god or that; rice fields and offerings, priestesses in Nagata and Hirota. And Silla.

Chūai died because he sought to conquer the Kumaso rather than Silla, but the gods allow Jingū to defeat the Kumaso in mere months. Past and future blur in the gods' minds; they knew, and know, that this is how things will happen. Chūai's death was arbitrary and meaningless, proof that the gods are either ironical or cruel, or simply do not care. The gods may define her actions, but they do not care what she feels, the sorrow and anger and love and grief that are always with her, always as intense as the first moments she feels them.

For a time after his death she performs divination after divination, all asking, *Shall I conquer Silla?* Catching trout with a needle is part of this. She will also watch a rock crumble and allow water to irrigate a rice field she has planted. Later she will bathe in a river and feel the water in her hair, drawing conclusions from the currents that pull it this way and that. She knows what the answer will be—has seen it already, as familiar to her as a song she will sing to her infant son when he is born—but her only power over the gods is this, that they must tell her what they want for her to give it to them. And so she asks them to repeat themselves and takes a chill comfort in hearing their voices and pretending they care.

There are places in Japan where the gods do not permit men to fish during spawning, for they cannot understand and will not properly respect the fish's feelings. Jingū often fished as a child, before she becomes consort and then empress, and old skills come back easily when the past is eternally now. It is still some months before Ōjin will disrupt her balance, so she stands precariously on the little river's bank, the thread coiled in one hand, the baited needle in the other.

The sun has moved barely a hand's breadth in the sky since she first saw the trout; still, this is a long time for a fish to stay in one place. Perhaps the trout must be here as surely as she is. She frowns as she calculates and tosses the hook through the air. It settles just before the eyes of the trout, light as an insect.

Six months from now, Jingū sits her horse before the walls of Silla's capital, longing to kill. She strokes the feathers of the arrow in her hand, and dreams a little dream: the king will open the gates and emerge at the head of all his armies, all dressed in armor from beyond China, riding tigers and breathing fire. With Chūai alive beside her, she will ride to meet the Sillans, and her own people with them. She will empty her quiver and then draw her sword; and she will cut and cut and cut. Men's blood will soak her hair, and there will be no gods, nothing but the random terror and delight of a life without certainties. Chūai might die or he might not. And she might die here, today, instead of forty long years from now, years already laid out before her, as clear and cold and pitiless as a mountain stream.

It is only a dream, of course. She knows the shape of this victory in all its details. She has seen it since the first of her trances, when the gods broke down the walls between the past and the future. The king of Silla also has diviners, perhaps his own instructions to follow; in any case he has problems of his own: violent Paekche neighboring, to the north and west China's looming shadow. He opens the gates and sends out not armies but emissaries.

Silla falls to Japan without an arrow fired. The king surrenders and swears fealty, annual shipments of horses and gold. The only weapon hurled in anger is the spear that Jingū drives into the ground before the king's palace, the symbol of the conquest. Her rage is intact when she returns to Japan and bears her son, the emperor who will become the god of war, Hachiman.

The bent needle and its bait lie on the stream's surface just above the trout's head. Jingū can only wait, for she knows she will catch it, bring it to shore, and watch it die, gasping in the unbreathable air. This will prove yet again that she is to go to Silla, to conquer a land she does not care about for gods she hates, who have killed her husband and will steal her son and make him one of them.

All moments are this moment. Past and future jumbled together: Jingū cannot say which is which. And because everything—sorrow and anger and love and grief—is equally immediate, she finds herself strangely distanced from her own life. It is as if she listens to a storyteller recite a tale she has heard too many times, the tale of the empress Jingū.

She lives this tale divorced from past and future, separated even from what is and what is not. The fragments of her life are stolen from the later empresses: this woman will take Silla without a fight; that woman will manage the land for weary years after her husband's death. Jingū is no more than the tale of the empress Jingū, forced through the patterns of the storytelling, again and again and again. But she nevertheless feels, and she aches to kill something, anything.

The trout strikes and the hook sets. She hauls it in.

*   *   *

Women ruled Japan for more than eighty of the 177 years between AD *593 and 770. These tennō—"emperors"—were effective leaders, including the first to call a national census, document regional geography and resources, institute legal and administrative codes, open and sustain relations with the nations of the Korean peninsula and China, and gather what have been for more than a thousand years the basic references to Japan's ancient history and literature. Jingū ruled Japan some two hundred years before the earliest of the women tennō, in what is called the mythological era of imperial succession.*

TWILIGHT OF IDOLS

Stephen Dedman

Here is a skillfully wrought horror story featuring the man who was arguably the twentieth century's most murderous conqueror, and in which the only other contender for that particular title makes an offstage appearance. Stephen Dedman is the author of the novels *The Art of Arrow Cutting*, which was a finalist for the Bram Stoker Award, *Shadows Bite*, and *Foreign Bodies*, all published by Tor; he has also brought out a collection of short fiction, *The Lady of Situations*. His short stories have appeared in *The Magazine of Fantasy & Science Fiction*, *Asimov's Science Fiction*, *Eidolon*, *Science Fiction Age*, *Interzone*, *Dreaming Down-Under*, and *The Year's Best Fantasy and Horror*. He lives in Western Australia.

I

The thin, pale-faced man had been sitting quietly on the edge of his seat as though prepared to flee, obviously in awe of the august company. The conversation at the table had somehow drifted from opera to politics, and the little man had started to orate, almost to preach, condemning communism and all communists in venomous phrases. Though hung with tapestries, the villa's marble halls unfortunately had excellent acoustics, and the man's voice became louder and increasingly strident until it was impossible for anyone anywhere in the building not to be painfully aware of him. Rudolf looked over his shoulder at the stranger, then returned his attention to the wine; the villa's cellar was even better than its acoustics.

"Methinks he doth protest too much," he muttered. "Even for the stage. Still, he might make a Cassius; he has the lean and hungry look."

His wife, Thea, spared the orator a brief glance, and shrugged. "The eyes are interesting, but the moustache has to go. Who is he, anyway?"

The director peered at the man through his monocle, shrugged, and with a barely visible gesture, summoned the butler. "Yes, Herr Lang?"

"The loudmouth in the riding leggings," said Fritz Lang, with a slight nod. "Who is he?"

Anton shrugged. "One Herr Hitler, sir. A set designer, or so he led me to understand. He waited outside for an hour to see the Baron, and refused to leave; the Baron finally asked me to admit him."

The director nodded: the Baron, Clemens zu Franckenstein, was the manager of the Royal Theatre. "He has some interesting ideas on staging Wagner," the butler continued, and then a hint of distaste crossed his normally carefully impassive face, "but unfortunately, no manners. I was going to see if the Baron wished him to leave."

The other woman at their table said nothing, but watched as Anton walked over towards the table where the orator was still holding forth. More of the Baron's staff gathered around him, and the man quietened down rather than yell into their faces. A few minutes later, he was persuaded to leave. Anton opened the huge windows, to admit the warm fresh breeze from the spring *föhn,* and the conversation drifted back to talk of film and theater and music, as though all thoughts of the man had been blown away.

II

"Herr Hitler!"

The orator was walking along the Thierchstrasse, dressed much as she'd seen him at Clemens' villa; his face was over-shadowed by a slouch hat, and he carried a riding crop, but the woman could have recognized him by his walk alone. He turned around slowly, looked her up and down, and nodded stiffly. "Yes?"

"My name is Irene," she said, walking briskly towards him. "I'm a friend of Clemens zu Franckenstein's; I saw you at his villa, two weeks ago."

Hitler shrugged slightly, and looked her up and down. She was taller than he, and looked to be in her forties, at least ten years his senior, but with a handsomeness that suggested that she'd once been a great beauty. Her contralto voice spoke of opera training. "Yes?"

"I have a proposition—a business proposition—to put to you. Do you have somewhere where we can talk?"

"What sort of business?"

"Call it a job offer."

"I have a job."

She smiled thinly. "I know. You're a V-Mann, a political education officer . . . but I think this job may be more to your liking."

"You were with those movie people," said Hitler, suddenly recognizing her. "Rudolf Klein-Rogge, and that, that director . . ."

"Fritz Lang. Yes, that's right. Fritz wants to make a series of films of the *Ring* cycle, and I'm helping with the script." She looked along the street, and nodded at a cafe. "In there?"

"You want me to design sets for the film?" he asked.

"No," she said, with a soft laugh. "Fritz was a painter, like you, and he's also been trained as an architect; his designs are quite brilliant. I—"

"How did you know I was a painter?"

"I have my sources," she replied with a small shrug, as she led the way into a café. She didn't speak again until they were seated in a booth and the waiter had taken their orders. "Do you enjoy being an informer?"

Hitler stared at her, and he paled. "I'm—"

"Lance-Corporal Adolf Hitler, Reserve Infantry Regiment No 16," said Irene softly. "Two Iron Crosses, one First Class. Regimental Diploma for Conspicuous Bravery. Military Service Cross with Swords, and Medal for the Wounded: you were shot once, and gassed a few weeks before the war ended. You were a messenger, carrying orders to the front lines. There were some things I couldn't find out, such as why you were never promoted past *gefreiter* . . ."

"I wasn't interested in becoming an officer," replied Hitler, stiffly. "What do *you* want?"

"A hero." Her voice was soft; he listened for mockery, heard none. "Are you interested, Corporal Hitler? Or are you happy where you are, giving lectures and spying?"

"Somebody has to do it," said Hitler, after a long pause. It seemed unlikely to him that his superiors would have chosen a woman like this to spy on him or try to test his loyalty, but Captain Mayr, his commander, was a Jew, with a Jew's cunning. "I'm a soldier. I obey orders. And because the Versailles *diktat* won't let us have weapons that are fitting for soldiers—"

"I'm not questioning your patriotism," Irene replied, with a flick of her fingers. "Have you ever killed anyone?"

He shrugged. "I don't know: you don't often see the enemy, when you're in the trenches. I'm a good shot—my favorite game when I was a boy was shooting rats—but I'm not a murderer, if that's what you want."

"No. I'm offering you a chance to face an opponent worthy of your courage again. You remember Siegfried's battle with the dragon Fafnir?"

"Of course."

"My father was a history professor, as well as a lover of Wagner's music, and his life's obsession was to see how much truth there was in the sagas, as Schliemann did with the Iliad and other archaeologists have done with the Bible or tales of King Arthur. Father was determined to find the historic Siegfried, or at least the historic Gunther. He believed, when he died, that he'd found much more than that; he'd found Gnitahead. Fafnir's lair."

Hitler snorted. "And the dragon's hoard, as well?"

"My father believed so," said Irene, sadly but levelly. "He and my brother went in search of it more than twenty years ago, but neither returned.

"In those days, I was married, and my son—my only son—was less than a year old. A few months ago, I received a letter from my father's lawyers, with a map of the way to Gnitahead. It was intended for my son, not me—but like you, my son served in the infantry at Ypres. Unlike you, he did not survive."

Hitler looked down at the table, then nodded. Irene reached into her purse and extracted two American banknotes, a twenty and a hundred bill, which she carefully tore in half.

"If you will come with me to Gnitahead, this is yours," she said, sliding half of the twenty across the polished table towards him; they both knew how valuable foreign currency was compared to the deutschmark. "If we find any treasure, half is yours, and whether we do or not . . ." She handed him half of the hundred.

"And if we find a dragon?" asked Hitler, not quite mockingly, as he pocketed both notes.

"If that part of the legend is true," said Irene, softly, "then perhaps the rest is true also—that bathing in Fafnir's blood will make you invincible, like Siegfried. If you want to find out, meet me at the railway station tomorrow—and bring a weapon."

"What is this place?" asked Hitler, as Irene led the way through a cold squarish tunnel. "Some sort of mine?"

Irene nodded, and the lamp attached to her helmet sent shadows scrambling. "It was a salt mine. I don't know how recently it's been worked. But the lowest shaft leads into a cave with an underground river, and the river runs through the dragon's lair."

"And what is this dragon supposed to eat?" asked Hitler, dryly. "Its own tail?"

"Blind fish. Bats. I don't know. There are always people disappearing from this region, mostly young men and women, and rumours that somebody has been killing them and dumping their bodies down some empty shaft. Maybe that's how the dragon feeds."

Hitler's snort showed what he thought of that theory. "How many other men have you led down here?" he asked, his hand on the butt of his revolver.

"None. None came this far. The brave young men all went to war and haven't returned, and those locals who are left are too scared of whatever lies down here."

"There are plenty of ex-soldiers who would have taken your money."

"Thousands, yes," she replied. "Some of them with war records as good as yours, or better. But most were fools who'd never heard of Fafnir, or cowards that I couldn't rely on, or criminals who would have robbed me and run."

Hitler nodded. He knew from experience that many de-mobbed soldiers, desperate for money or action, had turned to crime: many had joined the new political parties, and he saw dozens every night in the beer halls. A moment later, his curiosity won over his discretion, and he asked, "And you're sure I won't?"

"Fairly sure: I think if you were going to, you would have done it a few miles ago. And even if you do, I don't think you'll rape me as well. I don't know what drives you, Lance-Corporal, but it isn't sex, and I don't believe that money would be enough either. Patriotism? Glory? Maybe, like Siegfried, you want to rule. Whatever it is, you have enough imagination, enough vision, to have come this far." She led the way into a cave, and followed the sound of running water until they found the river. Then she removed the pistol from her belt and placed it in a watertight metal box, which she then wrapped in oilcloth. After a moment's hesitation, Hitler did the same.

The river had carved a tunnel passage through the rock, but it was very narrow and the ceiling was never high enough for Hitler to stand upright even in those places where they could wade rather than crawl or swim. Usually there was a pocket of air at the top large enough at least for their faces and flashlights, but a few times Hitler found himself wondering whether they were more likely to drown or just to be trapped in some crack too narrow for them to turn around in: either fate seemed far more likely than falling prey to a dragon, and every time something shifted beneath his feet or hands, he looked to see whether it was the remains of Irene's father or brother or some other fool. He sniffed cautiously at the air every time he emerged, careful not to breathe in any poisons: having nearly been killed by gas once, he had decided it was no fit fate for a human being, and resolved to kill himself cleanly with one of the weapons he was carrying rather than let that happen. Then Irene stopped so suddenly that he blundered into her, almost dropping his flashlight. "What—"

"Quiet!" she hissed. He blinked, shone his light upwards, and realized that they'd emerged into a larger chamber than any they'd seen since first wading into the underground river. He took another cautious sniff: apart from the stench of what must have been centuries of bat guano, the air was fresh. He scrambled to his feet—the water was barely up to his knees—and both looked around.

The lights disturbed a few bats, which fluttered around, and the dragon opened its eyes and growled low in its throat. Hitler swung the light around until he could see the animal, and nearly burst out laughing. Though its snake-like neck and the heavy tail that balanced it were long and thick, the dragon's body was scarcely larger than that of his beloved Alsatian dog and closer to the ground. They stared at each other for a moment, then the dragon drew back its head like a snake about to strike. Hitler ducked, and a glob of corrosive slime spattered across his protective helmet.

Irene unwrapped the oilskin parcel with a flick of her wrist, and was trying to open the metal box when Hitler grabbed her and pulled her back down into the river. "What are you—"

Rather than waste time speaking, he reached into his sodden coat and removed a "potato-masher" grenade. Irene's eyes widened, and she nodded. Hitler unscrewed the cap, then raised his head above the water to stare the dragon in the face again. As it opened its mouth, he pulled the string, hurled the grenade, and began counting. One . . . two . . .

To his disappointment, the grenade fell short of the dragon's raised head, but rolled between its great clawed feet. Three . . . Hitler plunged back into the water and continued to count. The grenade exploded on five, but he didn't raise his head until he'd counted past twelve.

The air was alive with startled bats, but a few seconds later, he and Irene could see the shattered body of the dragon, its precious blood leaking from its mangled belly. Irene removed the entrenching tool from her belt and thrust it into Hitler's hands. "Quick!" she said. "The blood! Dig a pit!"

Hitler scrambled out of the riverbed and scurried across the guano-covered floor. The rock was too hard to dig—even his pick made barely a scratch—so he removed his helmet and placed it beneath the largest of the wounds, to catch the blood. He did the same with his boots, then hastily peeled off his wet clothes with one hand while holding the other over another jet of blood. Within a minute, he was naked and had emptied the blood-filled helmet over his head. Remembering the tales of the deaths of Siegfried and Achilles, he smeared blood over himself liberally, careful not to leave any part of his skin vulnerable. "So this will make me immortal?" he asked, as Irene also began removing her clothing.

"No," she said. "Not immortal. We'll still age, and we're not immune to disease. But your skin will be better than any armor they can make for a panzer: no bullet, no blade, no fire, will be able to penetrate it.

"Pain, however . . . you will still feel primary pain as you would now. If you were to accidentally put your hand on a hot stove, it would jerk away instantly . . . but if you chose to, you could stand in flames or even swim in molten iron and not be burned, and the pain would stop as soon as you've moved away from the heat. And once we've eaten the flesh, we'll be safe from poison—but not from gas. If you try to breathe mustard gas again, it will still corrode your lungs, though it won't blister your skin."

Hitler shuddered.

"At least," said Irene, "that's what my father believed. He never had a chance to test it." She dipped her hands in the helmet, and wiped the blood over her face. Hitler laughed at the sight, then turned away from her for a moment and reached for his belt. He waited until Irene's face and neck were wet with blood, then drew his dagger and stabbed her under the chin. She stared at him in horror, then realized that the point had failed to penetrate.

Both were silent for a moment, and Hitler withdrew the knife and ran the edge across the back of his left forearm. It made no impression.

Irene smiled. "It works!" she crowed. "My father was right!"

Hitler grinned back, then thrust the dagger up under her ribcage and into her heart. He stood there until he was sure she was dead, then began searching for the dragon's hoard.

III

The prostitute looked at Hitler with her usual carefully neutral expression; after all, she'd heard much stranger requests. They agreed on a price, twenty marks, and then Hitler handed her his riding crop and stripped down to his leather breeches.

As he requested, she whipped him for several minutes, wondering why he was laughing. Then he lay on the ground, face-up, and begged her to kick him as hard as she could. "It's your money," she said with a shrug. "Anywhere in particular?"

"Everywhere except the face," he said.

She shrugged again, and complied. Hitler laughed—giggled, almost—as she did so, and her impassive mask almost faltered. She thought she'd grown inured to her job, and that nothing would ever disgust her again, but there was something about this strange little man that made her feel as though she were treading in something indescribably foul.

IV

Fritz Lang peered at the letter, and shook his head.

"What is it?" asked Thea. The paper was thick and looked expensive, and she could see a swastika on the letterhead and a jagged, angry-looking signature.

"Adolf Hitler," said Fritz, sourly, dropping the letter onto his dinner plate, his appetite gone. "He's offered me a job as director of the Reich's film industry."

His wife smiled. "Well, why not? He's always said he admired your *Ring Saga*, and *Metropolis* . . ."

"And banned my last film," the director pointed out.

Thea shrugged. "A lot of people thought you were lampooning him, that Dr. Mabuse was meant to be him . . ." She smiled. "Of course, they were right. Rudolf saw Hitler for the first time just before we made *Dr. Mabuse,* and I'm sure the resemblance wasn't entirely coincidental . . ."

Fritz blinked. Rudolf Klein-Rogge, Thea's ex-husband, had first played the hypnotist and master criminal Dr. Mabuse in 1922; highlights of that film had included a car which filled with poisonous gas, and Mabuse ordering his mistress to commit suicide to avoid being taken prisoner. "What? Where?"

"At Clemens zu Franckenstein's. We'd just finished *Weary Death.* I know it was twelve, thirteen years ago, but surely you remember him? He was a stage designer; you called him a loudmouth. Are you going to accept?"

"No," said the director. "Hitler is a monster; I want nothing to do with him."

"I'm sure some of your actors would say the same about you," said Thea, dryly. "Darling, if it mattered to him that your mother was Jewish, he'd never have offered you the job. People don't like Hitler because he's not scared of anyone or anything, and they're not used to politicians who aren't scared. You talk about him as though he were some sort of robot; I'm sure, underneath it all, he's quite human." She smiled. "If you pricked him, would he not bleed? If you poisoned him, would he not die?"

"And if you wronged him, would he not revenge?" growled Lang. He left Germany that night.

V

1944 had begun badly for the Reich, with the Russians advancing into Poland again as well as reclaiming Leningrad, and America establishing the War Refugee Board to help Jews escape. Five months later, the Americans had landed at Normandy, and a report by escapees from Auschwitz had been delivered to the Pope. Increasing numbers of Germans were beginning to doubt the Führer's infallibility—even some of his generals, Hitler knew, privately and traitorously thought he should never have broken his pact with Stalin and tried to fight the war on two fronts.

Because none of the rooms in the bunker at Wolfsschanze were large enough for the map table and all the officers assembled, staff meetings had to be held in a converted barracks above ground. Hitler looked down at the map through a magnifying glass, scowling as General Jodl described the Allies' capture of Caen and St. Lo. "And on the Russian front?"

"They'll be in Madjanek within a week," said General Heusinger, gloomily. "If we used some of the trains that are shipping prisoners to Auschwitz, we might be able to hold it . . ."

"We could use gas," suggested General Jodl. "We have stockpiles of Substance 83 . . ."

"And so do the Allies," snapped Hitler. "If they learn that we've used it, even on the Russians, they'll use it on us, gas us as though we were Jews. And the Russians may also have it. We won't be the first to use it."

Heusinger and Jodl looked at each other, but neither spoke; neither did any of the other twenty-two men in the room. Most, even the clerks, knew that Hitler still had a revulsion for chemical warfare more than thirty-five years after being exposed to mustard gas himself, and no one was prepared to argue with him on a last-ditch measure.

Colonel von Stauffenberg, standing near the door, excused himself and left. No one noticed that he'd left his briefcase under the heavy oak table.

"Maybe we should destroy the gas chambers at Madjanek," said Heusinger, after a long silence. "Before the Russians get there. If they find them, they'll tell the world . . ."

Hitler shook his head. "Maybe," he replied. "But there have been stories told before. People either don't believe them, or don't care. Stalin has no love of Jews, either, and his own hands aren't clean; how many graves did we find in the Ukraine? And how many of their own people are they torturing in Siberia?" There was a faint hint of approval in his voice: the Russians, who he'd predicted were too primitive to build a working motor vehicle, were far less efficient in their attempts at extermination than the Reich, but they didn't lack for zeal, and some of their methods of both physical and psychological torture were remarkably ingenious for such a backward people. Not as sophisticated or useful as the Gestapo's, of course, much less Mengele's, but worthy of respect nonetheless. He shrugged. "We'll invite the Red Cross to see one of our camps, and show them that the rumors are only that. Tell Himmler to arrange it."

SS Hauptsturmführer Günsche, Hitler's adjutant, nodded, and suddenly the briefcase under the table exploded. Hitler, standing next to the bomb, flew through the air and landed on Field Marshall Keitel. Ceiling beams cracked, and the lamp crashed down on Jodl's head, stunning him. Von Stauffenberg, standing a few hundred yards away, watched as bodies and debris came hurtling out of the windows, and turned and ran.

As the smoke cleared, Hitler painfully hauled himself back to his feet. His hair was burnt and smouldering, his

ears were ringing, and his pale blue eyes were glazed. Günsche and the other SS officers, who'd been standing in the
corner furthest from the bomb, stared in amazement at
Hitler's torn uniform, and the unmarked flesh beneath it—
and then at the mangled remains of Colonel Brandt, who'd
also been standing next to von Stauffenberg's briefcase, and
the other wounded men.

Hitler looked around the room, and, though shocked and
concussed, pulled himself together. "You will tell nobody
what you've seen," he barked, then glanced at Brandt's
corpse. "Say . . . say I had left the room, or was away from
my chair . . . no, say the bomb was moved to the far side of
the table leg." Günsche nodded, and walked unsteadily towards the radio set, only to find that it had been wrecked by
the blast. "And say that Providence . . . no, *Destiny* has protected Germany from a . . . a great tragedy. Say that the failure of this attempt is . . . a sign that that I am under, under
the . . . the protection of a divine power." He smiled.

V

The vial was sheathed in a yellow metal tube which looked
for all the world like a lipstick, and Eva smiled as she sucked
the glass ampoule into her mouth. Hitler, sitting next to her
on the couch, did the same. Eva dropped the metal tube onto
the floor, and bit down hard. The thin glass shattered, and a
stench of bitter almonds filled the poorly ventilated room,
noticeable even over the reek of the blocked toilets. Hitler
closed his eyes; he felt the ampoule crunch between his
porcelain-and-metal teeth, and swallowed cyanide and glass
splinters. Eva's jaws clamped down in a horrible rictus, and
Hitler felt her convulse as she gasped for air, but he didn't
open his eyes until she had collapsed onto the floor. A few
minutes later, when Eva had stopped moving, he reached for
his revolver, placed the muzzle in his mouth, and squeezed
the trigger.

The bullet slammed into his hard palate, ricocheted, and
rolled down his throat; Hitler coughed as he felt it sear its

way down his esophagus and into his stomach. Incredulously, he removed the gun from his mouth, stared at it, then pointed it at his chest and fired again.

The bullet punched a burning hole through his soup-stained tunic, but failed to leave a mark on his skin. Screaming an oath, he threw the pistol away and stood, almost tripping over his wife's corpse.

He listened, wondering if anyone else remained in the bunker. Goebbels had announced his intention of poisoning his children before he and his wife committed suicide; Bormann, he was sure, would flee as soon as he felt it was safe to do so, and might already have gone. He staggered towards the door. If only Heisenberg had been able to build one of the bombs he'd once talked about, a single bomb able to destroy an entire city; he could have turned all Berlin into his pyre, killing the treacherous Russians and his own cowardly people and leaving a vast ruin as his monument. . . . He realized, to his horror, that he was weeping, and turned away from the heavy steel door as it opened. "My Führer?"

It was Major Günsche, still in his black SS uniform, proudly bearing the special wound badge issued to the survivors of the Wolfsschanze bombing. Hitler stared at him wearily, then nodded at Eva's body. "Do you have the petrol?"

"I've sent Kempka to fetch it."

"Burn her," he said, wearily. "And the Goebbels family—I take it they *are* dead?" he added.

"Yes, my Führer."

"Good." Hitler looked around the small bedroom, then totttered into the conference room with Günsche following him. "Where's the doctor?"

"He left with Reichsleiter Bormann."

Hitler grimaced. "See if you can find a body that could pass for mine, and burn that, too. Maybe it will fool the Russians when they get here—for long enough for me to escape."

"Sir?"

"Don't look so shocked," Hitler snapped. "I can't let them

take me alive. The cyanide didn't work, the bullets didn't work,
even a bomb didn't work . . . what else should I do? Hang myself?" He grimaced. "Get me some civilian clothes. Women's
clothes, if that's all you can find; it worked for Lenin."

Günsche allowed himself a ghost of a smile. "It might fool
Russians: have you ever seen Russian women?" Hitler didn't
reply. "Where will you go?"

"I don't know, and it's best that you don't either." The
bunker rocked as a shell hit the upper level. "Goodbye, my
friend."

VI

The Russian attaché opened his briefcase and removed a fat
manila file. "These are the photographs, and Dr. Shkaravski's
report," he said, smoothly. "Unfortunately, by the time our
soldiers reached the bunker, the bodies were already too
badly burned for the remains to be readily identifiable, but
we're confident that this is Eva Braun, and the other body
would seem to be that of Hitler."

Fritz Lang looked suspiciously at the translation of the
pathologist's report, snorting with amusement at the description
of the undescended testicle. He'd called in a lot of favors for
the privilege of seeing these Soviet Intelligence files, but he'd
long had an uncomfortable feeling that he was in some way responsible for Hitler's career. "It's a kinder death than he deserved," he muttered, "and I hope he burns in hell forever."

The attaché allowed himself an undiplomatic smile. "I'm
sorry that I don't believe in hell," he said, softly, "but, just this
once, I hope that Marx was wrong, and that you are right."

Fritz chuckled. "I'll drink to that," he said. He poured himself a drink, and offered one to the Russian, who accepted it
with a gracious nod. "The important thing is, we're sure he's
dead."

*   *   *

The prisoner was never named, and his number was
known only to a select few. In his first year in the cell, various attempts had been made to remove his tongue for fear

that he might say his name loudly enough to be heard through the thick walls and door, but all the methods they'd tried—scalpels, saws, drills, flame, acid, intense cold, even flesh-eating insects and plants—had failed. By the time Beria suggested filling the mouth permanently with molten lead or something similar, Stalin had decided that he liked the sound of the man's guttural screams too much, and had settled for binding the prisoner's toothless jaws between his visits.

Beria walked into the cell and looked at the twisted form. While nothing they'd tried was able to pierce his skin, not the smallest needle nor the most powerful anti-tank weapon, starvation and thirst had withered his flesh, and driving a tank over his legs and arms had gradually broken his still-human bones. The head of the secret police chuckled as he remembered the crunching sounds, and mad pale blue-grey eyes stared back at him.

Beria considered telling the prisoner that Stalin had died a month before, but that might have been a kindness; better to let him wonder. "We're going to move you," he said, in German. "It's time you did some useful work; from each according to his abilities, as Marx said."

The pale blue eyes stared, uncomprehendingly. Beria wasn't sure whether the prisoner understood anything any more, after nearly eight years in the cell, but it hardly mattered. "I know," he said, as he freed the prisoner's jaw, "you may not think you can be of much use to anybody, but you're wrong. You can perform a great service to Soviet science." He grinned. "We're giving you to the Army Chemical Corps, to help test some new gases."

The prisoner opened his mouth and emitted a thin, whistling scream that reminded Beria of some Wagnerian opera. He chuckled, wondering whether the scientists could find some way to kill the man, or whether he might somehow scream forever.

SPIRIT BROTHER

Pamela Sargent

Much of what we know about Genghis Khan has come down to us through histories written largely by those who were enemies of the Mongols or who were conquered by them. This isn't to say that his reputation as one of history's villains is completely undeserved, only that one gains a more complex image of him from other sources. One primary source about his life is *The Secret History of the Mongols* (translated by Francis W. Cleaves, Harvard University Press, 1982), a history of his childhood and early years apparently written down during the reign of his son Ogedei. What makes this document especially valuable is that it contains stories related by several people who knew him as the young chieftain Temujin, before he became Genghis Khan. Even allowing for faulty memories, the *Secret History* offers a more nuanced portrait of the man.

One of the more poignant and tragic aspects of his life is the tale of Temujin and his boyhood friend Jamukha, who later became Temujin's deadly enemy.

That conflict ended with Jamukha's death, but I found
myself imagining how their story might have continued after death. All of the characters here—Jamukha,
Temujin, the shaman Teb-Tenggeri, and the rest—are
actual historical figures, and the events depicted actually happened. What lay behind those events is my
invention.

T he flat land below him was white, the color of purity
and luck. Jamukha flew in the form of an eagle, feeling
the wind under his wings. The steppe and mountains had also
been covered by snow on the day he had first met Temujin,
the companion and comrade in arms who had later become
his greatest enemy.

But all of that had happened when he was a boy, years
ago, in the world of the living.

"My spirit will watch over you," Jamukha had said at the
end, knowing even as he spoke that Temujin would not let
him live, that he would have to punish Jamukha for turning
against him. Temujin had granted him an honorable death by
strangulation, so that his blood would not be shed, but Jamukha could not recall the moment when the silken cord had
tightened around his neck. Temujin's shamans had chanted
over Jamukha's body, and buried him with a horse, some
dried meat, a skin of kumiss, and his weapons on a mountain
overlooking the Onon River.

Jamukha had lingered near his grave after his death, un-
heeding of the days and nights that passed. He had feared
that the world of the spirits might be as empty as the steppe,
and usually it was, for the bravest of the dead had flown to
Koko Mongke Tengri, the Eternal Blue Sky that covered all
of Etugen, the earth. But at other times, as Jamukha flew
over the land, he would see other lost spirits camped near a
grave, pale wraiths feeding on the smoke of the offerings
being burned by mourners for the dead.

He glimpsed one such spirit now, hovering in the form of a
black bird over the ashes of a sacrificial fire near the moun-

tain gravesite of a chief. Jamukha watched the bird avidly gulp the last of the tendrils of smoke and knew then that the creature was the ghost of Toghril, the Kereit Khan, as greedy in death as Toghril had been in life.

"I greet you, former ally and enemy," the ghost of Toghril Khan said. The spirit-bird's eyes were sly and crafty, its talons ready to clutch at whatever was near.

"I greet you, Toghril Ong-Khan." Jamukha alighted near the small yurt that had been raised near the grave. "How many times did you betray me in life?"

"No more often than you betrayed me," Toghril replied. "No more often than Temujin betrayed both of us, after claiming to be our comrade and brother. Yet you swore before your death that your ghost would watch over Temujin."

"That is true." The few spirits Jamukha had encountered had been able to glimpse his inner thoughts and to remember all the events of his life; Toghril was no different.

"Why would you want to protect the man who sentenced you to death?" Toghril asked.

"Because he was my anda, my sworn brother," Jamukha said, "before he became my enemy. I made my last promise to him for the sake of our old oath." That was part of the truth, but not all of it.

"There's no place in your world for men who won't bow to you." Those were the last words Jamukha had spoken to Temujin. "But my ghost will remind you of what you lost to gain your triumphs. A ghost is not so easily cast aside." That had been part of his promise to his old comrade.

"In your place, I would long for revenge," Toghril said. "I think that's what still holds me here. Temujin took everything from me."

"He was my anda," Jamukha said. "I turned against him only when I knew that his heart had hardened against me. We might have ruled together, but he prefers to rule alone."

"In heaven, there is only one sun," Toghril said, "and on the earth, there can be only one khan."

That was not what had been said when Jamukha and Temujin were youthful comrades. "In the sky, there is a sun

and a moon," the men had sung, and for a year and a half he
and Temujin had ridden together and led their clans together.
They had shared the same grazing grounds, the same triumphs, the same blanket and bed.

"I didn't leave Temujin," Jamukha said. "It was he who
left me." At that thought, the pain and rage he had felt when
Temujin had abandoned him nearly overwhelmed him once
more. His sworn brother had left him without warning,
sneaking away in the night, and many of the men they had
led together had chosen to follow Temujin. That had been the
beginning of the wars between them, the wars Temujin had at
last won.

"He swore oaths to me, as he did to you," Toghril's spirit
murmured, "and now he rules over my Kereits, as he rules
over all the tribes."

Jamukha said, "I loved him."

"As all the chiefs now love and honor Temujin, who became Genghis Khan."

"They do not love him as I did," Jamukha said.

"You loved him, and swore to watch over him, but I think
you also still long to punish him for what he did."

Jamukha was silent, unable to deny the other ghost's
words.

Toghril stretched his black wings, rising toward the sky
with the last of the smoke. Jamukha gazed at the ashes of the
dead fire. He had come to love Temujin when they were both
fatherless boys, after Temujin and his brothers had been
abandoned by their people. He had known that the brave
Mongol boy would not be an outcast forever, that Temujin
would become an honored chief. He had ridden with Temujin
against their Merkit enemies in their first great battle together. A beloved comrade, his other self—that was what he
had seen in his sworn brother, and Temujin had finally used
it against him.

He should have been past such feelings; they belonged to
the world of the living. But he clutched at that world, unable
to free himself of it.

He had not been like other men; Jamukha had always

known that about himself. Others might occasionally take their pleasure with boys or young men, with a captive or a boy too weak to resist, but such pleasures were no more than the whims of a moment, or a way to take revenge on a defeated enemy. But for Jamukha, they had been a way to douse the fire that sometimes flared inside him, the flames that could not be quenched by anything else, and then with Temujin, he had found more—a companion who might share his feelings, who might honor their love above all others.

But it had not been that way for Temujin. He had shared himself with Jamukha for a time, surrendering as little of himself as possible, never allowing himself to admit the true nature of their bond, and then he had left Jamukha's side in the night. There had been many battles and betrayals after that, and too many times when Jamukha had allowed his old feelings for Temujin to cloud his judgment and lead him to defeat.

They might have ruled together. Instead, Temujin had become Genghis Khan, the greatest khan his people had ever known. He had united all of the Mongol clans, and had then brought all of their old enemies—the Merkits, the Tatars, the Naimans to the west—under his yoke. He would not rest now; Jamukha was sure of that. Temujin would not be satisfied until all the world bowed to him.

Such thoughts, and the anger and sorrow they evoked, were useless now; they only kept Jamukha chained to the earth, haunting the living, unable to fly to heaven.

The wind carried Jamukha to another snow-covered mountain. He wondered if he was doomed to haunt the world forever. He had roamed the land as a tiger or wolf, soared toward the sky as an eagle or falcon, and even when he longed most fervently to fly to Heaven, he remained bound to the Earth.

He had not kept the promise he had made, to watch over Temujin. Perhaps the spirits had condemned him to wander the world of the living until he honored that oath.

A yurt made of felt panels stood below the mountain; a

stream of smoke rose from its smokehole. Three white horses were tethered outside the round black tent. A man sat on the mountain slope above the yurt, his eyes closed, his body still. Jamukha recognized him at once, and the fear that suddenly welled up inside him nearly drove him from the mountain.

The man was a shaman, and a shaman more powerful than most, able to sense the presence of spirits and ghosts and to let them take possession of him. This shaman's spells had helped Temujin to win so much of the world.

"Teb-Tenggeri," Jamukha whispered as the wind whipped the feathers of the shaman's headdress. No one called him by the name he had been given at birth; he was now Teb-Tenggeri, the All-Celestial. He was a man almost as beautiful as a woman, smooth-skinned and with no traces of a mustache; age had not yet touched him. His spells, it was said, had brought Temujin many of his victories, and his curses could make men sicken and die.

Jamukha knew that he should flee. Ghosts might be invisible to most of the living, but shamans could feel their presence. Great shamans could summon ghosts and spirits and bend them to their will. The spirit harbored by this mountain was already whispering to Jamukha in the wind, warning him to fly away from this place. Then Teb-Tenggeri turned his head toward Jamukha and opened his large dark eyes.

Jamukha circled him slowly, hoping that he remained invisible. The shaman frowned, as if sensing that Jamukha was near, and then he turned away and slowly got to his feet. Jamukha waited, powerless to flee, expecting the man to chant a spell that would bind him, but Teb-Tenggeri made his way down the slope toward the yurt below, seemingly unaware of the ghost fluttering near him.

"Flee," the spirit of the mountain whispered, but there was no need to escape the shaman now. Perhaps Teb-Tenggeri was not as powerful as people claimed. Some, Jamukha knew, attributed more powers to shamans than they actually possessed, and his wanderings as a ghost had shown him shamans who seemed blind and deaf to the spirits around them. Teb-Tenggeri had seemed to sense that Jamukha was close to him, and yet had not tried to bind him or to ward him off with a spell.

Perhaps I have the power to possess him, Jamukha thought. A spirit could enter the body of a man, speak through him, drive him into madness, even make him sicken and die. The weak were easy prey for ghosts, as were the mad, and also those shamans who sent out their souls too often to wander among the dead.

It came to Jamukha then that, through Teb-Tenggeri, he might be able to keep the oath he had sworn before his death. He could watch over Temujin, as he had sworn to do, and honor his oath even as he awaited chances to torment his former comrade. There would be risks, but perhaps risks worth taking. Few were as close to Temujin as Teb-Tenggeri, and Temujin had always feared the powers of shamans.

"Flee," the mountain's spirit whispered once more, "fly away now," but Jamukha was already following Teb-Tenggeri down the slope. The shaman seemed unaware of his presence now; that would give Jamukha the advantage. His form changed, becoming a mist with silvery tendrils slowly entwining themselves around the shaman's body; still the man did not sense him. As he prepared to take possession of Teb-Tenggeri, the world abruptly vanished, trapping him in a darkness as thick and black as a felt blanket.

Jamukha cried out, and heard the shaman's answering cry. He struggled against the darkness and felt it press against him more heavily. The man had been waiting for him, he realized, ready to trap him.

"I have you," Teb-Tenggeri murmured, and his voice surrounded Jamukha. "I know who you are, who you were."

Jamukha struggled in the blackness, blind, gasping as he had at the moment of his death. "Let me go," he whispered.

"But you don't want to go," Teb-Tenggeri replied. "You don't want to leave me, Jamukha. You're still dreaming of revenge against the man who was once your sworn brother."

"No," Jamukha said.

"You can't hide your thoughts from me. You want to be near Temujin, to recall your old friendship and remember what he once was to you. But you also want vengeance—you dream of taking everything Temujin has won away from him, of seeing his men betray him as yours betrayed you, of leaving him with nothing."

Jamukha was silent.

"I serve Temujin, Genghis Khan," Teb-Tenggeri continued. "I have sensed the will of the spirits, I know that Temujin is the Son of Heaven and destined to rule over all the world. I cannot stand against the spirits, but it is I who will rule through him in the end. That is the only revenge I can grant you, sworn brother of Temujin—that you will see the great Khan grow ever more regretful as his conquests increase, that he will be haunted even at the height of his power by the ghosts and spirits of those he betrayed, and that, because of his fear and remorse, he will give me whatever I want and do whatever I wish him to do."

"That will be enough punishment," Jamukha said, wondering if the shaman could sense his fear of the smothering darkness in which he was embedded. Invisible ropes held him, and he understood that Teb-Tenggeri had bound him with a powerful spell. To attempt escape would be risky; if he failed, Teb-Tenggeri would bind his soul even more tightly, and see that he never got another chance to fly away from him.

Jamukha had what he had wanted, a chance to keep his promise to haunt Temujin. But already the hatred that had flared up inside him burned less brightly, replaced by a growing fear.

Teb-Tenggeri kept him blind and deaf, wrapped in the heavy darkness. Jamukha had no way of knowing if a day or a month had passed. He felt as though the shaman had buried him again, interred him in a grave from which he could never escape.

At last Jamukha sent out a tendril of thought, then realized that the shaman could not now hear him. Teb-Tenggeri, as did most shamans, endured moments when he would fall to the ground senseless, or else start to twist in one of the fits that he could not control, whenever certain spirits had possession of him. Perhaps Teb-Tenggeri had lost consciousness; maybe his spirit had left his body temporarily.

Jamukha waited for the shaman to come to himself, then felt the man's body stir.

He would leave this place, Teb-Tenggeri was thinking, and ride to his khan. Jamukha sensed the shaman's intention before the darkness as thick as heavy felt cloaked him once more.

Jamukha and Temujin were enemies long before Teb-Tenggeri had become the Khan's chief shaman, but Teb-Tenggeri's reputation had quickly grown among the tribes. The shaman had come to his calling early, while still a boy called Kokochu. He had told his father Munglik, a Khongkhotat chief who had chosen to follow Jamukha, that a dream had shown him that Munglik should ride to Temujin's side. Munglik had been amply rewarded for heeding that omen and deserting Jamukha; Temujin had welcomed him as an old friend and given the Khongkhotat his own widowed mother as a wife.

Kokochu, as a trusted stepbrother of the young Mongol khan, had quickly won fame as a mighty shaman whose spells were greatly feared by Temujin's enemies. He could raise the wind, and sweep enemy horsemen from their mounts. He cast spells that protected the Mongol forces from enemy arrows. He would stand fearlessly in the open as lightning struck the ground around him, and turn a storm of ice and hail against enemy forces. It was said that he often rode to heaven on his white horse, and that the spirits themselves had given him the name of Teb-Tenggeri, the All-Celestial.

Jamukha had once scorned and mocked such tales. Now, imprisoned inside Teb-Tenggeri, blind and helpless, he no longer doubted them.

The shaman was speaking in his musical voice. Jamukha did not know how much time had passed, how long he had been waiting in the darkness, and then he heard the familiar and once-beloved voice of another man.

Temujin, he thought, straining to hear his anda's words. Teb-Tenggeri must have ridden to the Khan's camp; he was addressing Temujin now. Jamukha was suddenly afraid.

"I must speak to you," Teb-Tenggeri was saying, and then spears of light pierced the darkness around Jamukha, making the world visible again. He gazed through the shaman's eyes and felt Teb-Tenggeri's body around him.

Another man sat on a cushion across from Teb-Tenggeri. The man stretched his arms toward the fire that glowed inside the curved metal bands of the hearth; the light caught his face, and Jamukha felt sharp pangs of grief and regret as he recognized Temujin. His anda's strange pale eyes were the same, his mustaches as long, and the dark braids coiled behind his ears on his shaven head still had their reddish tint, but there was weariness in Temujin's leathery aging face.

"What is it?" Temujin asked. "What do you wish to tell me," and Jamukha, moved by the familiar sound of that quiet but forceful voice, nearly called out his sworn brother's name.

"I am with you again," Teb-Tenggeri said, but Jamukha was also saying those words, hearing his own voice in that of the shaman's. "I speak to you now through your shaman Teb-Tenggeri."

Temujin's eyes widened as he held up his hand, palm out, and made a sign against evil.

"You wanted me at your side," the shaman continued with Jamukha's voice, "even as you ordered my death, and I have not forgotten my promise to you."

Temujin clutched at the shaman's arm, and Jamukha felt his old comrade's strong grip. "Can it be?"

Jamukha longed to tell the Khan of how his spirit had been wandering ever since his death, of how he had not forgotten his oath to watch over him. Then the pain of all the betrayals stabbed at him again. You ordered my death, Temujin. You said that you could not allow me to live, and now, when it is too late, you mourn me and long for me and indulge yourself in regret. Jamukha was about to utter a curse when he felt the words catch in the shaman's throat.

Teb-Tenggeri could still rein him in, could bury him again in the suffocating darkness if he resisted the shaman's will. Teb-Tenggeri could trap him and see that he never escaped.

"I promised to watch over you," Jamukha said through the shaman, "and I am here. You longed for me to be your comrade once more, and I have come to you."

"Jamukha!" Temujin cried.

Teb-Tenggeri held out his hands as Temujin sagged against him, then closed his arms around him. "I am with you again, Temujin, as you wished me to be."

Temujin clung to Teb-Tenggeri, his fingers digging into the shaman's coat. "You were my first true friend as a boy, Jamukha," Temujin said softly, "as close to me as my own brothers. You were my friend when I had no one, when my father was murdered and my family abandoned by all. I didn't want to leave your side, I never wanted to fight against you, I did not want to order your death. There were so many times when I was ready to forgive you."

Temujin wanted to believe that, Jamukha thought. It was a weakness of Temujin's, perhaps his only weakness, the way in which he often hesitated before deciding on what he must do. He was always one to seek counsel from those closest to him—his mother Hoelun, his brother Khasar, his close comrade Borchu, and his chief wife Bortai, who had done everything in her power to turn Temujin against Jamukha. The Khan would listen to their advice, and weigh it, but in the end he always overcame his doubts and did only as he wished to do. However much Temujin might falter making his decisions in the beginning, in the end he was always implacable in the service of his own will. Then he would delude himself into believing that he had been forced only by necessity and the will of the spirits to act in his own interests.

"I have forgiven you." The shaman was still speaking with Jamukha's voice. "I am here to honor my oath to you. When you wish to have me with you again, you need only summon your shaman to your side."

"Jamukha." Temujin held on to Teb-Tenggeri's coat, and Jamukha glimpsed tears in the Khan's gold-flecked greenish-brown eyes. Temujin would never have shown such weakness in front of any of his men. Jamukha should have felt triumphant, seeing his betrayer in such a state; instead, pity pricked at him.

"Promise me that you won't leave me," the Khan murmured, "that your spirit will always watch over me."

"I shall," Teb-Tenggeri said with Jamukha's voice. "Be at peace, my brother." Then Jamukha was again plunged into darkness.

Jamukha waited, curled in on himself, buried in the darkness he could not escape. Once, unable to bear the thick gloom any longer, he found himself pushing against it, sinking more deeply into the blackness even as he struggled to free himself.

"You cannot get away." Teb-Tenggeri's voice surrounded him. "There is no way out for you until I choose to let you go. Right now, I need you if I am to strengthen my hold on Temujin. He will heed my words above anyone else's because he hears your voice in me, because he knows that your spirit truly lives inside me. When I have seen more deeply into your soul, when I have finally learned everything that has passed between you and Temujin, when I know enough to make my Khan believe that you still possess me even when you do not—then I can show you some mercy and release you."

"I'm grateful for that," Jamukha murmured, wondering if he could trust the shaman. He held his doubts close, cloaking them, knowing that he had to keep his deepest thoughts hidden.

"It seems," the shaman said, "that you have some doubts about my ambitions."

The man was too sensitive to his innermost thoughts. Jamukha reined in his doubts. "I am only thinking," he said, "that as trusted as you are by the Khan, and as much as Temujin fears your powers and your spells, you are not the only one who advises him. He also listens to his brothers and to his comrades in arms—Borchu, Jelme, Mukhali and the rest. Temujin has always had so many trusted followers." He struggled against his bitterness, then allowed Teb-Tenggeri to sense it. "I also suspect that his chief wife Bortai still has his ear."

"Bortai Khatun is too frightened of me even to think of poisoning her husband against me. As for his brothers, Temujin has only to suspect that one or more of them covets his throne, and that would be enough to make him turn against them."

Could that be true? Could Khasar or Temuge even dream of ruling in their older brother's place? Jamukha did not believe it; the two had been deeply devoted to Temujin ever since boyhood, and had remained loyal even when the Khan had suffered his worst defeats. Could Teb-Tenggeri rouse the Khan's suspicions against his brothers? That might be a kind of revenge, seeing Temujin harden himself against those who were most faithful to him and to doubt the loyalty of those he loved most.

Jamukha should have felt a fierce joy at that prospect. Instead, he was remembering a time when he and Temujin, as boys, had practiced together with their bows. Khasar had joined them on the windswept plain of yellow grass, aiming his arrows at a distant tree, never missing, proving that he was the best archer among them. It had been easy for Jamukha to praise Khasar for his skill, to feel joy at the pride he saw in the younger boy's sharp dark eyes. For that moment, on that day, the three of them had been happy, oblivious of their enemies and all of the hardships that still lay ahead.

The memory left him, captured in the web of Teb-Tenggeri's thoughts. The shaman would find a way to use it to play on Temujin's regrets. Jamukha wondered why he did not feel happier about that prospect, then quickly cloaked his feelings in the thick darkness.

* * *

Embedded as he was in the blackness, unable to see or to hear, Jamukha found himself recalling the sights and sounds of the past.

He was in the northern forests, waiting with his men to raid an encampment of mushroom-shaped yurts along the Uda River. He had ridden there to aid Temujin, whose young wife Bortai was a prisoner in that Merkit camp. Far above him, bright veils of light fluttered in the night sky; the spirits who danced at the Gate of Heaven were urging him on to victory.

Now he was standing with Temujin under the great tree in the Khorkhonagh Valley as hundreds of men swore oaths to them both, raising a forest of lances and stamping their feet.

Then he was lying with Temujin under that tree, listening to the distant howl of wolves, gazing up through the leaves at the tiny bright smokeholes of Tengri that dotted the night sky. They had shared themselves with each other under the blanket, giving themselves pleasure with their hands as they had when they were boys, but now they were men, binding themselves to each other more tightly, being to each other what no one else could be to either of them.

That love had been their secret. Others had seen them only as the closest of comrades and sworn brothers, and Jamukha was content to leave it so, feeling that such secrecy kept their love unsullied. No mockery would wound them; no puzzled, suspicious looks from Bortai or Temujin's other women could touch them. Nothing would sever the secret bond that bound them.

But that bond had been cut, and the love they had once shared had made their parting angry and bitter. The urges of his body, the desires that made him long for Temujin, became only more weapons the spirits had used to strike at him, tormenting him with what he had lost. His rage had turned his love to hatred, lashing him into his doomed battles against his anda.

Most of his thoughts now were of the times before he and Temujin had parted so bitterly, before they had fought their wars against each other. Allowing himself to think of the be-

trayals and the wars only brought pain. There had been times
when Temujin had been ready to forgive him, when Jamukha
had wanted to reach out to his once-beloved friend to say that
he was willing to forget the past, but always the anger and
hatred and bitterness had come between them again.

From time to time, light and sound would flood into him,
and Jamukha would observe the world through Teb-
Tenggeri's eyes. Usually, the shaman was inside his yurt, sitting on silk cushions amid the chests of treasures that had
been given to him in return for his spells. Temujin was always with them, trembling as he reminisced with Jamukha,
laughing or weeping over the past, striking his chest with a
fist as he spoke of his regrets, gripping Teb-Tenggeri by the
shoulders as he begged again for Jamukha's forgiveness.

"Once, the spirits spoke to me," Temujin would say,
"and then they grew silent. Once my dreams were clear,
and then I saw them only through a mist. An evil in me has
made me doubt the truth of the spirits, but now I hear the
ghost of my anda, and know that I was wrong to doubt.
Forgive me, Jamukha."

Always the response was the same. "I forgive you," Teb-
Tenggeri would say with Jamukha's voice, and then the
shaman would offer his own advice to the Khan, speaking of
what his dreams had told him.

The Khan should make another foray across the Gobi
against the Tanguts in the south; the spirits had promised
Teb-Tenggeri that there would be much loot for his men to
share.

Toghar, Teb-Tenggeri's cousin, had proven his loyalty to
the Khan and deserved to be rewarded with five hundred re-
tainers and their households.

Hoelun Khatun, the Khan's old mother and Teb-Tenggeri's
stepmother, might once have been wise, but she had grown
more feeble in both body and mind and her advice could no
longer be trusted. Such were the slow poisons Teb-Tenggeri
fed to Temujin with his advice.

Temujin was willing to believe the shaman's words, because through him, his comrade Jamukha lived again. Jamukha would listen as Temujin gave the orders that granted honors to those who were loyal to Teb-Tenggeri and also withheld favors from any whom the shaman doubted. The Khan was clearly ready to do anything to keep the ghost of his old friend near him, fearing to lose Jamukha again.

Yet when the darkness enclosed him once more, cutting him off from the world, Jamukha found himself thinking of how little joy there seemed to be in seeing Temujin give vent to his regrets, in watching the shaman play on the Khan's fears and remorse. His soul's imprisonment inside Teb-Tenggeri had finally burned the fire of his old rages into ashes.

It was Teb-Tenggeri's wish that Temujin hold a kuriltai, and once again be proclaimed khan. The bones and the stars had revealed that it was heaven's will that Temujin be once more confirmed as Genghis Khan, now that all the tribes had submitted to him.

The shaman had allowed Jamukha to gaze through his eyes as he read the bones, to listen as Teb-Tenggeri told Temujin of the ceremony that would mark his greatness. He had even let Jamukha's spirit fly from him for a time, to soar above the steppe and look down at the chiefs and Noyans in their lacquered leather armor as they rode toward the Khan's great pavilion. But Jamukha felt the invisible, strong tether that still bound him to Teb-Tenggeri. A longing for freedom came over him, but the tether drew taut, pulling him back to the shaman.

Other shamans performed the horse sacrifice, strangling a white steed and burning its flesh in a pit to the right of the pavilion. Temujin's brothers and close comrades raised him on a carpet of felt and carried him to his throne. But it was Teb-Tenggeri who hoisted the khan's tugh, a standard of nine white yak tails on a long pole, and again proclaimed Temujin as Genghis Khan.

Temujin's favorite wives sat with Bortai to the Khan's left, their high square birch headdresses adorned with feathers and jewels. The men seated at Temujin's right lifted their goblets of kumiss and airagh as they hailed their khan. Jamukha fed on the smoke of burning meat and the drops of fermented mare's milk that the men spilled from their cups as offerings to the spirits.

Perhaps Teb-Tenggeri was granting Jamukha this unaccustomed freedom in order to stoke his rage against Temujin. He was allowing him to see his old comrade at the height of his glory, with all the tribes honoring him, knowing the sight would feed Jamukha's anger. It no longer mattered what the tribes called themselves, Kereits or Merkits, Onggirats, Naimans, or Ongghuts; they were all Mongols now, and the man who had united them and made an army of them would hurl them against the world.

It should have been a bitter sight for Jamukha, yet he found himself pitying his friend. Temujin's face revealed his weariness, and his pale eyes were cold as he recited the laws that would now govern his people.

He is mourning me still, Jamukha realized. During all of the times that Jamukha had spoken to the Khan through Teb-Tenggeri, Temujin had murmured of their old bond, his loneliness, his increasing isolation. He could trust fewer and fewer of those closest to him; he claimed to need Jamukha even more now. That was, Jamukha supposed, part of his revenge, knowing that Temujin was becoming weaker and more suspicious of others.

Teb-Tenggeri quickly drew Jamukha inside himself and wrapped him in darkness again. Jamukha had glimpsed some of the shaman's thoughts—his lust for power, his arrogance, his growing belief that he was destined to rule through the Khan whom the spirits favored.

But that was not the will of the spirits, to have Teb-Tenggeri rule. Jamukha was convinced of that truth. He had read the bones that morning through the shaman's eyes, had seen the burnt clavicles crack down the middle. The omen had been clear, that Temujin was favored by God; Koko Mongke Tengri, the Eternal Blue Heaven above, had chosen Temujin to rule over the world.

Perhaps that was why Jamukha had been left to wander the land of the living, why he had been set out for Teb-Tenggeri like small game for a hawk; the spirits needed him to fulfill their ends. It came to Jamukha that he would not be free to fly to Heaven, to ride and hunt with the other spirits of the dead, until he carried out heaven's will and preserved Temujin's throne from Teb-Tenggeri.

But what could he do? How could he act against the man who kept his soul imprisoned, who could read his thoughts if Jamukha grew careless in hiding them?

He had no power to stand against Teb-Tenggeri, but there might be a way to turn Temujin against him. Perhaps he had to urge the shaman more forcefully along the trail he already intended to follow. Teb-Tenggeri had been patient and cautious so far in his demands, but Jamukha might be able to goad the shaman into overreaching himself and thus rouse Temujin's anger.

Talons seized him in the darkness, making him throb with pain; Jamukha twisted in their grip. "I sense disloyalty," Teb-Tenggeri's thoughts whispered. "There is something inside you—"

Jamukha allowed a wisp of thought to escape. "You think that you can wait," he murmured, "that you have all of the power you need over Temujin for now. But if you don't move quickly against those who resent your growing influence, the Khan may come to doubt you."

"He will not doubt me as long as he can hear your voice through me, as long as he can speak to the ghost of his sworn brother."

"But you don't want him to listen to too many other voices. You don't want to give others the chance to rouse his suspicions against you."

The invisible talons released him. The shaman was silent, his thoughts hidden; he would now be turning his attention to the feast and to the honors being parceled out by Temujin to his men. Jamukha suddenly feared that Teb-Tenggeri would never release his soul. How could the shaman risk losing the strongest hold he would ever have over his khan?

* * *

"Move against Khasar first," Jamukha said inside Teb-Tenggeri. "If you can bring Temujin to doubt his favorite brother, it will be easier to rouse his suspicions against others."

"Khasar is too close to him still." Teb-Tenggeri's voice seemed more distant. "I can wait. It is enough for the moment that I'm the Khan's chief advisor, that he listens to me above all others."

"He may turn to Khasar again," Jamukha said. "I was the ally of Toghril, the Kereit khan, when Khasar was living in Toghril's camp. Many said that Khasar was a prisoner there, but Toghril treated him well and wanted Khasar to ride with him against Temujin, and it was said that Khasar nearly agreed to do so."

"Yet he finally escaped from the Kereits and returned to Temujin."

"True," Jamukha said, "but some whispered that was only so that he could spy on his brother for the Kereits, and that Khasar was waiting to see whether Toghril or Temujin would win out. Temujin was aware of such rumors, I'm sure. You should remind him of them."

A sudden wave of heat seared Jamukha; the darkness surrounding him was as hot as fire. He had not sensed the depth of Teb-Tenggeri's hatred for Khasar, and the force of it startled him.

"Temujin may fear me," Teb-Tenggeri's thoughts murmured, "but Khasar does not. I've even heard tales that he mocks me behind my back. He doesn't know that I can sometimes sense unspoken thoughts in others, that I know what he thinks of me."

He had to be cautious now. He had not understood the intensity of the shaman's enmity toward Khasar, and it frightened him.

"And what does Khasar think of you?" Jamukha asked.

"That I use my spells to satisfy certain urges." The darkness around Jamukha throbbed. "That I bring boys and men, and not only women, to my bed, and that they use me as a woman. That may be the way of some other shamans, but it has never attracted me." The flood of anger and loathing nearly overwhelmed Jamukha. "I've hated Khasar for whispering such things. I would happily see him dead for uttering them."

"Then why have you not moved against him before?"

"Because he still enjoys Temujin's great favor. Because others fear me too much to believe such tales. I have told myself that it's better to wait, that to act too soon against Khasar might only give more credence to his lies."

The shaman's pain and rage flared up once more. Jamukha struggled to shield himself against the onslaught. Teb-Tenggeri had not yet sensed the true nature of the bond between Jamukha and Temujin; perhaps he could not even allow himself to glimpse it. To be trapped inside such a man, one who loathed and feared what Jamukha had been—Jamukha buried that thought.

"To let Khasar spread such rumors," Jamukha murmured cautiously, "only makes it more likely that some will come to believe them. Others may begin to doubt that you're as mighty a shaman as they thought. They'll whisper that if you had the powers you claim to have, you would have punished Khasar for his lies long ago."

He could feel Teb-Tenggeri weighing this possibility. "Perhaps you are right, Jamukha," and another surge of loathing and disgust nearly flooded into him. "Maybe I've been too patient with Khasar."

He does not allow himself to know what I was to Temujin. Why would he fear that so much? Jamukha wondered. Perhaps Teb-Tenggeri longed to be what Jamukha had once been to the Khan, even while despising such feelings.

Jamukha clutched that bit of knowledge to himself. It was a weapon that he might be able to use against the shaman.

It was Khasar who finally provoked a confrontation. He rode to Teb-Tenggeri's camp one evening and demanded entrance to his yurt.

The shaman, who had grown more accustomed to the pres-

ence of the ghost he had captured, now often allowed Jamukha the use of his eyes and ears. Jamukha listened as
Khasar raged outside, shouting to be admitted.

"Some of my men have left my ordu for yours," Khasar
cried, bursting through the doorway almost before a female
slave had rolled up the flap to admit him. "They've ridden
away with their households from my camp and say that they
now want to serve you." His words were slurred, his broad
face flushed from drink.

"If they wish to join me," Teb-Tenggeri said softly, "I
can't stop them. What does it matter, as long as they still
serve our khan?"

Men were shouting outside the tent. Jamukha heard the
voices of Teb-Tenggeri's brothers. This meeting was likely to
turn into a brawl; he wondered if the shaman could control it.
Perhaps, amid the shouting and the fighting, he could find a
way to free himself.

No, Jamukha thought. The spirits had sent him to Teb-
Tenggeri, and would not free him until he had accomplished
their purpose.

"Those men were my followers." Khasar took a step toward Teb-Tenggeri. "I demand that you send them back."

Teb-Tenggeri shrugged. "If you're such a poor leader that
you can't hold them, I see no reason why they shouldn't
choose another."

Khasar cursed and lifted his right arm. Jamukha waited for
the broad-shouldered man to strike the shaman. Khasar drew
back and lowered his hand. A smile crossed Khasar's face as
he tugged at his mustaches, but his narrowed dark eyes were
still angry.

"Did they choose you," Khasar asked, "or did you bring
them here with one of your spells? I've heard all about your
spells, Kokochu." Jamukha felt the shaman tense at this use
of his childhood name. "I've heard of how you lure men to
you, by bending over and parting your buttocks. That's your
kind of spell, telling them they can use you—"

Teb-Tenggeri's fist caught Khasar on the jaw. The force of
the shaman's rage plunged Jamukha into darkness; the pound-

ing of Teb-Tenggeri's pulse nearly drowned out the sound of the commands being shouted to the shaman's brothers.

"Drive this man from my camp!" Teb-Tenggeri screamed. "Beat him and the friends he brought here, and tell them never to show their faces here again!"

Jamukha hid himself in the darkness. This was exactly what he had wanted, to push the shaman into such a confrontation. Khasar would turn to his brother Temujin for justice, and the Khan would surely order Teb-Tenggeri to return Khasar's followers to his camp. A few more such incidents, and Temujin might begin to doubt his shaman's wisdom and loyalty.

Another thought came to him; Teb-Tenggeri had been much too angered by what was only a crude drunken jest. The shaman, he was sure now, secretly feared that he might be exactly what Khasar accused him of being. Perhaps he lusted for Temujin, and maybe he also feared that he would lose his hold on the Khan if Temujin ever glimpsed that hidden longing.

Jamukha held that thought closely. It was another weapon he might use.

Khasar appealed to his brother the Khan, but Temujin gave him no justice. Instead, he sent him away with mocking words about how the mighty Khasar had allowed himself to be beaten. Rather than losing Temujin's favor, Teb-Tenggeri had strengthened his position. Temujin had listened when Teb-Tenggeri went to him to say that Khasar had designs on his throne, that he had been plotting against him, that some of his followers wanted Khasar to be their khan.

Now Khasar was in disgrace, and even the pleas of the Khan's old mother Hoelun had not swayed Temujin. He would not risk angering his shaman, and Jamukha knew why. Temujin could not bear the possibility that Jamukha might again be lost to him.

"I had come to doubt the spirits," Temujin whispered. He had summoned the shaman to his camp and had sent everyone, even the slaves, away from his great tent, for he always

spoke to Jamukha's ghost in solitude. "I began to think that
the dead would always be silent," he continued, "that in truth
there were no ghosts who haunted the world or who had
flown to heaven. I came to think that this world might be all
men have, and now I can believe that isn't so."

"That my spirit is with you proves that," Jamukha said
through Teb-Tenggeri. The reins controlling him were looser
now; the shaman allowed him to speak more freely when Jamukha's talk seemed to be serving his end.

"More often now," Temujin said, "I find myself thinking
of the time you were my only friend, when we first swore our
anda oath."

"I remember." They had sworn their oath by the iced-over
Onon River in winter, both of them fatherless boys. "I had
only a brass die to offer you as a gift to mark that promise."

"And I had only my knucklebone dice." Temujin leaned
forward, reciting the words he had said so many years ago.
"When we ride together, no one will come between us. I will
cherish you and love your sons as my own. Our bond will
last for all our lives."

"Our two lives will be one," Jamukha said. "I will always
defend you, and will never raise my hand to you—I swear it
now. May my promise live in my heart."

"All that I have now was only a dream then." Temujin's
hands gripped Teb-Tenggeri's shoulders. "Sometimes I think
that my old dreams of glory brought me more joy than the
actual conquests, those old dreams I shared with you." His
face seemed more youthful in the soft glow cast by the
hearth. "My comrades, my brothers, my sons—I value all of
them, but none has ever taken your place. You were—"

Temujin fell silent, searching Teb-Tenggeri's face. Jamukha knew what he could say, which words would bring
Temujin under Teb-Tenggeri's sway forever: You were my
other self, Temujin. You shared yourself with me as you did
with no one else. I have not forgotten our nights under the
tree in the Khorkhonagh Valley, the nights under my tent, the
nights out on the steppe when we were guarding the horses.
Temujin would expect to hear such words, which would

prove that Jamukha's spirit was speaking to him. Teb-Tenggeri would be given everything he desired, because he had restored Jamukha to his sworn brother the Khan.

Jamukha cloaked his thoughts quickly, then sensed that the shaman's mind was elsewhere. Teb-Tenggeri was relishing his growing influence, taking pride in how easily he had divided the Khan from his favorite brother Khasar, of how he would soon become the true ruler of Temujin's realm. But would he be so willing to use Jamukha's ghost to further his ends once he saw the hidden part of his bond with Temujin? Jamukha recalled the rage and shame that had torn at Teb-Tenggeri during Khasar's coarse joke, of how fearful he had been that Khasar might have glimpsed something inside him that he could not acknowledge.

To bring such things out of the dark pools inside Teb-Tenggeri into the light would be risky. The shaman's rage and fear might destroy both his soul and Jamukha's.

Temujin was gazing intently into Teb-Tenggeri's eyes, clearly waiting for Jamukha to speak of the deeper love they had kept hidden from everyone. "You were my comrade in battle," Jamukha murmured, "my companion during the hunt, my sworn brother. There can be no stronger bond than that."

Temujin glanced down, looking disappointed. He lifted his head and, for an instant, Jamukha thought that he saw doubt in the Khan's pale eyes. That uncertainty might grow, might become another weapon to use against the shaman. If Temujin came to believe that no ghost truly lived inside Teb-Tenggeri, the shaman would lose his hold over him.

Temujin sighed, then slowly got to his feet, and Jamukha realized that the shaman had missed the flicker of doubt in the Khan's eyes. Jamukha now had all the weapons he needed in order to work the will of the spirits, to destroy Teb-Tenggeri and allow Temujin to be the ruler heaven had chosen.

Hoelun, the Khan's mother, was ailing; some whispered that the old woman was dying. Others murmured that the

shaman Teb-Tenggeri had put a curse on Hoelun because she
had confronted Temujin, demanding justice for her son
Khasar and uttering harsh words about Teb-Tenggeri. To af-
front the Khan's chief shaman, who had brought the Khan so
many victories with his spells, was dangerous; he would
summon the powerful spirits he commanded and bring ruin
upon his enemies.

Those seeking to ingratiate themselves with the shaman
carried such rumors to him, and Jamukha saw that the tales
only fed Teb-Tenggeri's growing arrogance.

Jamukha had, while haunting the Earth, recalled the times
his own passions and ambitions had been his undoing. His
hungers and longings were gone, burned away at last by Teb-
Tenggeri's imprisonment of his spirit. But the shaman was
still driven by his desire for power, which had grown even
greater after his capture of Jamukha's ghost. Now, spurred on
by his triumph over Khasar, Teb-Tenggeri sought to tighten
his grip on the Khan.

To bring down the shaman who had captured him, to bring
Temujin to see that Teb-Tenggeri thought of the Khan's
realm as his own, was now Jamukha's only purpose and also
the only way that he could free himself from the shaman.
Temujin had become the greatest Khan of his people, chosen
by Heaven to unite them and to make an army of them. Without Teb-Tenggeri, he might at last bring all of the world
under his standard, but under his shaman's influence, he
might lose all that he had won.

Jamukha had done what he could to sow distrust and doubt
in Temujin's mind. Three times since Khasar's banishment,
Temujin had come to Teb-Tenggeri's camp to commune with
Jamukha's spirit, and three times Jamukha had refused to
utter the words of love that his anda clearly expected to hear,
and Teb-Tenggeri's suspicions had not been aroused. But Jamukha could not tell if Temujin's doubts were growing, if the
Khan was beginning to suspect that his shaman might only
be mimicking Jamukha and pretending that he had captured
his ghost.

More men joined Teb-Tenggeri's camp and swore their

oaths to him; better to ride with the man whom Genghis Khan favored above all than with another leader. Among those who came to the shaman were several comrades of Temuge, Temujin's youngest brother. A more cautious man would have sent them away, would not have provoked another confrontation with one of the Khan's brothers so soon. Instead Teb-Tenggeri, as Jamukha had expected, welcomed Temuge's men to his camp.

"Kokochu!" a man was shouting outside Teb-Tenggeri's yurt. "Come outside!"

Teb-Tenggeri was sitting with his brothers and other followers, picking over the remains of a feast. Before the shaman could rise, one of his brothers moved toward the tent's entrance.

"Who are you," the brother shouted through the open entrance, "and what is your business?"

"My name is Sokhur, and I rode here under the orders of Temuge Odchigin, brother of the Khan. Temuge demands that you return his followers to his camp."

Sokhur came through the entrance then, ducking down and then straightening again as he approached the hearth and the men who were seated with the shaman on cushions in the back of the tent. Jamukha, peering through the haze that Teb-Tenggeri's drunkenness had produced, saw a huge man with a wrestler's massive build under his long belted tunic. Sokhur would be a match for any man in the tent, perhaps for all of them.

"If Temuge can't hold his men himself," one man called out, "then they should be free to choose another chief."

Another of Teb-Tenggeri's brothers was whispering to him. "Send the men back," he murmured to the shaman. "They'll return to your camp before long, and when they do, Temuge will have to let them go."

Good advice, Jamukha thought, but Teb-Tenggeri was beyond such wisdom, drunk on wine and kumiss and intoxicated with his ambitions. "Temuge's men will stay here,"

Teb-Tenggeri said as he got to his feet. "Leave now, or we'll take a whip to you."

Sokhur's face reddened at the insult; to take a whip to a man was a grave offense. "The Khan will have something to say about this!" he bellowed.

"The Khan will say nothing." Teb-Tenggeri drew himself up. "You know what happened to his brother Khasar. You'll only bring the same fate upon your master Temuge."

Sokhur lunged toward Teb-Tenggeri, but was quickly brought down by three other men. They dragged him toward the entrance as Teb-Tenggeri laughed. "Whip him out of the camp!" the shaman shouted after them. "Send him back to his master with his saddle tied to his back!"

Jamukha withdrew into the darkness. He did not need to hear more. Perhaps Temujin would finally act, would see that if his shaman could strike out at the Khan's brothers, he might not shrink from eventually striking at his sons, even at the Khan himself. And if he did not act, but let Temuge suffer the disgrace that Khasar had—Jamukha refused to think of that.

"My power grows." The voice whispering that thought of Teb-Tenggeri's was so low that Jamukha could barely hear it. "Soon I may not need you at all, but don't think I'll release you so quickly. There are many ways to imprison a ghost, to keep it against a time when it may be needed again."

Jamukha's fate was still bound to Temujin's. He hid in the blackness of Teb-Tenggeri's soul, wondering what the Khan would do.

Teb-Tenggeri was summoned to the Khan's ordu. His six brothers rode there with him, leaving their tents well before dawn. The shaman was certain that Temujin would not stand against him, but preferred to face him with his brothers at his side. Temuge had probably gone to the Khan to demand the return of his followers, but he would get no more satisfaction from Temujin than had his brother Khasar.

As they rode, Teb-Tenggeri allowed Jamukha to gaze at the world through his eyes. Spring had come to the steppe, and blue and white wildflowers dotted the grassland; soon the grass would reach to a man's waist. In the distance, a black ridge of mountains thrust up from the land, reaching toward heaven, and Jamukha thought he could hear the spirits of the mountains calling to him, chanting that he had stayed too long among the living. He suddenly felt a fierce longing for the earth he had lost, as if this might be the last time he would ever look upon it.

A herd of the Khan's favorite white horses grazed beyond his camp; on the horizon, streams of smoke rose from the circles of black tents in the Khan's ordu. They had approached the encampment from the south. By the time they had reached Temujin's great tent to the north of the camp, the sun was in the western part of the cloudless blue sky.

Temujin's guards watched in silence as Teb-Tenggeri and the others dismounted, then called out the names of the visitors as they approached the entrance. Teb-Tenggeri led his brothers inside, stepping carefully over the threshold. He did not bow; he had never bowed before his stepbrother the Khan, and would not do so now.

The shaman and his brothers hung up their bowcases and quivers of arrows on the western side of the entrance. An expanse covered by carpets separated them from Temujin, who sat on his felt-covered throne on top of a platform at the northern end of the tent. His chief wife Bortai was at his left, her large golden-brown eyes focused on her husband; Jamukha had not expected her to be there. To his right, the Khan's brother Temuge sat in the place of honor, with three big broad-shouldered men near him. Members of the Khan's day guard, wearing black lacquered leather armor and blue sashes, stood in front of the platform.

Was Temujin, Jamukha wondered, finally ready to confront Teb-Tenggeri? Would he have urged Temuge to stay there for this meeting only to humiliate him? Munglik, Teb-Tenggeri's father and Temujin's stepfather, was seated not far from Temuge, pulling at his long gray mustaches and smiling to himself; surely he would not have come there if he expected to see his shaman son disgraced. Temujin's intentions were well hidden.

"I greet you, my khan and brother," Teb-Tenggeri murmured as he approached the back of the tent. Jamukha sensed no fear inside the shaman as he lifted his head and gazed steadily into Temujin's pale eyes. Teb-Tenggeri had worn his white coat made from the hides of snow leopards, his hat of eagle feathers, and his necklaces of silver and jewels, all gifts from the Khan. Temujin wore a plain brown wool tunic, worn trousers, felt boots, and a simple blue headband around his shaven head; he had always scorned adornment for himself. Jamukha could read nothing in Temujin's eyes; they seemed to be staring past Teb-Tenggeri at something unseen.

"My brother Temuge Odchigin has complained to me about you," Temujin said in his quiet voice. Temuge sat up straight on his cushion, anger in his eyes. He had grown fatter since the years when Jamukha had known him; he had always been a slower, lazier, more placid man than his brother. Now his eyes flitted from Temujin to the shaman, as if he were waiting for a command.

Jamukha sensed danger. The wisest course for Teb-Tenggeri now would be to smooth over his differences with Temuge. That might weaken the shaman's position for a short time, but Temujin could be brought around again. Even as he realized this, being careful to keep his thoughts masked, Jamukha knew that Teb-Tenggeri was now beyond reason.

"Your brother has no reason to complain." The shaman's musical voice almost sang the words. "Some of his men chose to join me. Does it matter if they serve me or Temuge Odchigin, as long as they serve their khan?" He paused. "I suspect they came to me only because Temuge may harbor ambitions much like those of his disgraced brother Khasar."

"I won't listen to this!" Temuge shouted, rising from his cushion. Temujin motioned him back with one sharp movement of his hand. Teb-Tenggeri had gone too far to turn back.

Jamukha trembled in the darkness, suddenly fearful for himself and his spirit.

The shaman drew nearer to Temujin, so close that he could

have reached out and touched the tops of the Khan's boots. Bortai clung tightly to the edge of her husband's sleeve.

"I serve my khan above all others," Teb-Tenggeri said softly. "My loyalty is to you and to no one else. It is not your brother who casts the spells that have brought you victory. It is not your brother who allows the spirit of your anda Jamukha to dwell inside him and to bring comfort to you."

Temujin recoiled. Jamukha saw the pain and longing in his pale eyes and thought that the shaman would win out after all, and then the greenish-brown eyes grew hard once more.

"Once, I believed that." Temujin's voice was so low that Jamukha could barely hear him. "I heard his voice through you, I saw his spirit gazing out at me from your eyes. But there are things he would have said to me, words you never spoke, words that only he—"

The Khan suddenly motioned to Temuge. His younger brother jumped to his feet, shouting, "I'll settle this myself!" Temuge rushed at the shaman. "We'll see who's stronger now!" His big hands closed around Teb-Tenggeri's neck; Jamukha fluttered helplessly inside the shaman as Teb-Tenggeri gasped for breath.

"Settle this outside my tent," Temujin called out. "You may prove who is stronger there."

"What is this?" Munglik was rising from his seat. "What are you doing?"

Temujin spun around to face the old man. "Temuge has been insulted," he replied. "Your son Teb-Tenggeri has overstepped his bounds. I will do nothing against him myself, and won't shed his blood, but Temuge must be allowed to settle this."

The shaman's brothers were advancing toward the back of the tent; the Khan's guards quickly massed around the throne. "You will never hear the voice of your anda again!" Teb-Tenggeri screamed, but Temuge was already dragging him across the threshold, followed by the three burly men who had been sitting with him.

Outside, Teb-Tenggeri's terror flooded into Jamukha; his fear was the wind under the wings of a bird, lifting Jamukha

swiftly from the darkness and setting his soul free. He heard
a shriek as one of Temuge's men forced the shaman's shoulders back, bending him into a bow until his back snapped.
The two other men were laughing as they talked of how poor
a fighter Teb-Tenggeri had been, and how easily he had been
defeated. Temuge bent over the body, poked at it to be certain that Teb-Tenggeri was dead, then kicked the corpse toward a cart.

A pale mist formed over Teb-Tenggeri, then became a falcon. The ghostly raptor flew up from the shaman's broken
body and stretched out its translucent wings as it circled
Jamukha.

"You escaped me," the falcon said with Teb-Tenggeri's
voice. "I might have kept you bound to me even after my
death, but you escaped me. Now I have no power over you."

Jamukha fluttered his own ghostly wings, then alighted
near the cart. "The will of the spirits is done. Even you could
not stand against it."

"And what was the will of the spirits?" Teb-Tenggeri's
ghost asked.

"That Temujin should rule his people, and not you."

"My spells brought him his conquests."

"You should have been satisfied with the many rewards he
gave you," Jamukha said. "Now he will have to conquer the
rest of the world without you."

Men were coming out of the Khan's tent to peer at the
body, unaware of the spirits lingering near the corpse. "I
could have ruled with Temujin," the falcon said.

"Once I said the same," Jamukha murmured.

"You might have had your revenge for what he did to you,
Jamukha. Instead, you hid the truth from me, the truth that
would have kept Temujin bound to me. I see that now, what
you were to him and what he once was to you."

"You would never have accepted that truth in life," Jamukha said.

"That wasn't why you kept it from me. You used it as a
weapon against me."

"I used it to free myself."

The falcon spread its wings and sprang up, riding on the wind toward the bright blue sky. Temujin was coming toward the shaman's body now, followed by his guards. The Khan's face was slack, his eyes as dead as if his own spirit had flown from him.

Temujin leaned over the corpse of Teb-Tenggeri. "Rise," he whispered, "rise now. Come back to life so that I can know that my sworn brother truly lived inside you. I would willingly suffer any curse you might put upon me to know for certain that the dead are not silent, that Jamukha spoke to me through you."

Teb-Tenggeri's glassy eyes gazed up sightlessly at the Khan. He would trouble Temujin's realm no more; those who loved their Khan would no longer have to fear his spells. Temujin would have the triumphs that heaven had ordained for him, but he would also have to live in an empty world where ghosts no longer spoke to him, in which his doubts about their existence would always torment him. He would fear the death of his soul as much as that of his body while he lived, for he would believe death to be only a void, one that would extinguish his spirit.

With only a few words spoken through Teb-Tenggeri while the shaman still lived, Jamukha could have banished those doubts and Temujin's torment, but only at the cost of giving the shaman the power he craved. It came to him then that he had won some measure of revenge while also honoring his oath to watch over his anda.

"Your torment will not last long." Jamukha extended his wings. "It will last only a man's lifetime. You will be with me again, Temujin, when your soul flies to heaven."

But his anda could not hear him. The wind lifted Jamukha, and he let it carry him away from the Khan.

GOOD DEEDS

Jack Dann

Robert F. Kennedy, in my opinion, was one of the most fascinating and promising political figures on the American scene and one of the greatest losses of potential the U.S. endured when he was assassinated in 1968, less than two weeks after the tragic death of Martin Luthur King Jr. The son of a wealthy and powerful father, and member of a family both blessed and cursed, he went from being an aide to the appalling Senator Joseph McCarthy to becoming, in his last campaign, a spokesman for the poor and dispossessed. It is the complexity of his character, the combination of great strengths and great flaws, that makes RFK such a compelling figure. Here, we catch a glimpse inside the mind of an imagined Bobby Kennedy, a man swimming in the darker currents of American politics, one of the few venues left (business may be another) in which a mid-twentieth century American conqueror could operate. Jack Dann is the author of the highly praised novels *Junction,*

Starhiker, The Man Who Melted, the Civil War novel *The Silent* (described by Peter Straub as a book "filled with mystery, wonder, and the kind of narrative inventiveness that makes other novelists want to hide under the bed"), and an international bestseller about Leonardo da Vinci, *The Memory Cathedral.* His most recent novel is *Bad Medicine* (Tor), and a collection of his short fiction, *Jubilee,* has also been published; he is now at work on a novel about James Dean for HarperCollins. Dann has won several awards, including the Nebula Award and the World Fantasy Award, and lives in Melbourne, Australia while "commuting" to Los Angeles and New York.

B obby Kennedy sat with Max Gohr, Buz Connover, and Pete Lastfogel at Dirty Jerry's on Church Street in lower Manhattan.

It was a cold, bitter night, too cold for snow. The air, usually clotted and smog-heavy, was sharp and crisp and clear, but not in the bar, which was stuffy, crowded, and overheated. Cigarette smoke hung in layers below the high tin ceiling; the bar was crowded with a coming-and-going assortment of young, greaseball, sideburned toughs; whores; girls from the neighborhood; the occasional upscale call girl looking in to see if she might service one of the agents of the Federal Bureau of Narcotics; old lizards who looked like bag ladies; subdued first-shift blue-collar workers in for their beers and shots before going home; and the welfare hangers-on who'd been drinking since Shirley, the barkeep and owner, had opened at 11:00 AM. The windows were ice-slicked, and the bright beams of automobile headlights flickered across them. A loud medley of "Ain't That a Shame," "Sixteen Tons," "Shake, Rattle, and Roll," and "The Yellow Rose of Texas" played on the neon jukebox near the door. Shirley was hot for the songs, especially "The Yellow Rose of Texas," and played them constantly.

Bobby and his friends sat at their usual corner table near

the adjoining poolroom—away from the couples who occupied most of the other tables—and they had already put quite a buzz on, each matching the other drink for drink. Bobby sucked a few inches of lager from his schooner, dropped a shot glass filled with bourbon into the beer, and then carefully took a drink.

He was completely happy. This was where he most wanted to be, among friends he could respect . . . men of action. "So you've really been through it," Pete Lastfogel said to Bobby. Pete was a tall, mild-looking man with thinning blond hair, a thin face, pale skin, and baby blue eyes. Everything about him seemed mild and taciturn and considered. But Bobby knew better.

"Yeah, it's been one bitch of a month. I figure I deserve you guys."

Everyone laughed.

"Well, no one deserves *you*," Buz said, combing his fingers through his frizzy brown hair. He was a big man, burly and overweight, a football player gone to seed.

"Thanks for that," Bobby said.

"My pleasure, man." Then after a beat Buz asked, "Tell us about your trip to Russia."

"Nothing to tell, except they're all a bunch of atheist assholes. The food was shit . . . poison. I wouldn't eat it. I ate watermelon and fruit, that's about it. Lost twenty pounds."

"We can see that," Buz said.

"—And there are pictures of Lenin and Stalin everywhere, until it comes out of your ears," Bobby continued. "One of their professors in Kirghizia told me that Communists looked upon people who practice religion as backward. So I showed them how incredibly backward I was by carrying a Bible everywhere I went and visiting every church and mosque I could find."

"Good for you," Max said. Like Buz, he wore a leather jacket over a button-down shirt. He was ruddy-complexioned and balding; he'd once told Bobby that since his hair fell out, women were crazy for him. Bobby, for his part, was not inclined to believe that.

"The women there live on farms and work in the fields.

It's really something to see them all toiling away, hour after hour, in their bright red and blue dresses. All the while, their children are taken away to state-run nurseries. Gave me the creeps. Although I've got to hand it to them, the places were well managed. Don't underestimate the Soviets. For all my traveling companion talks about making peace with them"— he meant Supreme Court Justice William O. Douglas—"we won't have any kind of lasting peace unless we're strong."

"You practicing a speech?" Max asked.

Bobby smiled. "I leave all that to my brother."

"Yeah, you only write them for him," Buz said.

"I think Jack is more than capable of writing his own speeches," Bobby said, bristling. "And who the fuck are you to say otherwise?"

Buz shrugged, looked away, and Bobby forgot about it immediately. He was with friends. He was safe here. Buz was an asshole. So what? That was his nature. Bobby wasn't here to be with eggheads and politicians and administrators. He was here to be free, to be himself, and to have some goddamned fun.

"But the trip was worth it," he said, talking to Pete, as if he was the only one with the intelligence to understand. "We don't know the Russians, and they're equally ignorant about us. But I liked the people themselves. They're people with problems. Their regime is detestable, but for all the propaganda those people have to endure, they were friendly to us. So I don't think the Commie propaganda is working very well."

"I thought you said everyone there was a bunch of atheist assholes."

Bobby ignored Buz.

"I'll tell you where they thought they had us, though," Bobby continued, still directing himself to Pete. "They kept bringing up how we discriminate against Negroes. They think we lynch a couple every few minutes. I tried to explain that was all exaggeration and told them they have segregation all over the Soviet Union. But I have a great idea that would change what Soviet citizens think about Americans. We should ask the Harlem Globetrotters if they'd consider going to Russia and touring around the country for a month. That would be a wonderful thing. It would break down barriers and change the Russians' idea of American race relations. But I doubt if Khrushchev would give them permission because that would put the United States in a good light." Bobby reminded himself to mention his idea to his brother . . . and to his father, too.

"You going to tell us about how you got sick there?" Buz asked.

"Will you stop ragging him," Pete said. "For crying out loud!"

"Where did you heah that?" Bobby asked.

Buz grinned and said, "You think only the FBI gets the dope on you."

"Very funny," Bobby said. "Yeah, I got sick in Siberia. Thank God we carried our own supply of penicillin."

"Shouldn't've fucked the whores," Max said.

"Couldn't get *near* any whores," Bobby said. "Wasn't for lack of trying, either."

Everyone laughed, and Max said, "Well, we should be able to help you out in that department. We might even be able to score some penicillin."

"A little early for you guys, isn't it?" Bobby asked. "Not even seven-thirty."

"Early to bed," Max said.

"Okay," Bobby said, "I'm ready for anything." He reached into his back pocket for his wallet, but Pete stopped him.

"Your money's no good tonight." He gestured to Shirley to bring the bill and said, "Listen, Bobby . . ." He paused awkwardly, as if he was embarrassed. "This is on behalf of all of us here, but we're really sorry about what happened to your wife's folks."

Ethel's mother and father, George and "Big Ann" Skakel, had died in a plane crash in Oklahoma, their bodies burned beyond recognition.

"I told George that B-26 bomber was a death trap," Bobby said. He could feel the beer and the booze working through him, flushing him with acid, irritating his hiatal hernia, opening him up, giving him the courage to be with the others, to be one of the boys, to talk, to say whatever he goddamn well wanted, anything, everything—unless it was about money or politics—because he was safe here, right here, right now, because he could blackmail, or buy, everyone sitting at this table; that's how you got safe and stayed safe. His daddy had taught him that.

"But George, the great goddamn entrepreneur, thought it was good value for money," Bobby continued, "and said he was going to buy every B-26 the Air Force decommissioned and convert them all into a fleet. Stupid bastard. You know what was left of them at the wreck . . . all that was left?"

None of the agents answered.

"George's Diners Club card. Probably make a good advertisement for Diners Club, don't you think? 'The card that just won't die.'"

Max shook his head and said, "It's a bitch."

"No, the bitch is Ethel, poor goddamn thing that she is and blessed mother of my children." Bobby stared hard at the three agents, who looked like deer caught in the beam of a headlight. "I tried keeping her away from those drunk bastard brothers and sisters of hers, tried to protect her from herself, and so I guess I'm the sonovabitch because I didn't let her stay with them at Rambleside after the funeral to sop it up. I should have let her go. At least she wouldn't be getting arrested every five minutes for shoplifting and driving under the influence."

"I think you did the right thing," Pete said.

Bobby shrugged. "Doesn't matter a shit."

"Well, I'll tell you what does matter," Buz said, "and that's that we go and get ourselves some spic and nigger criminals." He grinned at Bobby.

"Man's got a point," Max said. "And then one day Bobby can prove to Old Bullethead and his other fairy assholes at the FBI that all these criminals are organized."

"I think we'll let them figure all that out on their own," Pete said. "Unless you fancy being out of work." He stood up, looked around, then folded a twenty-dollar bill in half and placed it under his glass. "I wonder where Shirley ran off to? Must be off in the store room."

"Or taking a piss."

Bobby stood up with the others when an eavesdropping construction worker said, "Hey, rich kid." He was drinking shots and beers at the bar with four of his cronies, who were as big as he was. Bobby paused, looked over his shoulder at the man, who was around six four and some two hundred and twenty pounds, and then shook his head and continued toward the door.

"I mean you, you shanty Irish nigger piece of shit." The worker's friends tried to stop him, warning him as they looked nervously at the FBN agents, but he shook them off and said, "I know who you are. Go back to your piece-of-shit daddy in Boston."

Bobby stopped, and Pete said, "Bobby, forget it. We got a deal with Shirley that we don't fuck up her place."

"Then we go outside," Bobby said quietly. He could feel the adrenaline pumping in his chest, hot and wet as if he was peeing himself on the inside, and there was the blinding anger exploding in his head, white and bright, the anger that he didn't have to contain or focus; and he turned to the construction worker, who was flat-faced and smooth-skinned and wearing a grimy tan jacket over a plaid work shirt. "Moron, are you trying to talk to me?"

"Nobody else, shithead."

Max, Buz, and Pete stood calmly behind Bobby, and one of the construction workers said, "Look, he don't mean nothin', he's just drunk and stupid." He apologized to Bobby, but directed himself to the agents.

"Fuck you, don't go kissin' their freakin' mick asses," said the construction worker who was antagonizing Bobby. He combed his fingers through long, straggly blond hair; in another five years he would certainly be bald. "And I ain't drunk, and if I was I could wipe the floor with this skinny mick bastard."

"We really don't want no trouble with you guys," one of

the other hardhats said. "Really, man, he's just got a mean drunk on."

"Let's just shoot the cocksuckers," Max said quietly.

"Outside, not in here," Pete said.

Bobby was trembling with the anger and fear and anticipation, that heady, delicious, deadly mixture, but he wasn't going to run; he wasn't going to walk out of here with that asshole jeering at him; and he wasn't going to let his friends take care of business for him either because this was his chance, right now, right the fuck now. This was his chance to prove himself to them, to prove himself to . . . himself; and in that white hot wet sliver of time, in that vacuum quiet transparent place where he was standing, before tiny A-bombs of wet, slippery red viscera exploded, he remembered playing baseball with his brother Jack and his sister Pat and that little asshole Gareth Skenk at the family's summer home in Hyannis Port. Gareth was on third base, Jack was pitching, and Bobby nailed him cold when he tried to slide into third, but Gareth whined that he was safe; and Jack, ever the peace-maker, told little wheedling asshole Gareth that of course he could have a replay, and when Gareth slid over the plate, Bobby stepped aside and shoved the hardball right into Gareth's big mouth, breaking his front teeth.

"You're right, Gareth, you were safe."

"You want to step outside, you piece of shit," Bobby said; and the man lurched toward him. His friends called him back; one of them raised his hands, palms out, as if Buz was holding a gun on them. Bobby walked quickly to the door and held it open for the hardhat, who stepped around him, and as he did Bobby sucker-punched him hard and clean in the jaw, breaking bone, then hit him again square on the nose; the crunch of delicate bone and cartilage, an instant of chill blowing in from the lamplit street, Shirley out of the bathroom now and shouting, "What the hell's going on here?" and Pete assuring her, calm, soft-spoken Pete lagging behind.

But Bobby was out of there.

In the cold, in the dark. Victorious. Jubilant.

He stepped down the street, not even thinking whether his

friends were with him, walking with pure white light joy, thank you Heavenly Father, and for a beat everything was still absolutely silent; and then everything was movement and noise, Buz congratulating him first, then the others catching up, including Pete who finally said, "You know, guys, the cars are back that way."

"Christ, Bobby, I really didn't think you had it in you," Max said, his bald pate shiny in the street light.

"I guess we'll have to be careful around you from now on," Buz said, "or you might sucker us like you did that poor asshole."

"I just might," Bobby said. His right hand was pulsing, aching, already swelling where it had connected with the hardhat's jaw.

"He was a big fucker," Buz said. "Where'd you learn to do that?"

"From my 'piece of shit daddy in Boston.'" Bobby smiled. He tried to control his ragged breathing and excitement. This was what he needed, moments like this, pure golden moments of freedom . . . and the camaraderie of friends. He had to urinate, but he could hold it until they got to the bust, wherever that was; and he was also shivering from the cold, as he was only wearing brown khaki trousers, a sweat shirt, and his old, rumpled seersucker jacket. He buttoned all three buttons and rolled the collar up. It started to drizzle, and in the bone-cold humidity the sidewalks became slippery; the rain threatened to turn to snow.

"We promised Shirley never to make trouble in her place," Pete said, as if he were still working out what had happened.

"We didn't make the trouble," Bobby said.

"Doesn't matter. They were a bunch of assholes, and god-damn Max was ready to shoot it out like *High Noon*."

"I was just—"

"Stick it," Pete said to Max, an uncharacteristic edge to his voice. "And you, Bobby, you're on the bus, man, you're on the fuckin' bus."

Everyone pulled hard on Bobby's ears, welcoming him into their secret Boy's Life society; and Bobby, for his part,

decided to pee right there in an alley, just like they do in
Paris, France.

They raided a huge six-bedroom railroad apartment in
Spanish Harlem on 116th Street and Amsterdam. A fifth-
floor walkup. The stairs were marble, broken and round-
worn, and stained sour milk gray; and the high-ceilinged
hallway smelled of stale tobacco and semen and urine. Loud
music from different apartments combined into a cacophony
of Latin, rock and roll, and blues, the rhythms stepping on
each another, melodies clashing in different keys, Joan
Weber's "Let Me Go Lover" overwhelming "Rocket 88."
Pete knocked on the door and said that "String" had sent
him, and when a hollow-eyed young black woman unlocked
the deadbolt, unlatched the chain, and opened the door a
crack, he pushed inside and struck her neatly on the side of
the head with his pistol. She collapsed without a sound, her
cotton bathrobe revealing nasty looking sores around her
navel and varicose veins and needle marks on her legs. Guns
at the ready, they rushed through the hall and surprised three
Puerto Rican couples in the living room.

"Cover them," Pete shouted to Bobby as Buz and Max ran
down the hall, kicking open doors. Then Pete followed, leaving Bobby alone in the living room with the juiceheads, the
potheads, the cocaine-sniffing, heroin-injecting, mainlining
hopheads. He could smell the cloying odor of marijuana. He
pointed his Army issue .45 caliber pistol at them and asked,
"Can you understand English?"

They sat on a long, expensive-looking blue velvet art deco
couch, which was out of place with the cheap blond veneer
end tables, torn chairs, and a round Formica table that should
have been in the kitchen. There were several stuffed en-
velopes on the Formica table, and a joint was burning in a
circular glass ashtray on the end table beside a girl in a fuzzy
white sweater. The men, all in their twenties, glared at
Bobby, as if this sort of thing happened to them every day.
Machismo. The women didn't scream; they looked down at

the floor, as though they had been caught having intercourse
by their priest.

"Well?" Bobby asked, his voice harsh. He was nervous,
scared of these dirty junkies, even though he had the gun,
even though he had just beat the crap out of that hardhat
who'd called him out in the bar.

One of the women nodded as she hastily pulled her white
sweater down to the belt of her skirt. She looked up at him,
imploring. Her long, coarse black hair was tied away from
her face with a pink ribbon, her complexion was tan, her eyes
large and dark and deeply set, and her bright red lipstick was
spread clownishly over the edges of her lips. Her light
skinned boyfriend—he was probably her pimp—pulled her
toward him possessively. He had a delicately handsome face
and very bad, discolored teeth. His shirt was open, revealing
gold jewelry. His pants were pegged, without hint of a
crease. He was the leader, Bobby thought. No doubt. "You
tell your boyfriend and his two pals to stand in the corner
there on the other side of the room."

The woman nodded and spoke to them in Spanish, but
they didn't move.

Then Bobby heard Max scream, "You dirty fucker" at the
other end of the apartment. There was a grinding noise like a
jammed window being forced open, and someone shouted,
"Please, man, no, I'm sorry, no, please, no." A tumble of
Spanish words was followed by a gagging strangled yelp.
Somehow that gave Bobby courage . . . and made him angry.

The couples sitting in front of him looked frightened now
and started talking and arguing in Spanish. Bobby told them
to shut up. He pointed his pistol at the young man with bad
teeth and said to the woman sitting beside him, "Tell your
boyfriend and his brothers or cousins or whatever the hell
they are to move their respective asses right the fuck now or
I'll shoot their pimply heads off." And he meant it.

She said something in Spanish to the men and started to
cry.

They stood up.

"I said in the corner, against the wall."

The man with the yellowed teeth glowered at him, but led the others to the other side of the room.

"And you girls, I want you standing up right over there right the fuck now." Bobby pointed to the Formica table and the stash of marijuana.

The women nervously watched him and cried, but they didn't make a move until the girl who understood English mumbled something to them in Spanish.

They all have such similar, familiar faces, Bobby thought. Probably more Spanish than Negroid. But who could tell? All dark people looked similar to him. Still, the girl who understood English was definitely the prettiest; she had long, straight beautiful hair and tiny breasts. Bobby liked tiny breasts.

"What's your name?" he asked her.

But before she could answer Pete Lastfogel appeared and said, "We're not going to be here for long, Bobby. Pick up any stash you can, we'll figure it all out later." Buz came in after Pete. He looked mean and jumpy. He shouted at the men to move and shoved them easily out of the room. Bobby was sure he would have shot any one of them who didn't obey. The Latino leader looked scared; and for some reason it only made Bobby feel sad . . . and anxious.

"What the hell was going on in there?" Bobby asked.

"You don't want to know," Pete said.

"—and don't ever come back here again, you stupid-ass *puta. Comprende?*" Bobby recognized Max Gohr's voice.

After a beat a tall barefoot woman in a flowered print dress ran through the hallway. She carried a screaming baby in her arms like a football. Her head hunched forward; her face was a death mask the color of burnt umber, her shiny, kinky hair a dark halo.

The door opened with a click. Slammed shut.

"Believe me, you don't want to fucking know."

Then the woman Pete had knocked out with his pistol walked dazedly into the room. She blinked, then turned around, and Bobby heard the door open again with a click, then slam shut, as if there was a vacuum in the apartment.

"Let her go," Pete said to Bobby.

"Can we go, too?" asked the woman in the fuzzy white sweater.

"You're all under arrest."

"For what? We didn't do nothing."

Pete picked up the stub of a joint, lit it, inhaled deeply, and flicked it at her.

The other girls started crying.

"Your boyfriend is going to be an old man next time you see him. And there's one of your dope dealer pervert friends that you ain't ever going to see again. You know why? Because he's dead dead dead, honey." Pete talked softly, but he was on a roll, and cold anger was coming out of him like sweat from an athlete. Perhaps he was also sweating out his calm and quiet gentleness. "Maybe something can be done for you . . . but first you have to do a little something for us."

"Like what?"

"As I said, it's got to be quick," Pete said to Bobby. "Which one do you want?" He smiled without humor. "After all, you're the guest of honor."

"I want to know what the hell happened back there," Bobby said.

"We found one of the dealers getting himself sucked off by a goddamn little infant," Pete said, looking disgusted. "Christ, it was a goddamned infant. It didn't know any better. That was the mother, if you can call her that, who ran out with it. We let the poor slut go."

"And the pervert?"

"Was probably her boyfriend," Pete said. "Dumb sonovabitch just happened to fall out the window. Justice be done, hallelujah. But we got a little time because the window looks out into an enclosed alley. We just added a little more garbage for the boys in blue. Made quite a score back there, too. Enough coke to put all those niggers up the river for a long time. So which one of these beauties do you want?"

"What's your name?" Bobby asked the girl in the white sweater again.

"Marinda."

"That's all? Just Marinda?"

She looked down at the floor.

"I'll just have a little talk with Marinda," Bobby said. He saw she was trembling and felt ashamed of himself. But he'd come here to catch drug pushers. Everything else . . . that was just the dirt that went with it.

"The rest of you, come with me," Pete said.

The other girls looked to Marinda, who spoke softly to them in Spanish. They glared at Bobby and left the room with Pete.

Bobby led Marinda to the couch; he could smell her fear, a sour perfume.

"You gonna let me go, maybe?"

"Maybe."

She was still trembling.

"Look, I'm not going to hurt you," Bobby said. "Nobody's going to hurt you."

"If you say."

Bobby lifted her chin, and she looked directly at him. She's too young, Bobby thought. She's a baby, and she smells, and she's dirty; and although he didn't understand why, he suddenly thought of his brother Jack's wife Jackie. He was reminded of Jackie as he looked into this little frightened junky whore's face, Jackie the day she married Jack in Saint Mary's in 1953, how she stood and gazed around, how she looked in her frosting white wedding dress, her perfect shoulders exposed, her face so . . . innocent, pure, perfect. How could he look into this whore's coffee eyes lined with too much mascara and see Jackie, perfect, fragile, fawnlike Jackie? If she reminded him of anyone, it would be Ethel. Mother of God, how could I even think that? he asked himself. She was nothing like Ethel . . . just as Ethel was nothing like Jackie. Ethel was athletic and plain. She loved hot dogs and chicken on the barbeque. Jackie loved everything fine, and as Bobby lifted up Marinda's sweater, he remembered the string of pearls Jackie had around her neck when she got married. Marinda didn't wear a bra, and Bobby squeezed and kissed her small breasts; he tried to calm her and stop her trembling, but she knew what she was supposed to do. She

kneeled in front of him, unzipped him, and as Bobby felt her
mouth moving expertly over his penis and felt her teeth,
which might as well have been as sharp as needles, he
prayed. He prayed for forgiveness. He whispered Jackie's
name, and as he came, bucking like a child who had been
crying and could not stop the spasms, he resolved that he
would make everything right.

He hadn't *really* cheated on Ethel. . . .
Fondling and screwing those poor whores was outside the
marriage; it was part of the danger and the excitement, and it
was good for the girls because they didn't get arrested. (Pete
Lastfogel's philosophy.) You couldn't just let them go. You
had to show them you were a little bit bent or they'd think
you were an asshole. They'd lose their fear, and then where
would you be?
And who was Bobby to argue? He was just along for the
ride.
It was all over in an hour, anyway, and then Pete dropped
him off at Times Square, the sleazy crossroads of the world,
the quintessential center of all the action. Bobby loved the
smells, sounds, and dangers of the streets; he loved the
anonymity because under all the red, white, and blue neon,
he was just another shadow, just another guy looking for a
piece, looking for money or shelter or excitement, looking
for the party, the crap game, the absolute perfect other-
worldly whore; and this seedy, crowded billboard-lit inter-
section was the loneliest place on earth. But not for Bobby,
not for golden Bobby who was here to do good . . . one good
deed for the night, then a good night's sleep, and back to
Washington, back to his life, that paper construction of details and routine. But his life would start tomorrow. This was,
indeed, time out, and he stood on Seventh Avenue and
looked at the Bond Building, awash in white light—two
well-dressed male and female statues as large as King Kong
stood on a ledge and glowed in their respectively resplendent
Bond suit and gown, while a circular sign blinked 9:30.
Below were the words

EVERY—HOUR
1190 PEOPLE
BUY AT

A coruscating red, white, and blue wall of neon proclaimed BOND . . . BOND APPAREL . . . TWO TROUSER
SUITS across the width of the building.

Straight ahead and south were the Pokerino palaces, the
Astor Hotel, the Criterion, and Loew's State. The neon sign
for the Park Sheraton Hotel was gauzy as mist in the distance. Skyscraper tall signs for CHEVROLET and ADMI-
RAL TELEVISION APPLIANCES and COCA-COLA and
BUDWEISER blinked and glowed and rippled. The Winston
man blew huge, perfect smoke rings out of his empyrean sign
above the streets with clockwork regularity, and a thirty-foot-
wide waterfall drenched passers-by in pure, cleansing light.
The streets were jammed with cabs and cars, all driving
through the electric mist. The streets glowed, wetly reflect-
ing; pedestrians hurried, as if rushing to the most important
appointment of their lowlife lives, while others lounged,
leaning in doorways, casing everything and everyone, all the
hangers-on, the out-of-work, the junkies, the troublemakers,
villains, pimps, bouncers, the niggers and the spics and the
dagos . . . and the mick shantytown Irish.

Bobby smiled. Here he was. Right in the heart of it. Right inside the glowing heart of it. Here were the girls, the whores, the
runaways, and the rich kids slumming for a good time. Here
were the bums wearing layers of shirts and filthy sweaters
under torn filthy coats. Here were all manner of down-and-out-
ers. He passed a young woman sitting on a subway grate. She
was pretty, but addled and had been obviously living rough for
quite some time. She wore a fur coat that looked like mink, but
was so tattered and matted that it was difficult to tell. Over the
coat she wore a plastic rain protector. Her delicate face—pug
nose, rather thin lips, high cheekbones—was mottled with
some sort of eczema, or perhaps burn scars. Her short, greasy
brown hair curled out from under a black woolen hat. Without

looking up at him, she asked for a dime. He gave her a dollar.
She just nodded, as if it was her due.

Bobby kept walking, then turned around. "Hey, have you
had anything to eat today?" he asked the woman.

She looked up at him. "What's it your business?"

"Not my business."

"If you're worried, give me a few dollars and I'll go buy
something."

"I just gave you a dollar."

"Well, there you are."

"You hungry or not?"

"You looking to get laid or what, you weird fuckin'
pervo?"

Bobby sighed and walked away, but she got up and followed him. She shouted obscenities, told every passer-by
that he had propositioned her and was a pervert, and then she
grabbed his arm and said, "Yeah, I'm hungry. What you
going to do about it? Come on, pervo, put your freakin'
money where your mouth is."

He stopped short, turned around and said in a low voice,
"You say one more thing, just one fucking word, and I'll
break your face."

She closed her eyes tightly and scrunched up her face as if
waiting to be struck. Then she opened her eyes and nodded.

"Well, you hungry or not?"

She nodded again.

"You think you can behave yourself in a restaurant and not
humiliate yourself?"

She nodded.

"You can talk now, it's okay."

"Yeah, I'm hungry, yeah I can behave, no, I won't humiliate you."

It was Bobby's turn to nod. "What's your name?" They
walked up Seventh Avenue.

"Gracie." After a beat she said, "You're supposed to say,
'Say Good night, Gracie,' but you didn't, so ask me a question, go ahead, ask me a question."

"Is that your real name?"

"Wrong question, no cigar. You're supposed to ask me what I think of television."

"What do you think of television?"

"I think it's wonderful—I hardly ever watch radio any more. Get it?"

"Yeah, I get it," Bobby said, smiling in spite of himself.

"Too corny, huh?"

"Too corny."

"Works for me."

"So you're Gracie Allen and I'm George Burns."

"Got it in one, pervo . . . oh, I'm sorry, uh, what's your name?"

"Bob."

"Bobby Socks?"

Bobby didn't respond. She hummed as they walked, then asked, "Where we going?"

"55th, between 6th and Park, a little restaurant. French. That okay?"

"I guess."

"Now tell me your name."

"Grace," she said, as if giving up something precious. Her shoulders hunched forward. She pulled off her hat and ran her fingers through her matted, curly hair. "Don't have a comb."

"You look fine," Bobby said.

"I look fine," she said. "You ever see a birthmark?"

"Yes, I suppose," Bobby said.

"I'm a birthmark."

"You're a . . . what?"

"Yeah, that's exactly right, mister. Or maybe you'll like this better—I was on my way to a beauty contest, and an oil-can blew up in my face." She giggled. "I didn't always have it, though." She blinked at Bobby in mock innocence and said, "It just grew. But you'd be surprised, 'cause lots of people like it. It's very, *very* sexy. And I think, what I think, is *you're* one of those people is what I think."

As they reached the green awning of La Chaumière, Bobby wondered whether to go through with this. He could buy her a frankfurter from one of the street vendors; he didn't

have to take her to his family's restaurant. But he guided
her past the doorman and introduced her to the maître d',
who bowed and made a fuss over her. He was privy to
Bobby's little fancies. Once he seated them at Bobby's
usual table in the far corner, he whispered, "Your brother
Jack has been phoning and asking for you, and he asked me
to give you this number, you're supposed to call him as
soon as you can."

"It can wait until tomorrow," Bobby said.

"The Senator said it was personal." Code for important.

Bobby sighed and allowed the maître d' to lead him to the
phone in the office.

I expected you to call me two hours ago.

*I'm not working for you, anymore, remember? The elec-
tion's over.*

I need a favor, Bobby.

Yeah?

I was supposed to meet Marilyn.

Where?

At the Algonquin. I booked a suite for the night.

So . . . ?

*I can't make it, it's a long story, but Jackie's here in New
York, and she's having a conniption.*

*So what am I supposed to do? Just call your bimbo and
tell her you got tied up.*

I can't do that.

Why not?

Because she'll get all upset.

And make a scene.

Yeah, Bobby, and make a scene.

I told you, Jack, you got to get rid of her.

Will you meet her and explain? Please. I'll owe you.

She's trouble, Jack, I've told you—

Tell me you wouldn't want to get into her pants.

Look, she wants you, not me, Johnny.

Bail me out, Bobby, okay?

*And if something intimate should happen between her and
me, what then?*

Then I guess I won't owe you one, little brother.

When Bobby returned to his table, he found Gracie guz-
zling champagne and eating petit fours and a double portion
of crème brûlée.

"Don't you want a main course?" he asked.

She nodded. "That's coming next. I ordered everything:
steak bloody rare, seafood terrine, chicken fricassee, lobster
thermidor, an endive and walnut salad, and a cheese plate the
size of your head."

"That's good." Bobby noticed that she had managed to get
custard in her curly hair.

"Half for you, half for me," and she pushed her saucer of
crème brûlée across the table to Bobby.

"No, you finish it." There was hardly any left, and he certainly wouldn't eat from her plate.

"Well, did I do okay?"

"Yeah, you did fine."

"You like all those things?"

"I like all those things."

Gracie smiled at him, revealing rotten, yellowed teeth,
which reminded Bobby of Marinda's drug dealing boyfriend.
"I haven't had a goddamn crème brûlée since I was a kid."

"Where was that?" Bobby asked, surprised.

"In George-and-Gracie land."

A waiter, overseen by the maître d', brought the food she
had ordered.

"Give him the steak, that's how he likes it. Rare."

Bobby said he'd have the terrine . . . he couldn't stand rare
steak.

"Your loss."

"Champagne?" asked the waiter, as he turned a glass upright. Bobby nodded.

As Bobby sipped champagne, he watched Gracie spear the
steak with her salad fork and drop it on top of the lobster.
Cheese sauce splashed onto the table, but she didn't seem to

notice; She was concentrating everything she had on the business of getting food from the various platters into her mouth. Bobby wondered whether she could be fixed. Clean her teeth, wash and cut her hair, burn her clothes, get her a room, a job, surely she could do something.

"I know who you were talking to on the phone."

"And who would that be?" Bobby asked.

"Me."

"Ah, so I called you at the table."

"That's right. How the hell do you think I knew what to order if you didn't tell me on the phone?"

"I guess that makes sense."

"Goddamn right it does. What do you want to do when we're finished eating?"

"*We're* not doing anything. But if you'd like, I'll get you a hotel room for the night and give you a number to call tomorrow. Someone who can help you out, get you settled somewhere decent."

"Oh, gee, hot diggidy dog, thanks, mister. Now tell me who you were talking to on the goddamn phone."

"You. That's what you just told me."

"And who else? Tell me or I'll throw the biggest tantrum you ever saw."

Bobby sighed and shook his head, thinking that this waif wasn't so different from Jack's girlfriend. He wrote a number on a slip of paper, handed it to her, and stood up. "If you want a decent room for the night, ask the maître d', and he'll see to it for you."

"Where are you going?" Gracie demanded. "Tell me. I mean it, I'll throw a goddamn tantrum right on this table."

"Okay, Gracie, how's this? I've got a hot date with Marilyn Monroe."

Gracie leaned back in her chair and grinned rainbows at him. "Oh, yeah?"

"Yeah. Now say goodnight, Gracie."

"Goodnight, Gracie . . ."

And Bobby left her with the maître d' and a phone number.

Left her for Marilyn.

WALKING GODS

George Alec Effinger

Students of Greek (there are still a few of us around)
are familiar with Xenophon's *Anabasis*, in which the
Greek historian and former mercenary soldier writes
of leading his men on a fifteen-hundred mile march
through enemy Persian territory to safety. The following story is related by Saladin, the Muslim leader
who captured Jerusalem from the Crusaders in 1187,
but as you will see, Xenophon also has a role to play
in this tale of two very similar battles far removed in
time. Saladin's haunting thoughts about earlier battles
have an eerie resonance with current events, as we
struggle with our own conflicts inherited from earlier
times. George Alec Effinger was one of the most
gifted and versatile writers ever to work in science fiction and fantasy. His talent was evident from the very
beginning of his career in the early 1970s, when his
stories began to appear in all of the major maga-
zines and anthologies. His novels include *What En-
tropy Means To Me, Relatives, Death in Florence,*

Felicia, Heroics, The Wolves of Memory, The Nick of Time, and *The Bird of Time;* among his short story collections are *Mixed Feelings, Irrational Numbers, Dirty Tricks, Idle Pleasures,* and *Maureen Birnbaum, Barbarian Swordsperson.* The late 1980s and early 1990s saw the publication of his inventive and much-admired novels set in a futuristic Middle Eastern city, *When Gravity Fails, A Fire in the Sun,* and *The Exile Kiss.* He has been honored with the Nebula Award, the Hugo Award, and the Theodore Sturgeon Award.

I am Salah al-Din Yusuf. To the Franj, my enemy, I am Saladin. To my people I am a great and generous king. To my Creator I am the instrument of his wrath upon the defamers of our faith. To my friends and counselors I am an old man about to die.

They tell me I have led a legendary life, but what they recall and what I remember are not the same. This morning when I opened my eyes I found that I had become old, that my body was weak and crippled, and that I was surrounded by men with pity in their eyes. My biographers asked me about my great battles, but they did not believe me when I explained my strategies. I told them that I had won my greatest victory with an army of dead men, but they only murmured to each other and shook their heads in sadness. I tried to tell them of the bargain I had made and how I repaid those strange allies, but my doctors begged me to rest. They believed that age and illness have caused me to dream a whole new life, but I know the truth. I know what is a dream and what is certainty.

Yesterday I kept my promise to the lost warriors of the Rum, and helped them win a great battle at Cunaxa near the city of Babylon. That triumph secured their freedom and guaranteed their safe return to their homes in Greece. In some way that I do not understand, those troops, the glorious Ten Thousand, had fought the same battle more than one thousand five hundred years ago. One of their commanders related to me how their prince had been killed and their cause had gone down to defeat. Yesterday, however, with my soldiers reinforcing theirs and my counsel added to that of their generals, Cunaxa became a great victory. How can the same battle be fought twice? How can downfall be turned to triumph? I cannot say. Everything is in God's hands, everything happens as pleases him alone. God is most great.

Last night, after the celebrations, I returned to my tent weary but filled with gladness. On the morrow I would assemble my army again, take leave of the archaic Greeks, and march home to continue the war against the European invaders, they who call themselves the Crusaders. I was young and strong when I took to my bed and closed my eyes. Today, when I woke, I was not at Babylon but Damascus, and many years had passed in a single night. This also I do not understand.

I will tell how it began more than ten years ago. Then I was but the youngest general in the army of my uncle, Shirkuh the Lion. One cold, stormy afternoon he said to me, "Yusuf, you must gather what is necessary and come with me. We are going to march on Egypt and take Cairo for the honor of our sultan."

"My uncle," I replied, "I do not wish to go, not even for all the riches of the kingdom of the Nile." But of course my wishes meant nothing, neither to my uncle nor to the sultan himself. I could only do as I was ordered.

The power in Cairo had been seized by a scheming, greedy vizier named Shawar. I could not see why he wanted that power—of his fifteen predecessors, only one had died a natural death. Indeed, he did not enjoy his stolen position and wealth long before he too was overthrown; he was lucky to escape with his life. King Amalric of the Franj decided to take advantage of the unsettled situation by invading Egypt, and that is when the sultan ordered my uncle to reclaim the land to the west. The clockwork of fate had been set in motion.

Fortunately for my uncle, Amalric was a fool. He had surrounded a strategic town on a branch of the Nile and was laying siege to it. The people of the town sent word to Shirkuh, but before we could draw near, they liberated themselves. It was September and the river was swollen to flood stage. The people of the town broke down some of the embankments and inundated the lowlands. If the Franj had stayed in their positions, they would have drowned in their battle armor. Amalric ordered a rapid retreat, and while we were still on the march we heard that the enemy had fled in confusion back to Palestine. We gave thanks to God, but we did not turn our faces toward home. Our orders were to capture Cairo and restore Shawar as vizier.

My uncle proved his prowess on the battlefield in the next few months. He feinted toward the north of Palestine and Amalric, gullible and ill-advised as always, followed. Then my uncle made all speed to the west. We crossed the undefended Franji territory unhindered and soon made our camp outside Bilbays, Egypt's easternmost port city. Only a week later we were at Cairo, and we hadn't lost a man. Amalric was in the countryside somewhere, no doubt wondering how we had managed to swing around his great army and pass through his conquered lands so easily.

I did not know it at the time, but this campaign was my schooling to become the scourge of the Crusaders that history knows. I give all credit to God and to Shirkuh, my uncle. Cairo was also where I learned best about treachery, for no sooner had we returned the vizier Shawar to power then he ordered my uncle to leave Egypt at once. Of course, my uncle did not. It was then that Shawar made a shameful alliance with the Europeans to drive us away. I could not believe there was so much deceit in a single man.

"He will be punished in due time," my uncle told me.

"When that moment arrives," I said, "I pray that I am near enough to witness it."

My wish was granted, but not immediately. Before that, we would meet on the battlefield again. My uncle realized that he was hundreds of miles from home and threatened by the combined might of the Europeans and the soldiers of Egypt, who were our cousins. We did not wish to go to war with them, but we had little choice. "There are other ways of defeating an enemy than striking at its head," Shirkuh said.

"I do not see what you mean, my uncle."

He shrugged. "We are far from home, far from reinforcements and supplies, so we will make Shawar and the Franj suffer the same hardships." He turned our army and dashed away from Cairo, as if we were fleeing in disorder. But we were not fleeing. I did not believe the trick would work, because it seemed to me obvious and transparent. Once again, though, I had credited Amalric with too much intellect. At last, when my uncle reached his chosen destination, he stopped near al-Babayn. Our men were hungry and filled with fatigue, but so too were the Franj. When we joined battle, I think the troops were glad of it. They preferred fighting to forced marches.

Our strategy was simple: we would use the vanity of Shawar and Amalric against them. They thought we were afraid and desperate. They assumed they were superior in number and armament, and so when I ordered my division in the center to fall back, the Franj came after us, eager for killing and plunder. The farther I pulled back, the farther the enemy extended itself, somehow blind to the fact that my uncle's units on the right and left wings were wheeling about to trap them. Amalric's army was decimated, but he himself escaped to Cairo where fresh Franj companies were waiting.

I expected that after the engagement my uncle would allow our men to refresh themselves and recover their strength before the next battle, but I was wrong. Shirkuh taught the whole world a lesson in military tactics that day. Striking as lightning strikes, he urged his weary men to even greater haste, rushing back northward beyond Cairo. There we found Egypt's largest city and port, Alexandria, virtually undefended. The Lion had crossed the entire country from south to north in unheard-of speed, and we were welcomed into Alexandria as liberators.

There was nothing for Shawar and Amalric to do but follow us and lay siege to Alexandria. This is when I got my first taste of command, for my uncle left me in charge of the city while he took his best cavalry, passed through the enemy lines, and thundered south yet again. Now the Franj had a war on two fronts, in the north at Alexandria and in the south of Upper Egypt. Shirkuh sent a message to Amalric, pointing out that further bloodshed would not benefit either the Franj or us, and only Shawar himself could profit by it. Amalric mulled that over for a time and finally realized it was the truth. He agreed to abandon Alexandria on the condition that my uncle take his army out of the country as well. And so the siege was lifted and a truce declared. I will not call it peace.

There would be no more fighting for a year, until Amalric decided that he wanted to make another grab at wresting Cairo and the Nile Valley from the Saracens' grasp. Perhaps he would have succeeded this time, because a flood of fresh warriors had arrived from Europe to aid him, but he made a grave misjudgment. After a minor battle near an inconsequential town, the Franj massacred the entire population. There had been no provocation. It was just one of those horrors of war that happen and cannot be explained by logic or military necessity. The brutal killings did nothing but strengthen the Egyptians' resolve to resist the Crusaders. Even Shawar's loyalties wavered again. He withdrew the inhabitants of Cairo to the newer part of the city, and then he had twenty thousand jugs of naphtha poured through the old town. He burned the ancient city rather than let it fall into the hands of his former allies. The bazaars, houses, palaces, and mosques of old Cairo burned for a month and a half.

Shawar's act and the determination of the Cairenes caught Amalric's attention. He paused to reevaluate his position, and again he fled eastward to Palestine. As I look back upon those days, I believe the Franj king spent more time shuttling between Cairo and Jerusalem than he did on the field of combat against my uncle.

I visited Shirkuh as soon as I received the news. "This will give us all the time we need to prepare a final plan," I said. "We may rid ourselves of that brainless Amalric for once and all."

The Lion laughed. "Yes, possibly," he said, "but would

you not rather face a loud incompetent general than a quiet capable one? God alone knows who will command the Franj in his absence."

There was a great truth in what he said, yet another lesson for me. "And we owe our gains to that blighted scoundrel Shawar."

My uncle handed me a dispatch from our sultan in Syria. "I do not doubt that Shawar will look for a reward now. The king agrees he should have one. Read his words."

I studied the message and smiled. "It is Shawar's death warrant," I said.

"Yusuf, I remind you of your wish to be present at Shawar's punishment. You must consider the king's decree a direct command. I delegate the task to you, my nephew. I would not deprive you of the honor."

Not long after, on some pretext, Shawar was invited to our camp. When he arrived he was arrested and put in a tent under guard. I went to see him, heard his pathetic pleas for mercy, and then choked the life from him with my own hands. That is how I performed an execution the first time. I feel no guilt or remorse. I do not need to argue that I was acting under orders from my lord king. I have earned a reputation as a kind, generous man, but God and man know that I am ruthless toward those who make of me an enemy.

It was Shirkuh himself who took the vizier's place, but like so many men before him my uncle had been doomed by the honor. During an elaborate banquet he suddenly rose up and clutched his throat. He could not speak, but only utter the most horrible choking sounds. In but a moment he collapsed dead upon the table. It was obvious to everyone that he had been poisoned, but the murderer was never identified. To this day I do not know who was responsible for elevating me to the position of vizier of all Egypt. The caliph chose me on the advice of his counselors, who believed I was the youngest and most inexperienced of all the candidates, and that I would be easiest to control. History asserts otherwise.

These are the events which steered me toward my pact with the Ten Thousand, the valiant soldiers who should have been dead yet fought on, who were dead in fact yet ate and drank beside campfires no one else could see. Those soldiers served me well and I have returned their support, but when I speak of them the doctors think me mad. I have only hours to live, so the doctors will hear of them no more.

I was trained as a military man and not a governor, so at first I was uncomfortable with the wealth and authority of my new rank. Even my sternest critics note how liberal I was in bestowing favors and riches. Indeed, this morning my treasurer told me that he despaired for my empire in the coming days, as there was not even enough gold and silver on hand to pay for the reverent funeral I was due. And I have always hated disappointing anyone who requests my help. Once I even returned a vanquished city to the Franj, merely because they came to me humbly and asked for it.

I did not squander my subjects' money in lavish living, as so many before me have done. I suppose that is because I have never forgotten that I am only a man, consigned to a man's fate. Death has been a frequent though unwelcome guest at my court, reminding me daily of my mortality. Even as a young man I knew that someday God would whisper to me the command that cannot be shunned. Not long after my uncle was murdered it was Amalric who died, also not in battle. Then it was the sultan himself. His son took the throne, but as he was but a boy of eleven years, I found myself suddenly the most powerful of men.

I had to learn from painful experience that many men desired my death just because I wielded the emblems of authority. I needed an honest and reliable friend, and I prayed to God to send me someone as dependable as my uncle had been. God did not fail me.

I was with the army near the city of Tiberias, far from Cairo and my enemies, or so I believed. I did not yet know that the faction that planned to wrest Egypt from my control had allied itself with the heretic Assassins. One night after I had taken to my bed but before I had fallen deeply asleep, I heard movement in my tent. I had a moment to wonder why my guards had failed at their posts, and then a tall, thin man dressed in black lunged at my head. His knife cut through the material of my pillow and I rolled to the floor unharmed. Before I could get to my feet, however, I heard my attacker grunt and fall heavily to the ground.

"Rise, noble sir," another man said. I do not know what language he spoke, for while we discovered that he did not speak my tongue nor I his, yet we always communicated quickly and easily.

"I give thanks to God for sparing my life," I said, sitting on the edge of my bed, "and I thank you for being his means."

The man laughed, though there was no humor in it. He was dressed in the attire of a foot-soldier of the Rum from ancient times. I did not question his appearance at the time, and that seems strange to me now. Although our word for these men is Rum, they were not in fact Roman, just as all Europeans are not French in origin. "I'll bet a month's pay this wasn't the first assassination attempt you've survived," the soldier said.

I glared at the unconscious form of my attacker. "No, it wasn't, but that is part of the risk one assumes along with glory. And you must know there's little enough glory."

"What do you plan to do?"

"They will keep trying to kill me as long as I am alive," I said. "They are my cousins, but now it seems they're in league with the Franj. I must punish them without causing outrage among my own people."

The Rum warrior removed his helmet. "A wise king I've heard about had success in a similar situation. He let it be known throughout his lands that he would not persecute his enemies any longer, and then he just bought them. He decided that he could spare the gold more easily than he could spare his head. I don't see why it wouldn't work as well for you."

Before I could reply, two more Assassins sprang at me from the shadows. My new friend accounted for the first and the other had his hands around my throat as we fell to the ground. My guards arrived at last and dragged the intruders away. I did not need to question them before they were executed.

The man in the Rum armor watched in silence. When he and I were alone again, I spoke up. "Who are you?" I asked. "How did you come here?"

"I'm a Greek mercenary," he said with an aching sadness in his voice. "My name is Xenophon. My fellows and I fought a battle not very far from here fifteen centuries ago. We'd been hired by Cyrus, who was rising up against his brother, the Great King of Persia. We were the ablest troops Cyrus commanded and we were triumphant on the battlefield, but around us the remainder of his army failed him. We Greeks slaughtered the Persian troops who faced us, but Cyrus himself was killed, his headquarters overrun, and suddenly we found ourselves abandoned in an enemy land with no allies and no way home. That was only yesterday. Somehow tonight it is a thousand and a half years later. My army lies to the west, the Persian army is to the east, and the battle must be fought all over again. Possibly the gods know why, but I confess that I do not."

Some men would have called Xenophon a lunatic, but it never occurred to me to doubt him. As impossible as his story sounded, I believed him. "I owe you my life," I said. "How can I reward you?"

He stared down at the ground for a moment. "I believe we must win our battle against the Persians before we're allowed to return home."

"Perhaps. I have a battle to fight tomorrow as well. I will make you this bargain: that if you and your companions join my ranks against the Franj, I will lend my army to use against your enemy."

Xenophon's expression did not change. "That is what I had in mind. Then we can try a different strategy, and if fate is with us, both you and I will see happy conclusions."

"Do not rely on fate," I said. "Rely on God." The Greek only shrugged his shoulders.

It was autumn and the season of warfare had almost ended. When the weather turned cold I would return to Egypt and the Europeans would go back to their strongholds to await spring. I wanted to crush them for good before that. My forces were arranged upon the beautiful, fertile plain that stood before the city of Tiberias. I showed Xenophon a map and indicated where he should marshal his troops, to cut off any Franj retreat. Behind me was Lake Tiberias and the Jordan River. Before me were King Guy and the Franj, camped upon a hillside. The trap I had set for them would spring shut at dawn.

I slept very well that night. My servants woke me early and I ate a small breakfast. It was a fine, clear day, and I took that as a good omen. The sun would be fierce by noontime, but that would be a greater hardship for the Franj than for me. The enemy numbered more than twelve thousand, and I knew that the city behind me was their nearest source of food and water. Xenophon's heavily armed hoplites struck the first blow, thrusting at the Franj in close formation. King Guy's knights fought back ferociously. I wondered what they thought of their foe, dressed in ancient armor and carrying Greek spears and shields. It did not matter that Xenophon's men belonged to a vanished age—the men they killed were just as dead as any other.

I maneuvered with my cavalry so that neither Xenophon nor my other commanders would suffer many casualties. I struck the Franj from the left flank, then from the right, but it wasn't my plan to slaughter them. I let them advance a little now and then while my army fell back slowly toward Tiberias. The invaders would die, but before that they would suffer.

The afternoon wore on and the heat grew. I knew the Franj were beginning to crave water, but to drink they would have to fight their way through me. I suppose sometime during the day the same truth became clear to the Crusaders, and as the sun set they realized they would not quench their thirst that night. Just before dark I retired to my tent and sent for Xenophon.

When he arrived he did not look the worse for the day's

struggles. "I don't understand," he said. "I think you could have emptied the valley of them whenever you chose."

"Yes," I said, "that would have been victory, but I want more than that. I must teach this King Guy a lesson, too. He is just the current general from a distant land. The Franj have other generals, and I know they are watching what I do. I want them all to see that there is easier plunder elsewhere."

Xenophon frowned. "They've gathered their soldiers from every nation in their empire. They seem to be prepared to spend the whole winter here."

"Let them. I'll be spending the whole winter here, too, but this is my home and I will not lack for anything. The Franj must decide if what they take from us is worth months of hunger and want in a hostile country. Today they began to learn about deprivation. Tomorrow they will know it well."

"As you say, noble sir. I'm a mercenary and I don't pretend to know about such tactics."

That made me laugh. "History has a thing or two to say about you, Xenophon. Of course, much of what is recorded was written by you in the first place. I don't suppose many leaders have that great advantage."

He only raised his eyebrows, although I knew he was longing to ask me what I knew of his fame. "If that is all," he said simply, "I will rejoin my men. I wish you a pleasant evening and the taste of triumph tomorrow."

"God willing," I said. Then he left me alone.

The battle resumed at first light. It was a terrible thing to witness, and I took no joy in it. The Franj were desperate, willing to charge into overwhelming numbers in the vain hope of reaching the river. I watched for a while, but finally I returned to my tent. At midday Xenophon brought word that the invaders had been driven back against the hill, that his foot-soldiers had gained back every bit of ground they'd given up the day before.

"Good," I said. "Have they offered to yield?"

"No, noble sir," he said, "though they must be insane with thirst."

"Then let us apply more pressure. The grass in the valley

is brown and parched. Have your men set fire to it. The wind will blow the smoke into their faces."

Xenophon smiled. "It's wise to let the elements attack instead of your men."

I looked away. "The grass will grow back next year. My cities are many centuries old, and not so easily replaced."

It was only an hour later that he came back with news that fewer than two hundred European knights were left alive. "And King Guy?" I asked.

"He still fights."

"Not for much longer. Stay here with me until we hear of his surrender." We took a small meal in my tent and spoke of various things. I waited for Xenophon to ask me how the world had changed since his day, and what had become of his great civilization. He would not, as if he feared the truth or already knew it.

At last a messenger interrupted us. "It is the king of the Franj," he announced. "He is here to plead for his life."

"Yes," I said. "Let's finish this." Xenophon and I stood up and went out. King Guy was not an impressive man. He was short in stature, his tunic in tatters, and his skin had been darkened by the smoke. He said nothing. "Do you wish to live?" I asked him.

"You are Saladin?" he asked.

"Yes."

"If you have any compassion, let my men have water."

"If you ask it." I gave the order and allowed King Guy to drink as well. While he gulped the water down, I studied him. "Now the Franj have no army," I said.

He looked up at me over the rim of the cup. "Are you going to kill me?"

"Are you fearful? It does not suit a great general to plead for his own life."

He shook his head. "Now that I'm no longer thirsty, I'm no longer afraid."

Xenophon laughed aloud. "Saladin, your enemies have no more wisdom than they have skill at arms."

I looked at King Guy. "I will allow you to live. Take your

surviving followers and go back to your European kingdom. It is time for me to reclaim what you have stolen." My men led the Franj king away and I never saw or spoke to him again.

That evening I celebrated with all my commanders, including Xenophon. It was my greatest success, but I knew this war would go on. As I had said, there were other enemy armies and the Europeans had more suitable generals. When I finally sought my bed, I did not know that it was at once the most glorious and most terrible night of my life.

I woke before sunrise, not in my tent but beneath the stars. I got to my feet, confused, wondering how I had come here. Unlike my uncle, Shirkuh the Lion, I did not make a practice of getting drunk with my soldiers, nor did I feel drugged. I looked around and saw other men, asleep on the ground wrapped in blankets and cloaks. "Guards!" I called, but only one man raised his head. It was Xenophon.

"You must rest, noble sir," he said. "There will be more fighting in the morning."

"What . . . where are we? This isn't Tiberias."

"No, we are at Cunaxa, near Babylon. Now *you* are the one in the wrong time."

"Ah," I said. I did not need to ask how I came there. Xenophon wouldn't know the answer, either. Just as he had accepted his translation to my world, I accepted my journey to his. There are many strange and wonderful things under the sun, and God arranges them as he will whether we understand or not.

Xenophon laid his head upon the ground once more. "If you lead the Ten Thousand to victory tomorrow, perhaps we will finally depart this place, each to his own home and time."

"I must lead the Ten Thousand?" I confess that I did not welcome that task. These were not my troops, this was not my cause, and I knew nothing of the enemy or the place where we would do battle.

"It's our only hope," Xenophon said. "When we followed our own leaders, we were doomed to defeat."

"But—"

"Go back to sleep," he said. I took his advice and went back to sleep.

When the time came, Xenophon led me to a high ridge where I could watch the battle unfold. "Our hoplites," he said, pointing, "and the peltasts. Then on either side, units of our prince's men. Across the field are the chariots of the Great King, arrayed in front."

"Scythed chariots, a clever device," I said.

Xenophon shrugged. "The regular cavalry hates them. They cause more panic than actual injury. It's just another factor the field general—you, I mean—must keep in mind."

I took a deep breath, held it, and let it out slowly. "I thank God that warfare didn't change beyond recognition in the fifteen centuries between our lives."

Xenophon gave his customary shrug. "You developed better materials, but the basic happenings hand-to-hand stayed familiar."

I looked at a small map of the battlefield on a table nearby. "Cyrus, your prince, put you in the middle to face the Great King's line."

"Yes, we were clearly the best fighters."

"Good or bad, the result is the same."

Xenophon was puzzled. "What do you mean? We were the supreme warriors anywhere on that ground that day. We could have faced any army in the world."

I spread my hand and gave him a small smile. "This is exactly why I was made to study with my uncle, Shirkuh. I still see every detail of that first battle, when he had me retreat to trap Shawar's men."

"We did not retreat. We advanced. We cut our way through everything the Great King threw at us!"

I patted the air impatiently. "Yes, yes. Sometimes a badly timed advance is as ruinous as a backward flight in full panic. In both cases, the soldiers leave the battlefield. You are proud, because you left in pursuit of a defeated foe, eager to inflict even worse punishment. Your place, my friend, was not halfway across the countryside chasing after the enemy's gold and women. Your place was where Cyrus, your prince, expected you to be. Where your brothers-in-arms expected you to be."

Xenophon was quiet for a time. "No one has ever found fault with us before. We were always the champions who had been let down by the other units, and by the prince himself. Maybe my comrades never think of it, but I know we should not have followed the Persians. We neutralized our own force running after baubles."

I put on a grim expression and looked deeply into his eyes. "Yes, my friend. That is what you must know before today's battle. I will control the entire army, but you must keep your Greek friends in check. If we both succeed, Cunaxa may have a different ending."

Xenophon gave me one of his rare smiles, then hurried off to give the revised plans to his captains. I was alone. Actually, I had little to do that day, because the fate of the rest of Prince Cyrus' forces was still under his control alone. What I had done was to keep his best bodyguard from leaving his side at the critical moment. As soon as I realized that I would be only a spectator at this historic conflict, the terror grew in me until I nearly screamed. It is always so much simpler to be part of the fight, to be the one to decide to fight longer or to lay down one's arms. Everyone at Cunaxa would be asking themselves if they would live or die before sundown. Only I was uninvolved, and above me God, who knew the results already.

I did not write about Cunaxa in my memoirs, as I described my other battles. After all, this second Cunaxa did not truly exist. It belonged to another world, some earth that God created for the heroes' reward, perhaps their paradise. It is beyond me to speculate on the motives of God, and I will stop here. I will say only that this time, the Rum mercenaries did not run from the field, greedily chasing the vanquished Persians. They stayed in place, remembering their discipline, and they defended their prince, so Cyrus did not die this time. It seemed to me that when night fell and the armies took different roads north and south, Xenophon's army had taken a slight defeat. They had not overthrown the Great King of Persia, but they had served notice that Cyrus and his obstinate, determined, superior allies would be back soon and the war between the feuding brothers might stretch on for years—or until the Greek mercenaries began to long too much for their own farms and wives.

Xenophon met me one last time at a crossroad near Babylon. With him was a tall, fierce warrior also in the infantry uniform of the Rum. "Be well, my friend," I said, "wherever your destination."

Xenophon laughed. "At the moment, I don't know where that is, but isn't that the soldier's life?"

The tall stranger turned to me. "You did well, Syrian," he said. He was awful to look at and awful to hear.

Xenophon introduced us. "It is not given to many men to meet the god of war himself. Saladin, you are being given a great honor!"

The bearded giant growled. "I am Ares, God of War. Kneel to me, man. I have watched your actions with special interest these last few days."

I looked up into his face and smiled. "There is no god but God," I said simply.

Ares' face darkened and he shouted at me. "I have done terrible, ghastly things to you puny men for insulting me!"

"God is alone, sufficient." I did not feel the slightest fear of this phantom Rum deity.

Ares raged on. "Do you think it was your god who brought you here, who sent this other man to your day? Do you not believe the witness of your own eyes? Are you as foolish as all that?"

I gathered my few things and began walking away. My heart was calm. I recited a few verses from the book and soon the shouting behind me died away. Soon the road I walked became more familiar, and I found my tent and rested myself upon it. I fell asleep.

In the morning, it was all as I had told you. I was not at Cunaxa nor with my troops, but in my capital city of Damascus, now an old, dying man with not enough memories. I talked a little about what had happened, how a few days and nights had lasted many years that I do not remember. That is when my doctors agreed that my sickness had driven me out of my head. I have spoken little since. I am preparing myself to die, to go to the true next world, to meet my God if he permits it, and also, if he permits it, to ask some questions. Now that Xenophon's army won their battle, instead of losing it as history teaches, how is our world different? I don't have time to learn the truth. What more did I do in those missing years after Cunaxa? Did I ever open the city of Jerusalem? Who wil rule after me, and have I prepared him? I am so weary now, none of those problems matter any more.

It is time at last. Goodbye to a good world and a good life. I take refuge with the Lord of the Worlds.

AN APPEAL TO ADOLF

Ian Watson

In this story, Ian Watson gives us a glimpse into a world where heavier-than-air flight is impossible and aircraft have never been built, but in which Adolf Hitler still dreams of conquering England. Ian Watson earned a first-class honors degree in English literature and a research degree in English and French nineteenth-century literature from Oxford University. He has been a lecturer at universities in Tanzania and Japan and now lives in a small rural English village sixty miles north of London. Among his many novels are *The Embedding*, which won the Prix Apollo in France, and *The Jonah Kit*, which was honored with the British Science Fiction Association Award and the Orbit Award. His novels have been translated into fourteen languages and his widely anthologized short stories have included finalists for the Nebula and Hugo Awards. From 1990 to 1991, he worked with director Stanley Kubrick on story development for the motion picture *A.I. Artificial Intelligence* (directed by

Steven Spielberg after Kubrick's death), for which
Watson received credit for screen story; Watson's
memoir of his experiences with Kubrick was published in *Playboy*. Recent publications include his
ninth short fiction collection, *The Great Escape*, and a
science fiction novel, *Mockymen*, both from Golden
Gryphon Press.

Masses of dirty smoke pour from the many funnels of
Der Sieger—our conqueror—and drift westward
across the waters of the Atlantic. Will people far away in the
Caribbean smell our passage faintly and wonder whether
Africa itself is on fire? I fantasize—yet soon enough *England*
will be ablaze!

It goes without saying that *Der Sieger*'s funnels are spaced
so that their smoke should not blanket the fire control positions, but in the distant haze that we are creating it could be
difficult to spy the exact fall of our shot if any enemy vessels
appear on the vague westerly horizon. Accuracy at long
range is always such a problem. The colossal muzzle blast,
the vibration, the long barrels whipping. It is that haze into
which we must stare eagle-eyed, August Lenz and I, through
our big Zeiss binoculars.

What a sight it is when one of our superheavy guns test-
fires a supercharged shell. The gush of orange cordite flame
is a hot orgasm hanging in the air.

Petty by comparison is the smoke that issues from the
steam train that transports crew members and slave laborers
and stores and all sorts of equipment along the deck between
fore and aft, seven kilometers apart. The train-stops on board
the deck of *Der Sieger* are named after the city gates of Munich—Isartor, Sendlinger Tor, Karlstor—but also Hofbräuhaus, although the only beer served in the vicinity of
this, its marine namesake, is alcohol-free.

Very tasty, nevertheless, coming from the huge brewery in
Swakopmund. German desalination technology is easily able

to support brewing in dry South West Africa for hundreds of thousands of thirsty throats.

So huge is our ship it seems not like a ship so much as a coastline of continuous steel cliffs—an Iron Coast, perhaps, akin to an Ivory Coast—and a heavily industrialized coastline at that, chimneys venting as far as the eye can see. What a demonstration of German might. Even in moderate storm the ocean scarcely makes us tremble. Today the gray waters swell gently like innumerable backs of whales.

"They say," murmurs August, my beloved Gustl, "that the Führer's real purpose is not so much to defeat England by a devastating blow—England's already starving—but to capture Ludwig Wittgenstein in Cambridge and hang him by piano wire so that he'll speak no more. That's why the Führer will board *Der Sieger* for the final assault, at risk to his own safety."

"What risk? Never mind our half-meter of armor plating, the Führer is always protected by destiny." I look around— just as a lookout should do! "Maybe even by magic? Who knows what rites the senior SS fellows get up to in Wewelsberg Castle?" Those blond butch black-clad SS boys, no, don't think of them. My Gustl's hair is chestnut and his eyes are hazel.

"But the guns of Dover . . ." He's sometimes a little timid, is Gustl. How ravishing he looks in his tropical uniform, the white cotton shirt with blue cuffs, the white bell-bottomed trousers. Any day now we'll be obliged to change into northerly uniform, quite horrid coarse trousers.

Let me reassure my Gustl.

"We'll knock out those guns from forty kilometers away. We'll have fifth columnists on land equipped with radios as spotters. Bound to have! The British won't even know where we are."

Hmm, even assisted by spotters we might bombard the whole of Dover and environs without a single shell actually hitting the guns themselves.

Gustl ventures to stroke my thigh, secure that no one can see more than our upper bodies here on our lookout turret high above the aft bridge platform, quite like one of the slim

fairy-tale towers of our Führer's beloved Neuschwanstein
Castle.

"Dietl, my darling man . . ."

Even alone together up here, skirted by armor and with
armor overhead, Gustl and I need to be very careful. The
love of a man for a man is forbidden love! Such feelings
must be sublimated into comradeship, solidarity of soldiers
or seamen, so says the Party. Or woe betide. So many men
who experience uranian feelings have been castrated or have
disappeared. Instead, emulate our Führer! He's widely ru-
moured to be denying himself consummation with Eva
Braun until his mission is totally accomplished. He must
concentrate all his energies upon the guidance of Germany.

When the war is won, when all of Europe from England to
the Urals is a cleansed Greater Fatherland, will Gustl and I
ever be able to go to a bathhouse openly together? And
where would such a bathhouse be?

Only in sultry Angola or the Congo perhaps, where offi-
cials turn a blind eye or are of our own inclination. Oh the
joys that Gustl and I experienced in the tropics during shore
leaves while training to crew the vastest battleship ever!

A far cry from the Naval Academy in stern Prussian Potsdam. In one particular bathhouse in Luanda—oh the black
bucks who were the attendants!—I heard it asserted by an
impeccable eye witness that in Weimar and Bayreuth estab-
lishments survive, catering for uranians who are high enough
up in the Party hierarchy to be exempt from the harsh anti-
uranian laws. How can something which Gustl and I do together in privacy for our delight whenever we get a chance
be punished, yet the selfsame be permitted for those in
power? How can the Führer in his wisdom overlook this injustice? Maybe that magician and king of men does not know
about it. Great rulers sometimes must rely on self-interested
advisors. Those people do their jobs splendidly and cleverly,
yet they also foster their own desires and ambitions.

If only someone would tell the Führer about this
hypocrisy. What is permitted for some should be available to
all, as used to be the case. Or to nobody! I prefer *all*. No,

what am I talking about! A lot of men, probably most, sincerely enjoy women. How else could our race propagate? Maybe the real intention behind the anti-uranian laws is to encourage population growth. We have lost many men in gaining our victories. Empty spaces on the map must fill up with German and Nordic population. The Führer is wise.

It's highly likely that England remains in utter ignorance of these victory weapons of ours—our own seven-kilometer-long battleship and its four- and five-kilometer-long companions accompanying us both ahead and astern like great lengthy floating Gothic castles.

Had we built such vast vessels elsewhere than in tropical Africa, word would have leaked out. In Angola we were safe from scrutiny. Neither the millions of black slave laborers, nor the hundreds of thousands of Jewish artisans whom we relocated there as a merciful alternative to extermination, had any means of contact with the rest of the world.

Annexation of Belgium during the World War, the first one, gave us that ridiculous little country's huge Congo colony, so therefore during the years of battleship building the closest place from which hostile spy balloons could be launched—at great risk—was Brazzaville. Or else from out in the Atlantic, but our U-boats cruised the waters off equatorial and southwest Africa like sharks.

Unobserved by our enemies, that genius Albert Speer was able to excavate his ten-kilometer dry docks running inland from mighty gates that held back the sea, and to dredge trenches in the sea floor so that our mammoth vessels could launch straight into deep water. For decades battleships had become steadily bigger, evolving rather like Brontosaurus. The ships of our secret fleet are of ultimate size. The world will see none greater.

Gustl points. "What's that?"
I train my binoculars.
"An albatross."
Biggest of birds, gliding through the air on wings that

seem motionless, like—like something that does not exist, something impossible, yet which we must watch out for nonetheless.

I don't quite understand why. If, given all the science and technology of our Reich, a flying machine with fixed wings cannot be made, then how can the Americans, ruled by Jews, succeed? Does this imply a lurking fear that Jews, and the hotchpotch of people whom they manipulate on the other side of the Atlantic, might be more ingenious than Germans?

Yet suppose the albatross to be a hundred times as large— or bigger, bigger! Suppose it to be made of wood or aluminum, fueled by something like kerosene, able to fly *hundreds of kilometers*. Imagine it able to carry torpedoes to launch from the air against ships.

Visualise a hundred such machines attacking *Der Sieger*. Despite the protection of our waterline coal bunkers and our bulging belt of inclined underwater armor, could enough harm be caused for us to wallow and break our back? Can many mosquito bites cripple an elephant?

I did try to pay attention during our instruction session, which touched on the impossibility of fixed-wing flight. Trouble was, I was feeling so horny for my Gustl, seated next to me. Just a handspan away. Might as well have been on the far side of the world. Didn't dare touch him, not even seemingly by accident. Too many upright Prussians in the room.

The instructor's wire-rimmed glasses made him resemble an owl as he hooted on about the way that air flows, and about pressure, was it pressure? And about some Swiss scientist years ago, Berne something or other—Berne's in Switzerland, which is how I half remember the name. Oh yes, and about the death of one of those American brothers. Tried every shape of wing, the brothers did. Trial and error— and error after error. Eventually they constructed wings that would flap like a bird's and one of the brothers did get airborne at last, only to crash and be killed. Still, we must watch out for that mythical flying machine in case somewhere in the great plains or deserts those Jew-Americans established an enormous secret project and have recently succeeded.

I so yearn to unbutton Gustl and cup his balls and cock in my hand and squeeze ever so gently. Need to clutch my binoculars one-handed. They're rather heavy. Can't just let them dangle round my neck by their strap while on watch. Regulations; must hold them all the time alertly. Shall I, shan't I? Rebuttoning quickly with one hand is quite an art.

Softly I whistle our song, Wagner's *Du bist der Lenz,* which Sieglinde sings to her Siegfried. You are the Springtime for which I longed in the frosty Winter season. Your first glance set me on fire et cetera et cetera. Sieg for victory. Sieg Heil.

I first met my Gustl at the Jena Conservatoire where I studied the reedy, plaintive oboe, and he the bright, piercing piccolo. Before long we were blissfully playing one another's instruments, in a manner of speaking. How happy we were in that attic room we shared in Zeitzerstrasse. Impending mobilization put paid to our musical studies—together, we volunteered for naval service. The navy would save us from soggy trenches, or, as it turned out, heroic but brutal dashes across vast landscapes filled with death.

I love my Gustl but, like so many millions of men and women, I adore my Führer—in an entirely different manner, of course! I have only seen him once in the flesh, when he drove from Berlin behind the wheel of his supercharged Mercedes to deliver a speech in Potsdam. His voice was so vibrant. His eyes shone. His face glowed. There was such charm in his every gesture, and oh the pure force of his will! On that day he was Siegfried and Parsifal.

Magical, truly magical. Yes, *literally* so. We all knew it. Who could deny it?

When the Führer spoke, it was as if words spoke through him spontaneously, his not the choosing. His words issued from out of the Aryan over-mind, a primeval heritage which all we Germans share, unifying us fervently, empowering us to feats of labour and valor.

Shall I compare the Führer to the conductor of an orchestra, whose gestures conjure from a host of players a thundering, unified symphony? Actually, delicious thought, the Führer was once a choirboy, although hymn-singing wasn't the only source of his vocal force. Not a conductor, no—he is more like an oracle whose statements become reality.

How else, indeed, could he have come to power than through a kind of practical magic? Think back . . .

The bloody muddy stalemate in the trenches of northern France had to end for the sake of all concerned, and the armistice did leave the fatherland in ownership of the Congo with all its riches, so despite our losses we could hold our heads as high as the British or French. The Trotskyist takeover of Russia caused the fomenting of revolution anywhere and everywhere and enough German Marxists were eager to oblige, so the Kaiser was assassinated. The new republic might easily have weathered all this, had not our future Führer begun to preach his crusade against the Jews. Jew Marx, Jew Trotsky, Jew America: behold the pattern. *Deutschland erwache!* Our German racial soul awoke. And spoke through him. The people heard and surrendered their petty individualities in magical rapport, for our Führer is at once *nobody* yet also *everybody*.

How odd to think of such a towering figure as being "nobody!" Yet consider Tristan and Isolde singing together, *Selbst dann bin ich die Welt.* Then I myself am the world! How oceanic the love between those two, how transcendent of the mere self. Our Führer transcends ordinary existence.

What of Gustl and me in this regard?

On the occasions when we're able to be together, naked unto one another for long enough, flesh and soul certainly both play their role. Gustl is the world to me, I to him. Curse the anti-uranian laws!

I think of Gustl's cock erect, my lips slipping over it, to

and fro. Kissing him intimately is such a joy. When his cock swells before he comes, oh moment of ecstasy.

Dead of exhaustion and heat, bodies of black stokers are thrown overboard every day. Did I mention sharks? Enough sharks may attend us to form a torpedo shield. Those sharks may accompany us out of the tropics as far northward as France and England. Considering how hot equatorial Africa is, you'd suppose that the black man could tolerate the heat of the boiler rooms better than us Europeans. Aboard a vessel accommodating a crew of fifteen thousand souls and twenty thousand non-souls, a certain number of people are bound to die from natural causes. By non-souls I mean the blacks and the smaller complement of artisan Jew slaves, them not being part of the Aryan soul. Everyone who was in the Hitler Youth knows how to smile death in the face. Our Führer aimed to forge hard boys, as hard as Krupp Steel. When I hear the phrase "hard boys" I can't help thinking of a different meaning.

Along with a little crowd of other ratings, in our free time Gustl and I take a hike to the Hofbräuhaus amidships. He and I don't wish to be conspicuous by strolling together, nor one of us trailing after the other—that could look even odder. This constrains any genuine conversation we might have. We must pretend to be merely fellow comrades in arms. I'm not sure whether this sort of neutral proximity to Gustl is pleasant and teasing—oh if only you knew our secret!—or deeply frustrating.

The steam train is reserved for ship's business, but hiking is positively encouraged as one way of keeping fit. Certainly we have enough deck space, two hours at brisk pace from bows to stern and back. Our Führer loves to hike when time allows. Visualize him in his Bavarian mountain dress, the lederhosen and white linen shirt, the pale blue linen jacket with staghorn buttons. Quite fetching.

"Best foot forward, Schmidt!" Hoffmann says to me. "Eins, zwei—" —and down the hatch, the Hofbräuhaus drinking song. "What a shame there aren't any busty lusty *barmaids,* eh?" Hoffmann is a short but burly chap with a birthmark like a thumbprint of dark blood on his brow.

Only black barmen send the foaming stone steins sliding along the steel counters into the waiting hands of other Africans to carry to the tables. No black can carry as many steins in each hand as your average blonde pigtailed Munich barmaid, not my type of person at all. Songs arise in the huge dim drinking hall adorned by a giant framed photograph of our Führer, kiss-curl upon his forehead, wearing his Iron Cross and Wound Badge. It must be some years since that photo was taken. In it our leader possesses an almost erotic charisma. Of course he is pure male, yet celibate even with Fräulein Braun, hence the adoration of the ladies of Germany. In their minds any of them might have him (or rather, he them) at least for one night so that they will conceive a superman. The same can happen in the love camps, so in a sense those besotted women are succeeding by proxy.

"How about you then, Lenz?" asks skinny, flaxen-haired Scharffenstein. "Got a girl back home, good-looking fellow like you?"

Danger, danger.

"Oh," says my Gustl, "it would be unfair. All of us have been away for three years now. Besides," with a wink, "she might be unfaithful or become fat in my absence due to lack of exercise!"

Guffaws all round, including from me.

"I have a girl in Hamburg," Hoffmann says. "She's a cracker. If she's unfaithful I'll kill her."

"Didn't you use the Jew brothel in Luanda?" Gustl asks innocently. Risky in my opinion. Still, we have to say something.

"That's different. A man must keep his juices flowing or else they sour. Never saw you there myself. Did you use the *black* brothel, then?"

Gustl shrugs judiciously. "The Jew brothel's a big place."

"You're telling me."

"I propose a toast," I declare. "To the downfall of England and to brothels full of Englishwomen."

"*Eh?*"

"Those of the wrong racial categories," I hasten to add. "There'll be plenty."

What, to *pollute* ourselves with? I must extricate myself from this topic.

Given the numbers of the crew, that of a medium-size town, there must be other uranians on this ship. I suspect who some of those are, yet it would be folly to confide in anyone in the hope that somewhere aboard this enormous vessel there exists a sanctuary to which Gustl and I can safely resort. The navy is a more tolerant environment than the Fatherland in some respects, but there are limits! Let me think instead about Ludwig Wittgenstein, our Führer's *bête noire*.

Transmitted from Rhodesia, no doubt weeks or months after each had been put on to aluminum discs lacquered with cellulose nitrate in London, in Angola we could hear the philosopher's broadcasts delivered in his upper class Viennese accent. We Germans have the defector William Joyce talking to the British from Radio Hamburg to demoralise them; the British have Wittgenstein.

To be caught listening to Wittgenstein on your Volksradio is a bad idea, but the punishment—at least in the navy—is surprisingly light: a docking of pay, a leave canceled, some dirty extra duty. I presume it's a whole lot tougher for land-lubbers whom the Gestapo catch red-handed, or red-eared. The navy protects its own and Naval Intelligence does not seem unduly bothered, no doubt because talks about the sanctity of language are over the heads of the vast majority of people.

Not everyone aboard is as down to earth as a Hoffmann or a Scharffenstein. Gustl and I don't exactly count ourselves as high-powered intellectuals. I mean, we're educated, but we're artists. Or we used to be. However, we do know a couple of chaps whom you might call intellectuals, if this wasn't a dirty word. Not uranian chaps, I hasten to add, but never mind.

Jahn and Hager. That's Rudolf Jahn and Gottfried Hager, both of them assigned to the nearest of the great quadruple gun turrets. Hager is very fond of music, which is how we got talking in the mess amidst the bustle of so many men eating. The tonnage of pigs consumed aboard *Der Sieger* every single day!

Hager asked me, "Do you actually *hear* the music in your head the way Beethoven did?" His is a face made for wistfulness, his close-set eyes peering out past a long sharp nose in a kind of diffident expectation of something good perhaps occurring, but probably not.

I was about to nod when in the nick of time I made the connection between Beethoven and deafness.

Instead I frowned. "Not exactly. Beethoven was special."

Hager sighed. "Aah, so not even most musicians . . . The noise of the guns, you see . . ."

Hager was worried about being permanently deafened when the occasional test firing became the real thing, repeated over and over again. My fib seemed to console him somewhat. If he lost his hearing, the knowledge that professional musicians who were similarly deafened could continue to enjoy music would be a torment.

One thing led to another, and presently he and Jahn and the two of us were confidants, at least as regards certain topics such as Wittgenstein.

Gottfried and Rudolf are both philosophers, or had been so before the war. Both of them taught in universities. Taught a lot of Nietzsche and Schopenhauer, needless to say. The Will to Power. The World as Will and Idea. And Plato too, the Führer's top favorite. They both listen to Wittgenstein on their Volksradio because, as Rudolf explained one day, Wittgenstein is an heir to Schopenhauer as surely as our Führer is.

Physically I don't fancy the melancholy Gottfried, nor Rudolf who has pockmarks all over a moon face and very wispy hair. Yet their minds seem to mesh with mine and with

Gustl's. Admittedly more so with each other—at times Gottfried and Rudolf seem to be talking to one another in code,
where a word does not mean what you would ordinarily take
it to mean! Acquaintance with those two serves as a useful
protective cover for Gustl and me, because Gottfried and
Rudolf aren't in the least good-looking and seem to have no
interest in sex. They're definitely monkish, an austere trait
that Wittgenstein shares. Also our Führer, come to think of it,
him being vegetarian and teetotal, but so effervescent.

Oh god, I'm visualising the beautiful white cheeks of
Gustl's bum and that puckery little mouth between the
cheeks which can swallow my cock so sweetly, so grip-
pingly. Think philosophy!

"Schopenhauer's central idea," I recall Rudolf telling us,
"is that we share a common mind. A person of will power,
who can suspend thought and who can submerge his individ-
uality, gains access to the common mind and he can influence everyone in word and thought. The Führer knows
Schopenhauer by heart and he can do exactly what I just said
in a very practical way in his speeches—which is how he
works his magic. *Quite literally*, magic. That's how magic
works: it bespeaks and alters reality."

Wittgenstein himself wrote a book of spells called the
Tractatus Logico-Philosophicus, which our two friends had
read before all copies of the academic periodical which published it were consigned to bonfires, at least in the Fatherland
and conquered territories.

"The book is full of logical propositions designed to grasp
higher truth. Words speak through you, you don't originate
them, the self is an illusion, that sort of thing."

When Wittgenstein quotes from himself in his broadcasts,
what an incantatory power there is.

Needless to say, the number of copies of the *Tractatus* that
ever saw print was utterly dwarfed by the popularity of *Mein
Kampf*.

I remember one exquisite time when Gustl and I each
teased one another's cock for five or ten minutes by plucking
the throbbing head two-fingered like a violinist twanging a

string, *pizzicato*, until the yearning for the firm and constant pressure of the mouth between the cheeks became unbelievably urgent, and meanwhile a forefinger, on which we could scarcely concentrate, and then two fingers slid up and down within that mouth, opening it. Aah.

The amazing thing is that the Führer and Wittgenstein, the man of the people and the rich Jew, both attended school together in Linz. Undoubtedly they read Schopenhauer together, Wittgenstein perhaps even *leading* the Führer (if such a thing can be conceived) in their mutual investigations, for Wittgenstein was two years senior. In time this led to some sort of contretemps, whereupon the Führer awakened to the evil of the Jewish sub-race. That's one reason why the first speech our Führer made after German troops marched into Austria was in Linz.

"You international seeker after truth," our Führer sneered, "Ludwig Wittgenstein, Jew-boy with a truss—if only you could be here today to see my victory!" By then Wittgenstein had long been an exile in England. Yes, those were the exact words that issued from the Führer's mouth, striking home like a lance. Our Führer must have spied Wittgenstein's truss when the schoolboys undressed for sport or hygiene. That was the reality inside the trousers.

Inside of Gustl's trousers, on the other hand . . . no, no, no, no.

That's quite a famous speech. It wasn't until after the war started that Wittgenstein began broadcasting, ever so saintly in his precise, logical way, scorning to allude to such things as trusses or what they held. The Führer, clever man, manipulates reality while his ex-school companion operates on a more abstract plane, criticising our Führer and Göbbels for betraying the meanings of words. I know who will win. The Führer. That's because he seeks power, whereas Wittgenstein seeks what you might call illumination. Maybe Wittgenstein will be burned alive rather than hung from piano wire.

"There's a battle being fought for the common Aryan mind," Rudolf also said. "Wittgenstein comes over as a Magus, but the SS boys at Wewelsberg Castle hold séances to stymie him, and any speech of the Führer's blows all those logical propositions away like fluff."

I shrugged. "I'm not so sure about *that*. Or why does the Führer want to nail Wittgenstein so much?"

Our vast ship surges onward, and we do change our trousers (and other garments) for northerly attire. Our super-heavy guns elevate to 30 degrees and swivel like athletes limbering up and stretching their muscles. Smoke pours due southward now, for the wind has shifted. Towards the stern sometimes it's hard to see anything very clearly. Certainly we spy no big artificial albatrosses of Jew-American manufacture, which of course do not and cannot exist. On account of the smoke Gustl and I are constantly clearing our throats and our eyes water a bit. The steam train puffs its way to and fro along the deck in preparation for when it will carry invasion troops. Of course tanks and trucks and motor bikes will also race along the broad deck.

By now surely everyone aboard—with the possible exception of the blacks and the Jewish slave workers—understands the details of Operation Sea Bridge. It is a plan of staggering genius, typical of the Führer's vision.

An ordinary sea-borne invasion by innumerable escorted troop carriers, vulnerable to vagueries of weather and requiring multiple landing sites, could result in confusion and losses. But to bridge the Straits of Dover with our battleships several kilometers long, linked together by ingenious mini-bridges: that is to thrust a permanent bridgehead right into England through which men and equipment will pour unstoppably! At the same time our guns will be shelling the towns of Kent and even the East End of London! Whatever little British battleships try to thwart us will simply be swept aside or sunk by our U-boats.

Such surprise there will be on those supposedly unflappable English faces with their stiff upper lips.

How long will *Der Sieger* remain as the foremost part of this bridge? Several months? At some stage surely we must be freed to resume our role as a mobile vessel. Bombarding New York, who knows?

During those several months Gustl and I hope to enjoy shore leaves in newly conquered southeastern England, where our opportunities to enjoy one another may be many and varied. Abandoned barns in balmy weather, deserted or commandeered hotels . . .

We must be wary of partisans! It may take a while for vengeance executions to deter English resistance. How I yearn for idyllic pleasures in the region behind the war front, oh yes why not a hay loft, soft if perhaps tickly bedding for our naked bodies entwined together, both of our manhoods rampant, my tongue in Gustl's mouth then his in mine, shafts of sun shining in through cracks and through a few bullet holes to illuminate the motes of dust which our mutual ecstasy raises like so many tiny stars. To gaze into his hazel eyes, my body against his body, to stroke his chestnut hair. I love him so much that I ache with yearning even when I'm with him. Gustl, du bist der Lenz, du bist der Lenz.

The wind from the north persists and many complain about the smoke. Finally the order comes to switch around those of us who are most exposed, such as lookouts, gun crews, and bridge officers, from the stern to the bows, to be replaced by our counterparts. Gustl and I board the steam train, along with Rudolf and Gottfried and other ratings and officers, all with our kit, and we travel those seven kilometers forward in style.

Quite a holiday mood—until the awful thought strikes me that Gustl and I might be assigned to different duty rosters, or even worse, to different lookout turrets towards the front of the boat. This tormenting notion brings a cascade of other might-be's crowding in its wake. The frustrations we suffer at present are as nothing compared to those we might endure if the requirements of war or even an error of paperwork ever separates us! We have been so lucky so far, so very lucky. I cannot bear to be separated from Gustl.

*   *   *

My fears were pointless. Here we both are together, scanning sky and sea. The air is considerably cleaner and fresher, not merely because we are up front. Our great battleships no longer steam in line astern but are flanking one another, each a couple of kilometers apart, an early redeployment. Simply to copy with the smoke problem, or for tactical reasons? I am not privy to Fleet Admiral Dönitz's mind.

What a spectacle the *Lohengrin* is off to the west, five kilometers of armored battleship the length of an entire island. An island five kilometers long, very much longer than it is wide, rather like Wangerooge in the East Frisians but more vertical. Oh yes, an island of steel cleaves the water, smoke streaming from all its funnels. Whales would be minnows around its sides. Gulls fly through the air like white confetti.

Yesterday evening, Gustl and I explored below decks and discovered an unlocked storeroom piled high with greatcoats.

"What if we're discovered—?"

"Who needs greatcoats yet?"

What we did next I shall not describe, save to say that the brass buttons of a greatcoat refolded inside-out feel a bit harder than the buttons on a mattress which stop the springs from poking you. When you're so hard yourself, who cares about a few buttons? Afterwards you're too softly melted to bother.

The sea is flat, and here we are at last in the Channel, five kilometers offshore from bombarded, blazing Dover. Our bows are five kilometers from shore, our stern perhaps eight kilometers. The difference is increasing as we swing about to become the spearhead of invasion.

Our great guns roar. Oh me of little faith. The castle of Dover is in ruins. The White Cliffs themselves are crumbling and collapsing as if to form a ramp for our Panzer tanks to ascend into the English countryside—to the extent that we can make out such details clearly. A couple of hours ago the sky was blue but now smoke is everywhere.

As we swing, *Der Sieger* and her sister ships are in a sense

damming these straits. We are giant lock gates. Water will
continue to flow underneath us, but the current from the
northeast pushes against us. Propellers recessed into our hull
along the relevant side of our mighty vessel counteract this.
We repel the very sea like Moses coming out of Egypt, sending the water back upon itself, higher on one side than on the
other. This causes *Der Sieger* to list by a few degrees, not
enough to cause any problem for our steam train.

Moses was a Jew, of course. That's the trouble with the
Bible, altogether too many *Juden*, an infestation of them. Including Jesus, I suppose. Wagner provides a perfectly ade-
quate substitute for Christianity. True, Parsifal is searching
for the Holy Grail, the blood-cup of Jesus. Parsifal is a holy
fool. Personally I think Jesus was an Aryan, brought from
India to Palestine as a baby by the three Wise Men to place
him as near to Europe as they could reach. With their gold
and frankincense the Wise Men bribed the parents of Jesus to
accept a changeling.

Wie doof to think about such matters at such a moment!
How stupid, as kids will say. We are bombarding Doofer.
How dumb of the English to think they could defy us.

The stability of the steam train—and of the trains on *Lohengrin* and the other battleships that will soon form the
bridge across the Channel—is important because I presume
that the Führer will arrive by train. Unless . . . he drives, or is
driven, along the decks in an armored car. Or even in his supercharged Mercedes, swastika flags fluttering! What a wonderful sight that would be, inspiring utter confidence.

Orgasms of orange cordite-flame erupt. The thunder is
worthy of *Götterdämmerung*. Through our excellent binoculars, and through rifts in the smoke, Gustl and I watch bits of
England flying into the air.

Our bows are rammed into the very port of Dover in
flames. One of the harbor piers is now much shorter than it
was. Buoyed by floatation bags, the great connecting ramp is
rolling ashore. Sheer firepower of heavy machine guns,
rocket launchers, and tracer artillery has virtually annihilated

local resistance. Shells from elevated superguns to our rear soar high overhead so fast that you can scarcely follow them for more than a second or so.

Late in the day the English sent big balloons to try to bomb us. Bags of flames is what those balloons soon became. Evening draws nigh and our watch is nearly over. How will Gustl and I get to sleep amidst the extreme noise and excitement? By prior recourse to the storeroom of greatcoats? Ach, too many men are bustling about by now, here, there, everywhere.

Overnight, Waffen-SS heroes have seized the main road that rises from Dover. With dawn come the Panzers and the troop carriers of the army and of the Waffen-SS, rumbling along the deck and crossing the ramp. English reinforcements will be on their way but our superior tanks will cut through those like a knife through butter. Or perhaps through cheese. Cheese is stiffer than butter, though of course in certain situations greasy butter does have its virtues. The English protected many other potential landing sites, obstacles and barbed wire along miles of beaches yet they could never have expected a frontal assault of such a kind or magnitude on this port. A massive bridge coming into existence within a matter of hours! When they first spied our secret weapons looming, extending for kilometer after kilometer across the sea, how they must have wet themselves.

Another day, and our Kentish bridgehead is as secure as if it is part of the Fatherland. On our Volksradios we hear how Panzer divisions and motorized troops have reached Canterbury and Ashford. Resistance is fierce—give credit where credit is due—but basically futile and suicidal. A flotilla of smaller vessels constantly ferries equipment between Boulogne and Folkestone, while along the battleship-bridge pour whole armies as if it is an autobahn. I think no one who is not German remains alive in Dover itself.

The English Prime Minister Churchill has made a growling speech vowing to fight us in the streets of London and in the mountains of Wales and in the glens of Scotland, not realising what an admission of defeat such far-flung promises are. Elevated to their maximum, great guns are shelling London.

Wittgenstein, more sensitive to the nuances of language, has uttered certain propositions.

"The good or bad exercise of the will can only alter the limits of the world, not the facts. Nazism is not irrefutable, but is obviously nonsensical."

That's telling us, Ludwig! However, the Waffen-SS is not listening.

The Führer may be listening angrily. Nonsensical? Why, we are witnessing the beginning of the reign of a very different kind of world-view that has diverged utterly from both Christianity and rationalism. This will be the reign of superhuman Will, which you might perhaps call magical realism.

It is nonsensical that privileged uranians can enjoy themselves freely when Gustl and I can not.

Oh sacred hour: now that Dover is cleansed by fire, the Führer is coming, and yes he is coming by train, to the Isartor Station close by our turret.

Gustl has developed a terrible fit of the sneezes. I don't think he has a cold as such. I think his problem is the affinity between the nose and the penis. Don't we say, like the nose of a man, so is his dick? It's well known that certain smells excited our primitive ancestors sexually. I mean, what ape could get excited just by *looking* at another ape covered all over in hair? Consequently to think intensely and imaginatively about sex may in turn stimulate the nose to discharge itself, rather than the cock. Gustl has been thinking a lot about sex with me in that Kentish hayloft I promised him.

Chaperoned by naval officers, the Führer's security boys in their long black leather coats are swarming all over this part of the ship, and Gustl is ordered off duty. No one must sneeze anywhere near the Führer. Vegetarianism and clean living protect the Führer, but it's better to be safe than sorry.

For obvious reasons we lookouts have no real function at the moment—roll on our shore leave! I'm not likely to spy any sniper amongst the smoldering ruins. Even so, it would be bad practice to leave the forwardmost watchturret unmanned. Two of us aren't essential for the job, however, so I'm left on my own, after being frisked for any concealed weapon—better to be safe than. That blond security man's hand sliding up my inside leg . . . I thought determinedly of *Parsifal* and purity.

This is incredible. On my watch too.

Yet it figures, it figures. This is the highest, closest vantage point to look out from without actually going ashore and climbing uphill. Bound to be some unexploded stuff lying around in the smoking ruins.

At this very moment the Führer himself is ascending my watchturret—on his own, *selbst*. Guards follow, but he is the leader, what else should he be? He is a hero climbing the tower overlooking the conquered land.

Although obviously tired from sleepless nights and somewhat sallow, he beams almost boyishly at me. His eyes shine. His face glows. What a big fleshy nose he has. On his uniform, in honor of our achievement he wears the badge of the High Seas Fleet, a battleship steaming directly towards you, its guns abeam so that they show to better advantage, within a wreath of oak leaves crowned by an eagle.

"Dieter Schmidt," he says to me, as if he has known my name all along, rather than its being whispered in his ear just previously.

I could not draw myself more fully to attention.

"Jawohl, mein Führer."

"You are doing your duty to Germany, Dietl." Oh moment of sheer intimacy, the *du* and the Dietl, like a lover's caress. "You will be decorated."

With a somewhat womanly gesture he requests my Zeiss binoculars. Through them he stares up at the wreckage of Dover Castle.

To himself, he snarls, "Wittgenstein, you are not far."

And I am quite carried away. This is a moment given by
God.

"Mein Führer, rather than being decorated may I humbly
request that the anti-uranian laws be amended to allow uranians who prove their manliness by serving their Fatherland in
the armed forces—"

I get no further. Never have I seen or heard such a change
come over a human being. Words jabber out of the Führer in
a paroxysm, as if not uttered by himself voluntarily. How
balefully he turns upon me—and from the wild words and
from the rictus that distorts his features I understand instinctively and in appalled wonder that my Führer *is a uranian
just as I am* and he has ever been so, and of a sudden too I
understand the source of his loathing for Wittgenstein, because at school back in Linz once upon a time the Jew with a
truss must have squeezed the Führer's balls and he must have
had his cock up the Führer's bum—but no one must ever
know this, and therefore Wittgenstein must die. Already the
Führer is screaming for his guards, froth flecking from his
lips.

Thank God that my Gustl was taken off duty. Let them not
guess the truth about him. Gustl may cry himself to sleep to
have lost me yet dear God, let him not cry out for other reasons, in agony at sexual torture and castration if the navy
cannot protect him, as I doubt it can, for the navy cannot protect me.

I am gagged, and stripped to my underwear, and bound,
and greased. On the Führer's orders a great gun is already
loaded, perhaps even by Gottfried and Rudolf for all I know.
Into the muzzle I am lifted feet-first. The barrel is just big
enough to accommodate me. With a big mop normally used
for swabbing the decks I'm pushed down as far as possible.
This is an atrocity such as I never expected of my fellow
Germans.

The gun begins to elevate. Even greased, at twenty-five
degrees I do not slide any further. As I stare upward I can see
a star or a planet—it's as if I'm at the bottom of a very deep

well. The gun is swiveling. I know that it's being aimed at Cambridge.

Impossible for even a supercharged shell from a super-heavy gun to fly as far as there, but the intention is all-important, the vision that just conceivably I may hit Wittgenstein as he strolls in some college quadrangle.

Will any part of me survive these coming moments? My head perhaps, still conscious for a few seconds, speeding ahead of the orgasm of cordite?

"Our life has no end," proposes Wittgenstein, "in exactly the way in which our visual field has no limits." He means that we see nothing beyond our visual field, nor likewise do we experience anything beyond the end of our life.

"Death is not an event in life," he has said. "We do not experience death."

I sincerely hope not.

Oh what a cock-up.

Ich bin im Arsch!

Oh balls.

MARTYRS OF THE UPSHOT KNOTHOLE

James Morrow

Here is another story featuring Genghis Khan, and perhaps only James Morrow, whom Samuel R. Delany has described as a writer "attracted to large political and ethical questions, which he encounters with a robust feel for satire," could have given us this particular story, which manages to combine an actual (and famously bad) cinematic depiction of the life of Genghis Khan with one of the twentieth century's central moral dilemmas. James Morrow has won the World Fantasy Award twice, for his novels *Only Begotten Daughter* and *Towing Jehovah*; he has also been honored with two Nebula Awards, for his novella "City of Truth" and his short story "Bible Stories for Adults, No. 17: The Deluge." Among his other novels are *The Wine of Violence, The Continent of Lies, This Is the Way the World Ends, Blameless in Abaddon*, and *The Eternal Footman*. His short stories have appeared in *Amazing Stories, Synergy, The*

Magazine of Fantasy & Science Fiction, Full Spectrum, and in his collection *Bible Stories for Adults.* A new novel, *The Last Witchfinder,* will soon be published by Harcourt Brace.

I sit in the comfort of my easy chair, the cat on my lap, the world at my command. With my right index finger I press the button, and seconds later the hydrogen bomb explodes.

The videocassette in question is *Trinity and Beyond,* a documentary by Peter Kuran comprising two hours of restored footage shot in full color by the U.S. Air Force's 1352nd Motion Picture Squadron, "The Atomic Cinematographers." I am watching the detonation of February 28, 1954: Castle Bravo, fifteen megatons, in its day the largest atmospheric thermonuclear test ever seen on planet Earth.

Red as the sun, the implacable dome of gas and debris expands outward from ground zero, suggesting at first an apocalyptic plum pudding, then an immense Santiago pilgrim's hat. The blast front flattens concrete buildings, tears palm trees out by the roots, and draws a tidal wave from the Pacific. Now the filmmakers give us a half-dozen shots of the inevitable mushroom cloud. I gaze into the roiling crimson mass, reading the entrails of human ingenuity.

"You're free of cancer" and "You're the lover I've been looking for my whole life" are surely two of the most significant sentences a person will ever hear, and it so happened that both declarations came my way during the same week. An optimist at heart, I took each affirmation at face value, so naturally I was distressed when the speakers in question began backpedaling.

No sooner had my oncologist told me that the latest lab report indicated no malignant cells in my body, not one, than he hastened to add, "Of course, this doesn't mean you're rid of it forever."

"You think it will come back?" I asked.

"Hard to say."

"Could you hazard a guess?"

Dr. Pryce drew a silk handkerchief from his bleached lab coat and removed his bifocals. "Let me emphasize the positive." In a fit of absentmindedness, he repocketed the glasses. "For the moment you're definitely cured. But cancer has a will of its own."

In the case of the man who called me his ideal lover—Stuart Randolph, the semi-retired NYU film historian with whom I've shared a loft overlooking Washington Square for the past eighteen years—I logically expected that his subsequent remarks would concern the institution of marriage. But instead Stuart followed his declaration by arguing that there were two kinds of commitment in the world: the contrived commitment entailed in the matrimonial contract, and the genuine commitment that flowed from the sort of "perfect rapport and flawless communication" that characterized our relationship.

"If we enjoyed perfect rapport and flawless communication, we wouldn't be having this discussion," I said. "I want to get married, Stu."

"Really?" He frowned as if confronting a particularly egregious instance of postmodern film criticism. Stuart's an *auteurist*, not a deconstructionist.

"Really."

"You truly want to become my fourth wife?"

"As much as I want you to become my fifth husband."

"Why, dear?" he said. "Do you think we're living in sin? Senior citizens can't live in sin."

"*Imitation of Life* is a lousy movie, but I like it anyway," I said. "Marriage is a bourgeois convention, but I like it anyway."

"Should the cancer ever return, dearest Angela, you'll be glad you've got a committed lover by your side, as opposed to some sap who happens technically to be your husband."

Stuart was not normally capable of bringing romance and reason into such perfect alignment, but he'd just done so, and I had to admire his achievement.

"I cannot argue with your logic," I told him. And I couldn't.

All during my treatments, Stuart had been an absolute prince, driving me to the hospital a hundred times, holding my head as I threw up, praising the doctors when they did their jobs properly, yelling at them when they got haughty. "Checkmate."

"Love and marriage," he said. "They go together like a horse and aluminum siding."

Have no fear, reader. This is not a story about what I endured at the hands of Western medicine once its avatars learned I'd developed leukemia. It's not about radiation treatments, chemotherapy, violent nausea, suicidal depression, paralyzing fear, or nurses poking dozens of holes in my body. I have zero desire to relive those days, and I don't think you want to hear about them either, except to indulge in a variety of schadenfreude that is unworthy of you. My subject, rather, is the last performance ever given by an old colleague of mine, the biggest box-office star of all time, John Wayne—a performance that was never committed to celluloid but that leaves his Oscar-winning portrayal of Rooster Cogburn gagging in the dust.

It would be inaccurate to say that Duke and I hated each other. Yes, I detested the man—detested everything he stood for—but my loathing was incompletely requited, for at some perverse level he clearly relished my companionship. Our irreconcilable philosophies first emerged when we appeared together in the 1953 survival melodrama *Island in the Sky,* and ever since then our political clashes, too uncivilized to be called conversations or even debates, provided Duke with a caliber of stimulation he could obtain from no other liberal of his acquaintance. Throughout his career he routinely convinced the front office to offer me a marginal role in whatever John Wayne vehicle was on the drawing board, thereby guaranteeing that the two of us would briefly share the same sound stage or location set, and he could spend his lunch hours and coffee breaks reveling in the pleasurable rush he got from our battles over what had gone wrong with America.

As I write these words, it occurs to me that any self-respecting actress would have spurned this peculiar arrangement—a kind of love affair animated by neither love nor physical desire but rather by the male partner's passion for polemic. No public adulation or peer recognition could possibly accrue to the parts Duke picked for me. There is no Oscar for Best Performance by an Actress Portraying a Cipher. But while I am normally self-respecting, I have rarely achieved solvency, and thus over a span of sixteen years I periodically found myself abandoning my faltering Broadway career, flying to Hollywood, and accepting good money for reciting bad dialogue.

In 1954 I played a fading opera diva trapped aboard a crippled airliner in *The High and the Mighty*, which Bill Wellman directed with great flair. Next came my portrayal of Hunlun, mother of Genghis Khan, né Temujin, in *The Conqueror*, probably the least watchable of the films produced by that eccentric American stormtrooper and aviator, Howard Hughes. Subsequent to *The Conqueror* I essayed a middle-aged Comanche squaw in *The Searchers*, the picture on which Duke started referring to me, unaffectionately, as "Egghead." Then came my blind wife of a noble Texan in *The Alamo*, my over-the-hill snake charmer in *Circus World*, and my pacifist Navy nurse in *The Green Berets*. Finally, in *Chisum* of 1970, I was once again cast as Duke's mother, although my entire performance ended up in the trim bin.

It was Stuart who first connected the dots linking John Wayne, myself, and nearly a hundred other cancer victims in a fantastic matrix of Sophoclean terror and Kierkegaardian trembling. Six weeks after Dr. Pryce had labeled me cancer-free, Stuart was scanning the *New York Times* for March 15, 1975, when he happened upon two ostensibly unrelated facts: the Atomic Energy Commission was about to open its old nuclear-weapons proving ground in Nevada to the general public, and former screen goddess Susan Hayward had died the previous day from brain cancer. She was only fifty-six. Something started Stuart's mind working on all cylinders, and within twenty-four hours he'd made a Sherlock Holmesian deduction.

"*The Conqueror,*" he said. We were having morning tea in our breakfast nook, which is also our lunch nook and our dinner nook. "*The Conqueror*—that's *it!* You shot the thing in Yucca Flat, Nevada, right?"

"An experience I'd rather forget," I said.

"But you shot it in Yucca Flat, yes?"

"No, we shot it in southwest Utah, the Escalante Desert and environs—Bryce Canyon, Snow Canyon, Zion National Park . . ."

"Southwest Utah, close enough," said Stuart, shifting into lecture mode. "*The Conqueror,* 1956, Cinemascope, Technicolor, the second of Dick Powell's five lackluster attempts to become a major Hollywood director. In the early sixties, Powell dies of cancer. A decade or so later, you're diagnosed with leukemia. Somewhere in between, John Wayne has a cancerous lung removed, telling the press, 'I licked the Big C.' And now the female lead of *The Conqueror* is dead of a brain tumor."

The epic in question had Susan playing a fictitious Tartar princess named Bortai (loosely based on Genghis Khan's wife of the same name), daughter of the fictitious Tartar chief Kumlek (though the screenwriter was perhaps alluding to the real-life Naiman chief Kushlek), who slays Temujin's nonfictitious father, Yesukai, offscreen about fifteen years before the movie begins. "The curse of *The Conqueror,*" I muttered.

"Hell, there's no *curse* going on here, Angela." Stuart used a grapefruit spoon to retrieve his ginseng tea bag from the steaming water. "This is entirely rational. This is about gamma radiation."

According to the *Times,* he explained, the military had conducted eleven nuclear tests on the Nevada Proving Ground in the spring of 1953, an operation that bore the wonderfully surrealistic name Upshot Knothole. The gamma rays were gone now, and civilians would soon be permitted to visit the site, but during the Upshot Knothole era anyone straying into the vicinity would have received four hundred times the acceptable dose of radiation. The last detonation, called "Climax," had occurred on the fourth of June.

"And one year later, almost to the day, the *Conqueror* company arrives in the Escalante Desert and starts to work," I said, at once impressed by Stuart's detective work and frightened by its implications.

My lover exited the breakfast nook, removed the cat from our coffee-table atlas, and opened to a spread that displayed Utah and Nevada simultaneously. "You were maybe only a hundred and thirty miles from the epicenter. Eleven A-bombs, Angela. If the winds were blowing the wrong way . . ."

"Obviously they were," I said. "And the Atomic Energy Commission now expects *tourists* to show up?"

"Never underestimate the power of morbid curiosity."

A quick trip through the back issues of *Film Fan Almanac* was all Stuart needed to reinforce his theory with two additional casualties. Unable to cope with his cancer any longer, Pedro Armendariz, who played Temujin's "blood brother" Jamuga, had shot himself in the heart on June 18, 1963. Exactly eight years later—on June 18, 1971—cancer deprived the world of Thomas Gomez, who portrayed Wang Khan, the Mongol ruler whom Temujin seeks to usurp (thereby bestowing a throne on himself and a plot on the movie). Like Susan, Tom was only fifty-six.

"We are the new *hibakusha*," I mused bitterly. The *hibakusha*, the "explosion-affected persons," as the Hiroshima survivors called themselves. "Me, Duke, Dick, Susan, Pedro, and Tom. The American *hibakusha*. The Howard Hughes *hibakusha*. I'd never tell Duke, of course. Irony makes him mad."

Our obligation was manifest. We must contact the entire *Conqueror* company—stars, supporting players, camera operators, sound men, lighting crew, costume fitters, art director, special effects technician, hair stylist, makeup artist, assistant director—and advise them to seek out their doctors posthaste. For five months Stuart and I functioned as angels of death, fetches of the Nuclear Age, banshees bearing ill tidings of lymphoma and leukemia, and by the autumn of 1976 our phone calls and telegrams had generated two catalogues, one listing eighty *Conqueror* alumni who were already dead (most of them from cancer), the other identifying one hundred forty survivors. Of this latter group, one hundred sixteen received our warning with graciousness and gratitude, three told us we had no business disrupting their lives this way and we should go to hell, and twenty-one already knew they had the disease, though they were astonished that we'd gleaned the fact from mere circumstantial evidence.

John Wayne himself was the last person I wanted to talk to, but Stuart argued that we had no other choice. We'd been unable to locate Linwood Dunn, who did the on-location special effects, and Duke might very well have a clue.

I hadn't spoken with the old buzzard in years, but our conversation was barely a minute underway before we were trading verbal barrages. True to form, this was not a fond sparring-match between mutually admiring colleagues but a full-blown war of the *Weltanschauungen*, the West Coast patriot versus the East Coast pinko, the brave-heart conservative versus the bleeding-heart liberal. According to Duke's inside sources, President Jimmy Carter was about to issue a plenary pardon to the Vietnam War draft evaders. Naturally I thought this was a marvelous idea, and I told Duke as much. John Wayne—the same John Wayne who'd declined to don a military uniform during World War II, fearing that a prolonged stint in the armed forces would decelerate his burgeoning career—responded by asserting that once again Mr. Peanut Head was skirting the bounds of treason.

Changing the subject, I told Duke about my leukemia ordeal, and how this had ultimately led Stuart to connect the Nevada A-bomb tests with the *Conqueror* company's astonishingly high cancer rate. Predictably enough, Duke did not warm to the theory, with its implicit indictment of nuclear weapons, the Cold War, and other institutions dear to his heart, and when I used the phrase "Howard Hughes *hibakusha*," he threatened to hang up.

"We need to find Linwood Dunn," I said. "We think he's at risk."

In a matter of seconds Duke located his Rolodex and

looked up Linwood's unlisted phone number. I wrote the digits on the back of a stray *New Republic*.

"Well, Egghead, I suppose it can't hurt for Lin to see the medics, but this doesn't mean I buy your nutty idea," said Duke. "Howard Hughes is a true American."

He should have said Howard Hughes *was* a true American, because even as we spoke the seventy-year-old codeine addict was dying of kidney failure in Houston.

"You may have just saved Lin's life," I said.

"Possibly," said Duke. "Interesting you should get in touch, Egghead. I was about to give you a call. I'm thinking of shooting a picture in your neck of the woods next year, and there's a real sweet part in it for you."

I drew the receiver away from my ear, cupped the mouthpiece, and caught Stuart's attention with my glance. "He wants me in his next movie," I said in a coherent whisper.

"Go for it," said Stuart. "We need the money."

I lifted my hand from the mouthpiece and told Duke, "I'll take any role except your mother."

"Good," he said. "You'll be playing my grandmother." He chuckled. "That's a joke, Egghead. I have you down for my mentor, a retired school teacher. We finish principal photography on *The Shootist* in two weeks, and then I'm off to New York, scouting locations. We'll have dinner at the Waldorf, okay?"

"Sure, Duke."

Later that day, Stuart and I telephoned Linwood Dunn.

"You folks may have saved my life," he said.

I'm probably being unfair to Duke. Yes, his primitive politics infuriated me, but unlike most of his hidebound friends he was not a thoughtless man. He enjoyed a certain salutary distance from himself. Of his magnum opus, *The Alamo*, he once told a reporter, "There's more to that movie than my damn conservative attitude," and I have to agree. Beneath its superficial jingoist coating, and beneath the layer of genuine jingoism under that, *The Alamo* exudes an offbeat and rather touching generosity of spirit. The freedom-loving frontiersmen holding down the fort do not demonize Santa Anna's army, and at one point they praise their enemy's courage. I think also of Duke's willingness to appear in a 1974 public forum organized by the editors of the *Harvard Lampoon*. When a student asked him where he got the "phony toupee," he replied, "It's not phony. It's real hair. Of course, it's not mine, but it's real." Another student wanted to know whether Mr. Wayne's horse had recovered from his hernia now that the superstar was dieting. "No, he died," Duke answered, "and we canned him, which is what you're eating at the Harvard Club."

This refreshing streak of self-deprecation surfaced again when we met in New York at the Waldorf-Astoria. As we dug into our steaks and baked potatoes, Duke told me his idea for an urban cop picture, which he wanted to call *Lock and Load*. He'd seen Clint Eastwood's first two Harry Callahan movies, *Dirty Harry* and *Magnum Force,* and he was beguiled by both their vigilante ethos and their hefty profits. "If a liberal like Eastwood can make a fascist film," said Duke with a sly smile, "imagine what a fascist like me could do with that kind of material."

I laughed and patted him on the arm. "You'll make Harry Callahan look like Adlai Stevenson."

It was obvious to both of us that there would probably never be a John Wayne picture called *Lock and Load*. We were eating not in the hotel restaurant but in his room, so that the general public wouldn't see what a wreck he'd become. Maybe Duke had licked the Big C in 1964, but thirteen years later it was back for a rematch. He breathed only with the help of a sinister looking portable inhaler, and he had a male nurse in permanent attendance, a swarthy Texan named Sweeney Foote, forever fidgeting in the background like a Doberman pinscher on guard.

"You look terrific, Egghead," he said. He was wearing his famous toupee, as well as a lush Turkish bathrobe and leather slippers. "I'm sure you gave the Big C a knockout punch."

"The doctors aren't that optimistic."

Duke worked his face into a sneer. "Doctors," he said.

I glanced around the suite, appointed with tasteful opulence. Sweeney Foote sat hunched on the mattress, playing solitaire. I'd never been in the Waldorf-Astoria before, and I wondered if Duke had selected it for its symbolic value. When the Hollywood Ten's highly publicized appearance before the House Un-American Activities Committee started going badly (not only were the Ten actual by-God former Communists, they didn't seem particularly ashamed of it), the heads of the major studios called an emergency meeting at the Waldorf. Before the day was over, the money men had agreed that unemployment and ostracism would befall any Hollywood actor, writer, or director who defied a Congressional committee or refused to come forward with his or her non-Communist credentials.

"Tell me about *Lock and Load*," I said.

"Hell of a script," said Duke. "Jimmy's best work since *The Alamo*. I'm Stonewall McBride, this maverick police captain who likes to do things his own way."

"Novel concept," I said drily.

"Stonewall has stayed in touch with his fifth-grade teacher, kind of a mother-figure to him, regularly advising him on how to get along in a dog-eat-dog world."

"I've always enjoyed Maria Ouspenskaya."

Duke nodded, smiled, and gestured as if tipping an invisible Stetson, but then his expression became a wince. "I'll be honest, Egghead." He popped an analgesic pill and washed it down with beer. "I'm not here just to scout locations. Fact is, the Big C has me on the ropes. The medics say it's in my stomach now, as if I didn't know."

"I'm sorry, Duke."

"Back in L.A. I kept meeting folks who're into herbal medicines and psychic cures and such, and they advised me to go see this swami fella, Kieran Morella of the Greater Manhattan Heuristic Healing Center."

"Southern California at your fingertips, and you had to come to *New York* to find a hippie guru flake?"

"You can laugh if you want to, Egghead, but I hoofed it over to Kieran's office the instant I stepped off the plane, and what he said made sense to me. Sure, it's an unconventional treatment, but he's had lots of success. He uses a kind of hypnotism to send the patient back to the exact moment when some little part of him turned cancerous, and then the patient imagines his immune system rounding up those primal malignant cells the way a cowboy rounds up steers."

"Steers? Hey, this is the cure for you, Duke."

"Next the patient tries to tune in these things called quantum vibrations, and before long the space-time continuum has folded back on itself, and it's as if he'd never developed cancer in the first place."

"'Unconventional' is a good word here, Duke."

He swallowed another painkiller. "To help the patient get the proper pictures flowing through his mind—you know, images of his lymphocytes corralling the original cancer cells—Kieran shows him clips from *Red River.* Kinetotherapy, he calls it."

"Jesus, he must have been thrilled to meet *you*," I said. *Red River* is one of the few John Wayne westerns that Stuart and I can watch without snickering.

"He almost creamed himself. Now listen tight, Egghead. You might think I'm just talking about me, but I'm also talking about you. All during my flight east, I kept thinking about that American *hibakusha* business, and eventually I decided maybe your theory's not so crazy after all."

"Howard Hughes has nuked us, Duke. Your fellow Bircher has pumped us full of gamma rays."

"Let's leave Howard out of this, Robert Welch too. Here's the crux. The minute I told Kieran about this possible connection between *The Conqueror* and the Big C, and how the Cinemascope lenses may have captured the very moment when the radiation started seeping into me—how it's all up there on the silver screen—well, he got pretty damn excited."

"I can imagine."

"He kept saying, 'Mr. Wayne, we must get a print of this film. Get me a print, Mr. Wayne, and I'll cure you.'"

Duke snapped his fingers. Taking care not to disturb his matrix of playing cards, Sweeney Foote rolled off the bed.

He went to the closet, reached into a valise, and drew out an object that looked like a Revell plastic model of the cryptic black monolith from *2001: A Space Odyssey,* a movie that Duke had refused to see on general principles.

"*The Conqueror* arrived this morning, special courier, along with the necessary hardware," said Duke. He took the little monolith from Sweeney, then passed it to me. "Brand new technology, Jap thing called Betamax, a spool of half-inch videotape in a plastic cassette. Sony thinks it'll be the biggest thing since the crockpot."

The Betamax cassette featured a plastic window offering a partial view of both the feed core and the takeup spindle. Somebody had written "The Conqueror" on a piece of masking tape and stuck it across the top edge. "Ingenious," I said.

"It's all very well to wring your hands over Hiroshima, but if you ask me the Japs have done pretty well for themselves since then, especially the Sony people. My first kinetotherapy treatment occurs in two days and—you know what, Angela?—I'd like you to come along. You could help me concentrate, and you might even get a healing effect yourself."

"I couldn't afford it."

"I'll pay for everything. You're not out of the woods yet."

"I'm not out of the woods," I admitted ruefully.

"Monday afternoon, two o'clock, the Heuristic Healing Center, 1190 West 41st Street near Tenth Avenue. There's a goddamn mandala on the door."

"Let me talk it over with Stuart."

"With the Big C, you're never out of the woods."

I pour myself a glass of sherry, rewind *Trinity and Beyond,* and press *Play.* As before, the fiery mushroom cloud from the Castle Bravo explosion fills my television screen, shot after shot of billowing radioactive dust, and for a fleeting instant I experience an urge to bow down before it.

How beautiful art thou, O Mighty Fireball. How fair thy countenance and frame. Give me coffers of gold, O Great One, and I shall heap sacrifices upon thy altar. Give me silken raiments and shining cities, and I shall wash thy graven feet with rare libations.

Stuart and I decided that as long as Duke was picking up the tab I should indeed give kinetotherapy a try, and so on Monday afternoon I took the N train to Times Square. Ten minutes later I marched into the foyer of the Heuristic Healing Center, its walls hung with Hindu tapestries, its air laden with patchouli incense, and announced myself to the receptionist, a stately black woman wearing a beige Nehru jacket. The name-plate on her desk read JONQUIL. Duke was waiting for me, outfitted in blue denims, a checked cotton shirt, a red bandana, and tooled-leather cowboy boots. He looked like a supporting player in a bad science fiction movie about time travel. Sweeney Foote lurked near the coat rack, Duke's inhaler slung over his shoulder, a large crushproof envelope tucked under his arm like a private eye's holster.

Duke and I had barely said hello when Kieran Morella, a pale slender man dressed in a flowing white caftan and sporting a salt-and-pepper-goatee, orange beads, and a silver-gray ponytail—a counterculture point guard—sashayed out of his office, all smiles and winks. He gave us each a hug, which did not go down well with Duke, then took the envelope from Sweeney and ushered us into Treatment Salon Number Three, a velvet-draped chamber suggesting an old-style Hollywood screening room. At the far end, two brown, tufted, recliner chairs faced a television set connected to a squat device that I took to be a Betamax videocassette player.

As Sweeney slunk into the shadows, Kieran produced a coffee tin crammed with neatly rolled joints, presenting the stash to us as a hostess might offer her bridge club a box of chocolates. Getting stoned was optional, the therapist explained, but it would help us reach a "a peak of relaxed concentration."

"Hey, Doc, I've never smoked that Timothy Leary stuff in my life, and I'm not about to start now," said Duke. "Don't you have any drinking whiskey around here?"

"I could send Jonquil out for something," said Kieran.

"Jack Daniels, okay?"

"Tennessee's finest"—Kieran issued a nervous laugh—"endorsed by Davy Crockett himself."

Duke and Kieran spent the next twenty minutes talking about their favorite John Wayne movies. They were both keen on the so-called Cavalry Trilogy made under John Ford's direction: *Fort Apache, She Wore a Yellow Ribbon, Rio Grande*—three pictures that leave me cold. (I much prefer Duke and Ford in Irish mode: *The Quiet Man, The Long Voyage Home.*) At last Jonquil appeared with a quart of Jack Daniels and a shot glass. Kieran guided us into the recliner chairs and removed *The Conqueror* from Sweeney's envelope. He fed the cassette into the machine, flipped on the TV, and bustled about the room lighting incense and chanting under his breath.

"Your job is simple, Mr. Wayne." Kieran seized a remote control connected to the Betamax by a coaxial cable. "Each time you appear out there in the Escalante Desert, I want you to imagine a kind of psychic armor surrounding your body, filtering out the gamma rays. Ms. Rappaport, you have exactly the same task. During every shot you're in"—he handed me a box of wooden matches—"you must imagine a translucent shield standing between yourself and the radioactivity. If you folks can get the right quantum vibrations going, your screen images will acquire visible protective auras."

"We'll really see *auras*?" said Duke, impressed.

"There's a good chance of it," said Kieran.

Duke poured himself a slug of whiskey. I took a joint from the coffee tin, struck a match, and lit up. Kieran positioned himself behind our chairs, laying a soothing hand on each of our heads.

"This is going to be fun," I said, drawing in a puff of magic smoke.

"Concentrate," said Kieran.

I held my breath, slid the joint from my lips, and passed it to Kieran. He took a toke. The credits came on, a roll call of the dead, the doomed, and the fortunate few, this last category consisting mainly of people who didn't have to sweat under the Utah sun to get their names on the picture: the associate producer, the writer, the film editor, the sound editor.

As the movie unspooled in all its pan-and-scan glory—the film-chain operator had astutely decided that the original anamorphic images would not prosper on the average TV screen—it occurred to me that my running feud with Duke encapsulated the history of the Cold War. During the making of *The High and the Mighty,* we fought about the imminent electrocution of the "atomic spies," Julius and Ethel Rosenberg. While shooting *The Searchers,* we nearly came to blows concerning the Senate's recent decision to censure Joseph McCarthy. ("Old Joe will have the last laugh," Duke kept saying.) *The Alamo* found us at odds over the upcoming Presidential election, Duke insisting that there would be jubilation in the Kremlin if Jack Kennedy, the likely Democratic contender, beat Richard Nixon, the shoo-in for the Republican nomination. Between takes on *Circus World,* we nearly drew blood over whether the Cuban Missile Crisis obliged the superpowers to start taking disarmament seriously or whether, conversely, it meant that America should ratchet up her arsenal to a higher level of overkill. On the sets of both *The Green Berets* and *Chisum,* the Vietnam War inevitably got us going at each other tooth and nail.

And what about *The Conqueror* itself? What issue fueled our hostility during that benighted project? Believe it or not, our bone of contention was atomic testing, even though we knew nothing of Upshot Knothole and the radioactive toxins seething all around us. Fear of Strontium-90—like Strontium-90 itself—was in the air that year. *Fallout* had become a household word. Each night after we were back at the Grand Marquis Hotel in St. George, our base of operations during the shoot, most of the cast and crew would stand around in the lobby watching Walter Cronkite, and occasionally there'd be a news story about a politician who believed that unlimited on-continent testing of nuclear devices would eventually make lots of Americans sick, children especially. (Strontium-90 was ending up in the milk of dairy cows.) One such report included the latest figures on leukemia cases attributable to the Hiroshima and Nagasaki bombs.

"Poor old Genghis Khan," I said to Al D'Agostino, the art director. "He had to spend *weeks,* sometimes *months,* bringing down a city."

"Whereas Paul Tibbets and his B-52 managed it in the twinkling of an eye," said Al, who in those days was almost as far to the left as I.

"Poor old Genghis Khan," echoed the assistant director, Ed Killy. Ed was likewise a progressive, although he usually kept it under wraps, thereby maintaining his friendship with Duke.

"You people seem to forget that Hiroshima and Nagasaki kept our boys from having to invade Japan," said Duke. "Those bombs saved thousands of American lives."

"Well, Temujin," I said, sarcasm dripping from every syllable, "I guess that settles the matter."

The Conqueror had been on Kieran's TV barely ten minutes when I decided that it wasn't a costume drama after all. It was really yet another John Wayne western, with Tartars instead of Comanches and the Mongol city of Urga instead of Fort Apache. But even the feeblest of Duke's horse operas— *The Lawless Range,* say, or *Randy Rides Alone*—wasn't nearly this enervated. None of those early Republic or Monogram programmers had Duke saying, before the first scene was over, "There are moments for wisdom, Jamuga, and then I listen to you. And there are moments for action, and then I listen to my heart. I feel this Tartar woman is for me. My blood says, 'Take her!'"

"Concentrate," Kieran exhorted us, returning the joint to my eager fingers. "Repulse those gamma rays. Bend the fabric of space-time."

"I'm trying, Doc," said Duke, downing a second slug of Jack Daniels.

"Why would anybody want to make a movie celebrating a demented brute like Temujin?" I asked rhetorically. I'd read the *Encyclopedia Britannica*'s account of Genghis Khan the night before, baiting my hook. "Bukhara was one of medieval Asia's greatest cities, a center of science and culture. At Temujin's urging, his army burned it to the ground, all the while raping and torturing everybody in sight."

"Ms. Rappaport, I must ask you not to disrupt the healing process," said Kieran.

"When the citizens of Herat deposed the governor appointed by one of Temujin's sons, the retaliatory massacre lasted a week," I continued. "Death toll, one million, six hundred thousand. Genghis Khan was a walking A-bomb."

"Let's not get too high and mighty, Egghead," said Duke. "Hunlun wasn't exactly Florence Nightingale, but as I recall you didn't run screaming from the part. You picked up your paycheck along with the rest of us."

Duke had me on both counts, historical and ethical. Shortly after Temujin became the titular Mongol ruler at age thirteen, Hunlun emerged as the power behind the throne, and she ruled with an iron hand. When a group of local tribes turned rebellious, Hunlun led an expeditionary force against the obstreperous chiefs, and eventually she brought over half of them back into the fold.

"Please, people, let's focus," said Kieran. "This won't work unless we focus."

Screenwriter Oscar Millard had given my character three major scenes. In the first, Hunlun sternly reprimands her son for abducting the nubile Bortai from her fiancé, a Merkit chief named Targatai—not because it's wrong to treat women as booty, but because Bortai's father murdered Hunlun's husband. "Will you take pleasure with the offspring of your father's slayer?" Hunlun asks Temujin. "She will bring woe to you, my son, and to your people!" In Hunlun's second major scene, she bemoans the Mongol casualties that attended both Temujin's initial seizure of Bortai and Targatai's attempt to reclaim her. "And what of *your* dead, those who died needlessly for this cursed child of Kumlek's?" Hunlun's final sequence is her longest. While applying healing leaves and ointments to Temujin's arrow wound, Hunlun takes the opportunity to tell him that, thanks to his obsession with Bortai, he is losing track of his destiny. "Did I not hold our tribe together and raise you with but one thought—to regain your father's power and avenge his death?"

I hadn't seen my work in *The Conqueror* since the world premiere, and I hated every frame of it. It took a full measure of willpower to ignore this embarrassing one-note performance and concentrate instead on conjuring an anti-radiation aura around my pan-and-scan form.

Despite all the encouragement from Kieran and the marijuana, I failed to build the necessary shield, and Duke didn't have any luck either. From the first shot of Temujin (our hero leading a cavalry charge) to the last (the Mongol emperor standing beside his bride as they proudly survey their marching hordes), Duke's Betamax simulacrum never once acquired anything resembling psychic armor. He made no effort to hide his disappointment.

"Doc, I think we're pissing in the wind."

"Kinetotherapy takes time," said Kieran. "Can you both come back tomorrow at two o'clock?"

"For grass of such quality, I'd watch this piece of crap every day for a year," I said.

"Make sure you've got plenty of Jack Daniels on the premises," said Duke.

The instant Kieran activated his television on Tuesday afternoon, the picture tube burned out, the image imploding like a reverse-motion shot of an A-bomb detonation. Of course, it's not difficult to purchase a new TV set in New York City, and Jonquil accomplished the task with great efficiency. Our second kinetotherapy session started only forty minutes late.

As Kieran got the cassette rolling, Sweeney assumed his place in the shadows, Duke poured himself a shot of Jack Daniels, and I inhaled a lungful of pot. Today's weed was even better than yesterday's. Kieran might be a lunatic and a charlatan, but he knew his hallucinogens.

"Want to know the really scary thing about the Upshot Knothole tests?" I said. I'd spent my evening reading *The Tenth Circle of Hell,* Judith Markson's concise narrative of the Nevada Proving Ground. "By this point in history such devices were considered *tactical*—not strategic, *tactical*."

"Take it easy, Egghead," said Duke.

"Time to watch the movie," said Kieran.

"The monster that killed seventy thousand Hiroshima civilians is suddenly a fucking *battlefield weapon*!" I passed the joint to Kieran. "Isn't that *sick*? They even fired a Knot-hole bomb out of an *artillery cannon*! They called it 'Grable'—from Betty Grable, no doubt—fifteen kilotons, same as the Hiroshima blast. A goddamn artillery cannon."

As the screen displayed the opening logo, Kieran drew some illegal vapor into his body, then gave me back the joint. AN RKO RADIO PICTURE FILMED IN CINEMASCOPE.

"Focus, my friends," said Kieran. "Tune in the quantum vibrations."

HOWARD HUGHES PRESENTS . . . THE CON-QUEROR . . . STARRING JOHN WAYNE . . .

"Then there was 'Encore,' dropped from a plane." I sucked on the joint, inhaled deeply, and, pursing my lips, let the smoke find its way to my brain. "They suspended one pay-load from a balloon, released another from a steel tower."

SUSAN HAYWARD . . . CO-STARRING PEDRO AR-MENDARIZ . . . WITH ANGELA RAPPAPORT—THOMAS GOMEZ—JOHN HOYT—WILLIAM CONRAD . . .

"Battlefield atomic bombs." I gave the joint to Kieran. He took a toke and handed it back. "What barbarous insanity."

WRITTEN BY OSCAR MILLARD . . . ASSOCIATE PRODUCER RICHARD SOKOLOVE . . . MUSIC BY VIC-TOR YOUNG . . .

"Your opinion's been noted, Egghead," said Duke.

PRINT BY TECHNICOLOR . . . DIRECTOR OF PHO-TOGRAPHY JOSEPH La SHELLE . . . PRODUCED AND DIRECTED BY DICK POWELL.

And then the movie came on: Temujin abducting Bortai from the Merkit caravan (a kind of medieval wagon train) . . . Hunlun criticizing her son's choice in sex objects . . . Tar-gatai attempting to steal Bortai back . . . Hunlun denouncing the bloodshed that has accrued to Temujin's infatuation . . .

Temujin traveling to Urga and allying with Wang Khan . . . our
hero falling to the Mongol arrow and hiding in a cave . . .
Bortai returning to her depraved Tartar father . . . Jamuga in-
advertently leading Kumlek's henchmen to his blood
brother . . . Teniujin struggling beneath the weight of an ox-
yoke as his captors march him toward Kumlek's camp (an
image that inspired one of Stuart's students, in a paper that
received a B-minus, to call Wayne's character a Christ figure) . . . our hero standing humbled before the Tartar
chief . . . Bortai becoming conscious of her love for Temujin
and forthwith aiding his escape . . . Temujin arriving half-
dead in the Mongol camp . . .

At no point in this cavalcade of nonsense did either Temujin or his mother acquire a perceptible shield against the om-
nipresent radiation. But then, as my third major scene hit the
screen—Hunlun treating her son's wound—something utterly amazing occurred. A rainbow aura, glowing and pulsing
like Joseph's Coat of Many Colors, materialized on Hunlun's
head and torso as she uttered the line, "Would that I could
cure the madness that possesses you!"

It's the pot, I told myself. I'm high on hemp, and I'm seeing things.

"Good God!" I gasped.

"You've done it, Ms. Rappaport!" shouted Kieran.

"I see it too!" cried Duke. "She's got a damn rainbow
around her!"

"Wang Khan—he will betray you into disaster," insisted
Hunlun, "or rob you of your spoils in victory."

But then, to my dismay, the crone's anti-radiation suit
started to dissolve.

"Concentrate!" cried Kieran

My cloak continued to fade.

"Focus, Egghead!" demanded Duke.

I stared at the screen, concentrating, concentrating.

Hunlun insisted, "Were you not blinded by lust for this
woman—"

"Lust?!" echoed Temujin. "You, too, are blind, my
mother—blinded by your hatred for her."

"Shields at maximum, Ms. Rappaport!" shouted Kieran. "We're going to make you well!"

In a full-spectrum flash, red to orange to yellow to green to blue to indigo to violet, Hunlun's aura returned. "Daughter of Kumlek!" she sneered.

"Way to go, Ms. Rappaport!" exclaimed Kieran.

"Congratulations!" cried Duke.

"Even if you were right about Wang Khan, yet I would venture this unaided," said Temujin. Sealed head to toe in her luminous armor, Hunlun glowered at her son. "For I will have Bortai," he continued, "though I and all of us go down to destruction."

The scene ended with a dissolve to Jamuga riding through the gates of Urga, whereupon Kieran picked up the remote control and stopped the tape. It would be best, he explained, to quit while my triumph was at its zenith and the quantum vibrations were still folding back into the space-time continuum.

"Sounds reasonable to me," said Duke.

"Soon it will come to pass that the gamma rays never penetrated your body." Kieran ejected the cassette. "Ms. Rappaport, I must applaud you. By reweaving the cosmic tapestry, you have conquered your past and reshaped your future."

"That aura wasn't real," I said, wondering whether I believed myself. "It was an illusion born of Jack Daniels and marijuana."

"That aura was more real than the bricks in this building or the teeth in my jaw," said Kieran.

Duke caught my eye, then waved his shot glass in Kieran's direction. "Told you this guy's a pro. Most swamis don't know their higher planes from a hole in the ground, but you're in good hands with Doc Morella."

"I hope you're not jealous, Duke," I said. "There was no aura. It was just the booze and the dope."

"I've had a full life, Egghead."

*   *   *

For the third time in a week I contemplate the Castle Bravo explosion while drinking a glass of sherry.

The mushroom cloud, I realize, is in fact a Nuclear Age ink-blot test, a radioactive Rorschach smear. In the swirling vapors I briefly glimpse my has-been diva from *The High and the Mighty* as she speculates that nobody will miss her if the airliner goes into the drink. Next I see my *Alamo* character, the insufferably selfless Blind Nell, giving her husband permission to enter into a suicide pact with the boys instead of wasting his life taking care of her. And now I perceive the school teacher in *Lock and Load,* telling Duke to be the best obsessive-compulsive loose-cannon police captain he can be.

Slowly the quotidian seeps into my consciousness: my TV set, my VCR, my sherry, the cat on my lap—each given form and substance by my dawning awareness that the film called *Lock and Load* does not exist.

Was it just the booze and the dope? I simply couldn't decide, and Stuart had no theories either. Despite his unhappiness with postmodern scorched-earth relativism, despite his general enthusiasm for the rationalistic worldview, he has always fancied himself an intellectually vulnerable person, open to all sorts of possibilities.

"Including the possibility of a mind-body cure," he said.

"A mind-body cure is one thing, and Kieran Morella's deranged quantum physics is another," I replied. "The man's a goofball."

"So you're not going back?" asked Stuart.

"Of *course* I'm going back. Duke's paying for the weed. I have nothing to lose."

Kieran normally spent his Wednesdays downtown, teaching a course at the New School for Social Research, *Psychoimmunology 101: Curing with Quarks,* and Thursdays he always stayed home and meditated, so Duke and I had to wait a full seventy-two hours before entering Treatment Salon Number Three again. In a matter of minutes we were all primed for transcendence, Duke afloat on a cloud of Jack Daniels, Kieran and me frolicking through a sea of grass.

Our therapist announced that, before we tried generating any more quantum vibrations, we should take a second look at Tuesday's breakthrough.

"Whatever you say, Doc," said Duke.

"It was all a mirage," I said.

"Seeing is believing," said Kieran.

I retorted with that favorite slogan of skeptics, "And believing is seeing."

Kieran fastforwarded the *Conqueror* cassette to Hunlun treating Temujin's wound. He pressed *Stop,* then *Play.*

Against my expectations, Hunlun's aura was still there, covering her like a gown made of sunflowers and rubies.

"Thundering Christ!" I said.

This time around, I had to admit that the aura was too damn intricate and splendid—too existentially *real*—to be a mere pothead chimera.

"It's a goddamn miracle!" shouted Duke.

"I would join Mr. Wayne in calling your gamma-ray shield a miracle, but I don't think that's the right word," said Kieran, grinning at me as he pressed the *Rewind* button. "'Miracle' implies divine intervention, and you accomplished this feat through your own natural healing powers. How do you feel?"

"Exhilarated," I said. Indeed. "Frightened." Quite so. "Grateful. Awestruck."

"Me too," said Duke.

"And angry," I added.

"Angry?" said Duke.

"Mad as hell."

"I don't understand."

"Anger has no place in your cure, Ms. Rappaport, " said Kieran. "Anger will kill you sooner than leukemia."

As with our first two sessions, Duke's third attempt at kinetotherapy got him nowhere. Temujin went through the motions of the plot—he seized Bortai, speared Targatai, met with Wang Khan, suffered the Tartar arrow, endured imprisonment by Kumlek, won Bortai's heart, fled Kumlek's camp, conspired with Wang Khan's soothsayer, captured the city of

Urga, appropriated Wang Khan's forces, led the expanded Mongol army to victory against the Tartars, and slew Kumlek with a knife—but at no point did Duke's celluloid self acquire any luminous armor.

My character, on the other hand, was evidently leading a charmed life. No sooner did Hunlun admonish Temujin for courting his father's murderer than, by Kieran's account at least, I once again molded reality to my will, sheathing the crone's body against gamma rays. When next Hunlun entered the film, lamenting the pointless slaughter Temujin's lust has caused, she wore the same vibrant attire. Her final moments on screen—treating her son's wound while criticizing his life-style—likewise found her arrayed in an anti-radiation ensemble.

"Duke, I'm really sorry this hasn't gone better for you," I said.

The late Jamuga, now transformed into Temujin's spiritual guide, spoke the final narration, the one piece of decent writing in the film. "And the great Khan made such conquests as were undreamed of by mortal men. Tribes of the Gobi flocked to his standard, and the farthest reaches of the desert trembled to the hoofs of his hordes . . ."

Saying nothing, Duke set down his whiskey bottle, rose from his recliner, and shuffled toward the Betamax.

"At the feet of the Tartar woman he laid all the riches of Cathay," said Jamuga. "For a hundred years, the children of their loins ruled half the world."

Duke depressed the *Eject* lever. The cassette carriage rose from the recorder console and presented *The Conqueror* to the dying actor.

"Maybe you'll get your aura next week," I said. I took a toke, approached Duke, and squeezed his arm. "Never say die, sir. Let's come back on Monday."

"We lost in Vietnam." Duke pulled the cassette free of the machine. He removed his bandana, mushed it together, and coughed into the folds. "Nixon signed a SALT agreement with the Russians." Again he coughed. "The Air Force Academy is admitting women. The phone company is hiring flits.

Peanut Head"—he gasped—"is bringing the draft dodgers"—and gasped—"home."

Duke lurched toward me, tipped his invisible Stetson, and, still gripping the cassette, collapsed on the carpet.

Inhaler at the ready, Sweeney bounded across the room. Falling to his knees, he wrapped his arms around his supine employer and told Kieran to apply the plastic mask to Duke's nose and mouth. It was a familiar tableau—we had just seen it on the screen: Bortai cradling the wounded Temujin as she comes to understand that this particular egomaniacal sociopathic warlord is a real catch. ("He has suffered much," says Bortai to her servant. And the servant, who knows subtext when she hears it, responds, "Deny not the heart.") Kieran handled the oxygen rig with supreme competence, and in a matter of seconds the mask was in place and Duke had stopped gasping.

"You want another shot of whiskey?" I asked, kneeling beside Duke.

"No thanks." He pressed the cassette into my hands and forced himself into a sitting position. "I know when I'm licked, Egghead," he rasped. "It's not my America any more."

"You aren't licked," I said.

"You must have faith," said Kieran.

Sweeney proffered an analgesic. Duke swallowed it dry. "I've got *plenty* of faith," he said. "I've got faith running out my ears. It's strength I'm lacking, raw animal strength, so I figured I should hoard it for Egghead."

"For me?" I said.

"I projected all my quantum vibrations onto Hunlun," he said.

"You mean . . . you augmented Ms. Rappaport's shield?" Kieran bent low, joining our Pietà.

"Augmented?" said Duke. "Let's talk plain, Doc—I made it *happen*. I threw that bubble around old Hunlun like Grant took Richmond. I blocked that radiation till hell wouldn't have it again." He set a large, sweating hand on my shoulder.

"The Big C conquered John Wayne a long time ago, but you've still got a fighting chance, Egghead."

"Duke, I'm speechless," I said.

"I've never bent the space-time continuum for anybody before, but I'm glad I did it in your case," said Duke.

"I'm touched to the core," I said.

"Why does the aura make you angry?" he asked.

It took me several seconds to formulate an answer in my head, and as I started to speak the words, Duke coughed again, closed his eyes, and fainted dead away.

Before the day was over Sweeney got Duke admitted to the Sloan-Kettering Memorial Cancer Center, where they gave the old cowboy all the morphine and Jack Daniels he wanted. A week later Duke received open-heart surgery, and by the end of the month he was back home in L.A., attended around the clock by his wife, his children, and, of course, his faithful nurse.

The Big C accomplished its final assault on June 11, 1979, stealing the last breath from John Wayne as he lay abed in the UCLA Medical Center.

Duke always wanted his epitaph to read FEO, FUERTE Y FORMAL, but I've never visited his grave, so I don't know what's on the stone. *Feo, Fuerte y Formal*: "Ugly, Strong, and Dignified"—a fair summary of that box-office giant, but I would have preferred either the characteristic self-knowledge of *There's More to That Movie Than My Damn Conservative Attitude* or else the intentional sexual innuendo of the eulogy he wrote for himself while drinking scotch during the Chisum wrap party: *He Saw, He Conquered, He Came.*

Hunlun's aura still angers me. Kinetotherapy still makes me see red. "If Kieran Morella is on to something," I told Stuart, "then the universe is far more absurd than I could possibly have imagined."

A Japanese city has been reduced to radioactive embers? No problem. We can fix that with happy thoughts. The Castle Bravo H-bomb test has condemned a dozen Asian fisherman to death by leukemia? Don't worry. Just pluck the quantum strings, tune in the cosmos, and the pennies will trickle down from heaven.

"The miracle is the cruelest trick in God's repertoire," I told Stuart. "God should be ashamed of himself for inventing the miracle."

Next Tuesday I'm going to the polls and casting my vote for Bill Clinton: not exactly a liberal but probably electable. (Anything to deprive that airhead plutocrat George Bush of a second term.) The day after that, my eighty-first birthday will be upon me. Evidently I'm going to live forever.

"Don't count on it," Stuart warned me.

"I won't," I said.

According to today's *Times,* the Nevada Test Site, formerly the Nevada Proving Ground, is still open to visitors. The tour features numerous artifacts from the military's attempts to determine what kinds of structures might withstand nuclear blast pressures. You'll see crushed walls of brick and cinderblock, pulverized domes fashioned from experimental concrete, a railroad bridge whose I-beams have become strands of steel spaghetti, a bank vault that looks like a sand castle after high tide, and a soaring steel drop-tower intended to cradle an H-bomb that, owing to the 1992 Nuclear Testing Moratorium, was never exploded.

Disney World for Armageddon buffs.

Kieran let me keep the kinetotherapy cassette, but I've never looked at it, even though there's a Betamax somewhere in our closet. I'm afraid those goddamn psychedelic shields will still be there, enswathing my on-screen incarnation. Tomorrow I plan to finally rid myself of the thing. I shall solemnly bear the cassette to the basement and toss it into the furnace, immolating it like the Xanadu work crew burning Charles Foster Kane's sled. Stuart has promised to go with me. He'll make sure I don't lose my nerve.

I simply can't permit the universe to be that absurd. There are certain kinds of cruelty I won't allow God to perform. In the ringing words of Hunlun, "My son, this you cannot do."

*   *   *

Once again I import the Castle Bravo explosion into my living room. I drink my glass of sherry and study the Rorschachian obscenities.

This time I'm especially struck by the second shot in the mushroom-cloud montage, for within the nodes and curls of this burning Satanic cabbage I perceive a human face. The mouth is wide open. The features are contorted in physical agony and metaphysical dread.

Try this at home. You'll see the face too, I promise you. It's not the face of John Wayne—or Genghis Khan or Davy Crockett or Paul Tibbets or the Virgin Mary or any other person of consequence. The victim you'll see is just another nobody, just another bit-player, another *hibakusha,* eternally trapped on a ribbon of acetate and praying—fervently, oh so fervently—that this will be the last replay.

NAPPY

George Zebrowski

In the following story, George Zebrowski envisions a far future with the ability to create detailed virtual worlds of countless alternative histories, a setting in which a recreated Napoleon Bonaparte confronts the fantastic variabilities of history. George Zebrowski was born in Austria, grew up in Italy, England, Miami, and New York City, and now lives in upstate New York. He won the John W. Campbell Award in 1999 for his novel *Brute Orbits,* and has been a finalist for the Nebula Award and a nominee for the Theodore Sturgeon Award. Many of his best stories appear in his collection *Swift Thoughts* (Golden Gryphon Press), which *Publishers Weekly* described as "brilliant . . . all [his stories] demonstrate impressive discipline, logic, and mastery of his craft." Among his novels are *Macrolife, The Omega Point Trilogy, Stranger Suns* (a *New York Times* Notable Book of the Year), *The Killing Star* (written with scientist/author Charles Pellegrino), *The Sunspacers Trilogy*, and *Cave of Stars*.

"The story of Napoleon produces on me an impression like that produced by the Revelation of Saint John the Divine. We all feel there must be something more in it, but we do not know what."

—Goethe

When we look back to the Virtual Dark Age, before we emerged from ourselves and the chaotic variety of infinite existence once again reclaimed our human devotions, bringing a new age of outward explorations and a new age of space travel, it is easy to see the virtual centuries as only the most recent structuring of duration, one in which all of recorded human experience became, for a time, a new way of life—following in importance the first ordering of social life with timepieces.

This was not an unusual consequence, from a historian's view. The realist understanding of history had led to an epochal disillusionment, and to the end of sovereign national states. Along with economic emancipation from the tyranny of scarcity and the repetitive, sterile temptations of power bought by wealth, true histories destroyed the human weakness of looking at their localities in the sentimental, myth-ridden ways. But even as political and economic gangs perished in the blinding glare of revelation, the old longings persisted and gradually reemerged in the form of the Virtual Reality States, designed to give everyone his heart's desire.

These new conditions of life took the form of individual solipsisms, interlocking solipsisms, and genuine social groupings colonizing the various backdrop creations. Everyone thought he could do better than the given reality, whose pressures could now be suspended by willful acts of analogous creation.

Of course, inner realities emerged that could only be understood and valued by experiencing them; fundamental differences between inside and outside states had to be learned before new steps could be taken toward deeper understandings.

Among these realizations was the central, inescapable fact that a virtual reality could never be the equal of external existence. By the principle of the identity of indiscernibles, well known for centuries, if two things are exactly alike, they still differ through their location in space: there are *two* things, and that is how they differ. An exact match would exclude *all* differences, including the difference in spatial coordinates. The two objects would be one and the same thing, in the same place. What this meant was that a perfect match with external cosmic infinity was impossible, short of creating a second, identical cosmos. Difference would always be felt, and there would be other artifacts, quite unpredictable and inescapable giveaways to spoil the illusion, however perfect-seeming for a time. A sudden return to the non-virtual universe was always a shock, a collision with a universe free of obvious perceptual flaws, with an infinite richness that could never be duplicated, only suggested.

The mystery of the singular, non-made cosmos remained.

But as with an earlier Dark Age, we find in the Virtual Reality States many worthy reconstructions of the past—much as ancient Greek and Roman cultures were reinterpreted by the Renaissance and became a platform for the first human attempt at modernity (1500-2500 AD)—reconsiderations that brought great insight and beauty to countless human episodes that might otherwise have been forever lost, as many were lost.

The historical experience with virtual continua itself became a valuable lesson. These worlds were the remnants of a great social error, lost worlds containing whole human societies. Many were never found, and merely faded away as their structural supports in the primary world deteriorated or were destroyed. Some may still exist, and may be the only surviving examples of such groups. A search has been underway for some time, without success, for the Jesuit Order of scholars and scientists, which translated itself into virtual realms because its members had lost faith in the afterlife's promise of immortality. The virtualities, of course, offered immortality from the purely subjective view, for as long as the frame was fed power. There is a legend that a serviceable simulacrum of Franz Liszt dwells among the Jesuits.

It has been argued that the entities contained in the virtuals only appear to be sentient and have no conscious subjectivity other than an apparent one; but of course this cannot be settled any more than we can prove the subjective self-awareness of minds outside the frame. Only behavior is visible to us, inside the frame and outside. Besides, inside there were no bodies. There had been bodies during the dark age, and they had been awakened from their worlds; but a large number remained who had long since given up the flesh.

One of these still accessible fates is that of Nappy, once known as Napoleon Bonaparte, whose many-faceted personality, often held up to both ridicule and praise, refused to be erased from history's modalities.

Despite his death in what we must call, however vainly, the primary world, there were still the initial printed, painted, and sculpted survivals of his persona (he just missed the photographic), the theatrical and filmic survivals, and then the great wave of virtual reincarnations. Nappy was not to be denied. He persisted—because he lived in the minds of others, as prior conquerors had infected his imagination.

His specific survival is one that illustrates the first steps in our discovery of "framing strategies," studies which later became the basis of our current understanding of the universe—itself a unique system that inherently resists any ultimate framing, but that can be stepped back from endlessly, by pieces, and thus reveals ever proliferating details but not a final grasp of a universe known only from the inside, since it cannot be exited.

It had all started innocently, as W.W.W., the great historian, descending from an earlier age, examined a Nappy reincarnation, little expecting its viral charm—and was caught by the corporal's thoughts:

What shall I do with myself, and with this humanity that gave birth to me? Napoleon asks himself as he gazes at the Pyramids. How much must I impress myself upon my fellow beings? How much must I teach myself to become capable of teaching them? I suspect that this humanity around me will bring me down one day. I will be humiliated, and my heart will be torn out.

And to this tragic sense of fatality within himself, to the foreshadowings written into his character by dramatic, technical elements belonging to the accretions of commentary, Napoleon answers: I must hurry ahead of my humanity.

The British were readying to burn his fleet, to trap him in Ægypt. What was there to do?

"Conquest wrested from ignorance is the only true conquest," he whispers to himself as he gazes out over the ocean. "But what am I to do?"

He hates the balance of powers that is Europe, that has always been Europe; it is inherently unstable. Chaos always waits to throw Europe into the abyss. Only a universal peace bestowed by a final conquest can remedy the instability of tottering balances. . . .

Even now the fleet might be burning. Evening would bring the glow.

A Europe of dictators awaited, the historian inside Napoleon thought, rule based not on the divine right of kings, but on personal will, ready to go just as wrong. Of the study of history there could be no end. Factuals, counterfactuals, converse, inverse, obverse, analogous—all would take hold of minds attempting to stop the fleeing past . . .

There was a mistake in the scale-gauge settings of the framework, but the historian noticed this too late. A happy accident, he thought, as Napoleon stepped into the water and waded out across the waves. His massive feet stirred the bottom, his head nearly brushed the clouds. The French fleet was just ahead, helpless for lack of men and supplies before the approaching British squadron.

Gradually, Napoleon comes between the two groups of

ships, but the British vessels are not deterred by the titanic figure. They come on as if he were not there.

Tiny cannon point at him. Puffs of smoke bloom. Explosions pop distantly in his ears. Small depressions appear in the legs of his uniform, as if stiff fingers are touching him. He remembers his mother's soft hands searching his bare body for imperfections, then wrapping him against the infections of the Corsican night.

He leans forward and picks up a ship. Tiny figures fall screaming into the brine. Their cries are like bird calls. He waits a moment, then throws the vessel at two warships that are sailing side by side. Wood splinters, masts fall and crash, fires flower, hulls bob and struggle to turn away from his colossal legs.

Why am I able to do this? Napoleon asks himself. Boyhood fantasies rendered real as my ambition wills it. He looks around the ocean, imagining the tabletop of toys on which this war game is being played; but there is only the sea, sky, and the ruination of ships below his knees. He recalls his mother's soup pot coming to boil.

With the British fleet no longer a threat to his own, the little corporal wades back ashore and lays his titanic body on the beach. He knows now what he has to do.

His mind turns eastward from Ægypt, glorying in the conquest of Syria, Iraq, and Palestine. He will open the great prison at Acre and gain new followers. He will rebuild the Temple of Solomon and draw all the Jews out of an undeserving Europe. He will secure Mecca and Medina against the European infidels, and gain still more allies. He will build Alexander's dream of one world.

Then, all of this will be at his back when he turns back toward Europe, and cleans out the nests of oppressive royalties that had for so long turned the peoples of the world against each other, and who had no champion to stand with them.

Why these thoughts? he asks himself. Does a god instruct me? He cherishes the thoughts, but wonders about their provenance. I have gone mad, he tells himself. But how to tell the difference? I have no other instrument with which to judge except myself.

A vision of the future flashes through him, stirring his deepest needs. The French Revolution runs its authentic but mad course. He finds the crown of France in the gutter and picks it up with his sword. He puts it on his head with his own hands, but they are the hands of his people, whose yearnings are the ultimate legitimacy. Reason, it becomes clear to him, will not by itself govern his fellow man. He includes himself in the problem, sees it clearly, and tells himself that if he can see it, then he might just be able to step outside its imprisoning circle. It is his obligation to do so.

As Emperor, he tries to dig the grave of a previous world, and is buried with it. He knew that outcome well, it seems, as he knew the branches of an infinite tree growing toward the light.

And yet . . . and yet, what is there to aspire to except everything? Less? One cannot run from mistakes.

He walks in the sky over Waterloo, reviewing the battle, noting the dead. It has been a foolishly close thing, as Wellington had also confessed. Countless Waterloos waited, or could be sidestepped, if he now turned to the East.

As he lies on the sands under the clear Mediterranean sky, he knows how his futures had gone wrong. I was contaminated by the royal mold of my enemies. They crept into my soul, and made their faults my own. My very humanity contaminated the soul I had made for myself, and then had to defend for lack of a better one. All was lost when my health failed. Josephine's seduction of Wellington, my escape from Elba to lead the Old Guard, was nothing before my body's betrayal of a malleable future forever waiting to be shaped.

And always I loved my family too much.

I should have quietly and swiftly killed all the royal families of Europe, before those nests of spiders sent out their killers to get me. I waited too long, grew too weak, lived through too many defeats. I should have killed them first, as we did in France. That is what Europe feared most, and I waited too long, and they killed me slowly, so the youth of

Europe would not have a hero to stand at their side, to remember and cherish.

He recalls his deaths.

There was arsenic in the wallpaper of the house on St. Helena, and in my hair.

My body betrayed me at Waterloo, imprisoning my mind. I could not move to command.

His many deaths were outflows of blood into the sea, draining away the hopes and dreams of possibilities.

But all this will not happen, because I will turn East, to a richer culture that needs me even more than France. I see history plain, as a general sees his battlefield in a clear glass. I will not question the sight given to me. I will act the part I had always wished to play. There will be no revisions of my visions, because I know my lost battles.

Battles . . . to seek a plan of battle, complete, is to blind one's brain. One must have a general idea, then discover its method and its means only well after the plunge into the fray, and see it whole nearest to victory or defeat. A battle is a work of art, made with a fatal love or it is unmade, seeking its ways to a hidden end . . .

How am I able to see these things—to imagine and then find myself doing them? Am I God's dream? Is my disbelieved-in God mocking me? How many gods fashion the world?

Napoleon stands in the new Temple of Solomon. He stands in Baghdad, in Mecca and Medina. Poetry flows through his brain in Damascus, and he summons a just conquest of Europe. The joys! The joys of battle—from when I first had proof that my inspirations brought victories written on the skies!

And then his role is revealed to him. He learns who and what he is, as the historian's somewhat apologetic voice says to him: "In the virtuals of the history machine's cliometricon, everything may happen, because all of the past has been stored as information, fluid and malleable. Even the greatest unlikelies may happen."

As the revelations pierce him, Napoleon recalls his pre-fluid self, lodged in a single likelihood, only dreaming of others. He freezes at the realization of what he has been, and what he might be now. He is still himself, but his eagle's wings are opening to carry him farther, across the sea probabilities, carrying his truth . . .

Time stops within him, while his thoughts hurtle across time, free of the dying body.

"But why are you telling me all this?" he cries out to the blue Mediterranean sky.

The answer hangs upon the light.

"To see if a creature's possibilities might be increased through self-knowledge," a voice says within him.

"A creature?" Napoleon asks. His mind had been foreshadowed, but the sudden fact was a beast rushing in to devour him.

"Yes—you are a cloud of electrons in a box. No less real than I am, mind you."

"And who are you?" he asks, wondering at the meaning of the terms—which he suddenly understands as if they were old friends.

"A kind of historian, by your understanding."

"Which you have increased. I know what electrons are, also by your grace." The hand of a god was reaching out to him across the blue sky.

"Shall we continue?"

"Yes!"

A database overwhelmed him, flanking his doubts with joy.

The Channel Tunnel was being built. Napoleon watched his army enter the brick-lined passage. From under England his forces burrowed up into the daylight and swarmed across the countryside, his Old Guard and the Heroes from Acre. London surrendered in a day, and the British Crown fled to the American Colonies—and the probabilities proliferated from that transplanted tree.

In Napoleon's great soul, history found a new, swaying freedom, that of a pendulum moving from infinity to infinity, dancing to permit his every heart's desire, every justice, every forgotten, lost moment to be redeemed. He remembered his futures, and visited his revised pasts, lying in the light of that Mediterranean beach. He was everywhere, melding his fantasies with possibilities. Poetry flowed through him, and was writ large in the charged particles of his box:

> I know sanity, and when to
>   depart from it.
> I know chains
>   and when to break them.
> Chains are good, they give form,
>   but one cannot live shackled.
> Freedom is a terror,
>   but brings new things.
> To shun one or the other
>   is to embrace a living death.
> I like to live where I live.
>   I go everywhere there.
> Nothing sings sweeter
>   than pure possibility.

"But keep in mind," said the historian, "that you are not the original Napoleon, but only a gathering from all the vast libraries of recorded materials, including his own works. If you doubt this, then search your memory for what is missing. Details of a childhood, for example."

I am a scarecrow, Napoleon thinks, but then rebels, and answers: "No! He is my brother, out of the same sea of time! I am his image, and all that is left of him. I feel that I am myself, and that is real! I can do anything!"

"You cannot reenter history," said the historian, experimenting with cruelty. "You are a ghost."

He went to his abode in Cairo and told Josephine her true nature.

"What?" she cried out. "Are you insane? What are you saying? I don't understand."

He tried to explain their new form of existence, as he had learned it from the historian. She struggled to comprehend.

"I'm quite real," she insisted. "I hope none of these lunacies mean we have to go back to France. It's so warm here, and I can wear the skimpy dresses that were killing me in Paris. I am Josephine of Ægypt! I will show anyone who doubts it my wardrobe." She came up to him and took his face in her soft hands. "Touch me and you'll know I am real," she said, smiling. "Here, look at all these endless long letters you wrote to me from Italy!"

"Oh, you're real enough, such as you are," he said, thinking to ask her about her son and daughter, but held back. The detail was missing. Were they here or in France?

They are not in this history, said the historian within him.

"Real . . . enough?" Josephine asked. "Such as I am?"

"Yes. To feel that you are . . . you. That is enough." He would not press the matter further with her.

But Josephine's denial of her state rooted in his mind, and as he began to examine his newly revealed form of existence, he saw its horrors. We feel, we are real, but only we can know it.

I was the hope of the world, he told himself. I slept on a hard cot. Now these endless worlds, all to choose from, and none. A universe that cannot make up its mind!

And I am *inside*.

Out there, which gave me birth, is lost to me. Yet I am myself. I feel myself to be myself. But there was another one, *outside*, from whom I sprang.

My brother was a god in the true world! And I am not he. I was not there at Waterloo, even though I remember the mud, the endless mud at Waterloo! It was everywhere, there and in all the infinities—the same mud in all the many *kinds* of infinities. I was always a good mathematician, but I did not know about differing infinities, until now. The mud and my ailing stomach. Always the same. I should have won at Waterloo! I would have won if I had watched my rear. If I had bloodied the royals earlier, I might not have needed so many cannon, so many dead. Much earlier. The alliances that brought me down represented an armed minority interest in the world.

"Your virtues," said the historian, "—you forgot your ideals. Beethoven dedicated his Eroica Symphony to the memory of a great man. You were that man."

"All my failings I learned from the past, from my humanity."

He remembered his mother's knife, the one she always wore in waiting for vendetta. I am not he who saw that knife. I have only the memory. Yet that knife is real in my brain!

The historian, seeing his agony, said, "The worlds are myriad, even outside the cliometricon."

"But you have taken me from myself," Napoleon cried across the probabilities, "by subtracting all the difference between dreams and reality. It's all dreams now, all lies. Dreams that are fulfilled, then erased. I am a shadow wondering about shadows. I'm weary of being everything anyone has ever imagined or thought I was!"

The database of implications fell in on him, as the idea of an infinite, real world preyed upon his mind. Insights rushed into him like sharks, eating at his reason. This world of endless dreams was part of that first world, and so was also subject to infinite variations, as well as subject to its own deliberately sought variants. His great brother's reality had been different in *kind* from all the copies. He felt the darkness closing in, and wept into great Pascal's abyss. Infinities hurtled overhead.

"What would you have?" asked the historian.

"At least give me one! You have taken me from myself, by taking me from my world. You have stolen the soul I made for myself!"

"That man died centuries ago. You are what has happened to all history. As soon it was recorded, it was revised, dramatized, storied and shaped, and lost forever. Primary history comes only once, as it is now coming in this very dialogue. Accept what you are."

"You should never have told me!"

"Truly?"

"The cruelty of your miracle suspends natural law! You have raided the game. Raiding an honest game is cruelty."

"An honest game?"

"Yes! It had the honesty of infinite difficulty, of transcendent problems to be attacked!"

"And it had your tyranny," said the historian.

"Yes. But tyranny doesn't express the truth. I fell into tyranny out of frustration with my enemies, with human nature. And with myself. Something more direct was needed. Time runs out on democracy much too quickly. We would have to live very long to have the luxury of practicing it. I wanted to reshape the world, and myself. It was impossible to have changes without cannon, so I began to rage." He sighed into the clouds. "My ideals were one thing. What I had to do daily was another. One has to survive before one can do anything. Besides, I was not the tyrant. *He* was the tyrant. I only remember, so you tell me. I was a good artillery officer."

"That you were. I should never have told you," said the historian.

"It is better to know."

"Consider this," said the historian. "What you wanted for Europe—an end to its warring and bickering—you did not have the human instruments to accomplish. And the character of your primary brother failed, physically and mentally. I cannot revise *him*. Of new injustices there is no end, or the killing of heroes. Goodness never had a lasting strength. It was without armies or power. It had none. And whenever it started to have the means, it disgraced itself. All reforms, religious, political, and military, sooner or later always disgraced themselves. Every time was like every other time. People found themselves in situations made for them by previous people. But you had some effect, in the laws, the schools, the secular ideals. You were a great administrator. You vaccinated your troops."

"Alas, I know all that," Napoleon said as he went everywhere and lived every possibility. A great attractor drew him, ever calling him toward a myriad Waterloos . . . all of them beloved mirages, because the conquest of Europe was a need of justice, a redemption of the past, even though he now understood that it could never be final. Here and there in the currents of possibility, yes; but the rest, he knew, would always haunt him, as he suffered on Elba and returned from near-death, then was exiled and died on St. Helena.

Once, long ago, he had imagined that he would save Corsica from the French; but they had been only the latest vultures to have feasted on his beautiful island home.

Then, when he had become France, he had wanted to save the world from itself. He did not imagine that the world would want to save itself from him.

Of course it was not the world, but only its royal masters. That was why they had not dared to kill me. The world's people, when they saw that I might be defeated, chose once again to be fleas on the elephant, living their lives. I do not blame them. To do so was only practical. But their hearts were with me, despite my faults, so the British dared not kill me openly. The love of the world saved my life. Then, like a toy soldier, I was put back in my box. Too many cannon!

It was the great insult of the probabilities that troubled him without end. Why not one final, just outcome, where all the yearnings, ambitions, and selfless hopes could be realized? Why so many Waterloos? Why live so many histories and not have what is most desired? He was at sea with his humanity, as he had been in the open boat during the storm when he had fled Corsica. He had imagined himself the captain of his own ship, but there was too much below decks. This monstrous residue of nature could never be understood in a single lifetime.

"Historian!" cried Napoleon in his clouds. He howled at the darkness. It was filled with small creatures. They swarmed around him, eating his flesh.

"Yes?" answered a kindly voice.

"Give me what I want."

"And what is that?"

"Blinders. The mercy granted to horses!"

"And you wish to be . . . blinded, to what?"

"To these pitiless, endless outcomes. Even one, whichever, would settle my mind, and my stomach."

"Which one?" asked the historian, seeing how, when offered the freedom of history, the hero would never be satisfied, believing that by a single act of will he might suspend all the currents of injustice and dissatisfaction . . .

The darkness swirled. Napoleon cried out in agony for release. The particles whispered through their regime of charged geometries, mimicking time, and the worlds inside could not be guessed from their outward simplicities of physics, so far beyond Newton.

The historian thought, I told him who and what he is, which is more than I can ever learn about myself.

As he lived Napoleon's fatal agony, the historian relented.

Napoleon sighed.

All the probabilities collapsed into one well-shaped tragedy of defeat and humiliation.

Waterloo awaited him, its greenery serene, its mud welcoming.

It could never have been otherwise, throughout all the variants, thought the historian. For that, another human nature was needed. Human conquerors, at their idealistic best, were born of exasperation with their humanity, and sought to remake nature. They had always lacked the tools, and became even more frustrated with age. The intractability of history, Napoleon's exasperation with his family and with himself, had led him into a trap. Humanity had always deserved its tyrants; it admired its tyrants for as long as they served the common tyranny in every individual. This was not what Napoleon's ideals had needed, and he wore out his own brain and body thinking he might do better, somehow rearrange the drama.

All these bits of evidence! Who knew what went on in Napoleon's heart, who could say with certainty from all the recorded pieces? Truth was elusive, often pure fantasy. These variants and probabilities grew from a baseline primary world; but any possible world could be a baseline. Our primary, he reminded himself, had just emerged from a dark age of virtual fantasies, a trap which had almost replaced life itself. Unchecked, only the death of the sun would have ended it.

The historian deleted the whole mass of proliferating variants from his plenum. The ever-branching tree toppled, cut off from its roots.

And as Napoleon slept, the historian knew what to do.

Simplify, simplify.

He rewrote, or rather, wrote a new history, such as it was, as real as his encounter with Napoleon was, and it became real, in at least one meaning of the term:

In the days before his exile to St. Helena, Countess Marie Walewska, who had come to the conqueror between his military campaigns like a ministering angel, who befriended him in the hope that he would help her country, and who had borne him a son, rescues Napoleon from the clutches of the British by dressing him as her maid. They escape to America, where Napoleon takes up a new trade—plumbing in wood and ceramic and metal. These are new skills, and he grows rich from his invention of useful devices, which Jefferson adopts for his own great beloved folly, Monticello. Napoleon's health improves, especially his stomach, as a result of Countess Walewska's Polish cuisine.

Simplify, simplify. Artfully, the historian spins the probabilities, so that this world will never be found by anyone, and launches it into infinity.

Nappy dies a happy man, leaving his heirs a great entrepreneurship, *Nappy Bone & Sons, Waterworks*. He passes quietly, with his mother whispering to him, "Sleep, my Napoleone, sleep my Nappy," as she slips her blade of vendetta from his brain.

DEL NORTE

Michaela Roessner

Here is a story featuring a little-known historical figure, Joan Grau, one of the soldiers who served under
Hernando Cortés, Spanish adventurer and conqueror
of Mexico. In other words, it is a "true" story, but as
its author tells us: "Truth is a slippery, changing, shifting thing." Michaela Roessner was born in San Francisco and grew up in New York City, Pennsylvania,
Thailand, Virginia, and Oregon. She is an artist,
teaches the martial art of aikido, and began to write
after attending one of the Clarion Writing Workshops at
Michigan State University. In 1989, she won the Crawford Award for her first novel, *Walkabout Woman*, and
the John W. Campbell Award for best new writer. Her
novels include the highly praised *Vanishing Point* and
the first two novels of a historical trilogy about Cather-
ine de Medici, *The Stars Dispose* and *The Stars
Compel*. Her short fiction has appeared in *Asimov's Science Fiction*, *Omni*, *Full Spectrum*, and other publica-

tions. She lives in northern California with her husband, artist Richard Herman.

Florentina brushed away a wayward strand of copper-auburn hair as she put down the phone. Peering out the kitchen window at an angle, she could just barely see her two American cousins sitting by the front door on the bench made from a single twisted, gnarled log. Their luggage leaned against the end of the bench as if tired from traveling. The cousins—a middle-aged woman and an elderly woman—looked almost as worn. Their three-day stop-over with their Catalan relatives had barely begun to refresh them, and now they were on the go again.

Florentina went outside to join them. "Don't worry. I just called the cab service again," she told them in Spanish. "She's on her way and will be here in fifteen minutes. You won't miss your bus to Balageur." Florentina spoke slowly. The older cousin used to speak Spanish fluently but had grown deaf in the last few years. The middle-aged cousin's grasp of the language was mediocre at best—dialogue with her consisted of halting starts and stops, the retracing of entire discussions whenever it became clear that she'd lost the thread of a conversation. Neither woman spoke Catalan.

Both women thanked Florentina again profusely for her hospitality, as they'd done at least a dozen times in the past hour.

"I'm only sorry you couldn't stay longer," Florentina said. "One can only do so much in three days." They'd gone saffron and wild mushroom hunting up in the hills; they'd hiked to the village of Bar just up the road to tour through the family's old in-town house and the local cheesery; they'd helped rake up the harvest of cut hay to feed into Florentina's brother Pere's wheezy old baler; Florentina had reserved the local cab to take them all on a side-trip to Andorra and Seu de Urgell; and she'd cooked huge family dinners so that all the dozens of relatives in the area could drop in to meet their Yankee cousins. "You didn't have the time to really do Seu

de Urgell justice. And we never made it to Tolerieu at all."
Tolerieu was just a couple of miles further back into the hills
from Bar. "*Que lastima!* Tolerieu may be even tinier than
Bar, but its history . . . and the stories it has to tell . . ."

The Americans shifted forward on the bench and leaned
toward Florentina, as if those movements would somehow
miraculously make it possible for them to understand her
words more quickly and clearly. Florentina had grown used
to these gestures over the last few days. It was the way her
cousins responded every time she told them a local tale or a
legend. She'd told them many during their short stay.

"What kinds of stories?" the younger cousin asked. "Like
the other ones you told us, of *dracs,* and *demonas,* and *gi-
gants*?"

"Those, and even better ones. When I was a very little girl,
the children of Tolerieu used to boast to us, the children of
Bar, that once upon a time, hundreds of years ago, a beautiful
princess lived in Tolerieu. A good-looking and ambitious
young man, Joan Grau, had left Tolerieu to make his fortune.
He traveled to strange far lands across the sea and came
home with the daughter of a king as his bride.

"Of course we scoffed at them. Such a story! A princess in
the middle of nowhere, in tiny Tolerieu! Nobody believed
them.

"But years later some archaeologists came to this area
who'd heard of the legend. They obtained permission to
dig . . ."

1525 AD—Tolerieu

"Look! It is she! She walks among us!" To Pau's ears,
Manel's words amplified to a roar as they bounced back and
forth against the stone walls of the buildings lining the alley.
Manel's sister Sol turned to gawk, open-mouthed.

Pau cringed. "Hush! Don't be so disrespectful," he whispered, then blushed at the snake's hiss the acoustics of the
narrow space made of his chiding. He yanked Manel and Sol
back behind the corner of the community cistern, almost trip-

ping over the wooden buckets they'd come to fill with water
for his oldest sister's laundry.

The lovely object of their attention gave no indication of
having heard them. Flanked by two ladies-in-waiting and
four men-at-arms, she continued along the stone-paved lane,
walking in the direction of the village church.

Pau felt that his eyes couldn't open wide enough to drink
in all her beauty. The princess's skin shone like gold. Her
precise and delicate features spoke of the sacred breeding of
kings and queens. Blue highlights gleamed in her long black
hair. *Flowing like night's river,* Pau thought. She could have
been mistaken for a goddess of ancient Cathay. Pau's breath
compressed in his chest. Though she wore a plain black Hi-
bernian cloak, the hem of a turquoise-colored Florentine bro-
cade gown flowed below it, making it appear that the
princess floated over the cobblestones on her own private
patch of sky. A princess in the tiny village of Tolerieu—an
impossible fairy tale! He hadn't believed it when his relatives
had told him on the first day of his visit. Yet here she was!
Since this was true, *anything* might be true. The narrow
scope of Pau's life—as narrow as the alleyway walls—suddenly expanded to infinite possibilities.

"Why is she wearing such a heavy cloak?" Sol muttered.
"It's half-way to summer. And if she's a princess, why isn't
she wearing purple?"

"Remember that her father's empire was a tropical paradise." Pau breathed the words. "A balmy spring morning for
us might seem like the coldest day of winter to her."

Sol made a face. After all, it was *her* parents that had told
Pau all about the princess. Pau had seen a similar grimace on
Sol's face when her mother, his oldest sister, regaled him
with stories of the princess's piety, how her great beauty
merely reflected her virtue: how God had watched over and
favored her—rescuing her from her royal yet barbaric origins
so that she might find Christ and a good Christian husband.
"The Graus only come down from their mansion for religious
festivals. It stirs the heart to see the way the princess gazes
with perfect devotion at the statues of our Lord and the Vir-

gin. It's as though she waited all her young life to be whisked away from her heathen life of splendor to our tiny town. During communion," Pau's sister's breath caught in her throat, "when she receives the wafer—you can see that her faith is perfect, that her belief in the transfiguration is absolute."

Pau wished he *could* see the Princess take communion. He imagined her eyes closing, her soft, sculpted lips opening just wide enough to receive the wine and the wafer, the blood and flesh of Christ . . .

Sol interrupted Pau's thoughts. "Or it might be that, refined as she is, she never gets to enjoy the warming effects of hauling bucket after heavy bucket of water up and down these streets," she said. "Personally, I think she looks unwell."

Pau glared at his niece. All the girls and younger women in the village envied the princess. But Sol's words stained his vision: When he looked back at the princess he noticed a slight violet shadow of pallor lurking beneath the gilded glow of her cheeks.

"It's not a feast day. Why is she here in the village, like this?" Manel wondered out loud. "The Graus have their own chapel and cleric, so she needn't come to Mass amongst us common folk."

Pau didn't care about a reason.

The princess and her retinue walked down the length of houses and rounded the corner.

Sol rattled the handle of her bucket as she picked it up. "We must get this water to Mother. We'd be out working in the fields today, but for her extra loads of laundry. Count your blessings that you got to see the princess at all."

Pau shrugged. "Therefore to see her was intended by God. Remember that the unluckiest of actions is to question one's own good fortune." He pushed his bucket up against the cistern and trotted down the lane after the princess's entourage. Manel followed on his heels, as Pau had known he would. Pau might be only the scantest of years older then Manel and Sol, but he was their uncle, and besides that, a visitor from the big city of Seu de Urgell. A moment later Pau heard an exasperated clang as Sol slammed her own bucket down, then her staccato footsteps chasing after them.

I'd seen the three children watching me, of course, with their pale faces the color of bleached bone, their hair the tawny beast-fur color shared by so many of my husband's people. The two boys are as tall as I am, and the girl nearly so. These people grow so tall.

Back in my homeland, my tutors told me myths of tribes to the north who grew to such a height. I asked my tutors then, "If we Mexica originally came from that same north, what happened to us? When we came south and first dwelled by the lake, were we a larger, grander people?" My tutors always glared at me with irritation. I was supposed to receive their knowledge silently, accept their words with docile acceptance. I know they wished I'd behave more like my sisters. But I had to wonder if the taunts and curses of our ancient neighbors by the lake had dwindled us. Or if as we became more refined, gained more knowledge, enslaved those so-proud people there before us—had we condensed down to these smaller frames? Or is such physical stature only enjoyed *in* the North? Had my people stayed away from their country of origin too long?

Let these mere children stare at me. In my father's court I was stared at by courtiers, warriors, merchants and slaves. While *those* throngs stared at me, I in turn gazed upon hummingbirds feeding on nectar in the royal aviary. And with equal serenity, during festivals, at war—prisoners' hearts torn beating from their living chests before me, so close that my face freckled with their blood. When the occasion was the latter, the poets exclaimed that it only added to my beauty in the most appropriate manner, for I was, and am, the descendant of warrior kings.

Among my father's many daughters, only I never flinched when the priests officiated before us at religious ceremonies. My sisters' faces strained not to crumple into revulsion when the priests, with their black painted skin and long ebony cloaks, hovered over us like ravens—the bones and skulls that adorned their garments rattling and threatening to bang into our foreheads and noses, the awful stench of their un-washed bodies and uncut blood-caked hair saturating our nostrils. Of all my father's daughters, only my demeanor stayed as smooth and silken as the surface of the mountain ponds where we drowned children to please the rain god Tlaloc.

So let *these* children look. For although I do not stare the way they do, I too look. In this land both new and ancient, I notice everything: the stone-walled houses with their slate roofs; the narrow street paved with bumpy rocks.

The walls of my homeland were also built with stone; the streets also paved. But there the walls were plastered and wore, like ceremonial cloaks, the flowers of ever-blooming vines and brightly painted frescoes. The paved streets stretched flat and far in broad gracious boulevards, their water-street canal twins gliding beside them.

Something inside me trembles. I stumble slightly. A man-at-arms leaps forward to steady me, but I've already regained my balance.

I will *not* miss my homeland. I won't let myself. *This* is now my homeland. The true, lost homeland of my people. Alone of all my people, I've been returned to the north, to this land of stone and giants. That place of my childhood—the beautiful and terrible dream of now-conquered Tenochtit-lan—it is no more.

When I was still quite young, rumors began trickling to the capital that far to the east huge hills had been sighted moving on the sea; that lofty towers floated on the waters there. When the tides drew the towers to shore, tall men with faces as pale as corpses and long yellow beards clambered down from them. When they came onto land they were car-ried anywhere they wished to go by huge deer such as had never been seen before.

"You shall see," my Totonac nurse told me as she combed and then braided a garland of flowers into my hair. "Your fate, the fate of your people, is coming for you from the north, as was foretold."

I shrugged. I'd learned in school of the prediction that one day the god-king Quetzalcoatl would return to reclaim his lands. To no educated person's surprise, the omens began in the year Ce Actl—One Reed—the sacred name of Quetzalcoatl.

"From the east," I corrected her. "Not from the north."

"How can that be?" My nurse might be uneducated and ignorant, but not so foolish as to say outright that I was wrong, though I knew that was what she thought. "Your people came from the north. How can these *teules* arrive from the east?"

I frowned, but explained patiently. "Because if they arrive by way of the sea, as the sightings tell us, of course they must come from the east. Directly north there is only land. So obviously they come from both the north and the east, sailing down along the coast."

"Ah, I see," she said. "And what will they do when they arrive here, my princess, these ancient relatives of yours?"

I knew then that she teased me. I couldn't see her eyes or her face, but I could feel the smile in her hands as she wrapped my braids around my head, adjusting the ends so that they peeked out over my eyebrows.

Though I was still too young then to grasp the complexities of political matters, I ignored her levity and answered, "They will undoubtedly join forces with my father, to make him an even greater leader."

She sighed—her only response. She took me by the hand and led me from my room. As we walked down to the royal kitchens for the midday meal we were joined in the corridors by my sisters and half-sisters, each accompanied by her own nurse. We, the daughters of the king, had our own dining room near the kitchen. Clean mats to sit on, and low tables, waited for us there. As we arrived, cooks set trays with fresh steaming bowls of food up on shelves. While slaves went to fetch bowls of water for washing our hands, my sisters settled themselves on the mats, laughing and talking with each other.

No one noticed me walking over to the trays. I leaned over
them and sniffed. Supper was a bowl for each of us of a thick
stew of simmered chunks of fish and squash in a tomato and
sage sauce, with half a tortilla apiece at the side to scoop it
up with.

I was famished. I rubbed my stomach to quell its growling.
This afternoon I'd attend classes in the mathematics of
calendarship, followed by dance lessons. This morning our
tutors had kept us busy learning and reciting the poetry of the
philosopher-ruler Nezahualcoyotl.

> Even jade will shatter,
> Even gold will crush,
> Even quetzal plumes will tear.
> One does not live forever on this earth:
> Only for an instant do we endure.

Suddenly I felt as though I could not endure a moment
longer—though my hands were unwashed, if I did not eat
that very instant my hunger would shatter and crush me. I
looked around at my obedient, oblivious, prattling sisters.
Why should I wait? I picked up a bowl and shoveled stew
into my mouth with the rolled up tortilla. It was still warm.
By the time the slaves returned it would be cold. The fish
tasted tender and sweet, the squash rich and meaty. The smell
of sage steamed my face. I felt my cheeks blossom from its
grazing warm perfume.

"Ai! Ai! What are you doing?" My nurse's shriek sliced
through my sisters' chatter, killing all other sound in the
room. "A girl who eats standing up is fated to marry a long
way from home!"

My sisters, the younger ones and the older ones, all turned
to stare. Fear for me shone in their eyes. What could be a
worse fate then that?

I looked at my nurse. Though we'd both been taught otherwise, neither of us averted our eyes. "I've heard that saying
before," I said. "I will marry a god, and I *will* marry far from

home." As soon as I spoke those words I knew them to be true. I kept eating, kept standing. My hunger didn't abate.

My sisters tried to talk me out of my fancy, of course. When I ignored their words they told their mothers. Soon I received a command to present myself before a meeting of all my father's wives and concubines, including my own mother.

One of the head wives began the interrogation. "We hear you think you'll marry one of these rumored new gods, the ones that our lord the king has recently sent an envoy in search of?"

"Yes," I said. "Legend has it that they are our ancestors returning to us. Therefore it wouldn't be unseemly to be matched with one."

"Our ancestors came from the north," one of the youngest concubines said, "a cold, dead, barren and unlucky realm ruled over by the fearful god of darkness, Tezcatlipoca. Is a life under that sort of influence what you'd wish for yourself?"

"If it's true that our ancestors came from the north, then it was from just that land that our fathers' fathers drew strength when Huitzilopochtli led them hence to become conquerors and leaders. I do not fear it."

The concubine shuddered.

"Besides," I continued, "these *rumored* gods, these *teules,* come as much from the east as from the north, so I'd fall just as much under the influence of the eastern god Xipe Totec, with his attributes of light, fertility, and life."

The head wife turned toward my mother. "At least it can be said that your daughter pays attention during religious instruction." Then she frowned at my mother. "We warned you when this one was born that waiting for a propitious naming day wouldn't offset the misfortune of the timing of her birth."

I flushed with embarrassment. This woman might be a head wife, but her coarse rudeness was unfitting and unforgivable.

My mother's face reddened as much as mine. "My daughter is still only a young girl. This incident that concerns us all arose out of a breach of etiquette." (Here my mother glared at the head wife, serving notice that I was not the only one guilty of a breach of etiquette.) "She was hungry and ate before she should have, then concocted this romantic 'prediction' to excuse her bad behavior." My mother turned her glare on me. "I'm sure she'll outgrow such childishness."

My nurse was not always fond of me, but when we walked back to my room later she tried to comfort me. "Ignore the head wife's hurtful words," she counseled. "She's jealous. It's clear even now that you'll grow up to be a great beauty, far more attractive than her own daughter. Since your birth I've kept company with you more then anyone else, even your own mother. I watch for signs of black magic in you, but never see any. I've even lain awake at night, observing you while you sleep in case you should change into a beast or spirit. But I've never discovered any hint that the influence of the evil day you were born on holds any influence over you."

I thanked her for her advice, but what did she know? She was only a nurse, and a slave at that. For all her watchfulness she'd never detected that on many calendrical "nine" days, favorable to those born on the day One Wind like myself, I too feigned sleep, lying awake, willing myself to transform into a jaguar, or a hummingbird, or a spider or a snake.

From that day on I lived an impeccable life. I grew to become the princess that my father's poets extolled in verse. For the next two years I committed no blunders in manners. I walked with grace and modesty. I excelled at my studies. My father's court assumed I'd taken heed of the wives' words, that I'd contritely mended my ways. But that wasn't the case at all. I was transforming myself into a fit bride for a god.

In the meantime my father did what he could to address the mystery of the *teules*. First came news that our enemies, the Tlaxcalans, attacked them. The stranger-gods defeated them with magic and with terrible, uncanny, fire-belching malodorous machines. Hopes rose in Tenochtitlan that these *teules* were indeed our ancestors come to support and join us.

Then reports followed that the Tlaxcalans had rallied by allying themselves with the *teules*. The Tlaxcalans spread stories throughout the land that the *teules* were the supernatural beings promised by *their* own legends to deliver them from Tenochtitlan's dominion. At each step the *teules* took closer to Mexica lands, they asked about my father.

My father sent them messengers. The messengers bore greetings and precious gifts to please and placate the *teules*, to dispose them favorably toward my father in case they were indeed our ancestors. The messengers also bore maps and directions to Tenochtitlan that were, in fact, dangerous pathways, in the hopes that the *teules* would be destroyed en route. The finest of my father's Huastec sorcerers cast spells to divert, transform, or destroy the *teules*.

The stranger-gods kept the gifts and avoided all the pitfalls—those of treachery and those of sorcery. Throughout the palace, everyone had an opinion: the warriors and guards, the court noblemen and noblewomen, the judges, the administrators, the royal wives, our tutors, my sisters, the servants, even the jugglers, dwarf-jesters, and slaves. Only I kept my own counsel. Only I hungered for the *teules* to arrive.

Even stranger rumors reached us. The *teules* declared themselves men, but claimed they worshipped a more powerful deity then any of ours. In the lands they conquered they forced the priests to cut their hair, cast off their black cloaks and don white robes instead, and cease sacrificing prisoners to the gods. If a township refused, the *teules* slaughtered dozens of people.

"They plot to weaken our gods," a dwarf-jester fretted. "Without sustenance, Huitzilopochtli will no longer be able to protect us. Drought or floods will follow, then famine. Our vassals will rise up and overthrow us."

Omens seemed to prove the dwarf-jester right. On a windless afternoon the waters of the lake suddenly rose and flooded the city. For weeks a phantom woman could be heard in the city streets at night, sobbing over and over, "Oh my beloved sons, now we are at the point of going. My beloved sons, whither shall I take you?" Many said it was the voice of Huitzilopochtli's mother, the goddess Coatlique, preparing to take our god and his brothers, the moon and the stars, away from us. In the palace it was whispered that my father suffered ill-favored visions during the day, woke shouting from terrible dreams just before dawn.

One day my father commanded an audience with his daughters, as he did several times a year. Our tutors and nurses helped us gather together gifts for him. Then we presented ourselves according to custom. We walked to his quarters in procession, singing, led by one of the older noblewomen of the court.

Our lord father received us in his reception hall. He sat on a low stool cushioned with soft cotton and embroidered with brilliant threads of all colors spun from quetzal and parrot feathers. Elderly counselors, the concubines who acted as his handmaidens, his guards, his hunchbacks and dwarf jesters stood on either side of him, fanning out like a vulture's wings. We ceased singing. The noblewoman who led us presented him with our gifts: flowers that we'd grown in our own garden, the best of our weaving and embroidery.

He accepted our gifts, gave us permission to sit down on mats ringing the room. After that he ignored us for a while and spoke with one of his counselors in a quiet, clear voice that carried. He talked about matters of state: judgments he'd recently ruled on, tribute the state had collected from vassal kingdoms, the building of roads and bridges in the lands near the southern border. Then he changed the course of the conversation.

"My most recent envoy to the east tells me that the Tlaxcalan chiefs have broken with decent custom. They freely offer their own daughters and nieces to the *teules* in marriage, or concubinage, or for even a single night's passing pleasure."

"I've heard that myself," the counselor replied. "Our enemies hope to gain family alliances with the *teules,* or at the very least a new generation of boy-warriors, hoping they might be born with the same attributes of size, strength, and sorcerous abilities as their *teule* fathers."

They talked for a while longer in that fashion while we listened with bowed heads.

When they finished my father excused his counselor and said he was ready to receive his daughters' obeisance. He allowed us to approach him one at a time, prostrating ourselves before him. He spoke a few words to each, too quietly for anyone else to hear.

My turn came. With my face only inches from the ground, I could just see the edges of his legs folded under him on his stool. He addressed me by name, then said, "You've grown to great beauty. Of all my daughters, it is in you I find the unflinching calm, the gravity and intelligence that I would look for in a son. My one disappointment in you as a daughter is that you were *not* born a son. You would have made a great warrior and leader."

I said nothing, astounded.

"Do you still wish to marry a god?"

A long pause followed, until I realized that it was a question he was expecting an answer to. "I was only a foolish young girl then," I replied. "I'd hoped that my childish conceits would have been forgotten by now."

"A father forgets nothing," he replied. "Even a father who seems remote because he carries the burden of an entire nation's problems on his shoulders. As a ruler I must be obedient to the needs of my people. I do what is expected of me. Are you as responsible for your own role in life? Are you a good daughter? Would you willingly obey any request I made of you?"

"Of course, my Lord Father," I murmured. My heart sang. I knew what he'd someday ask of me. I was ready.

Town by town the *teules* came closer. In our city the temple of Huitzilopochtli caught fire for no reason. It wouldn't stop burning no matter how much water was poured on the flames. Comets ignited the night skies, some said to light the way for the *teules* to find their way to us.

My father ordained that the daughters of his two chief wives, myself, and three of his other daughters could wear the royal color turquoise as we saw fit. He granted us allotments equal to those of the chief wives, for every luxury imaginable: indigo for washing into our hair; *axin* for gilding our skin; garments woven from shimmering feather-threads; *chocolatl* ground from the finest cacao beans, mixed with honey and vanilla; headdresses and necklaces formed of carved jade and turquoise and cast gold in the shapes of crabs, birds, scorpions, flowers and sea shells. Although most of us weren't of age yet, he deeded us land and properties.

The *teules* reached and conquered the nearby city of Cholula. Then they marched through the hills and down to the valley, with its great lake cradling Tlacopan, Texcoco, and of course Tenochtitlan. They rode through the great causeway on their giant deer. The lords of Texcoco, Izapalapa, Tlacopan and Coyoacan greeted them and joined them on the way. My father went to meet them, borne on his finest litter with its canopy of green feathers, gold, silver, pearls, and jewels, wearing garments suitable for an audience with the gods. The *teules* gave him gifts, then followed him onto the palace grounds. I only know of this from what I was told by our servants. The streets were lined with men and women, the canals filled with boats, but all of my father's wives and daughters remained cloistered in our quarters. I wouldn't see the *teules* with my own eyes for many weeks, after they'd taken my father prisoner.

It was then that my father called for us, after he became a hostage. He sent us to grind maize and prepare tortillas for the *teule* chiefs. We offered our finest weaving to be made into new clothing for them. This allowed the *teules* the opportunity to see us. It also allowed me the opportunity to see them.

At first I, though I was fascinated, also felt disappointed. They were not *teules* after all. Clearly they were men. Yet men such as no one could have imagined: tall, with chalky skin, and almost as hairy as the captive beasts in my father's zoological gardens. I wondered if they'd all been born on a day predisposed toward black magic, such as my birthdate, One Wind, or on Three Alligator, and had proven more successful then I had in my childhood attempts to transform myself into an animal. Their language sounded like the song of drunken birds. I learned that they called the land they came from España, their language Español. They were not unintelligent. Some of them had studied a little of the languages of the many tribes they'd conquered. These men were making every effort to understand our language too.

One in particular jumped to his feet every time I entered their quarters. He made a great though clumsy show of treating me with courtesy. He possessed the look of one who wished to gaze upon my face, but had been told that was against our customs (he'd never seen the way that I'd been stared at in court), so his head bobbed this way and that like a captured creature. His hair was different colors of gold, his skin even paler than that of his compatriots. I wouldn't have said that he was either handsome or ugly. Rather that he was interesting to look at, like a jaguar or wolf.

One day I heard him speak to another of his compatriots in a language I didn't recognize—neither Español nor any native tongue I'd ever heard. They sounded like two beasts growling at each other.

"What are you saying?" I asked him. "That isn't your usual manner of speaking."

The jaguar-man smiled at me, forgetting he wasn't supposed to look me in the face. His eyes were green, like the cat he resembled. "You are correct, your Highness," he said in a broken approximation of my language. "We weren't speaking Spanish, but rather the speech of our own land, for we are countrymen."

"You're from a different country than the rest? You're not from España?"

He seemed unable to stop smiling, unable to stop gazing down at me. "No, Highness. We are Catalans. We're of the north—del norte. We live high in the mountains above Spain, to the east and to the north; the mountains to which we'll return when we leave here."

Del norte. To the east and to the north. In an instant my disappointment vanished. These men might not be gods, but they could still be our ancestors or cousins, returned to us as the legends had predicted.

"Consent to be my tutor," I said to him. "Teach me about your country, your customs, your gods."

My nurse, my tutors, my mother, and my sisters were scandalized. My father told them to silence their objections. He told them to follow my example. "The more we learn about the *teules,* the sooner we'll discover their weaknesses."

I learned, instead, of their strengths.

The Catalan first taught me his name. "Joan Grau," he said.

"Jszhwan," I twisted my tongue around the first name, trying to imitate him. He laughed, but I could tell that he laughed with delight. "Grau" proved easier. It sounded like a coyote snarling.

He tried to pronounce my name in *my* language. I was then the one who laughed. He admitted defeat. "I will call you Maria de Moctezuma. De Moctezuma to indicate that you're the daughter of your father. And Maria is the name of the mother of our God."

He told me what he knew of the Spaniards, and a great deal more about his own people. My people, the Mexica, have only lived here by the lake for a few hundred years. Joan Grau's family have dwelled in their town for a thousand years and half that again—scant years after the time that their god Jesus, son of their god, was born!

My greatest interest lay in learning about his religion. I had no trouble with some ideas. That their god Jesus had been conspired against, murdered, then returned to life again with even greater powers was a history shared with a number of our own deities, including Coatlique, the mother of Huitzilopochtli. I also accepted baptism as a familiar and comfortable concept. What could be more natural then dedicating a child at birth to a god, to ensure the eventual dispensation of its soul?

Yet I had trouble when Joan made distinctions where I saw none.

"Other then the fact that they serve a different god, your priests don't seem so different from ours," I told him. "Ours, too, wear black. Ours, too, take vows of celibacy. Ours, too, live modest, ascetic lives, pausing at all hours of the day and waking at all hours of the night to pray. Ours, too, listen to confession from their parishioners, though only once each lifetime, usually at its end. Why do your people take such an exception to our clergy, when yours are so similar?"

Joan liked to laugh and smile more then was the custom of my people or the Spaniards. But when we spoke of such things he became suitably serious. "For two reasons," he said. "They serve the wrong gods. There is only one God, the one that we worship. To save the souls of your people, you must come to believe in our God, and his son, our Lord Jesus Christ."

"And the mysterious creature-god you call the Holy Ghost," I said, unable to keep the puzzlement out of my voice.

Joan almost smiled. "I know that sounds like three deities, but it is a trinity within one greater entity."

I nodded. "I can grasp that. We also have such a god: the creator gods, Lady Omecihuatl and Lord Ometecuhtli, are in truth the single god of duality, Ometeotl. What is the other objection to our priests?"

Joan frowned. "Their habit of sacrificing their fellow men, then feeding the flesh to themselves, your rulers, and your gods."

Were the dwarf-jester's fears about to be explained to me as true? That Joan and his companions meant to conquer us by weakening our gods? If that were the case, how could they be our ancestors and cousins?

"How else can we keep our gods strong then?" I asked, afraid of what Joan might answer.

Joan looked up at the ceiling, then down at the floor, as if the words he searched for might be found in one of those two places. He took a deep breath. "Forgive me, princess, but I must be blunt," he finally said. "You cannot keep your gods strong, by that loathsome means or by any other, for your gods do not exist. Every time you see their mark upon your lives—good crops or bad, good weather, drought or flood— these are manifestations of the one *true* God. The one true God needs not be fed or strengthened since *all* strength already resides in him."

"But it is known, it was witnessed, that Huitzilopochtli, in the form of first an idol, then a hummingbird, led my people from their land of origin in the north to these shores and then guided them to greatness," I protested.

Joan furled his brows. "If that *is* true, perhaps that was the only way God could guide you at that time, since there was no way yet to hear His son Jesus Christ's message of compassion and salvation. Now He's led us to bring you that message. Isn't the way we've prevailed against hostile and overwhelming forces proof of His desire?"

I still didn't understand, until Joan later explained the custom of communion.

"During communion, through faith and God's will, the wine and wafer become blood and flesh," he said.

Except for the sorcerous transformation, this sounded exactly like the customs of my people, and even the customs of our enemies. The Tlaxcalans too sacrificed prisoners, offered up human flesh to their priests, rulers, and most especially their gods. Why did the Spanish so strenuously object to the practice, if they did the same—if not for their god, then for themselves?

"We don't eat the flesh of other men." Joan tried to look amused, though clearly he was shocked. "The transfigured blood and flesh we consume is that of the son of our God, of our Lord, Jesus Christ."

Clarity struck me in a single, overwhelming blow. I felt myself thrown down, my chest cleaved open, my soul and beating heart exposed by the overwhelming truth. I saw now that without knowing it, this was what I had been waiting my whole life to hear.

No wonder all the nations of our world, including my own,

fell before these men! No wonder our gods had fled! How brilliant they were, how foolish my own people! If one captured a prisoner in battle, no matter how valiant a warrior he might have been, he was still weaker than the one who'd captured him. In consuming him one would always partake of that weakness. In feeding such a prisoner to a god, it only made sense that one's god would likewise weaken. But a man who could find a way to consume a god would grow ever stronger, till he was as strong as the gods themselves.

I looked Joan Grau fully in the face. Tears streamed down my cheeks. I dropped to my knees before him. I heard my nurse gasp somewhere behind me. Past Joan I saw servants' and my father's guards' eyes widen in disbelief at my actions. "I wish to leave my gods and take your god as my own. I wish to be baptized and take communion."

Joan Grau turned as white as an egret's plumes. He too dropped to his knees. "Madre de Dios! Are you saying you want to convert? That you wish to become a Christian?"

"Yes. Now. This instant."

My father offered me to the chief Spaniard, Hernando Cortés, to wed. Cortés politely refused. He was already married. The god of the *teules,* my new god, permitted them only one new wife at a time, taking another only in the case of death. Then Cortés pressed Joan Grau's suit for me, using the flattering words of his bird-song tongue: Joan Grau esteemed me above all others and had personally undertaken my conversion. My life meant more to him then gold, fame, or even his own life. He came from a wealthy and respected family in his homeland. His people, the Catalans, were of a more ancient lineage then the Spanish, renowned as merchants and warriors—two castes also respected in all Mexica lands.

My father granted his consent gladly. Thus was my destiny, my goal, fulfilled.

In the women's quarters, my nurse and my sisters received the news with sobs and tears. "Your prophecy for yourself came true. You'll marry this *teule* and move far away from home."

"Yes," I confirmed their fears. "But you can come visit me. You'll see how well I live in the home of our ancestors and cousins."

This caused even louder wailing. "That we will never do! If these are truly our cousins, steeped in the rough ways of our ancestors, remember the fate of new brides in these circumstances. Remember how in ancient times the princess of Colhua, when given in marriage to the son of our king, was sacrificed on Huitzilopochtli's altar instead. Do you think we'll come to visit you, knowing that your groom might come out to greet us wearing your skin, your flayed face as his mask, as the king of Colhua was greeted when first he went to visit his daughter in her new abode?"

I laughed at them, though I knew they didn't understand. More likely *I'd* walk out to greet them wearing the skin and mask of my new god.

Before the wedding I bathed and purified myself. My nurse gilded my face with *axin*. She dressed me in jeweled, embroidered garments and covered my arms and legs with red feathers.

Joan and I married according to the customs of my people, but for two things. First: when the time came for me to be carried to my groom on the back of the matchmaker (which in this case was Hernando Cortés), instead I rode behind the Spanish chieftain on the back of his giant deer. The second thing was that I was married by Fray de la Merced, one of the priests of my new god. Fray de la Merced performed the ceremony and knotted Joan's cloak to the hem of my long wedding blouse. When I was presented to Joan as his wife, all I could think of, looking at his tawny hair and scarlet wedding clothes, was how very much he resembled Xipe Totec—how he had indeed brought me light and life.

Afterwards my father wed a number of my sisters to some of Cortés's other captains, though they protested bitterly. My father acquiesced to Cortés's requirement that my sisters first accept the *teules'* god. Yet no matter how much I tried to persuade him, my father refused to convert.

As a noblewoman of the court, and the wife of one of his captors, I enjoyed unheard-of access to my father. "Accept their god," I urged him. "Eat of his flesh. Drink of his blood. Grow strong again. Grow stronger then you were before."

He gazed at me with melancholy eyes. "Are you still loyal to me, daughter? Would you have me cast off these bonds, rid you of your *teule* husband?"

"You don't understand," I said. "If you accept their god you won't need to defeat them. They'll acknowledge you as their brother and raise you up. All that was yours will be yours again, and more. The Tlaxcalans will become humble allies. The Tarascans will at last fall before us. You, and our people, will receive unimaginable tribute from our vassals. You'll live, honored, to a great old age. When you die, instead of traveling four years in torment through the underworld of Mictlan, you'll ascend to the heaven of the *teules'* god, which sounds very much like the paradise that warriors slain in battle earn."

I know I came close to convincing him. But always Huitzilopochtli's priests lingered near by, fearful of all that they'd lose if my father followed the new god. They whispered and whispered to him, undermining my words.

Outside, in the city, the warrior Cuitlahuac supplanted my father. His followers began to attack the palace. On the day Cortés commanded my father to climb the palace roof to reassure the masses, I knew, as did my father, that the time for decisions and changes had passed. Joan tried to shield my face as my father was stoned to death by his own people. My eyes remained as dry as desert dust. My father had chosen his own fate. Crying would dishonor him.

Shaken, Cortés sent word to Cuitlahuac saying that, because of his grief over his own part in my father's death, the Spanish and their Tlaxcalan allies would leave Tenochtitlan forever in eight days. Four nights before that day, Cortés's contingent tried to slip away through the city under cover of rain, clouds, and darkness. This required the coordination of all of Cortés's men, all the Tlaxcalan allies who'd accompanied them, and my father's family and servants—hundreds of people in all.

We reached the main promenade before we were discovered. After that our retreat resembled an eternal journey through the horrors of the nine levels of Mictlan. The canals and the lake boiled with canoes filled with archers. Warriors chopped away at bridges to prevent us from escaping. Darts, stones, and arrows cascaded down on us from the flat roofs of the city's houses. Cold rain glued my hair to my face, my clothes to my body, as I watched many of my sisters and brothers die during the route. Cortés's great deer fell screaming, their huge bodies blocking our way like heaving, bleeding warm boulders. My father's great treasure that the Spaniards insisted on bringing tripped us—the Spaniards dragging it along behind them even as they died. Joan tried to protect me, but I walked without fear through the carnage. I had been born on the day One Wind and possessed special powers. I knew my new god protected me. I felt his flesh within me make me strong, invulnerable.

Afterward Joan left Cortés's commission. We both knew the retribution looming for Tenochtitlan. Joan wanted to spare me the site of the beautiful city of my birth razed, its graceful canals filled with stones, the flowers in its gardens trampled, the wild wings of the hummingbirds in the royal aviary stilled forever. He brought me here, to his homeland, to the north and the east.

Of late I've felt unwell. My stomach roils when I eat. Food has lost all appeal for me. My legs are weak and at times don't wish to support me. Sometimes I'm afraid that I'm not as strong as my husband's tall, hearty people; that I'm not strong enough to digest a god's flesh—that it's consuming me instead, from inside. At other times I'm glad. Perhaps these are the symptoms that I'm at last with child.

Last night I dreamed that *teules* from even farther north appeared. They were lean, dark-haired and pale, followers of the god of wizards, Tezcatlipoca of the Smoking Mirror. They dragged me from my rest, tore me to pieces. I woke up crying, sweating, babbling in Joan's arms. "Don't let them cut off my finger. Don't let them take my arm," I sobbed, still half-submerged in nightmare. "Don't let them use my powers against you."

"What are you talking about, beloved?" Joan asked, gently wiping tears from my face.

At that I woke fully. "Nothing, only a notion embedded in a dream. In my homeland, the souls of women who die in childbirth are transported to the western paradise, the House of Corn. There they become goddesses. Their bodies, left behind, transform into objects of great power. A lock of their hair and the middle finger of their left hand, attached to a shield, make a warrior invincible. Their left arms can be used for black magic." Especially the left arm of a woman born on the day One Wind, though I didn't tell Joan that. "Great effort is expended in trying to desecrate their graves."

"No one will do that here," Joan said. "That isn't our custom." He paused. "Does this mean . . . do you think you might be pregnant?" he said, soft hope in his voice.

"I might be . . . there are indications . . ." I clutched him to me. "Promise me that if I die you'll guard my body, and take my left middle finger and a lock of my hair for yourself."

He hugged me tightly and laughed, though through his laughter I could tell I'd brought him to the brink of weeping. "Maria, my Maria, those are the superstitions of your childhood. You'll bear me many beautiful sons and daughters. You'll live honored and happy beside me to a respectable old age. When at last you do die, we'll live for eternity together in heaven. Your body will be buried in a heavy, sealed stone sarcophagus. No one will disturb your bones."

As the priest leans over me I shiver. The cold stone church floors grind against my knees as I kneel before him. His black cassock smells long unwashed, as does his body beneath it. The cross swaying from around his neck looks like two bound, silvery bones as it threatens to bump into my forehead. I do not flinch.

"What can I do for you, my child?" he asks.

"Bless me, father, and hear my humble request," I say.

"Of course. I will do anything in my power for you, Doña Grau."

"If I should die, I wish to be buried not in the Grau family graveyard, but here within the church, safe and as close to god as possible."

"But my child, God is everywhere."

"And yet *here* is where the village gathers to meet him, not out in the fields, or the forests, or the barnyard or wine cellar," I respond. "Here I'd hear the sweet voices of the townspeople raised in prayer, in song, in adulation. Here I'd feel god's blessings and love."

The priest raises me to my feet. His woolly stench fills my nostrils. "There will be no need of that. Your soul will be in heaven *with* God, sitting in glory at His right hand."

I sigh. Will I have to argue with this man forever?

He pats my arm. "In light of your faith, I'll do all I can to grant your request. But what is all this talk of dying? You're still so young. And haven't I heard rumors that you may be with child?"

I nod. I pray it is so. I need to bear children, many children, to create my people anew, invigorated once again with the power of the North and the East. To raise them to heights unknown even in Tenochtitlan. My new god, whose flesh transforms me, will help me do this.

Pau leaned against the walls, his gaze fixed on the church doors. Sol and even Manel fidgeted, tired of waiting for the princess to reemerge. Pau ignored their impatience. They had their whole lives to catch glimpses of her, while he had only this one brief moment. Next month his father was sending him to attend the university in Barcelona, hoping Pau would excel at his studies. His father planned for Pau to become a great, well-connected merchant, the one who'd expand the family enterprises throughout Catalonia.

Pau folded his arms over his chest. He'd attend the university gladly. But not for his father's reasons, reasons which *had* also been his own. Now a career as a merchant—moving objects hither and yon, back and forth—seemed meaningless, empty. He'd been transformed by the sight of the Princess and the magic of her story. This was where true power lay. Above all else, he suddenly desired the ability to change others in the same fashion that he'd just been changed. He'd become a great writer, a poet, transfiguring others' lives with the truth and beauty of words.

The church door swung open. Manel, who'd been sitting on the cobblestones with his back against the wall, scrambled to his feet. Sol shifted from foot to foot, grumbling.

A man-at-arms stepped over the door stoop, turned to give his arm to the lady-in-waiting who followed him. Then another man-at-arms, another lady-in-waiting. The princess emerged next. Her face was drawn, its golden hues subdued to almost silver. She swayed for an instant in the doorway. A man-at-arms reached out to steady her. She held up her right hand to stop him, with her left hand braced herself against the door. Her gentle words carried with the clarity of a bell. "No, thank you. I must find my strength in god." She closed her eyes and placed her lips reverently against the church door.

The princess's retinue passed from sight up the street and around the corner. Pau stood thunderstruck, transfixed with shame. In the light of such beauty and purity, his fantasy of the power of poetry seemed as petty as the materialistic goal of merchanting. For the second time that day his world shifted. Now he truly knew what he *would* become. A priest.

Florentina stood up from where she'd been sitting next to her American cousins. The young woman who provided the taxi service to Seu de Urgell was pulling into the farmhouse driveway.

"But what happened to the princess?" the older cousin asked.

"Alas, she died young," Florentina said. "The whole village mourned. Out of respect for her piety her sarcophagus was moved into the church and became the base of the main altar. Joan Grau's heart broke. He commanded that all of

Maria's personal wealth be buried with her in fine turquoise velvet bags. He never remarried, never produced any heirs. Eventually his brother's children inherited his riches.

"Two hundred years later Napoleon's troops invaded, marching down through Andorra's mountain passes. When they bivouacked in this area they heard of the legend of Maria de Moctezuma. A cadre of them hiked up to Tolerieu. They broke into the church one night, smashed the lid of the sarcophagus, stole her jewelry and golden medallions from atop her body, scattered her bones, then fled away through the church graveyard. The bags containing her treasures were old and rotten by then. Some of them split, spilling their contents across the graveyard.

"The villagers left those treasures where they fell, for they knew that God watched. Later, when Napoleon's troops died in the thousands in Russia, the people of Tolerieu said it was God's judgment against the French.

"Decades passed. Rain helped sink the remnants of the treasure into the graveyard soil. Wind covered it with dust and leaves. Grass grew over it. Maria's story passed into legend, the rain, wind, and dust of time obscuring her story as surely as her jewelry and medallions. The people in other nearby villages, like Bar, came to believe she was just a fanciful myth—a way for the people of Tolerieu to give themselves airs. It was only when the archaeologists came and began their digging that the truth of the matter came to light again, when they found the Aztec medallions buried deep in the graveyard soil."

Florentina picked up one of the cousin's suitcases as the taxi driver opened the trunk of her car.

Author's note:
This story is real. That is, I was there when Florentina told it. There is a village in Catalonia called Tolerieu. It's just a mile or so up the road from Bar, the equally tiny village where my great-grandfather Francisco was born and raised. Joan Grau served as one of Hernando Cortés's bodyguards during the conquest of Mexico. There was a Maria de

Moctezuma, who Joan brought home with him from the New World. Actual people, places, events.

But is this story true? Truth is a slippery, changing, shifting thing. What is true in one person's mind might be, is likely to be, a miscommunication, a misunderstanding, a miscomprehension, or an outright lie to another. Words are slippery, changing, shifting things. Words, with their "truths" and "untruths," cause real objects and events to come into being, to happen in this world: bridges are built; children are conceived and born; a boy decides to become a shopkeeper, a poet, a priest; crops are planted in both good soil and bad; wars are fought; whole peoples enslaved, and so on and so forth. Such is the power of words. When my great grandfather Francisco died, my grandmother commanded that the plaque over his grave read "Frances." He had never existed as "Frances," yet a real thing, an engraved marker bearing witness to that "reality," now actually exists.

So I leave it to you to decide for yourself what is true and what is real in my story. I am, after all, a story teller.

For me, it led to but one truth. There are many ways death may come to me or to you: illness, strife, accident, old age. But in the human realm we all live under one god—under the iron-fisted dominion of Conqueror Word.

ABOUT THE EDITOR

Pamela Sargent has won the Nebula Award, the Locus Award, and has been a finalist for the Hugo Award. She is the author of several novels, among them *Cloned Lives, The Sudden Star, The Golden Space, The Alien Upstairs,* and *Alien Child.* Gregory Benford described her novel *Venus of Dreams* as "one of the peaks of recent science fiction." *Venus of Shadows,* the sequel, was called "alive with humanity, moving, and memorable" by *Locus. The Shore of Women,* one of Sargent's best-known books, was praised as "a compelling and emotionally involving novel" by *Publishers Weekly.* The *Washington Post Book World* has called her "one of the genre's best writers."

Sargent has also published *Ruler of the Sky,* an epic historical novel about Genghis Khan, which novelist Gary Jennings, author of *Aztec,* called "formidably researched and exquisitely written . . . surely destined to be known hereafter as *the* definitive history of the life and times and conquests of Genghis, mightiest of Khans." Elizabeth Marshall Thomas, author of *Reindeer Moon,* said about this novel: "Scholarly without ever seeming pedantic, the book is fascinating from cover to cover and does admirable justice to a man who might very well be called history's single most important character."

Sargent is also an editor and anthologist. Her anthologies

Women of Wonder, The Classic Years: Science Fiction by Women from the 1940s to the 1970s and *Women of Wonder, The Contemporary Years: Science Fiction by Women from the 1970s to the 1990s,* were published in 1995; *Publishers Weekly* called these two books "essential reading for any serious sf fan." Among her other anthologies are *Bio-Futures* and, with Ian Watson as co-editor, *Afterlives.*

Sargent's novel of an alternative nineteenth-century America, *Climb the Wind,* was published in 1999 and was a finalist for the Sidewise Award for Alternate History. *Child of Venus,* the third novel in her Venus trilogy, called "masterful" by *Publishers Weekly,* came out in May 2001 from Avon/Eos. Two collections of her short fiction, *Behind the Eyes of Dreamers and Other Short Novels* (Thorndike Press) and *The Mountain Cage and Other Stories* (Meisha Merlin), were published in 2002. She lives in Albany, New York.